Living Dangerously

Katie Fforde lives in Gloucestershire with her husband and some of her three children. Recently her old hobbies of ironing and housework have given way to singing, Flamenco dancing and husky racing. She claims this keeps her fit.

Praise for Katie Fforde

'A fairytale-like, gently witty read . . . Heart-warming – made for sunny days in the park' *Cosmopolitan*

'The mother-daughter bond the women develop is endearing and the heartache caused by a failed long marriage is touchingly conveyed' *Sunday Telegraph*

'Acute and funny observations of the social scene' *The Times*

'A heart-warming tale of female friendship, fizzing with Fforde's distinctive brand of humour' *Sunday Express*

'Delicious – gorgeous humour and the lightest of touches' *Sunday Times*

'A witty and generous romance . . . Katie Fforde is on sparkling form . . . Jilly Cooper for the grown-ups' *Independent*

'Top drawer romantic escapism'
You

'Warm, witty and entertaining . . . as satisfying as a
cup of hot cocoa on a chilly night'
Woman & Home

'Katie Fforde produces gentle cheering comedies that
feature heroines whose waistlines are not what they
were and who are gifted with humorous self-
deprecation' *Sunday Times*

'Katie Fforde writes entertainingly about country life
– and love' *Woman's Journal*

'Lively and engaging' *Woman's Weekly*

'Perfect for the beach' *Bella*

'Entertainingly written – a fine romance indeed'
The Lady

'Bright and airy' *Closer*

'A perfect piece of curl-up-on-the-sofa reading' *Real*

'A funny, fresh and lively read' *heat*

Katie Fforde

Living Dangerously

arrow books

Published by Arrow Books 2009

17 19 20 18 16

First published in Great Britain in 1995 by Penguin Books

Arrow Books
Random House, 20 Vauxhall Bridge Road,
London SW1V 2SA

www.randomhouse.co.uk

Addresses for companies within The Random House Group Limited can be
found at: www.randomhouse.co.uk/offices.htm

The Random House Group Limited Reg. No. 954009

A CIP catalogue record for this book
is available from the British Library

ISBN 9780099446651

The Random House Group Limited supports The Forest Stewardship Council
(FSC®), the leading international forest certification organisation. Our books
carrying the FSC label are printed on FSC® certified paper. FSC is the only forest
certification scheme endorsed by the leading environmental organisations,
including Greenpeace. Our paper procurement policy can be found at
www.randomhouse.co.uk/environment

Typeset by Deltatype Ltd, Birkenhead, Merseyside
Printed and bound by
CPI Group (UK) Ltd, Croydon, CR0 4YY

Published by Arrow Books 2009

17 19 20 18 16

First published in Great Britain in 1995 by Penguin Books

Arrow Books
Random House, 20 Vauxhall Bridge Road,
London SW1V 2SA

www.randomhouse.co.uk

resses for companies within The Random House Group Limited can be
found at: www.randomhouse.co.uk/offices.htm

The Random House Group Limited Reg. No. 954009

A CIP catalogue record for this book
is available from the British Library

ISBN 9780099446651

andom House Group Limited supports The Forest Stewardship Council
®), the leading international forest certification organisation. Our books
ng the FSC label are printed on FSC® certified paper. FSC is the only forest
ification scheme endorsed by the leading environmental organisations,
ncluding Greenpeace. Our paper procurement policy can be found at
www.randomhouse.co.uk/environment

Typeset by Deltatype Ltd, Birkenhead, Merseyside
Printed and bound by
CPI Group (UK) Ltd, Croydon, CR0 4YY

Katie Fforde

Living Dangerously

arrow books

To D.S.F. for laughing

Acknowledgements

To everyone at Mother Nature who inspired me.

To Alison Moylan, who taught me to throw a pot. To Nicholas and Maggie Gundry of Nicholas Gundry Wines, who taught me about wine merchants. To Radio Gloucestershire, who were so generous with their time. To Sarah Molloy, my agent, for taking me on, and keeping me. To Hilary Johnson, Elizabeth Harrison and the rest of the R.N.A. for every kind of support. To Jane Osborn, Barbara Gordon-Cumming and Peg Gardner, who taught me how to write. To Lyn Coleman for helping with my research. To my children and my friends, who put up with so much neglect, and to my cats, who were no help at all but thought they were.

Chapter One

Denied even a spritzer's worth of Dutch courage, Polly ran her fingers despondently up the side of her glass. It was going to be a dreadful evening.

She could see the man Melissa was *dying for her to meet* from the corner of her eye, having had him discreetly pointed out as she entered the room. And, really, she should tell Melissa outright that there was no earthly chance of them hitting it off. He was so tall, so well tailored, so thoroughly grown up.

Polly, aware that her just-washed, variegated hair would only defy gravity for so long, wished she'd made the time to get it cut. One comb had already slithered down her cleavage. Her large greenish-brown eyes were her best feature, but, as she was a firm believer in 'putting on a happy face' the kohl and mascara had gone on with rather a heavy hand. The result was a sleazy sexiness which matched her generous figure and low-cut, clinging velvet dress, but not her wallflower, party-pooper mood. Melissa's spare man would take one look at Polly and run.

But Melissa had got her here under false pretences. This was no 'cosy evening, just a few friends' – there couldn't be fewer than ten couples at this gracious gathering. And if you lay on a maid, even a small one, whose white cap keeps falling over her eyes and whose

English is more shattered than broken, the occasion is definitely formal. Melissa deserved to see her matchmaking fail.

Polly tried to attend to the difficulties the woman opposite had getting her child into the right kindergarten. The woman was supremely elegant. Her bouclé suit had the clean lines and distinctive buttons which, even Polly recognized, defined it as 'designer'. Her chunky gold jewellery may have been either Butler and Wilson or Cartier, but it was perfectly placed and balanced. Every gleaming, conditioned, dark brown hair on this woman's head was impeccably upswept and confined. Her make-up was subtle yet effective; she had enormous style.

Yet when talking about her children she showed touching vulnerability. According to her, child-rearing was a highly technical business, fraught with difficulties. At any stage, the whole thing could go horribly, irredeemably, wrong.

It wasn't enough to love them, and keep them warm and fed, and, eventually, send them to the local school. This primitive method was far too haphazard – any offspring who wasn't an absolute genius would fail to emerge from the primeval slime, let alone get into one of the professions. No, the way to have babies nowadays was to consult the experts at every stage, from the selection of your pre-pregnancy diet advisor through to the crammer who would get your child into the right Oxbridge college. Without this expertise, you might as well forget it. The wrong gynaecologist, anaesthetist, nanny agency, and the little son and heir would never fulfil his potential. And when you got into the business of the right school – well . . .

2

Polly offered a brief prayer of gratitude that so far she'd managed to suppress her maternal instincts. She'd never be able to afford all that specialist help, or even get through the reading list.

Oh, why hadn't she just told Melissa that she was ill and couldn't come to her awful dinner party? Because she knew that Melissa would have gone on issuing invitations until Polly caved in and accepted. Their friendship, left so happily behind at school, must be renewed. Melissa was no less daunting now than she had been at fifteen. If anything, the intervening years had added substance to her schoolgirl bossiness, and Melissa had always had the ability to make Polly do as she was told.

But if the years had added to Melissa's strength of character, they had done nothing for her sense of style. The opulent dullness of Melissa's drawing room deepened Polly's depression. It was all so *House and Garden*, so unrelentingly beige. In her efforts to avoid bad taste, Melissa had ended up with no taste at all. Not a single picture, piece of furniture or objet d'art appeared to have any personal connection. That way, it seemed, Melissa need have no fear of her preferences being criticized.

Even the cat, a pedigree Persian, was hustled hastily out of the way – 'in season, we *daren't* let her out. We've found a super tom and should get some really rather nice kittens' – had been chosen for her golden colouring rather than her personality. It was as if some interior designer had typed 'Georgian Cotswold Manor' into their computer, and given it the treatment. The cat was just another accessory.

A raucous laugh erupted from the civilized murmur of conversation. A large man in a dinner jacket was regaling two women with some anecdote he found hilarious. He either didn't notice or didn't care that his audience didn't join in his laughter and were hiding the fact that their minds were somewhere quite else behind a veil of politeness.

'So what's Freddy's reading age now?' Polly may have been childless, but she knew the jargon.

'Well, since he started at Boreham's . . .'

Polly kept her gaze fixedly on Freddy's mother. Boreham's was obviously a major milestone, the zenith of educational establishments for five-year-olds. Its regime seemed ridiculous to Polly, but as Melissa was smiling and nodding her way towards her, patent leather court shoes sounding unnervingly businesslike on the parquet floor, she assumed an expression of total fascination. Anything to deflect Melissa from her grisly mission.

But Melissa had all the energy and determination of a young and handsome headmistress, and while Polly was feeling several degrees under par, and possibly a few over 98.4, it was unlikely she could put up much of a fight.

'Polly!' Melissa reached her destination and took Polly's arm. 'I know Louise will forgive me if I drag you away. There's someone you simply must meet.'

'Melissa, I'm really not feeling . . .'

Melissa's grip tightened. Her back, eloquent in a lace blouse and no-nonsense bra, told Polly firmly to pull herself together and stop being such a wimp.

'He's talking to Thalia Bradley,' said Melissa over her shoulder. 'She does *such* a lot for charity.'

From a distance it was possible that what Thalia Bradley did for charity cut into the profits of honest

4

working girls. But close to, Polly realized that she was looking at real beauty, and possibly genuine charm. She sailed the fine line between good taste and sexiness and managed to emerge with both. Her soft, silk chiffon dress was draped in a way which would make many women look fat and probably represented more money than Polly spent on clothes in five years. Her golden hair swooped and waved above a perfect heart-shaped face, tiny retroussé nose, and a mouth which curved as sensually as her seemingly unsupported bosom. The effect was, in common parlance, 'Drop-dead Gorgeous'.

Polly drew abruptly to a halt behind Melissa like a child being introduced to a group of children by its mother; no way would the group accept her now her mother had barged in and broken up the party.

Thalia had her hand on the arm of the tall man and was looking entreatingly up into his eyes. 'You will do it for me, David, won't you?' Her voice, honey-drenched with nicotine overtones, was as sexy as the rest of her.

His head was bent to hear every fascinating word that dropped from her bee-stung lips. He would no more refuse her anything, however unreasonable, than he would sprout wings. He was totally ensnared, and Polly doubted that even Melissa would manage to inflict her old school pal on him right now.

She underestimated the ex-hockey captain of Heathermount. Melissa waited barely long enough for David to acquiesce to whatever Thalia was pleading for before she interrupted.

'Thalia, darling.' Melissa was a trifle sharp. 'I think Hugh's looking for you. Your nanny's just telephoned.'

Thalia could easily have held her ground. She had David in the palm of her hand. But she obviously knew

5

how to leave her audience wanting more. She acknowledged possession of a husband, nanny and presumably children with a reluctant, lingering smile that her companion would not forget.

'David!' Ruthlessly Melissa snapped his attention from the departing Thalia, who swayed away in a fair imitation of The Girl from Ipanema. 'This is Polly Cameron, who's practically my oldest friend.'

Polly forced her lips into a smile she couldn't get as far as her eyes, hoping she didn't look as old as Melissa made her sound.

'And Polly, this is David Locking-Hill, who's been a widower *far* too long. He was married to Angela – such a wonderful person.'

Why was it, thought Polly, that whenever people are described to you as wonderful you know you're going to hate them? But at least she wouldn't have to hate Angela in person.

'But you're just the one to cheer him up,' went on Melissa, oblivious to the fact that David was being more than adequately cheered up by the charitable Thalia. 'You were *so* amusing at school.'

Certain that she had sent two people on the road to true love – or at least to a pleasant evening – Melissa strode off. She took her work as a hostess very seriously.

Polly licked her lips and racked her brains. But fogged by medication and fever in equal amounts, even the common civilities deserted her, let alone the sort of witty epigram which Melissa assumed she could produce to order. Thalia was a very tough act to follow.

'As a conversation stopper that introduction should win a place, if not first prize.' David, prevented by his good manners from chasing Thalia across the room, grasped the nettle. 'Can I get you another drink?' He glanced down at Polly's almost full glass. 'No? Then let's sit down.' To his credit, his sigh was inaudible.

A moment later Polly, perched on the end of a slippery chaise longue, found herself forced to look her reluctant companion in the eye. His fortitude was infectious.

He had the stern good looks which had ruled the colonies for generations. He had thick, fly-away eyebrows above greeny-grey eyes which reminded Polly of the sea in winter – cold, and somewhat uninviting. A hawk-like nose and the sort of chin designed to take life on fitted in with the picture of rocky Britishness. A rather splendid throat, with just the right amount of Adam's apple, rose from the collar of a gleaming white shirt. His mouth was unnervingly noncommittal: he either had no sense of humour whatsoever, or had one which was so dry, so subtle, that only true wit would activate it. But his tie, which, to fit in with the rest of him, should have been 'old-and-very-spartan-public-school', owed more to the influence of Sir John Harvey-Jones than an Alma Mater.

Polly felt like a shaggy Shetland pony asked to stand in for a racehorse on Derby Day, and had about as much chance of keeping David amused for the required ten minutes as the pony had of getting into the winners' enclosure. Being naturally uncompetitive, she decided to sit back and enjoy the view.

Something about David's overt cleanliness was rather appealing. Most of the unattached men Polly came across were artists or craftsmen. Bearded, ponytailed and earringed, they were right-thinking, left-voting and had an odour of honest toil about them which could be as oppressive as their pessimistic predictions for the planet.

David could obviously be trusted not to go on about the ozone layer in mixed company.

'That woman you were talking to just now is very beautiful,' said Polly at last.

'Very beautiful,' he agreed.

She was not really surprised that he didn't add that she was an air-head, had been divorced three times, or that her breasts stayed upright even when she lay down, but part of her was disappointed. Of course he was too much of a gentleman to indulge in such bitchiness, and shame at her own mean spirit left her quite unable to think of anything else to say. Fortunately, he was not similarly affected.

'So how do you come to know Melissa?' He managed to sound genuinely interested. Give the man a merit mark.

Polly sipped her tepid Perrier. 'We were at school together and lost touch completely, but then ran into each other by chance.'

'Oh, where?'

'In Tesco's.' Hardly the most exciting location in the world, but the truth.

'Oh?'

'Mmm. We were both looking for balsamic vinegar.' She hadn't the energy to describe the eldritch shrieks of recognition, the frantic scanning for signs of ageing in each other's faces, the furious exchange of data on the past fifteen years. 'But they hadn't got any.'

David looked down his crooked nose at her. 'How interesting.'

Nothing in his voice, and not the merest twitch of eyebrow or mouth revealed his sarcasm. But there was no way that Polly could have missed it.

She closed her eyes briefly. It was totally understandable. He was probably planning to sue Melissa under the Trade Descriptions Act. And quite right too.

It wasn't his fault they'd been thrown together any more than it was hers. No doubt she was part of a long string of single women produced as understudies for Wonderful Angela. It was only fair that she should keep him at least mildly entertained, just until dinner. Especially when it was because of her that the most attractive woman in the room had been dragged away from him.

She made a vague, disparaging gesture with her hands. 'Not really, but it was fun catching up with Melissa. She told me she and Sheldon moved back to this area from London about a year ago. We exchanged telephone numbers and she said she'd invite me round for a meal.'

Polly had been surprised by Melissa's enthusiasm for a friendship which had only ever been lukewarm. Polly was too much of a rebel for Melissa's liking, and Melissa had embraced the jolly-hockey-sticks philosophy too wholeheartedly for Polly. Melissa really cared if the school lost an away match and was one of the few girls who wore her school uniform correctly, and actually possessed all the numerous items of games kit. Melissa had probably felt sorry for Polly, still unmarried and obviously not very well off, and had invited her out of kindness. Polly, happy to be single, content to be poor, fervently wished Melissa hadn't.

And the invitation had been for a meal, not a banquet. And Polly, weakened by a nasty complaint and a course of antibiotics, found herself promising to come. By the time Melissa had added, 'There's someone I'm longing for you to meet', it had been too late to back out.

9

'So here I am.'

'I see.'

They regarded each other until the goad of middle-class politeness kicked in and he restarted the conversation. 'Those are magnificent beads you're wearing.'

He went up a degree in Polly's estimation. She had a passion for flamboyant junk jewellery and the string of huge, amethyst-coloured glass beads nearly reached her waist. With them went a pair of earrings as lusciously vulgar as South African grapes.

Remembering that Melissa's taste in jewellery inclined towards the tiny but genuine, Polly had added the beads to her discreet black dress specifically to annoy her hostess. Unfortunately, they were incredibly heavy. Which was probably why someone had given them to a jumble sale.

'Thank you.' She gathered the beads into a bundle at her cleavage to ease the weight on her neck. 'So how do you know Melissa?'

'She was a friend of Angela's. They did charity work together.'

'Oh. Which charity?' Please God it was something Polly could approve of, and not some home for rehabilitating fraudulent pension-fund managers.

'I'm afraid I can't remember.' There was a pause as he thought how to continue this unpromising strand of conversation. 'Do you do any charity work? Or don't you have time?'

Polly considered her reply. She certainly spent a great deal of her meagre spare time working for nothing, but she didn't really consider the fight to prevent half of Laureton High Street being pulled down as 'charity' work. Something about him suggested he might not be as sympathetic to this controversial cause as she was, and decided not to mention it.

She smiled somewhat blandly. 'I support as many charities as I can. Oxfam, Save the Children, Help the Aged . . .'

A glimmer of something told her she may have been rumbled, and David Locking-Hill did not think she was on a score of committees and spent every spare minute selling raffle tickets. 'You mean you buy their Christmas cards?'

'Not at all. I always make my own Christmas cards.'

He allowed himself to look surprised. 'How very – enterprising.'

Even in her weakened state, Polly couldn't resist a little gentle teasing. 'Yes, it's amazing what you can do with stick-on stars and glitter.'

She was rewarded by a shudder so well controlled a less observant person might have missed it. She went on: 'The secret is to buy the envelopes first, otherwise you can never get them to fit. I'm just passing that on, in case you're planning to make yours next year.'

'I'll make a point of remembering. Thank you.' He had got himself under control. He answered perfectly seriously, not even a nostril twitched.

Feeling that she had at last gained the conversational upper hand, she pressed on. 'Do you do much in the charitable line?'

He nodded. 'I make a point of having at least one charitable thought every day.'

'Oh? About anyone in particular?'

'Yes. Tonight I'm going to try very hard to think nice thoughts about Melissa.'

Polly had her faults, but she was not slow on the

uptake. 'A lot of women would take offence at that remark,' she said cheerfully, to make it clear that she was not one of them.

'Would they? Why?'

'Because it implies you're annoyed with Melissa for interrupting your conversation with' – she searched for the name – 'that beautiful woman. Thalia, was it?'

'Does it?'

'Of course. You were annoyed, weren't you?'

'My dear Polly – I may call you Polly?'

'It is my name. On the other hand, I'm not too sure about being "your dear".'

'As I was saying . . .' He chivalrously ignored her lapse into feminism. 'If I was annoyed at being interrupted, I certainly wouldn't tell you.'

Polly chuckled. 'You wouldn't need to. Your body language is very clear. But don't get me wrong. *I* wasn't in the least offended. I shall be struggling with charitable thoughts myself.'

'Oh? Why?'

'Because in order to be introduced to you, I was dragged away from a very interesting discussion on education.'

David Locking-Hill, rising to his feet, froze. 'The implication being . . .' He was spared from having to finish his sentence by the maid announcing in a high, anxious voice that 'Dinner is ready'.

Polly smiled. 'Exactly.'

David regarded her from his great height and offered his arm. Polly, anxious not to offend him further, stood up and leaned on it.

Chapter Two

David performed his part of the ceremony with a detached efficiency. He ushered Polly to her place, put his hand under her elbow at exactly the right height and pulled out her chair at exactly the right moment. It was a racing certainty that he would never leave your left hand sawing frantically at the air as he held your coat. His manners were immaculate. But Polly wasn't at all surprised when he allowed Melissa to claim his attention, leaving Polly to take in her surroundings with disbelieving awe.

She could see why Melissa shied away from intimate little dinners. It would be easier to be intimate in a school cafeteria. Melissa's dining table was so shiny and so vast it could easily double as an indoor ice-hockey rink – perfect for dull winter evenings.

But in spite of its size, very little of the mahogany surface was on view. Melissa had managed to bejewel it with enough candelabra, wine coolers, bon-bon dishes, flower arrangements, cutlery and glasses for a small hotel. Each place setting could furnish the average family with a knife, fork and spoon. And one sip out of each glass would have most people well on the way to drunkenness, let alone over the legal limit for drivers. She must be Thomas Goode's best customer.

On the other hand, on discreet, closer inspection, Polly

discovered the table had leaves and could probably be reduced to half its size without much difficulty. There was no real need for Melissa to do things on such a massive scale.

Except that making things smaller was not Melissa's way. Polly remembered that from their schooldays. If she ever permitted herself such a vulgar thought, Melissa's motto could have been 'If you've got it, flaunt it'. Melissa always had the best-equipped pencil case, the shiniest leather satchel, the most expensive hair brush, looking glass and comb set with its own manicure 'pochette', and made sure it was noticed. Hiding her extremely lavish pocket money under a bushel was not a good use for it.

Melissa had obviously changed very little since those days. Her glasses were crystal and perfectly polished, but over-cut for Polly's taste. The silver was fiddly and too ornate. The flower arrangements were too high for comfortable, cross-table conversation.

And gazing around at the array of beautiful women and prosperous-looking men, Polly could see Melissa was still eager to be friends with those whom she considered the 'right' people. When at school, Polly hadn't recognized Melissa's anxiety to chum up with certain girls as social climbing. It was only now she realized that the girls in question either had titles of their own, or had titled parents.

She dimly remembered unkind digs about people 'smelling of the shop', which upset Melissa very much. Polly could never understand why – she thought shops smelt heavenly, of freshly ground coffee, newly baked bread, or scent. It was only the ironmonger's which sold bone meal loose by the pound that smelt unpleasant.

The happiest day of Melissa's schoolgirl life had been

14

when her father received a knighthood in the New Year's Honours List. 'Her mother's a lady at last,' commented one acid-tongued young nymphet. 'Which is more than can be said for yours, dear,' replied another.

Polly cast her gaze up the other end of the table. Sheldon, Melissa's husband, was admiring Thalia in an annoyingly obvious way.

Polly wondered about Sheldon. Why had Melissa married him? Had she given up the hope of a title and settled merely for a substantial entry in Debrett? Sheldon could surely provide that, otherwise he had little to recommend him. His neck bulged over the top of his collar, he had fat hands and it seemed he only had to see a woman in order to pant after her.

There was no accounting for taste, of course. He may have swept her off her feet. In his younger days he may have had a sort of dashing charm. Or he may have had an eye for the main chance. Melissa was a splendid catch – her wealthy father's only child and the sort of woman who lurked behind successful men, goading them on to stardom. Perhaps he was relying on her to get him a title, as Melissa's mother had for her father.

Whatever their reasons for marrying, she hoped Melissa was happy with him. Melissa may have been – and obviously still was – extremely bossy and overbearing, but she had a deep streak of kindness which deserved better than a fortune-hunter. At school one winter, when Polly was confined to the san with a persistent cough, Melissa had rung up her mother and demanded that Polly be sent Melissa's entire collection of Georgette Heyers. Polly had never forgotten the joy of having enough to read.

'How do you do. Hugh Bradley.' The carrying voice

broke into her reminiscences, and a long arm reached across the space until her hand met it halfway.

'Polly Cameron.' Surreptitiously she rubbed her fingers.

'Your other half here?'

Polly straightened her cutlery and unfolded her huge linen napkin. 'No, I'm not married.'

'Divorced, widowed, cohabiting?' Was he checking for availability, or just making conversation?

'No. I'm single. Is your wife here?'

She smiled warmly, knowing he'd have to have elastic extensions in his arms and legs if he'd planned to fondle her knee, or play footy-footy.

Hugh nodded and inclined his head up the other end of the table. 'Thalia – sitting next to Sheldon.'

'Oh.' Lucky man. Polly waited for him to come up with another opening gambit.

'So what do you do?'

Her luscious earrings had started to hurt. She discreetly removed them as she considered which of her many answers Hugh would like best. 'Waitress' was too blunt and missed out other aspects of her career, like washing-up. 'Salad maker' would involve far too much explanation. It would be nice to declare herself to be a potter, but until she made her living from it she wouldn't. 'I work in a wholefood cafe,' she said, opting for simplicity. 'What about you?'

Before Hugh could tell her, they were interrupted by the maid. She tottered in, staggering under the weight of a pile of huge soup plates. She put one in each place, and Polly discovered that they were cold. Another maid, possibly the twin sister of the first, followed with a tureen of soup, which she doled out over the flinching shoulders of the guests.

Polly watched in agony lest a drop, or even, heaven forbid, a ladleful go astray and ruin hundreds of pounds' worth of sartorial elegance. Fortunately, although diminutive, the maid was an accurate ladler. But by the time everyone was served and Melissa had ordered people to 'dig in', the soup was as cold as the plates.

Hugh, forgetting he was about to give Polly a potted life history, added a large quantity of salt to his *crème de stock cube and dried parsley* and scooped it up in three large spoonfuls.

Polly was impressed. Here was a man who didn't care about the finer points of etiquette, and had a hearty appetite. 'Would you like mine?' she asked him. 'I'm not very hungry.'

'I'm ravenous,' Hugh confessed. They both checked that Melissa, pushing her soup spoon delicately away from her, was too engrossed in a conversation about antiques with the man on her left to notice them swap plates. Hugh then dispatched Polly's soup with the same speed he had disposed of his own. 'Been playing golf all day.'

'Golf?' What could she possibly find to say about golf? Nothing. 'So, what did you say you did?'

Hugh was obviously dying to tell someone about the difficulties he'd had getting out of a bunker and, thwarted of his opportunity, became noncommittal.

'Oh, a bit of this, a bit of that. Basically, I suppose you could say I was in property.'

Polly, wondering vaguely if this was grammatically possible, said, 'Oh?' in a suitably interrogative way.

'Yah.' Hugh scraped optimistically at his empty plate.

17

'I'm working on a rather neat little deal in Laureton. Do you know it?'

'Yes.' Polly did indeed know it. She lived in it and loved it.

'Then you probably know that row of shops currently held up by scaffolding and fly posters?'

None better. She walked past it every day and thought about it often. She rested her elbow on the table, her beads clutched in her hand. 'Yes.'

'Then I think I can promise you a definite improvement in that area. A very *big* improvement.'

'Oh?' This was ominous news. So far the council hadn't found a buyer for those buildings, and while they were still searching for one the Laureton Action Group were desperately raising money so that they could buy and then preserve them.

'Have you bought the buildings, then?' she asked.

But Hugh winked at her, tapped the side of his nose and refused to be drawn. He was obviously delighted that having caught her interest he could leave her in suspense. Polly wanted to hit him, or give him a good kick on the shins. Prevented from relieving her feelings by courtesy to Melissa and her inability to reach his shins, she lapsed into a dignified silence.

The maids gathered the plates inexpertly on to their arms. Polly, whose nerves were already at breaking point, longed to help – partly to keep Melissa's china intact, and partly to get on to the side of the green baize door where she was most at home. She had had many jobs in her time, quite a lot of them to do with catering, and Melissa's staff obviously needed some sorting out.

The meal ground endlessly on. Polly took off her beads and hid them in her bag. She felt she was in a sort of social Disneyland, a theme park. Except that it was all very real to everyone else. It was only she, the outsider, who found the whole thing ridiculous. Hugh, having disposed of Polly's chicken in beige sauce and vitamin-free vegetables, found a more receptive audience to his bunker story on his right.

Some strange radar told David that Polly was now his responsibility, and he smiled at her, surprisingly warmly.

'Do you play golf?' she asked.

He shook his head.

That was a plus. 'So what do you play? I mean, what do you do to keep fit?'

David shrugged. 'I don't have much time for keeping fit, I keep busy instead.'

'And what do you keep busy at?'

'I'm a wine merchant.'

'Is that a lot of fun?'

David was obviously used to keeping his feelings concealed behind a mask of good manners, but the mask flickered. 'Not always.'

'Oh.' Polly was disappointed. 'So it's not all likening wines to freshly laid tarmac and old wellington boots?'

He shook his head. 'You're confusing what I do with being a television presenter talking about wine. I sell it.'

'But at least it's intrinsically pleasant. You could be selling surgical appliances or chemical lavatories.'

He nodded gravely. Polly had a hint that he might have a sense of humour after all. 'I could. And what do you do?'

Really, thought Polly, I ought to think up an answer, something calculated to end the conversation in one succinct sentence that she could trot out in situations like

19

this. Polly hated talking about herself, and she particularly hated talking about her job to people who had no notion what it was like to work in a kitchen. She talked about her pottery only to those she knew well, or who were artisans themselves and would understand.

'Nothing very exciting,' she said. 'Oh look, here comes pudding.'

Pudding was a pale mousse surrounded by a scarlet coulis and cream. It had probably looked stunning when it had appeared on *Masterchef*, but had obviously lost something in the translation.

'Consuela, dear.' Melissa's tone was as acid as the pureed strawberries. 'I thought I had explained about the cream being dotted on to the coulis? You remember? Like the picture?'

Consuela, who had her own defences, bobbed a curtsey. 'Yes, madam.'

Melissa started muttering to Thalia about the impossibility of getting good staff across her left-hand man. Because of the vast distance between each place, her complaints must have been clearly audible to Consuela and her sister. Polly cringed, picked up her spoon and approached her mousse.

She was wondering if she could force Hugh into telling her what his plans for the shops were when she became aware of David at her elbow, trying to catch her attention.

'Sorry, what? I was miles away.'

'I said, Melissa is trying to catch your eye.'

Polly looked towards Melissa, who was talking to Thalia, and back at David. 'Is she?'

He nodded. 'She wants you to withdraw.'

Polly had the feeling she was in a play, and didn't

know her lines. 'Me? Why? What have I done? Did Melissa see me give Hugh my dinner?'

She must have said something funny at last, because David was smiling. 'Not just you, all the ladies.'

The word 'ladies' rang a warning bell. 'Do you mean . . . ? No, you can't possibly.'

David nodded. 'I'm afraid Melissa intends to leave the gentlemen to their port so you girls can have a good gossip.' Not a muscle moved as he waited for the explosion.

Polly sat perfectly still. Anger, indignation and simple disbelief formed into a bubble which must surely burst. But somehow she kept it down. She didn't have the energy for a scene, and if Melissa was in dire need of enlightenment this was not the time or the place for her to be enlightened.

She regarded David as if the situation was somehow his fault. His serious expression mocked her indignation. For a moment she caught a glimpse of something behind the well-cut suit, the polished good manners, and saw a man she could be attracted to. But when she looked again it had vanished. His mask of respectability had descended to conceal whatever it was as if it had never been.

A thread of disappointment stirred in Polly and, recognizing it, she smiled to herself. Was Melissa's attempt at match-making having an effect? Or was it that she wasn't quite ready to turn into an eccentric old lady with only cats for company? Otherwise why on earth was she imagining there was more to David than a well-pressed shirt and nice tie?

She made a quick reconnoitre of the other men in the party, to see if any of them stirred her spinster soul. But no – they confirmed her conviction that being single had to be the best option. The last embers of a long-damped-down flame – a flame which had never burned strongly in the first place – had flickered again briefly before dying for ever.

Polly rearranged her collection of untouched glasses contemplatively, but not even a matching set of cut-glass water goblets, surely a wedding present, was enough to tempt her into marriage.

'But before you go -' David caught her attention again.

'Yes?'

'What is it that you do for Oxfam, Save the Children and Help the Aged so enthusiastically?'

She would never see him again. It didn't really matter if her answer embarrassed him. It was his fault for asking such a personal question.

She smiled. 'Where do you think I buy my clothes?'

Make of that what you will, she thought. Melissa's eye hit its mark. Polly rose to her feet with the other women and followed them out of the room.

As a body they went upstairs, presumably to tidy themselves after the exertions of the meal, although nobody seemed to have a hair out of place. The range of 'little' Jean Muirs, Caroline Charleses and Ronald Kleins looked as wonderful as ever. But Melissa always had managed to make people feel their hair needed combing and their socks pulling up, and these women were probably no exception.

But Polly had no desire to see how much mascara had landed under her lower lashes or what had happened to her hair. The discovery that she looked as if she'd been involved in a brawl and had done so for the past two hours would be an unpleasant shock best avoided. To aid her in this, she always brushed her hair and wiped under her eyes with a tissue *before* facing a mirror, rather than after.

Polly had intended to tell Melissa exactly what she thought of her antiquated notions of hospitality. If she hadn't seen it for herself, she would never have believed that people still separated men and women in such an out-dated, sexist way. It was high time Melissa and her friends joined the twentieth century.

But supposing they didn't want to? She could quite possibly be in the very heartland of the feminist back-lash. They might turn on her, hold her down on the bed and varnish her toe nails, or pinch her until she confessed that looking after a man was indeed the only career for real women. She shuddered. No, if they genuinely felt that port shouldn't be drunk in mixed company, who was she to try and convince them otherwise?

A Persian cat dashed out of Melissa's bedroom as Polly got there. The cat had apparently been caught taking an illicit nap and had covered somebody's coat in hairs.

'Oh, it's mine.' Polly saw her coat being held up in horror, and recognized the hairs as coming from her own cat. 'It doesn't matter, really.'

'It does matter,' contradicted Melissa. 'She knows she's not allowed up here. I'll get the girls to brush it for you.'

'Nonsense,' said Polly firmly, twitching her coat from Melissa's manicured grasp. 'The girls will be busy. I'll do it.' And then I'll go home, she added silently. Why didn't I think of that before?

The women regarded her, somewhat surprised.

'Have you all met Polly?' said Melissa, suddenly

wondering if inviting Polly had been such a good idea after all. 'We were at school together. Only, unlike me, she's managed to stay single.'

The women nodded and smiled, agreeing with Melissa that singleness was an unfortunate condition.

'Very wise,' said one. 'Husbands are so time-consuming. Not to mention children. One never has a minute to oneself, organizing everything for them.'

'Yes,' agreed Thalia. 'Being married is a full-time career.'

Polly smiled, but didn't ask what happened when that career comes to an end as the children leave home and your property-developer husband, no keener on preserving a once-beautiful wife than he is on preserving once-beautiful buildings, leaves you for a model which is easier to maintain. A few other skills might come in useful.

Though to be fair to him, Hugh-in-property may not have been that kind of developer at all. She may have been making quite unfair assumptions about what form his 'big improvement' would take. He may be planning to restore the buildings.

To her relief, the women reverted to the conversation they were having before her coat interrupted them.

Thalia went over to the full-length mirror. 'I finally got David to agree to it. And he's going to supply the wine. Goodness knows how I managed to talk him round.'

Thalia regarded the reason for his capitulation in the mirror with a sigh of satisfaction.

'I thought Hugh and David were at school together,' suggested the woman who Polly had been talking to about education. 'Perhaps that was why he agreed to do it.'

24

Thalia's beautiful eyes narrowed and Melissa broke in quickly, sensing the approach of an awkward atmosphere.

'You have got the perfect house for it, Thalia. If you want any help give me a buzz. I'd be delighted.'

'Just bring a party, Melissa dear,' said Thalia, 'And get them all to spend lots of money. I intend to make an absolute fortune.'

'Of course you will. It's *such* a good cause.' Melissa ran a comb through her hair and obediently it bounced into place. 'But if there's anything else that I can do, just let me know.'

Melissa's trying too hard, thought Polly, just as she had at school. If only she could be convinced that kind hearts were indeed worth more than coronets, and stop chasing up the rungs of the social ladder, she might be very much happier. In this set she was highly vulnerable to the sort of snubs she had endured at school.

Polly brushed at her coat. She would wait for a chance to slip out of the house unobtrusively. If she did the decent thing, and said her goodbyes and thank-you-for-having-mes, everyone would fuss and it would take her ages to get away. Melissa might even insist on someone – probably David – driving her, and she didn't have the strength.

She waited until everyone had geared themselves up for another hour or two of scintillating chit-chat with other people's husbands and had started to waft downstairs on a haze of duty-free scent.

'I won't be a moment, Melissa. I'll just tidy myself a little.'

'I always find long hair so difficult to manage,' said

Melissa, looking at her and implying that Polly found it almost impossible.

Polly sniffed Melissa's bottles, wondered if she washed her brushes every day, and glanced at her watch. She replied to Melissa's shrill enquiry from the hall that yes, she was quite all right, she was still trying to do something with her hair, and heard the drawing-room door close.

When she felt sure they were all sitting about Melissa's beige sofas, speculating which of their friends was sleeping with which other friend's husband, Polly tip-toed downstairs.

She felt as if she were bunking off school and remembered how at this stage she always collapsed into giggles, and a reminiscent bubble of hysteria threatened to break her cover. When she got to the front door she stopped wanting to laugh and only wanted to get out. She might as well try and bunk off from Alcatraz: the array of locks and bolts would have kept Fort Knox burglar-proof. Melissa's insurance company must have taken a lot of heavy losses to insist on such security. Either that, or she and Sheldon were extremely attached to their possessions.

But whatever the reason, Polly knew she'd never get them all undone silently, and before the chaps returned from whatever secret ceremony they were performing in the dining room. And it would be terribly undignified to be caught running away.

The door was a lot taller than she was, with a bolt right at the top. A sensible person would retire to the drawing room, vanquished. But Polly was no quitter and she badly wanted to go home.

Unfortunately there was nothing so useful as a chair in

that elegant hall, only a polished table and a marble pillar topped with an expensive, professional flower arrangement.

She considered the door, the table and the flower arrangement. She chose the flower arrangement. Lifting it carefully and placing it on the floor, she eased the pillar away from the wall and walked it the short distance to the door. Then she hitched up her skirt and got her knee on to it, levering herself up until she could reach the top bolt.

Bingo! Methodically, she worked down each specimen of modern security systems which fortunately were all well oiled and squeak-free. Then she clambered off the pillar and was about to replace it and the flowers when she heard the scraping of chairs and raised voices from the dining room.

Determined that she was not going to be caught with her dress round her thighs and the objet d'art askew, she made a run for it, and using both hands managed to hit on the right combination of latches to get the door open.

Unfortunately, it caught on the mat, which meant she had to drag it back until the opening was wide enough for her to get through. Unknown to her, she was not the only one anxious to cross that elegant threshold. The door was open a bare six inches when three ragged tom cats flew, like greyhounds from the traps, through the door and up the stairs, sending the flowers crashing to the floor.

Hypnotized, Polly saw them flash past and then flew in the opposite direction, somehow forcing her body through the tiny gap. Her bag hooked on the door handle, and as she freed it a yowl from Melissa's bedroom told her it was now the scene of a feline gang-bang. Melissa would probably issue her with a paternity suit. Too bad. She had escaped. She wrenched the door closed and made for her car.

A vicious January wind threw rain at her, and the thick gravel conspired with her high heels to trip her up as she stumbled across the drive.

Any minute the front door would open and she would be discovered leaving the scene of the crime, covered in confusion and circumstantial evidence. Where were her bloody keys? In despair, she leant against the car next to hers to have a really good look.

Instantly, its headlights went on and a high-pitched scream tore into the winter night.

'Oh, damn!'

Then, as her fingers closed on the keys, a wedge of light shone from the front door. The mat had obviously caught again, just giving her time to get into the car and switch on the engine.

Someone came down the steps as she reversed at full speed out of her parking space. She flicked on her headlights and lurched down the drive, gravel spurting from beneath her wheels.

'Melissa will never speak to me again.' A small urn fell over as she took a corner too fast. 'And a jolly good thing too.' She reached the road and started to laugh.

Chapter Three

❧❧❧

'. . . So, Bridget, remind me never to try to leave anywhere under the cover of darkness. A brass band ensemble and majorettes would be so much more discreet.' Polly completed her description of Saturday night's fiasco and picked the last of the cabbage out of the grater.

'Well, at least you won't be invited back.' Bridget took a tray of perfectly risen brown scones from the oven and set them to cool on top of the deep freeze. As the Whole Nut food shop and café's chief cook, she was responsible for most of the hot dishes served in the café. She also kept the other Whole Nut establishments supplied with quiches, homemade soups and freezer meals.

She did it all with an unruffled efficiency which in anyone else would have been maddening. But Bridget was remarkably uncritical. Everyone took a turn at cooking sometimes, but Bridget never expected anyone else to achieve so much in so short a time. She simply sorted out the muddles, threw away the mistakes and kept everyone happy. Everyone worked part time, but Bridget worked four days a week, and without her the place would fall apart.

Small and slight, with short dark hair, she had amazing stamina. Although she occasionally admitted she was tired after nine hours on her feet, she never slackened her pace of work or skimped on the cleaning up. Six years older than Polly, she was also her best friend. Monday morning was always spent hashing over the weekend.

Polly poured a stream of mayonnaise on to the heap of grated carrot and cabbage in the bowl in front of her. 'No, but I'll have to find homes for half a dozen misaligned kittens.'

She had sent Melissa an extremely pretty 'thank-you-and-I'm-sorry-about-the-chaos' postcard which had taken her a long time to compose, but she doubted it would do the trick. Even at school, Polly had realized her life would be very much easier if only Melissa had a better sense of humour. Gloomily she plunged her hands into the bowl. The mayonnaise was ice cold. 'So how was your weekend?'

Bridget deftly tossed half a dozen frozen baguettes into the oven. 'Okay. Someone rang me about overseeing the catering for a promise auction. It's a bit short notice, but I said I'd do it.'

'You're too soft-hearted,' said Polly. 'Never been known to say no, that's you.'

'Yes, well ... It was the school jumble sale on Saturday, and we went to see Alan's mother on Sunday.'

Bridget's change of subject distracted Polly from her usual lecture about being put upon – as she'd known it would.

'A jumble sale! And you let me miss it?'

'I didn't let you miss it. You were poorly, and resting for your big date. Remember?' Bridget picked up her knife, and with a few downward slashes followed by a rapid hammering action reduced an onion to the consistency of coarse salt.

Carrot and cabbage oozed between Polly's fingers as she dug down to the bottom of the bowl. 'Oh, yes. How was Alan's mother?'

'Motherly.' Another onion met the same fate.

'And how's Alan?'

'Fine.' Bridget's knife paused in its slaughter and her smile took on the dreamy satisfaction of a woman who had been thoroughly made love to.

Polly sighed. Bridget's relationship with her husband seriously threatened Polly's commitment to celibacy. Friends and lovers after twenty years of marriage, they made Polly wonder if there was something to be said for it after all. But, she frequently reasoned with herself and anyone else who would listen, how many couples were as happy as that? Far more were trapped in relationships which brought neither pleasure nor profit. Bridget and Alan were the exception.

Polly crossed the kitchen and submerged her freezing cabbage-coated hands into the hot, clean washing-up water with which their co-worker Beth had so thoughtfully filled the sink.

It was a mortal sin. Beth liked her washing-up water without a coleslaw scum on the surface, and had provided a tub of hot water for Polly to rinse her hands in. Too late, Polly noticed it, and slightly shame-faced scuttled back to her work bench, hoping Beth wouldn't notice.

Polly always worked better in a mess and found it a struggle to keep up with the standards so effortlessly achieved by the others. She excused herself by claiming there was no time to clear up if she was to produce six minor Alps of salad by twelve o'clock. Her workmates didn't agree. They did not subscribe to Polly's theory that you couldn't make an omelette without making a mess on the floor. But they had long since despaired of reforming her.

Beth, returning from the serving area with a loaded tray, saw the scraps of cabbage floating in the water. As usual, she muttered at Polly's thoughtlessness. Polly grimaced ruefully, aware that without Beth's good-natured efficiency the Whole Nut café would be even more stressful than it was already.

'So what did you get up to last night, young Beth?' asked Bridget. The onions were now sweating in a pan and she was slicing carrots into matchsticks. Everything she did was precise and perfect. Anything that didn't come up to her exacting standards went into the pig-bin.

'Went to the pub, got really, really drunk. Had a great time.' Before either Bridget or Polly could comment, the bell rang in the café. Beth swayed into the serving area. At eighteen she had all the rustic sensuality of Tess of the D'Urbervilles, but none of her innocence. She had long, dark red hair, clear, unfreckled skin and a cleavage which even her plastic apron couldn't hide. She had a startling effect on some of the customers.

'I'm frightened that Beth'll get herself into serious trouble one of these days,' said Bridget, beating a white sauce into submission with a whisk.

Polly shook her head. 'She won't. She's more street-wise than you and me put together, and is far too bright to get herself into a situation she can't get out of.'

'I hope you're right.'

'I'm sure I am.'

Beth gave Bridget and Polly cause for motherly concern. Polly was quite sure she didn't get up to half what she claimed to, and was convinced she deliberately

32

told them stories to make them cluck. But Bridget was not willing to take the chance, and gave her packets of condoms for her birthday and bought her a supply of sticking plasters. This was after Beth took to using bright blue catering plasters to cover up her love bites – not so much to conceal the problem as to advertise it. The management had then asked how she'd managed to cut herself on her neck.

'So what was the bloke like, then?' Beth loaded the dishwasher with cups. 'The one you were supposed to meet?'

Polly's undignified departure had briefly pushed the reason why she had been invited out of her mind. 'Oh, yes. Well, I met him. But I can't think why Melissa thought we'd get on.'

'So what was he like?'

Polly rinsed the last of the coleslaw out of her bowl and wiped it dry, thinking how best to describe that perfect example of English manhood in one simple phrase. 'My mother would love him.'

'Oh? Why?' said Bridget. A mother herself, she had a lot of sympathy for Polly's.

'Clean-cut and financially viable. He's a wine merchant. A mother-in-law's dream. Particularly one who likes a nice amontillado.'

Beth slammed the dishwasher shut and switched it on, not very impressed. 'Did you fancy him?'

'I hardly know him!'

'So? Did you fancy him?' Beth couldn't understand why Polly found this question hard to answer. She perfectly understood Polly's desire to stay single – why buy a book when you can join a library? – but she found her reluctance to sleep with her men friends incomprehensible.

Polly thought hard. 'I find it very difficult to fancy people I don't know, Beth. But if I had to sleep with someone, I dare say I could manage it with him without screaming.'

'Anyone would think you were still a virgin, the way you carry on.' Beth disdainfully attacked the knives and forks with a tea towel.

'If I was still a virgin, I'd be keener on sex. I wouldn't know how thoroughly disappointing it is – either sordid or boring.' Having thrown out this challenge, Polly started slicing mushrooms.

Bridget had long since stopped telling Polly that with the right person sex was a beautiful and meaningful expression of love, and continued to make her quiches. But Beth never missed an opportunity to put Polly right, and sex was her favourite subject.

'You don't get enough practice, you don't. If you went to bed with a few fellas, you'd get better at it.'

They'd been down this road before. 'But Beth,' Polly explained patiently, 'I couldn't sleep with someone I didn't like, and I couldn't sleep with someone I did like just for practice. It wouldn't be right.'

'You'll be over the hill and never 'ad an orgasm, you will,' said Beth brutally. 'Think of that.'

'Nonsense!' Bridget broke in. 'Polly's only just approaching the peak of her sexuality!'

Polly wasn't at all grateful for this attempted rescue. But Bridget often declared how much fun life became when your children were older and less exhausting; she wanted people to see approaching maturity as a positive experience.

Although Polly didn't mind growing older, now highlights in her hair were part of her life, she didn't terribly like the idea of becoming sexually active after years of celibacy.

Even at eighteen she had felt self-conscious about her pear-shaped body. Then it had at least been a smooth pear. Now her thighs were beginning to take on the colour and texture of cold porridge. And although her breasts were fuller, the thought of exposing her dimpled flesh to the possibly critical gaze of a man was not appealing.

And why put herself through all that embarrassment for something she lived perfectly happily without? But she would never convince either Bridget or Beth, and Monday morning was no time for this well-trodden argument. So Polly turned up the radio.

'Time for "Our Tune", girls. And no talking through it, Beth.' Polly retrieved a huge bowl of boiled eggs from under her bench. 'I've got sixty-five eggs to peel, I need a nice sad story to keep me going.'

'You two must be the only ones who actually cry when they listen to this rubbish,' Beth began.

'Shut up!' yelled Polly and Bridget in unison.

Beth raised her eyes to heaven and retreated to the sink.

The disc jockey's special 'Our Tune' voice, laden with sympathy and understanding, introduced the story.

'I'm going to change the names, not because they're ashamed . . .' In the background the theme tune to the film of *Romeo and Juliet* plucked plaintively at Bridget and Polly's heartstrings.

'. . . it all started when Sharon was fifteen . . .'

Beth, who wasn't sentimental, didn't care about the

dead babies, sick husbands and fathers who died without knowing they were loved, clanged the dishwasher door. As one, Polly and Bridget disabled the machine and tied a teatowel round Beth's mouth. They put up with a lot from Beth, but 'Our Tune' was sacred.

'I'll write an "Our Tune" for you, Poll,' said Beth, freeing herself from the towel. 'When you finally get a man.'

'I don't want a man. I'm quite happy as I am,' insisted Polly. 'Come and give me a hand with these eggs.'

'Well, at least have a lover,' Beth continued ten minutes later, after Polly and Bridget had wiped their eyes and the kitchen returned to noisy normality. 'As a pet. Just for sex.'

'Beth –' Polly quoted Bridget, her features solemn. 'Sex is a sacred expression of love between men and women who –'

'Otherwise you'll go funny. Even funnier than you already are.'

'Nonsense.' Polly wasn't at all offended. 'People who abstain from sex are more creative.'

'Where'd you get that load of crap from?' Beth called a spade a spade.

'I read it somewhere. Some quite well-thought-of medical correspondent wrote an article about how she and her husband had decided to abstain from sex to free their creative urges for other things.'

Beth's lip curled and her eyes narrowed. 'You know, Polly, I worry about you.'

'. . . and it's a well-known fact that nuns rarely, if ever, suffer from hypertension.'

'Cowmuck!'

36

'That might be because they spend all day praying,' Bridget put in. 'Very soothing, all that prayer.'

'Well anyway,' Polly persisted, knowing she was in a corner she couldn't argue her way out of, 'I can live perfectly well without it.'

'That is a matter of opinion.' Beth stripped the peel from an egg as the bell in the café rang imperiously. 'Sex is fun.' She tucked the eggshell down the front of Polly's apron, and went off to answer the summons.

Polly fished for the eggshell without rancour. She was saving up her annoyance against the time Beth found herself head first in the wheely bin.

'Beth's right, you know. Sex is part of healthy living.' Bridget switched on the liquidizer.

'What about the nuns?' Polly shrieked in protest, and then repeated herself when she could be heard.

'You're not a nun.'

'I know, but I'm perfectly happy. I don't need a man to complete me. I've got my home . . .'

'Rented.'

'My job . . .'

'Part-time and underpaid.'

'My pottery.'

'Part-time and not paid at all.'

'My garden . . .'

'A north-facing precipice.'

'And a full and stimulating social life . . .'

'With women, couples or men looking for replacement mothers.'

'Exactly!' Polly pounced on Bridget's slip. 'I don't want to be any man's mother, which is why I'm staying single.'

Bridget removed a tray of small quiches from the oven. 'But wouldn't you like to be a *baby's* mother?'

'Well, yes.' Polly chopped an egg into four and added it to the pile. 'Sometimes I think I'd like a baby. But it's a very selfish thing to do, having kids.'

If she was hoping to get a rise out of Bridget she was disappointed.

'I mean, what kind of a world are you bringing them into?' she persisted. 'They don't ask to be born. Having them is only a primitive desire to recreate one's genes. And for a single woman –'

'You could get married first.'

'. . . for a single woman to have a child, simply for the sake of her own hormones, is the most selfish thing of all.'

'That's true.' Bridget always looked at everything from all sides. 'I would never encourage you to have kids just for your sake. But the family unit –'

'Oh, stuff the family unit. I admit there are times when it would be nice to have a man about the place, but once you've got the hang of a Black and Decker, those times are very few and far between. And think what you give up. Just because the ballcock on the loo needs replacing from time to time. I couldn't make the compromises, not at my age.'

'Thirty-five is not old.' Bridget was forty-one.

'I know, but it is mature. I've lived on my own since I was twenty-five. I have my little ways – you might even say I'm a touch sluttish . . .' Polly made a face at Bridget, daring her to argue.

Bridget shot her a frown and was about to do exactly that when Beth bounced in with a loaded tray.

'So why don't you like sex, then?'

'You're obsessed, Beth! Don't you ever think about anything else?'

'Sometimes. But I really want to know. It's interesting.'

Polly gritted her teeth, wondering what it was about kitchens which brought out the lowest aspects of human nature. 'You really want the grisly details?' She didn't expect the answer to be 'no', but being of an optimistic turn of mind thought she'd ask.

'Too right!' said Beth. Even Bridget looked interested.

'Go on, Poll,' said Beth. 'Tell us how it happened.'

'You asked for it. I was in France.'

'Very romantic.'

'Look, do you want to hear this story or not?'

'We do, we do. Shut up, Beth. Tell us, Polly.'

'I was on holiday with a group of friends. Two boys, two girls, two tents. All perfectly respectable.'

'Shame!'

'I was twenty. I'd been going out with this boy for about four months when we decided to go on holiday. I knew I would have to sleep with him sooner or later . . .'

Beth and Bridget suppressed little noises of distress.

'So one night, after drinking a lot of cheap red wine, I told Stephen I'd let him make love to me.'

Bridget whimpered under her breath.

'The others had gone for a moonlit walk along the beach, so Stephen took me into the boys' tent.'

A particularly stubborn egg took her attention away from her narrative for a maddening moment.

'Go on!'

'Yes, come on, Poll. I've got a pizza to make.'

'Well, firstly the whole campsite might have been in the tent with us, for all the privacy we had. And the boys had been peeing on the grass outside the tent rather than go all the way to the toilet block, and the stench was terrible. And stones kept digging through the camping mat into my back, and it was absolute agony. It wasn't much fun for Stephen, either.'

Bridget nodded sympathetically. 'I expect you were both two-in-tents.'

Beth acknowledged this pun by wiping her wet hand round Bridget's neck and went out to answer her bell. 'Didn't you try again?' she demanded when she returned.

'Yes. Back at Oxford.'

'I didn't know you'd been to Oxford.' Bridget was impressed.

'Yes. To secretarial college.'

Beth scowled at Bridget for interrupting the story. 'Go on, then.'

'He took me to his lodgings. He was at Christ Church.'

'Well, wasn't it better the second time?'

'No. He'd just introduced me to his landlady. She was a sweet old thing, and she gave us tea and biscuits. I couldn't get in the mood with her in the next room moving about. I kept thinking she might knock on the door for some reason.'

'So you didn't even try?' Beth positively revelled in compromising situations.

'I let him have his evil way with me, and it wasn't quite so painful. But all I could think about was making a mess on the sheets and wishing he'd hurry up. Afterwards he asked me how it was for me, and I said very nice thank you, can you take me home now? The relationship fizzled out soon after that. My faked orgasm obviously wasn't convincing enough.'

'Poor Polly,' said Bridget. 'Did you never try again with anyone else?'

'Well, there was a what-the-hell attempt with a romantic Frenchman. But all that got me was a second-hand portion of snails in garlic butter, and an attack of cystitis. I still feel vaguely uncomfortable whenever I smell a Gauloise.'

The telephone started ringing. She answered it, read out the order for savouries and put it down. Beth and Bridget were still eagerly awaiting further details. She shrugged. 'I gave it up as a bad job after that.'

'And you haven't had a man since you were in your twenties?' Beth was surprised Polly was still alive and relatively sane.

'I really don't think you've given sex a fair chance, Poll,' said Bridget.

'Well, perhaps not. But why should I put myself and some other poor soul through agonies, only to discover I was right the first time? Sex is a let-down.'

'You just need the right bloke,' said Beth.

Bridget nodded. 'One who you love and –'

'One who knows what the hell he's doing!' Beth gave them both a pitying look and answered the bell. She returned a few minutes later.

'Now *there's* a guy who knows what's what,' she said. 'Go and check him out, Polly.'

Polly hesitated. The mess on her bench had got to the stage when even she felt she had to do something about it.

'Oh, I'll deal with that lot! Go and clear the tables.'

It was an offer too good to refuse. Polly went into the café armed with a damp cloth.

Sitting with a pile of papers in front of him was a man

with curly black hair and a thick gold earring. He was wearing a leather jacket, white T-shirt and denim jeans. Apart from his designer stubble, Polly couldn't see much of him, but she looked him over for Beth's sake.

She wiped the tables and retreated to the kitchen. 'Too young for me, Beth. He's only in his twenties.'

'Well, if you will go round with wrinklies, no wonder you don't enjoy sex very much.'

'Age has nothing to do with it,' said Bridget and Polly in unison. 'Or is that size?' added Polly.

'I give up!' Disgusted, Beth loaded herself up with clean cups to take into the serving area and let Polly get on with her salads.

Chapter Four

❧❧❧

Her shopping banged against her legs as Polly struggled homewards up the hill. The town was at its best at dusk, when its steep narrow streets and higgledy-piggledy houses took on a Christmas-card appearance. In daylight, gatherings of adolescents in the pedestrianized High Street and outside the amusement arcade revealed Laureton to be the unemployed capital of the South Cotswolds.

But in the evening the street lights, and what passed for a rush-hour, seemed to Polly to restore its status as a working class wool town. A good fall of snow, and it would be positively picturesque.

In spite of the fact that most of its youth were out of work, Laureton was not depressed. It hummed with a Green, homespun, anarchic vitality which thumbed its runny nose at more prosperous parts of Gloucestershire. While they created little but photo opportunities for tourists and pretty settings for antique shops, Laureton sold rope and ironmongery and had devised its own currency.

Usually Polly loved it. Now she wished it wasn't quite so hilly.

She approached the row of shops which had been empty ever since she moved to the town. Only if you looked closely could you see the beauty of the roofs above the hanging hoardings and peeling posters. There was now a huge red notice, like a bloody slash, across them: 'Under Offer.'

It was no doubt they were an eyesore, black and dilapidated amid the relative prosperity of the rest of the High Street. But Polly dreaded what the ravenous Hugh might consider an improvement. The cost of restoring them would be more than was profitable to someone 'in property'.

As she reached the buildings, she saw a figure staring up at them. It was Mac.

Mac was a rabidly left-wing carpenter friend of Polly's, whose hobbies included Appalachian clog dancing. Mac had a way with 'young people', wore his hair in a ponytail and dressed in tattered jeans and anarchic sweatshirts. He was the main force behind the Action Group and Polly found him extremely attractive.

'Hello, Mac.' She stopped beside him. 'They've been sold, then.'

'Near as makes no difference, but we're not giving in.'

Polly was glad to hear it. 'But what can we do? If contracts have changed hands . . .?'

'They haven't, yet. There's still time to try and raise the money ourselves.' Mac grinned. 'How's your head for heights, Poll?'

'Awful, why?'

'We're going to take up occupation. I wouldn't put it past that Bradley bloke to try and damage the buildings – but he can't if they're occupied, can he?'

Polly wondered, not for the first time, if Mac wasn't rather too radical for her. 'Is that the only way?'

'Reckon so. We've wasted enough trees writing letters no one reads.'

Polly swallowed hard. 'Well, I'll do everything I can to support you, but from the ground.'

Mac grinned again. 'Thanks, gal. But we've still got most of the Save the High Street mugs you made. You could design a few fly posters. I'll get Jake to print 'em, and then you can help distribute them.'

'Of course, Mac. Nothing I like better than being prosecuted for bill-sticking.'

'"Bill Stickers is innocent!" eh?' Mac chuckled. To him getting arrested was an occupational hazard, like getting wet hands is for window cleaners.

Polly made a face and continued up the hill, feeling a little more cheerful. If anyone could save those buildings, Mac could.

The surrounding villages which nestled in, or perched on, the five hills which culminated in Laureton, housed a cross section of country society. The genuine county ran the pony clubs for the children of harassed ex-yuppies who worked along the M4 corridor, although neither yuppies nor motorway got nearer to Laureton than the out-of-town supermarket. There they bumped trolleys with ex-captains of industry and ex-colonels of the army, united in their search for cut-price gin and petrol. They, too, shunned the town, preferring to shop where parking was easier and the drug culture better disguised. Melissa would never shop in Laureton unless she was really up against it.

But ever since she'd escaped from secretarial work to go to the art school there, Laureton had suited Polly. And so did her fellow residents. Ex-hippies who couldn't quite hack life in West Wales sold their organic vegetables in the market. Every sort of alternative therapy was available in the High Street. Actors ran stress-management courses while waiting for their agents to phone. Sculptors restored stately homes or drystone walls between commissions. And artists opened their kitchens to teach print-making and silk-screening. Teachers and social workers formed consciousness-raising book groups.

Binding the peripatetic, ephemeral in-comers into a community were the born-and-bred Lauretonians, who looked on the comings and goings of the others with philosophical tolerance. And among these, Polly found a circle of friends she could depend on. And none of them would sit back and see the heart torn out of their town.

To Polly's mother, who lived in Oxford – unthreatened, historic, academic and flat – her friends were an odd lot. She was always trying to persuade Polly to move back to Oxford – 'Give you a chance to meet some really nice men.' But Polly had found her niche where academic qualifications were less important than street cred, and class not important at all. However, when she had been on her feet all day and her ankles were beginning to throb, the idea of being able to bicycle home without pushing it three-quarters of the way became more tempting.

She finally made it up the last stretch to where her tiny rented cottage snuggled between an ex-pub and a Steiner Kindergarten. And as she heaved her bags through the gate, which had to be lifted open, it occured to her that a man about the place might be useful. The gate did need repairing and brawn had its place when it came to heaving baulks of timber about.

But she had rejected the notion by the time she had reached the porch. This elderly structure made of 'rustic' poles was held up entirely by the competition between a honeysuckle and a rose to pull it down. And both tried to pull people on to their side by catching at their clothes. No man would tolerate such rebellious behaviour from his plants and so the porch would collapse, never to be rebuilt. Polly knew about men. Better to fix the gate herself than put up with so much interference.

As she struggled to wriggle her front-door key to the exact angle it required before it would open, she heard the telephone ringing.

She didn't hurry. Only her mother would ring her before six, and she would ring again. And as her mother would be wanting a detailed account of Melissa's dinner party, Polly needed time to think. How could she describe that fiasco in a way which would satisfy her own regard for truth, and not offend her mother? Sylvia Cameron had not brought her daughter up to run away from dinner parties because they offended her feminist sensibilities.

As the key turned and the ringing stopped, Polly wondered, for the thousandth time, if she would ever stop trying to please her mother. Or if her mother would ever accept that Polly did not want a husband. Being the only child of a widow was a great responsibility.

She fell over the step into the welcoming muddle which was her sitting room. She dumped her shopping bags on the floor and failed to avoid Selina, her cat, who took her opportunity to leap on to her shoulder. Just sometimes Polly wished Selina wasn't quite so dog-like in her devotion. A bit of aloofness would go down well at this time of day.

'Hello, darling. Yes, I love you. Yes, I've brought you

some food. Ow!' The cat's claws clenched in ecstasy, penetrating her coat, two jumpers and a T-shirt.

With Selina weaving round her face making seeing difficult, Polly negotiated her way past piles of books, baskets of washing, boxes of pots and last night's supper things to the kitchen. There the warmth of the Rayburn embraced her like an old friend.

The Rayburn was the reason she had rented the house. It was a benign presence, a constant in an uncertain world. If she felt low, she would fold a towel on its lid and sit on it, her feet on a chair, a cup of tea to hand, and read. It suited Polly's sort of cooking and it produced unlimited hot water. A radiator leading off it kept her bathroom blissfully warm – the only room in the house which was. It also dried her clothes and her pots.

For this she forgave the riddling, the humping of coal, the emptying of ash, the putting out of heavy, ash-filled dustbins, the smoky smell which pervaded the clothes which hung above it. She could even forgive it its indigestion, manifested by huge, sulphur-filled belches which covered everything within range with soot. Regularly, once a month in winter, she cleaned out its chimney. It was a filthy job which required removing a cast-iron plate, but she did it, as Bridget's son once said as he watched her, 'as tenderly as if she was James Herriot delivering twin lambs'.

It was one of the many things about Polly that her mother couldn't comprehend.

'You maintain that having a husband would take up too much time and energy, but men aren't half as temperamental as that dirty old stove. If you got one who'd provide you with central heating and a decent

48

cooker you'd have lots more time to make your pots. Heaving coal about is so – *unfeminine.*'

And, as is the way of mothers, Polly's considered her daughter's lack of femininity to be all her fault. Somewhere she had gone disastrously wrong. Her frequent, exasperated cries that 'No husband would put up with anyone as untidy as you!' during rows about the state of Polly's bedroom, had not, as was the intention, made Polly mend her ways. Instead they sowed the seed of her resolution that no husband would ever have to.

Of course, if she'd known that Polly would forswear men before messiness, Sylvia Cameron would have let her daughter live in a pigsty. She would then have had a chance of grandchildren – or, as Polly unkindly suggested, at least a litter of piglets. As it was, Sylvia Cameron was still grandchildless, and if Polly didn't seem to notice that her best-before date was rapidly approaching, her mother did. Polly's childbearing ticket was about to expire without the family christening robe being taken out of its sandalwood box.

Now, thinking about this oft-repeated conversation and Melissa's dinner party, Polly wondered if a litter of kittens with a very aristocratic mother would satisfy her mother. Probably not.

Polly slid the kettle on to the hotplate and opened a tin of cat food. Selina deigned to leap off her shoulders on to the kitchen table and from there to the floor. For the time it took her to clear her dish, Polly would be free to pursue her own thoughts. Her mother could only be put off so long. She had been thrilled to hear that Melissa and Polly had met up again, and was in ecstasies at the thought that Polly was at last moving in the circle of friends Sylvia considered her daughter's true milieu.

'Poor Mummy.' Polly poured water on to a tea bag in a mug of her own making. 'When will she understand that I'm happy as I am?'

It was, she knew, her desire for grandchildren which kept Sylvia plugging on at Polly's independence. And when Polly's own hormones also nagged at her, she almost buckled under the pressure.

But supposing she decided bringing up a baby alone wasn't such a bad idea, how would she choose a father? 'Excuse me, you look as if you've got nice genes, would you care to make a baby with me?' Hardly. And artificial insemination was too cold-blooded, and fortunately her mother considered the whole idea disgusting. Otherwise she would be offering to pay for the operation and to look after the child.

Polly went into the sitting room, hugging her mug of tea, and sat down, still wearing her overcoat. In a minute she would summon up the strength to light the fire. And just as it reached the point when it couldn't be left without it going out, her mother would ring again.

'Are you tired, darling?' she would say. And Polly would either deny it brightly, or confess. Whereupon her mother would ask again why she had such a – an *ordinary* (meaning 'common') job, when she was so bright and talented? Sylvia would have been quite happy for Polly to have been a secretary, typing her life away, if she'd worked for men with public-school accents. But to divide her time between a café – albeit a very respectable wholefood café – and messing about with clay was not acceptable.

'Pottery is a lovely hobby, darling, but it's not – well – exactly *secure*, is it?'

It wasn't, but that wasn't a good enough reason to give

up something which gave her so much pleasure and satisfaction. Polly sat down and put her elbows on the table. If she could make a little more money from her pots, her potting could be wholly justified. But at present she was hardly earning enough from it to pay her rent on the studio.

Selina had finished her dinner and now wanted to catch up on the affection she'd missed all day. Polly dodged her dribble-laden chin as best she could as she looked at yesterday's crossword. Selina, insanely jealous of the newspaper, stepped up her offensive and managed to get both front paws round Polly's neck and, once there, got a good few dollops of saliva on to her coat.

Polly gave up and closed her eyes. The cat had finally settled for lying across Polly's neck, so at least her spit was confined to her shoulder, when the telephone rang again.

If I was strong, she told herself, struggling to her feet, I'd let it ring.

It was Bridget. 'I'm dreadfully sorry to bother you, but I wonder if you could do me the most terrific favour.'

Relief that she didn't have to talk to her mother made Polly expansive. 'Of course, Bridget. Anything.'

'You're not going to like it.'

'Tell me.'

'Well, you remember that promise auction I was going to be overseeing the catering for?'

Polly tried. 'Not really, but tell me anyway.'

'It turns out that Neil's school play is on the same night. The wretched boy didn't tell us until just now.'

'And?'

'I wondered if you'd do it.'

Bridget sounded so anxious, Polly couldn't help

teasing her. 'Neil's school play? I'm flattered to be asked but –'

'The promise auction, idiot. Will you go along and see that the caterers don't make a muddle for me?'

'Bridget, I'm not quite sure what a promise auction is.'

'Aren't you? The PTA at Cherry's school runs them sometimes. People offer things like babysitting, ironing, gardening, a week in their little places in France. And the lots are sold, just like at an auction. It raises money.'

'It doesn't sound the sort of affair to have caterers.'

'This one does, it's posh. It's at Cannongate Hall.' Bridget paused. Local curiosity about the new owners of Cannongate Hall was rife, and Polly was among the most curious.

'Oh.'

'Yes. And people will be offering their Tuscan villas for a month, shooting in Scotland, really scrummy things.'

'Bridget, have you ever heard me express a desire to go shooting in Scotland?'

'No, but since you couldn't afford the sort of prices these things'll be going for anyway, that's neither here nor there.'

'So what do I get out of it?'

'A million Brownie points from me, and a chance to see inside Cannongate Hall, which has to be worth an evening on your feet.'

'Wearing a little black dress and a pinny.'

'No pinny. I was going in a strictly supervisory role.'

'And how did you get roped in anyway?'

Bridget sighed. 'Alan's boss asked me. It's too long and boring to explain why. But it's a very good cause.' She mentioned a local group devoted to preserving the countryside and vernacular architecture. 'Can you possibly do it? It'll be a doddle – nothing like that ghastly wedding we did.' She paused again, sensing Polly had not yet capitulated. 'I don't want to take you away from anything more important. There isn't a committee meeting for the Save the High Street campaign next Saturday, is there?'

'No. I was only planning to snuggle up with a good book.'

'So you'll do it?'

Polly sighed. 'I suppose so. But you're not to make a habit of this, Bridget. I love helping you, but I've no intention of making a career out of vol-au-vents and doilies, even if you have.'

Bridget was so relieved that Polly was going to stand in for her, she ignored this remark. 'Bless you. You're a brick.'

'A soft brick.'

Bridget chuckled. 'You and me both. Call round on Wednesday, after you've finished at the studio, and I'll give you the details.'

Polly put down the telephone, smiling. Bridget was the only person who referred to the converted garden shed which she used for her pottery as a 'studio'. She loved her for it.

But on Wednesday, by the time Bridget had issued her list of dos and don'ts, Polly had stopped loving her.

'Really, Bridget, if you have so little faith in my abilities, why ask me to stand in for you?'

Bridget looked Polly straight in the eye. 'Because you may be totally disorganized, but I have taught you everything I know. And you are good at soothing ruffled feathers, and can get on with anyone from a duchess to a dustman.'

'And which will I need to be chummy with at this do?'

'Neither, but the committee were going to save money by roping in their teenage daughters to help.'

'Oh, God.'

'Exactly,' said Bridget. 'They'll get in the way and giggle and be a thorough nuisance. And you have to stop the paid staff from swearing at them, or the little dears' rich parents won't spend any money and the whole thing will be the most ghastly flop.' Bridget regarded her friend seriously. 'Will you be able to cope?'

'Of course!' said Polly blithely. 'Don't worry so, Bridge!'

She left the room whistling 'The Sorcerer's Apprentice'.

Polly took her black velvet dress out of the cupboard. It still smelled slightly of Melissa's dinner party: smoke, scent, other people. But in deference to its 'Dry clean only' label, Polly washed it on a woollens cycle, and she hadn't had access to Bridget's washing machine recently. But a good shake and a gentle steaming while Polly had a bath should restore its bloom sufficiently for the occasion.

She was quite looking forward to visiting Cannongate Hall. It had changed hands a couple of years ago, and if local rumour was anything to go by was more opulent than the whole of Hollywood Boulevard put together. The asses' milk on tap in the master suite was probably an apocryphal tale, but there should be something fairly exotic by way of a Jacuzzi.

The black dress would do, but, as her position as supervisor to the caterers required, she added only a single string of *faux* pearls (25p at a car boot sale – fine when you could be sure that no one was likely to bite at them when they were actually on) and a pair of pearl studs, which her mother had given her and were real.

She clipped her hair into a black velvet bow, and checked there were no slivers of clay caught in her nails. Black tights and her good shoes saw her discreetly elegant, if a little safe for her taste. Then she hauled her late father's British Warm overcoat, designed for the bridge of a battleship and weighing a fraction over three stone, out of her wardrobe and climbed into it.

Its weight made it difficult to move about in, or even stand upright, but it would keep the Arctic at bay. Polly felt confident that if the car broke down and she was forced to sleep the night in it, her British Warm would keep her from hypothermia and possibly even a chill.

As the heater in her car wasn't terribly efficient, Polly was glad of her coat before she finally found herself driving between the handsome, wrought-iron gates of Cannongate Hall. But before she got near the Palladian front, which included a huge portico, a man in the modern equivalent of Polly's coat took one look at Polly's car and directed her to the back of the house with a jerk of his thumb.

Chastened, Polly crept humbly round to the stable block in her Morris 1000, feeling that the massive edifice truly deserved the title of 'pile'. Pile of what, Polly hadn't seen enough to decide. But there was certainly plenty.

Much to Polly's relief, a caterer's van was already in situ. She had enough inside knowledge of the catering trade to realize what an unreliable profession it could be. She was quite prepared, though not entirely able, to find herself expected to feed two hundred people single-handed. Knowing that there would be at least one other person to help her lifted her spirits considerably.

She knocked on the door and waited. Eventually some sort of butler, who, Polly could tell by the discontent etched into his beetling brows, his hunched shoulders and the lines on either side of his downturned mouth, had been employed by the employers before last, opened it. He was not at all happy with the present incumbents but refused to leave until they offered him a decent pension.

'Yes?' he demanded, bitterly resenting the whole notion of opening the house for a charity event, and completely uncaring of who knew it.

'Good evening.' Polly smiled sympathetically. 'My name's Polly Cameron. I've come to supervise the caterers.'

The butler grunted and opened the door wider. 'The kitchen's through here.'

He led her through a series of dusty corridors which had been untouched, and possibly uncleaned, by several generations of 'family' and all the more recent owners of Cannongate Hall.

'This must be an awful nuisance for you,' said Polly, hurrying to keep up with him. 'Having hordes of people coming in from outside, getting in the way.'

The butler didn't reply, but he slowed down somewhat. Polly knew that while the butler would have nothing whatever to do with the caterers, and very little to do with his current masters, if the chips descended it would be him she needed on her side. It would be the butler who knew where the fuse box was and how to turn off the stopcock. Polly had been in similar situations

– where anything that can go wrong feels obliged to do so.

When they finally reached the kitchen, Polly gave the butler a very warm smile, and thanked him – a little gratitude on account.

The kitchen, while not as romantically undisturbed as the rooms on the way to it, was comparatively untouched by modern ideas of convenience. Had the National Trust adopted it and charged a large fee to visit, it would have inspired gusty sighs of nostalgia from everyone born before the Second World War and gasps of disbelief from anyone born since. Clean and properly lit, it would have been attractive and quaint. Now it just looked dreary.

Miles of grubby cream paint, a quarry-tiled floor designed to need washing several times a day and to make your feet ache in minutes; cupboards which rose to the ceiling, and which were impossible to reach without standing on a chair, if you could find one which wouldn't wobble dangerously on the uneven surface. Not the perfect setting in which to provide an elegant buffet for two hundred people.

However, a man whose dress trousers and starched shirt declared him to be in charge, and his three henchwomen, were apparently willing to do the best they could. They had obviously been there a while.

The youngest woman, who was about seventeen, was washing something, at a sink in a lonely corner of the room. Polly could tell at a glance that she'd never worked in catering before because she was wearing high heels and was standing in a way which ensured she would have awful backache by the end of the evening.

Whatever she was washing, probably *lollo rosso*, would take a long time to get clean.

The other two women were laying out canapés on massive oval trays known in the trade as 'flats'. They wore white nylon blouses with discreet brooches at the neck, black skirts and the kind of shoes advertised at the back of newspapers – utterly frumpy, but extremely comfortable. Polly's own lowheeled courts were comfortable enough, but lacked the twenty-four-hour ease guaranteed by the width and padded soles of her colleagues'.

'Hello, I'm Polly. I've come to help.'

The man, who was polishing glasses over the steam which rose from a bowl of hot water, looked up resentfully. 'Another of these blessed amateurs, are you?'

'No. I'm on your side. I'm here to' – she hesitated – 'make sure no one gets in your way.'

He grunted. 'I'm Steve. Those two are Shirl and Dot. That one over there is Lorraine.'

Hearing her name, Lorraine turned round and smiled. Her feet were already killing her, and no one had included her in the conversation. All this Polly could tell from her weak and pleading expression.

'Hello, Lorraine, glad to be working with you,' she said. 'And you two. How's it going?'

She should have known a question like that would put more of a burden on her shoulders than her British Warm, which she hung behind the door.

'Well, since you ask,' said Steve, 'there's only two pounds of butter. That miserable old sod of a butler won't open the red wine, though I was told he was going to, and if the lady of the house comes near this kitchen again I'm going home.'

Polly realized at last why she was there – not to make sure the caterers didn't steal the silver or get drunk on the vintage port, but as an interpreter.

Whoever she was, the lady of the house obviously found it difficult to go near people she considered 'the lower orders' without putting their backs well and truly up. Knowing this, she had roped in Bridget to smooth them down again, and to force a line of communication through the wall of blankness which was the defence of the hourly paid servant, a wall so impenetrable it made Checkpoint Charlie seem like an automatic door.

With a 'supervisor', it might just be possible to negotiate a workable truce. Polly's first job was to get the staff on her side. But she wasn't daunted. She'd earned extra money often enough as a silver-service waitress to understand the problems.

'Well, I'll slice the butter. They never provide enough at Cheltenham for Gold Cup day. And when I've done that, I'll open the wine. Then we'll find out if the miserable bastards have bought anything fit to drink!'

Steve looked at her with new respect. Mention of one of the most notorious local catering events marked her as a professional. He passed over the packets of butter and delved in his pocket for a corkscrew.

Chapter Five

❦

After half an hour, Polly felt she ought to offer her services as a diplomat to the United Nations. With a judicious mixture of flattery, cajolery and a few bare-faced lies, she had managed to get the butler to take charge of the wine, convince Shirl, Dot and Lorraine that she knew a lot more about catering than her black dress and pearls suggested, and Steve that she was on the right side. She had yet to meet the lady of the house. But after the staff she was bound to be a pushover, for the simple fact there was only one of her.

One of her there may have been, but she was not alone. When she swept into the kitchen, she was wearing a jewel-encrusted, full-length evening gown and was escorted by four very young females who had probably never seen a kitchen before, certainly not one so antediluvian, and were giggling nervously at the prospect. And Polly had met her before. She was none other than the Charitable Thalia.

Which meant at least that Melissa's 'frightfully good cause' was the same as Bridget's – a charity devoted to preserving rural life and traditional buildings. Perhaps Thalia's husband wasn't planning a dreadful fate for Polly's beloved buildings. He surely wouldn't support that sort of charity if he was.

The thought made Polly give Thalia a benign smile.

She was quite happy to vacillate between one side of the green baize door and the other and felt perfectly at ease.

But for a moment Thalia was totally at a loss. A thousand anxieties flittered across her beautiful face as she confronted Polly. She knew she had met this person before, but couldn't for the life of her think where. But she was quite sure it wasn't in the role she now presented.

Polly, with the advantage of being able to remember Thalia's name and who she was, came to her rescue.

'Hello. I'm Polly Cameron. You won't remember, but we met at Melissa's last week. I'm here instead of Bridget Mathews to make sure everything runs smoothly, which I'm sure it will.'

'Oh – er – yes, of course. So Mrs Mathews couldn't come?' Thalia summoned a charming but questioning smile.

Polly smiled back. 'Unfortunately not. But I'll make sure it all goes well. It's *such* a good charity, don't you think?' Polly gushed. 'We must make sure we make *lots* of money.'

'Yes, of course.' Thalia had got herself together. She still wasn't sure exactly to which tooth of the vertical comb of social classes Polly belonged, but she was obviously the right side of middle.

'This is Felicity, Sophia, my niece, Perdita and Maddy.' She introduced her giggling flock. 'They're here to *help*. Girls, this is . . .?'

'Polly Cameron.'

'. . . she'll tell you what to do.'

There was enough acid in Thalia's voice to quieten their mirth and make Polly feel sorry for them. These were pressed men rather than volunteers and she doubted that many adults had sufficient strength of character to refuse Thalia, let alone adolescent school-girls. From what Polly had seen of her, when honeyed phrases and longing looks didn't get her what she wanted, Thalia revealed telling glimpses of the iron fist which curled ready for action under her elegantly ringed fingers and painted nails. These girls' mothers were probably as scared of Thalia as they were.

'Hello.' Polly embraced the girls in a smile.

Felicity was about sixteen and was wearing a dress of midnight-blue satin, which was apparently especially designed to show off her acned chest. There was a hint of stubbornness about her chin which indicated she had worn it against the advice of her well-wishers.

Sophia, who was potentially as beautiful as her aunt, had a pair of chestnut-brown shoulders which could only have been acquired in the Caribbean. She was a little older than the other girls, and had all Thalia's self-assurance.

Perdita and Maddy, both about fourteen, wearing velvet mini-skirts, high-necked silk blouses and Doc Martens, were both still undergoing orthodontic treatment and looked more like waitresses than most waitresses. They smiled shyly back at Polly. This smile, and their sturdy footwear, gave Polly reason to hope.

'Now, Thalia,' said Polly, firmly using her Christian name, 'you must have masses to do without having to worry about the food. You go and do the things that only you *can* do, and leave the details to me. It's going to be marvellous, I promise you.'

Thalia was torn between her instinct to criticize the plates of canapés and a desire to remove herself from such unsavoury surroundings. But Polly's combination of flattery and firmness did the trick.

'Very well. You will make sure the champagne's *cold*, won't you, Mr er –?'

Steve bowed sycophantically. 'Yes, madam.'

His gesture was rewarded by a regal nod and just a glimmer of a smile. Steve stared after her longingly, his earlier attitude to her softened. She was extremely beautiful.

'Right, girls.'

Polly summed up the opposition. Without Thalia's dominating presence, they were quite likely to do absolutely nothing. Somehow she had to get them on her side without losing their respect. 'Steve here is in charge. Come with me, and I'll ask him what you should get on with.'

'We're only here to pour the champagne,' said Sophia, not moving. 'Aunt Thalia promised that was all we'd have to do.'

'Yes,' agreed Felicity. 'And I absolutely refuse to do anything else.'

Not hiring enough waitresses was just the sort of false economy the very rich indulged in, and Polly cursed it. If Thalia had any idea how hard standing around with bottles of wine was on the feet, she would have grumbled but paid up. Even with enough staff, catering for two hundred was difficult. With pubescent school-girls instead of silver-service waitresses, things were going to be very tough indeed.

Silently, she debated her chances of licking these girls into shape versus getting some extra help. The person she needed now was Beth, easy-going, friendly and efficient. She glanced at her watch. There was just under half an hour before the guests would start arriving. Beth would certainly be out. She would have to galvanize the girls.

'Listen, I know you've been bullied into doing this. I'd be absolutely furious if I were you.' She appealed to their better nature. 'But quite honestly, standing behind the food and piling it on to the plates is dead simple, and it's a great way to get talking to people.'

Maddy and Perdita were shy enough to see this as an advantage. The other two were more sophisticated than anyone ought to be, ever, and didn't need to put slices of ham on a plate to start up a conversation.

'And if there's anyone you really hate . . .' Polly was grasping at straws. 'You can make absolutely sure they get mayonnaise on their dress.'

For a moment, the girls hovered between total rejection of Polly and all she stood for, and a childish desire to get back at Thalia. Fortunately for Polly, the schoolgirl in them was stronger than the blasé sophisticate. As she watched their allegiance shift, Polly felt slightly guilty about the fate of Thalia's designer gown.

She set the girls to holding glasses over bowls of steaming water and polishing them with glass-cloths. As they got the hang of it, she realized they were enjoying having something to do. They obviously spent a lot of their time being bored.

Polly made her way to the dining room with the first of the food. The kitchen had been ignored by Thalia and her husband's desire to make a statement, but the dining room had not. With the possible exception of Brighton Pavilion, Polly had rarely seen such flamboyant magnificence.

The walls and ceiling were lavishly swathed in gold-coloured silk, which came from a central stud two foot across. The silk swept down to the floor with the aid of silken ropes with tassels the size of pineapples, creating the feeling that you were in a vast big top. At the corners of the room, segments of the silk had been parted to reveal a midnight-blue ceiling, dotted with tiny, random lights, like stars. Polly wondered if Thalia still owned a pair of harem pants. She must be one of the very few people who could wear them.

Most of the furniture had been removed for the evening. What remained was all gold, all highly decorated, all obviously antique. The only exception were half a dozen trestle tables put there for the food.

Unfortunately, whoever had been hired to do the flowers had seen these uncluttered surfaces as ideal sites for the arrangements of lilies, teasels, lumps of driftwood, dried seaweed and various sub-tropical flowers which may or may not have been carnivorous and which sprouted dramatically from gold-painted urns. Which meant there was nowhere for the food and wine.

If Thalia had been anyone else, Polly would have looked for her and asked advice. But Polly didn't feel Thalia would have much that was constructive to say and so undertook to sort the matter out herself.

The result was spectacular. The ancient butler, seduced by Polly's appealing manner, not to mention her expressive green eyes and low-cut gown, produced half a dozen wooden wine crates. These, covered with white cloths discovered by Polly in a musty hole which had once been a linen room, were put on the floor between the tables.

These makeshift and somewhat lowly *points d'appui* set off their exotic encumbrances perfectly. In fact, in Polly's opinion, they looked rather better than they had before.

But this artistic in-put took time, and most of the food was still in the kitchen when the guests started to arrive. Fortunately the ancient butler was now on the side of the angels, and helped Dot and the others bring it in.

Polly was just advising Lorraine to take off her shoes and hope no one would notice her stockinged feet when she was standing behind a table, when she spotted Melissa and Sheldon coming in through the front door.

By now she was no longer surprised to discover she was in the middle of the charitable occasion being so avidly discussed at Melissa's dinner party. David Locking-Hill was certainly due to appear, and Polly would find it difficult to avoid him. Why she should wish to do so she was too busy to consider, but for the first time that evening she felt momentarily flustered.

But seeing her collection of helpers looking to her for guidance, she pulled herself together.

'Maddy and Perdita, you dish out the ham and the beef. Dot and I'll deal with the salmon. Lorraine and Shirl, you do the chicken. They can help themselves to salads. When we've done the main course, we'll move on to the puddings. But they're all portioned out already, so it won't be difficult.' She took a breath and went on with the air of someone giving a special treat. 'Sophie and Felicity, you can hand out the champagne as Steve pours it. And then can you pop round and help Mr – the butler with the wine?'

For a few glorious moments the staff surveyed the buffet with satisfaction. Huge silver plates loaded with food, hedged with *lollo rosso* and *lollo biondo*, quiches and canapés, triangles of toast covered with caviare, vol-au-vents filled with smoked salmon and sour cream, would have made any reasonable board groan. The rickety trestle tables which lurked beneath the half-inch thickness of paper tablecloth were almost overwhelmed.

Beneath them, on and in cardboard boxes, the puddings awaited: individual chocolate mousses, little pyramids of white chocolate malakoffs, brandy-snap baskets filled with fruit, miniature rum babas oozing syrup. They were all incredibly rich and fattening, but Polly hoped, for the sake of her workers, they had not been counted out completely accurately. After a moment's thought, she concealed a plate of mousses on the floor. Dot, Shirl and Lorraine were at least getting paid for this evening's work. But the girls weren't, and needed some sort of reward.

It would be a bit of a scurry, dealing with the first course, clearing away the plates and getting out the puddings in the time allotted to the buffet. But they would manage. Polly had learned that Dot and Shirl were also old hands at the Cheltenham races, and were used to working under pressure.

The guests began to file in. The girls handed out glasses of champagne prettily, and Polly watched Perdita manipulate a roll of ham on to a plate without mishap. Everything was going fine. Polly relaxed.

Thalia cut through the crowd to where Polly was standing behind a row of salmon corpses, some of them now only a head and a delicate array of bones. She thrust her plate in Polly's direction.

'Just a smidgen, please. I can't have anything fatty.'

Polly was just about to lower a dainty portion, guaranteed not to put on an ounce of unsightly flesh, when Thalia turned round to talk to someone behind her, nearly causing Polly to drop it.

'Hector! How lovely. So glad you could make it. Have you heard the news?'

Hector, whose girth and flushed face indicated extreme prosperity, hadn't. 'No.'

'Hugh's deal on that land's almost sewn up. He's going to bulldoze those old buildings and put up a fantastic new shopping mall. All glass and steel.'

'Is he, by Jove?' demanded Hector. 'That should make Laureton sit up a bit. It's about time they joined the rest of the world.'

Thalia turned back long enough for Polly, who had broken into a cold sweat of anger and distress, to lay down the piece of fish. 'I thought I'd tell you in case you wanted to put in an offer. Hugh's already got several people very interested in taking up the units.' She glanced at Polly, who was holding a spoon from which a dollop of aïoli trembled precariously. 'Oh, no thank you. It's far too fattening.'

But it was too late. Just as Thalia pulled her plate away, the mayonnaise toppled and landed with a splat on her wrist, spreading itself all over a wide pearl and diamond bracelet.

'Oh, Thalia, I'm so sorry,' said Polly, suddenly deathly calm. 'You moved just at the wrong moment. Here, let me mop it for you.'

Thalia, irritation escaping from between her teeth like steam from a kettle, came to where Polly was waiting with a large paper napkin.

'It was dreadfully careless of me,' said Polly. 'But if only you hadn't moved.' *If only your husband hadn't decided to bulldoze some very lovely old buildings, I wouldn't have lost my concentration.* Then Polly noticed that there was now mayonnaise on Thalia's dress as well as her arm. She smiled up at her, capturing Thalia's attention so she didn't notice. 'Everything seems to be going awfully well, doesn't it?'

Intent on the condition of her bracelet, Thalia didn't respond to Polly's sycophantic question.

'I think saving old buildings is frightfully important, don't you?'

Thalia looked up, confused and annoyed.

'The charity,' Polly explained. 'It saves old buildings.'

'Does it?' said Thalia. 'I really don't know. I'll have to get my bracelet cleaned.'

Bitch! thought Polly. She must have been holding this promise auction for purely social reasons, and hadn't even bothered to find out the first thing about the charity. Hugh probably did it to get in with the council. Perhaps that was how he got them to sell him the land.

'I'm sure if you wash it gently in a little mild detergent the bracelet will be fine,' said Polly sweetly. But nothing will get that mark out of your dress, she added silently, wishing she'd smeared her with mayonnaise on purpose.

As she resumed her place alongside Dot, she wondered if, unconsciously, she had. Just then, she saw David Locking-Hill and Hugh disappearing together. Hugh had his hand on David's shoulder. Surviving public school together was obviously enough to make them blood brothers, honour bound to support each other in everything, no matter how unethical.

Polly bit back a mouthful of four-letter words and suddenly wanted to cry.

The auction started half an hour late. Not, thank goodness, because of any inefficiency on Polly's part, or even as a consequence of her shaking hand. Her collection of old pros and complete novices had formed into a team which worked comparatively well. To reward their efforts, she produced a bottle of champagne she had purloined from the bar and carried it, with the plate of chocolate mousses, to the kitchen. She opened the bottle.

'Find some glasses, we deserve this.'

'My feet are killing me,' said Sophia, easing off her shoes and starting to eat her mousse with her finger.

'And mine.' Felicity's black patent courts joined Sophia's under the table, but she found herself a spoon.

Dot, spurning the mousse and the champagne, put on the kettle. 'If you young things had spent as much time on your feet as I have, you'd wear something more sensible.'

Perdita and Maddy said nothing but looked smug. Their Doc Martens, worn in spite of dire threats of allowance-stopping from their mothers, had more than justified themselves. But Lorraine and Sophia regarded Dot's bunion-bulged sandals from their different ends of the social spectrum, and united in their distaste.

'The worst part,' said Maddy, sipping her drink, 'was that man who kept pinching my bottom every time I came out from behind the table.'

'And me,' said Lorraine. 'He was a terror.'

'He was gross,' agreed Perdita, who had chocolate round her mouth.

'He didn't bother me,' said Thalia's niece. 'I gave him a freezing look, and he went away.'

'It's all right for you, Soph,' said Maddy. 'Not all of us have had time to practise haughty looks in the mirror for hours and hours.'

'Don't drink all the champers.' Sophia snatched the

bottle from Maddy. 'You'll get tiddly, and Thalia will go mad.'

'I'll get another bottle,' said Polly wearily, knowing it would be hours before she could go home and hoping it wasn't Sheldon who was the bottom-pincher.

But instead of getting the wine, she crossed the hall to the ballroom to watch the auction.

It was a huge room. Even chairs for two hundred people didn't fill it. There was still plenty of space to admire its Scottish theme.

The walls were covered in a very red tartan. The heads of dead animals – moose and bison, as well as the more lowly stag – stared glassily at enormous pictures of particularly gory battles. Claymores and bagpipes, battle-axes and dirks, filled in any remaining wall space. But what really made Polly catch her breath was the chandelier – possibly, judging by its size and magnificence, a refugee from Versailles – which hung from the exposed rafters.

Was this a left-over from the previous owners of Cannongate Hall? Thalia's first step towards getting her ballroom done up? Or was this violent contrast of styles the latest quirk of interior designers? It may well have been an impulse of Thalia's brought on by their last weekend in Paris, but whatever it was the effect was certainly impressive.

So intrigued was Polly that she didn't at first notice that the man standing behind a lectern, gavel and pen at the ready, was David Locking-Hill.

At first she was shocked – no one as buttoned-up as he was could possibly play the auctioneer. But after a moment listening to his patter, she became fascinated. All the reserve and dignity which made him so starchy

71

and unapproachable had melted, leaving a salesman par excellence.

'Now come along, ladies and gentlemen. Surely you're not going to let this wonderful lot go for so little,' he was saying. 'You, sir, you're the kind of man to appreciate an adventure. I'm sure I can interest you in this splendid opportunity to stretch your muscles . . .'

Polly found a catalogue and, by looking at the items marked as sold by the woman in front, discovered that the 'wonderful lot' was a chance to drive a JCB for a day, to dig out a disused lake. She waited, eager to hear more.

'Do I hear a hundred pounds? Yes.' He pointed into the audience. 'A hundred pounds, a bargain at a hundred pounds, don't let it slip away. A hundred and ten, thank you. A hundred and ten pounds . . .'

In less than five minutes someone was going to get their pond dug for nothing, and someone else had paid two hundred pounds for the privilege of digging it – all for the opportunity to drive a large mechanical digger. David was a magician.

The next few lots were easier to sell. Fortnights playing golf in the Algarve, weekends in Venice, seats for Covent Garden, all went for far more than their market value. And went so quickly. Polly wondered how David had come to miss his vocation and become a wine merchant. He could make an absolute fortune doing this.

He had just started the bidding going on a weekend in Milan, including a trip to La Scala, when she heard a slightly slurred voice behind her say, 'One hundred and eighty!'

David turned in her direction, a look of absolute horror on his face. For a moment, Polly wondered if merely catching sight of her was enough to make him break off his sentence, but then realized that he hadn't noticed her.

'Bid ten pounds at a time, please,' he said severely to the merry bidder behind her.

So severely, indeed, that Polly turned round to see who had caused David to deviate so vehemently from his hearty auctioneer role.

He was tall and extremely thin, clad in tight-fitting black leather. Traces of acne among the stubble revealed his youth, and he was soaking wet. His fair hair, caught back into a ponytail, was darkened with rain, and moisture ran off his clothes and soaked into the tartan carpet. Apart from the difference in colouring, he could have been a mirror image of the man with the gavel. It was unlikely, however, that his father smelled so strongly of stale beer. His appearance must have caused David a shock, which any moment would turn into acute embarrassment.

He deserved to be embarrassed. He deserved to be boiled in oil for being so chummy with such a rat as Hugh Bradley. But she could never bear to watch the sort of public humiliation which made television game shows so popular, and another look at his son told her that he was about to be extremely, and possibly far-reachingly, sick.

If these people were all friends of Hugh and Thalia's, being vomited over was a fitting punishment. But they may not be personal friends of the Bradleys at all, but people who genuinely supported the preservation of rural England.

In which case it behoved Polly to get that lad out of there. And fast.

Chapter Six

❧❦❧

'Hello,' she whispered. 'You've missed supper. Would you like me to find you something to eat?'

Offering to find him the gents was a bit blatant, and might well meet with a flat refusal.

The youth regarded Polly with a glazed expression which couldn't be put entirely down to beer. 'Want a weekend in Milan?'

'Can you afford one? It'll go for a fortune. You'd be better off having something to eat.'

'Bloody father won't let me have anything I want, anyway.'

Polly sensed his defeat. Compassion for his youth and hopelessness and some suppressed maternal instinct made her want to look after him. 'Come with me. I'll sort you out.' She clutched his arm and guided him past a row of bisons' heads. 'I know your father a little bit.'

'Bully for you,' he said loudly, but fortunately when they were out of the room. 'I'm Patrick. Locking-Hill,' he added.

'Hello, Patrick. When did you last eat?'

'Can't remember.'

'Never mind. There's plenty left. Would you like to wash?'

She thrust him through a door labelled for the occasion as 'Gents', caught sight of taps in the shape of leaping dolphins and heard Patrick be violently sick. She waited for him. At last she heard the running water which indicated he had stopped vomiting and was washing his face.

He emerged a minute later. Dog-like, his conversation with the big white telephone had cured him. 'Did you say something about food?'

She couldn't take him into the kitchen, to be gawped at by the group who must by now have given up hope of more champagne. But luckily there was a small ante-room she could take him to. This room had somehow remained unaffected by numerous changes of ownership, its pale green paper and delicate birds still on the wall after a hundred years. In it was a rather fragile chair.

'Sit down. I'll bring some food.'

She collected a bottle of champagne from the store under the table and returned to the kitchen. While her co-workers exclaimed over her tardiness, she loaded a plate with left-overs, made a mug of strong instant coffee and escaped.

Patrick had his booted feet upon a little occasional table, threatening to break its legs.

'Hi. I've brought the food. If you take your feet off the table, I can put the plate down.'

Patrick obliged, and took a wedge of quiche. It disappeared in one mouthful and was followed by another. He was obviously starving.

Polly found another chair and watched him eat, speculating how David's son came to be at Cannongate Hall. One thing was certain: David had not been expecting him, and was not at all glad to see him.

Patrick took a gulp of coffee and spat it out on the carpet. 'Sorry. Hot.'

Polly, reflecting that Thalia probably planned to replace it anyway, seeing that it was so very old, tried not to mind.

'And no sugar,' Patrick explained.

'I'll get some. Eat some more.'

Polly ran to the kitchen, found some sugar and ran back. If Patrick had poured any more sugar into his mug, it wouldn't have dissolved. She watched him drink it, fearing for his teeth.

'So how do you come to be here?' she asked, her curiosity finally getting the better of her.

'Got a lift.'

'To Cannongate Hall?'

'Yeah. Got suspended from school – or at least the bastard was going to suspend me – so I walked out.'

'You mean you've run away from school?' Patrick's look of disgust told her how Angela Brazil she sounded. 'I mean, you've walked out of school?'

'I told you.' He scowled at her stupidity.

'But why didn't you go home? Why come here?'

'I told you. I got a lift. I was going home,' he conceded. 'But my lift dropped me off. I saw a sign for this place and remembered Dad said he was doing the auction. Thought he'd give me a lift home.'

It sounded perfectly logical, from Patrick's point of view.

'But he didn't know you were coming?'

'Course not! I just walked out of school, didn't I? They don't know I've gone yet.'

'I don't want to depress you, Patrick. But have you

thought how your father's going to feel, you turning up here in front of all these people, either drunk or stoned?'

Patrick frowned. 'Which am I?' He seemed really to want to know.

Polly shrugged. 'If you've been drinking and smoking, you're probably both. Whichever, it doesn't look good. I may be maligning him, but I would have imagined David was' – she picked her words carefully – 'a fairly old-fashioned parent. Or is he cool about drugs and alcohol?'

'My father's not cool about anything,' said Patrick, and closed his eyes.

Polly considered what to do. She could shut the door on Patrick, leave him to sleep off his excesses and let David take him home.

But David would never manage to get Patrick out of the house and into his car in secret; everyone would know. They'd make a terrible fuss, and Patrick would be rude. In spite of his wonderful performance at the auction, David still seemed to Polly to be a very private person. He wouldn't want the whole world to know his son got drunk, or took drugs. And however angry she was with David for having such awful friends, she wouldn't want anyone publicly humiliated by their unlikely offspring. It wouldn't be much fun for Patrick, either.

She glanced at her watch. Most of the clearing-up was already done. The glasses were mostly clean. They had been asked to serve coffee before people went home. Unfortunately she could only guess when that would be.

'Where do you live, Patrick?'

He lifted his head with a jerk and thought hard. 'Near Mannington.'

Mannington. It wasn't far. She might be able to run Patrick home and get back here before the auction was over. She could tell David that she'd taken him home discreetly, as she handed him a coffee cup.

'Is there anyone at home to look after you?'

'Nah. Monica 'snot there.'

She longed to ask who Monica was, but this was not the time. 'So there's no one at all?'

'You're bloody nosy, you are.'

Polly exhaled impatiently. 'I'm not nosy! I'm just trying to think what's best for you. Which unfortunately excludes leaving you alone in an empty house in that state.'

'You're nosy. But you're all right.'

Patrick was not the first young man to describe Polly as nosy, and she had to admit to a certain interest in people which made her ask a lot of questions. This time she felt perfectly justified.

She left Patrick, went back to the ballroom and discovered that David had been working fast. There were barely twenty lots before the coffee would be wanted. She returned to the anteroom.

'Come on, Patrick. Come into the kitchen. There are other people there, but at least they won't say anything to your father.'

Patrick seemed to sober up all at once. 'After this fiasco my father's never going to speak to me again.'

'Patrick, I'm sure it's not as bad as that.'

'Oh, are you? Shows how much you know, dunnit?'

'Come with me,' she said firmly, and took hold of his arm.

Patrick's entrance into the kitchen had a more silencing effect than even Thalia's would have done. The girls instantly recognized him as being a very attractive young man. And what was more, a rebellious one. Polly suddenly panicked lest his presence subvert them and encourage them to stop work. Fortunately, after a furtive glance, he subsided into his coffee mug, too wrapped up in his own problems to subvert anyone, least of all a gaggle of schoolgirls.

The two older women gave him a 'young people nowadays' look, and continued to fill sugar basins. They had two hundred cups of coffee to serve and had no time for layabouts the worse for wear with drink.

Patrick didn't react to this either. He was accustomed to disapproval and felt quite comfortable with it. He tucked a strand of blond hair behind his ear and slumped further into his chair.

Having reassured herself that he was not going to vomit again, or pass into unconsciousness, Polly turned her attention to more pressing matters. The people would be baying for their coffee at any moment.

'Come on, girls. Give a hand with those trays.'

The younger women dragged their eyes away from Patrick and regarded Polly somewhat resentfully. It was cruel of her to bring them such a lovely toy and then not let them play.

Polly tutted irritably. 'Steve, is the urn hot?'

'If it gets any hotter, it'll boil over.'

'Then get a shift on, girls!'

Reluctantly, they scraped their chairs back and joined their peers.

The next half hour was spent pouring cups of coffee and offering cream, milk and sugar. But although she looked for him, Polly didn't see David in the crowd. But when she finally got back to the kitchen, somewhat to her relief, Patrick was gone.

Polly half expected Thalia to come into the kitchen to thank the staff, but she didn't. The girls drifted off, limping, already contemplating how to relate the evening to their school-friends for maximum effect, with accounts of Patrick's part of the evening wildly exaggerated.

Polly was the last to leave. The butler had disappeared. Steve had driven his cohorts home. The only trace of Cannongate Hall's effort to raise money was a clean patch on the wall. Someone, Polly suspected Patrick, had written something rude in the dirt. Rather than leave it until Thalia's interior decorator finally got round to doing up the kitchen, she had wiped it off.

Shivering more from tiredness than cold, she huddled into her overcoat. She had her hand on the doorknob, and was about to let herself out, when the butler, refreshed, she suspected, after a couple of hours' snooze in his cubby hole, loomed up behind her.

'I was wondering, my dear, if you'd take a nightcap with me?' His eyes were rheumy and his lower lip was trembling in moist anticipation.

Polly suppressed her revulsion behind a smile. 'I'd love to, but I've got my car with me and wouldn't like to take the risk.'

Another smile, a quick twist, a wrench and the door was open and Polly was fleeing across the yard. As she pulled away with more haste than prudence, she wondered if these hasty escapes could possibly be habit-forming.

She got to the studio early the following morning. It was always difficult to drag herself out of bed in the dark, particularly when no one would notice if she didn't get up at all. But she had so little time to pot, she forced herself to start as early as possible – not easy in the middle of January.

Known to its co-users as 'the Shed', the studio was small, poorly lit and icy cold. But by the time Polly had boiled the kettle, got the coal stove alight and had weighed out and wedged a dozen balls of clay, she had taken off the ancient cardigan she wore over her dungarees and her cheeks had become pink with effort. Pottery was physically very hard work.

For two days a week, and every third Sunday, this was her territory, where real life went on. Pottery was the only thing Polly took seriously, the only thing she did with all her concentration. It was more than a way of making a little extra money, and had never been a hobby. She hesitated to call it a religion, but it uplifted her. Even when she tossed everything she threw into the dustbin of 'used clay' she felt she was doing something real. It was an obsession her mother failed to understand.

Because Polly didn't own the Shed, but only rented time in it from another potter, she hadn't been near it for days. After her exertions of the previous night, she needed time alone with the clay to restore her equilibrium.

Usually, by the time she had pounded twelve pounds of clay into submission, any trace of depression or discontent had vanished. And by the time the wheel was spinning sweetly, and the first rough-smooth lump of clay was centred firmly, the outside world and its tribulations faded into the background.

She accepted that she had to stick to smaller pieces.

The kiln was too small to make it economical to heat for just one or two huge things. Although she didn't sell much – she hated hawking her stuff about, trying to persuade shops they needed mugs with armadillos on them, consequently she gave a lot of her pots away – the Christmas craft fairs had cleaned her out and she wanted to build up her stock again.

But today her pottery was less than satisfactory. She pulled out a reasonably elegant cylinder but it gave her no pleasure. She longed to have a really large lump of clay in her hands, something which would take all her strength to control but would eventually become an enormous, glowing bowl.

She slid the wire neatly under the embryo coffee pot and set it aside before her discontent could spoil it.

The last evening she had been at Bridget's, she had spent some time in Cherry's bedroom admiring her pony pictures. She suddenly yearned for the space to paint one, right in the middle of a bowl. She'd use a dark blue base slip, then paint the horse in wax with a nice fat Chinese-style brush in a few, fat, Chinesey brushstrokes. With a pale grey slip on top, the horse should look as if it were galloping out of the mist. Or if she had a really big bowl, she could do a whole herd of them. They'd be just the thing if she ever got to the Gatcombe craft fair.

But without access to a larger kiln, she would never be able to become a truly professional potter. Virtually the only time she actually sold anything, outside the Christmas period, was when her mother commissioned things for wedding presents. And then she didn't like to charge enough because it was her mother.

Just for her, she had designed and made a beautiful two-handled christening mug with the child's name and date of birth and charming little animals painted on it. But instead of being thrilled at having her christening present problem solved for ever, her mother had wiped her eyes, biting back the words, 'I'm never going to have a grandchild of my own' with guilt-making fortitude. However, a postcard in the local post office had produced a few more commissions so Polly's efforts weren't quite in vain.

She squeezed a spongeful of warm water over another lump of clay. If only someone would commission something big and expensive. An urn, a fruit bowl, even the occasional casserole. But it was always tea-sets, coffee-sets, mugs and jugs. If they knew how tricky it was to get a teapot which poured, how time-consuming, they wouldn't have the nerve to ask for them.

The pot on the wheel wobbled off-centre. She recentred it and pulled it into shape with her teeth clenched, like a ferocious nanny dragging her reluctant charge into scratchy woollen clothes on a hot spring day.

When she had got the clay to behave properly and become a decent flower pot, she squashed it and tossed it into the bin. Then she got up and made herself a cup of tea.

She was – or had been – perfectly happy. She coped with being constantly broke, constantly balancing the need to earn money with the need for some creative outlet. She thought she'd found an equilibrium, created a way of living which fulfilled and satisfied her. Now, suddenly, she was discontented.

Like everyone else, she had always suffered from bouts of melancholy. In fact, she cried a lot, over little things – the deaths column in the paper, any sort of parade or ceremony, Australian soap operas -- she had even, under the horrified gaze of Bridget's children, been known to cry during the ads on television. But after a couple of tears and a good sniff, she felt fine.

Any deeper sadness would go away after a long walk on the common, an evening in front of the fire with a bad book or a weepy video, courtesy of Bridget's VCR.

What had happened to make her so unsettled? Perhaps the antibiotics she had been on took more recovering from than usual. Perhaps she needed a holiday. (Fat chance.) Perhaps she had finally allowed her mother, Beth, and even Bridget to wear away her resistance. Perhaps she didn't want to end up old and alone.

She had clung so long to her conviction that all marriages were doomed to failure, and the ones that worked did so only thanks to unacceptable compromises, it was rather scary suddenly to have doubts.

She instantly dismissed them. She was probably just tired. She had spent five hours on her feet yesterday evening, and had heard bad news about a subject close to her heart. And all that tact was emotionally draining.

Besides, she wasn't old yet. She had decades of happy, creative life before she had even to think about her old age. Bridget had said she was just reaching the peak of her sexuality.

Perhaps that was it. Perhaps her body was telling her there was no point in reaching the peak of your sexuality all on your own – especially if you'd never got off the nursery slopes. Perhaps she'd better do something about it now, before she was an eccentric old lady.

For the first time that morning she smiled. Eccentric old ladyhood was an appealing prospect. It would be fun to stop worrying about your appearance, to let the pounds roll on unchallenged, have your bad temper indulged because you were old. She would be a sort of great-aunt to Bridget's grandchildren and give them money for motorbikes and appalling clothes. You wouldn't have to conform to anyone else's ideas of proper behaviour – *they* would conform to *yours*. 'I must buy a bottle of gin and unplump the cushions, Great-aunt Polly is coming round.' It would be wonderful. But an old lady without a past?

It somehow didn't fit in with the Mary Wesley heroine she had in mind. Could you be a really successful old lady with such a boring sexual history? Her experiences to date, as related to Bridget and Beth, were pretty unexciting. Perhaps she should give the thing one last try, if only to add a little colour to her future reminiscences.

Surprisingly, no bolt of lightning found its way through the slipping tiles of the Shed roof in order to smite Polly for this volte-face. Instead, her decision gave inspiration to her hands and she produced a satisfactory quantity of milk jugs. Very saleable.

After all, there was nothing very revolutionary about her decision. It was only what people had been telling her for the past ten years: expand her social life, open herself to opportunity and concede there might be more to sex than embarrassing discomfort.

But no permanent relationships. About that she was still adamant. She believed it was very difficult for a woman to have a career and a man. And given that making a career as a potter was Polly's greatest, most dearly clung-to ambition, no way was she going to jeopardize it.

She centred a large lump of clay with a loud thump, remembering as she did so two of the women on her pottery course.

Both had stable, happy marriages until the children left home and they discovered they wanted something creative to take their place. Instantly, their husbands started to find excuses to prevent them going to classes. When the women's focal point of their day ceased to belong to them, they couldn't stand the competition and the relationships perished. One woman left her husband and stayed with her potting. But the other suppressed her creative nature and abandoned the classes. Polly had met her a couple of years later and thought she looked utterly worn down, though she put a brave face on the situation.

A job was fine. These women had both had jobs, latterly full time. Their husbands appreciated the extra income. It was the fact that their creative energy was no longer theirs that the men couldn't cope with. No way was Polly going to do anything which would detract from her limited potting time. The mere business of making a living and doing what she could for the environment took more than enough time already.

A brief, happy affair would do. That way she would stay in control and her main goal, to become a full-time, self-supporting potter, would remain clear and unclouded.

But that night, as she loaded leather-hard milk jugs into her car so she could decorate them at home, she realized it was easier said than done.

It was the 'happy' part which would make it so difficult. She had been dumped on often enough by her girlfriends to know that relationships rarely, if ever, broke up without someone getting hurt. With hindsight, she realized this was one of the reasons she had kept men at arm's length for so long: she was frightened the someone would be her. But the thought that she might cause pain was equally unpalatable.

She would have to find a man with the same motives and morals as herself. And it was going to be difficult, if not downright impossible.

In theory, men looking for casual affairs were under every stone. It was women who complained that men were only after one thing, and didn't want commitments. But Polly knew about theories: they never quite worked in her case.

Polly had never had any problems attracting men. She put it down to the simple fact that she was single and supposedly available. Unattached women were like parking meters with time on the clock. You had to park in them even if you'd done your shopping. Otherwise, when you next needed a space, the gods would strike you down for profligacy and there wouldn't be one. But could she attract the right sort of man?

A younger man might be the answer. He wouldn't be so desperate for a permanent, meaningful relationship. The snag would be finding the right kind of younger man. As well as all the obvious things, like kindness and a sense of humour, he must be adept in the use of condoms. She was not going to bring a baby into this adventure.

He must also be so overwhelmingly sexy that all her sordid memories would be swept away on a tide of passion. But could she possibly attract such a man? Did such men really exist? She certainly hadn't met any lately, if ever. When she was fifteen, she and her friends had read romantic novels avidly and had high expectations of what went on between satin sheets. But she was no longer fifteen. Real life had eroded her teenage fantasies.

Almost, she changed her mind. Spinsterhood was so cosy, so uncomplicated, so safe. She must be mad to even think of messing everything up with a man.

But she was thirty-five. If she gave men another chance at least she could look her mother, Bridget, Beth, and everyone else in her life who wanted to see her firmly shackled, in the eye and say she'd tried. And if it didn't work, she would have every excuse to stay happily single for ever.

Selina glared resentfully at the telephone, knowing it would make Polly get up and move her from the most comfortable position she'd been in all day.

Resignedly, Polly unhooked Selina's claws from around her neck and got stiffly to her feet. She'd been sitting in that chair for half an hour, ever since she got home with her jugs, thinking about her resolution to give men another try. She was starting to get cold.

'It's my mother, Selina. I must answer it. I was going to ring her later, anyway. This way it goes on her phone bill.'

'Hello?' She just managed not to add the word 'Mummy'.

'Is that Polly Cameron?' Oh, not Mummy. 'This is David Locking-Hill.'

Polly sat down hurriedly. It was as if her change of heart had somehow become public knowledge. And David Locking-Hill had decided to get in quickly, before the crowds. She choked on a gurgle of laughter at the thought. He was such a thoroughly unsuitable candidate.

'We met at Melissa de Vere's,' he prompted, when she didn't speak.

'Oh, yes.' So he hadn't seen her last night. She was obscurely relieved.

'Melissa gave me your number.'

'Did she?' Why? she wondered guiltily. What had she done wrong? It must have been his car she'd leaned against that dreadful night, and he was ringing up to complain that she'd damaged it. Melissa was perfectly capable of telling tales.

'Yes. You left your earrings.'

'Oh, is that all? I'd forgotten about them.'

'Yes, well, as I'm going to be in your area this evening, I wondered if you'd like me to drop them off.'

The Severn Bridge, yes, but not at my house.

'There's really no need. They're only –'

'It's no trouble. Are you in this evening?'

'Yes – no! – I've just remembered. I've got to babysit.' Inspiration, certainly divine, swooped to the rescue. 'You could drop them off at my friend's house if you like. It's easier to find than mine, anyway.' This at least was true.

'Fine. Can you give me the address?'

Knowing that in the circumstances Bridget would cooperate gladly, Polly complied. The advantage of Bridget's house was that, unlike Polly's, it didn't have to have three days' notice before someone strange crossed its threshold.

The moment he rang off, Polly called Bridget to tell her.

'Of *course*! Alan and I would love to have an evening on our own. But we can't miss *Alaska the Great* – you'll have to set the video.'

'I'll get Neil to do it.' Neil, Bridget's middle son, was

eleven and no slouch when it came to electronic equipment.

'Okay. What time did you say?'

Elated by the thought that David Locking-Hill wouldn't be fighting his way down her path to chaos, Polly rang her mother. Sylvia Cameron was a sucker for a double-barrelled name.

Chapter Seven

❧❧❧

'We don't need a baby-sitter,' said Mark, who opened the door to Polly. 'I'm old enough.'

'You may not need one,' Polly emerged from her British Warm. 'But you're getting one.'

'Why?' Cherry didn't object to Polly's sudden arrival, she just liked to know things.

'Because a man is dropping in to give me some earrings, and I don't want him coming to my house.'

'Very sensible,' said Neil. 'It's unwise for single women to let men they don't know into their homes.'

Mark punched his brother on the shoulder. 'It's because her house is such a mess, dick'ead.'

'He's right, Mark. It is unwise –'

'Yeah, but that's not the reason, is it? I don't think you should worry about it. My friends think your house is cool.' Mark found Polly's closeness to town very convenient.

'I don't think David Locking-Hill would. Cold, perhaps. But not cool.' Cool was a good word, though. It summed up David's elegant manner perfectly.

'Hi, Bridget.' Polly went into the kitchen. 'I brought you a bottle of wine as a thank-you present.'

'You shouldn't have,' said Bridget, taking it. 'We'll drink it when we're allowed home. What time is he coming?'

'About nine, I think.'

'Feel free to ask him in for coffee or something.'

'I don't think I will, thanks all the same.'

'Well, do if you want to. Are you ready, Alan?' Bridget shouted to her husband, whose footsteps could be heard in the bedroom overhead.

'Yup.' A moment later he thundered down the stairs and into the kitchen. He kissed Polly. 'How's my favourite bit on the side?'

Polly returned his kiss.

'You look gorgeous,' said Alan. 'Very Cavendish House.'

Polly was pleased. It had rankled when she discovered that David, who had for a brief moment created a little frisson of desire, was so close to the vile, property-developer Bradleys. She wanted to look haughty and aloof – as unlike the idiot in the low-cut dress who ran away from a grown-up dinner party as possible. She had spent precious minutes freezing in her bedroom in her Damart underwear thinking about what to wear.

So it was not only respect for Bridget's central heating which had made her shed her usual mille-feuille of cotton and wool and settle for a long, very soft polo-neck jumper over a long, very soft wool skirt. She hadn't had time to polish her boots, but she had rubbed moisturizer into the toes. With a suede belt round her waist and shoulder pads under her bra straps, the effect was not high fashion, but nor was it what Beth referred to as her bag-lady look. And her hair, which hadn't been washed since Saturday, was at least staying up.

'You're not just saying that to be kind?'

Alan winced. 'Of course not. I'm always perfectly honest. Aren't I, Bridge?'

'"Brutally" is a better word. And he's right. You do look unusually respectable.'

'So how are you, Alan?' asked Polly, finally convinced.

'Bearing up. Are you coming, Bridget, or shall I take Polly out instead?'

'I've been waiting for you for the last ten minutes,' said Bridget mildly, and probably truthfully. 'Have a nice time, Polly, bed at nine, Cherry. Come on, you.' She tugged fondly at her husband's sleeve. 'It's your turn to drive.'

Polly went into the kitchen to find out what her charges were doing.

Her easy relationship with Bridget's three children was based on mutual liking and disrespect. Mark, Bridget's eldest, at fourteen, teased her with a patronizing kindness which would have maddened his nine-year-old sister. Neil, the middle one, was quieter and harder to get to know, but a smile from him was well worth waiting for. Cherry, the only girl, was easy-going unless provoked by her brothers, then she turned into a miniature Valkyrie. They all three advised Polly on what was in fashion, what music she should listen to and what films were guaranteed not to scare her.

In return, she let them invade her house with their friends for drinks and hot cheese sandwiches. When they were younger, she used to let them cook in her kitchen. Bridget was a tolerant mother, but had discovered that gingerbread men ground into her carpet tiles was where her tolerance ended.

Polly found the relationship extremely satisfying, and doubted if children of one's own could be so enjoyable. But this evening she hoped they'd keep their refreshing frankness well under control.

Mark was sitting at the kitchen table reading a book with a dragon on it. He was taking notes and could well have been doing his homework. Cherry was working her way through a plate of naked tagliatelle, her mother's culinary skills wasted on her.

'Shall we do some cooking, Cherry? We could make a coffee cake.' It was such a nice, *grown-up* activity.

Cherry and Mark exchanged glances. Their mother didn't share Polly's relaxed attitude towards mess. If they spilled anything in Polly's kitchen she just sieved it through the coconut matting on to the floor. But here Polly would make them clear it up.

'Nothing you want to watch on the box, Poll?' Mark enquired.

'No, as it happens.' Polly usually appreciated an evening in front of Bridget's large colour television. When her own portable black-and-white one finally gave up and died, she hadn't bothered to replace it. And while at home she managed perfectly well with a radio for company, she relished television when she had a chance to watch it.

But this evening was different. She couldn't watch whatever happened to be on, happily and indiscriminately, knowing that David Locking-Hill was about to appear on the doorstep, her glass earrings in his pocket. Not if she was going to keep up her haughty deb act. 'What homework are you doing?'

'I'm not. Why do you want to cook? Are you trying to impress the boyfriend?'

'No!' She didn't want to impress him, just erase the memory of that terrible dinner party from his mind. 'Well, no. I'm not – I mean –'

'You don't want to be caught watching moving wallpaper?'

'No.'

Mark was far too perceptive for his own good, but she needed him on her side. She toyed with the idea of getting him to answer the door and receive the earrings, but then rejected the notion. She couldn't afford the bribe to get Mark to cooperate.

Cherry, now, she might be persuaded in exchange for an uninterrupted hour in Polly's make-up bag. But Cherry would ask why, and Polly didn't have a good enough answer.

'So you don't want to cook? I'll just tidy up a bit for Bridget, then.'

The kitchen was Polly's favourite room in Bridget's house. It managed to avoid the aseptic dullness of most fitted kitchens by the addition of a genuine Welsh dresser and a cosy armchair with a patchwork cushion. There was nothing in it which wasn't functional, but there was nothing on display which wasn't attractive. And unlike Polly's own kitchen, nothing in it was covered with dust.

Polly loaded Cherry's newly empty plate into the dishwasher, which was the only tidying required, and wiped the surfaces. Why was she so nervous? As she polished Bridget's taps (it was all she could find to do in such pristine surroundings) she decided it was something to do with David intruding into her real life.

Melissa's dinner party could have taken place on a different planet, it was so far removed from Polly's everyday existence. Because of her upbringing, Polly had, albeit very briefly, managed to exist in that rarefied atmosphere. But she wasn't sure David could do it in reverse. Which was why she had spared him the nitty-gritty of her own home. Bridget's was a sort of halfway house.

It had well-proportioned rooms which were decorated with taste and style. A few inherited antiques lived happily among the other furniture, as the one or two original paintings shared wall space with prints. It was also immaculately tidy. But it was a long way from Melissa's bogus grandeur.

'Find a box of matches then, Cherry, and I'll give you a game of vingt-et-un.'

The two of them gambled happily until it was time for Cherry to go to bed.

The doorbell rang when she was upstairs, in the loo for the ninth time. She heard his deep voice as she washed her hands. Mark must have opened the door.

Well, there was no point in tripping over herself to get downstairs now. Irritated, she pulled up her tights and made sure her vest wasn't interfering with her Cavendish House look. Having decided it would be best for her to deal with him entirely alone, it was just her luck that he chose to arrive at the one moment she was out of the way.

She tucked a few loops of hair back into their restraining combs, and splashed her cheeks with cold water. Either panic or Bridget's central heating had given her a flush bordering on the hectic. Then she pushed up her sleeves to a pleasing position just below the elbow, checked that her skirt wasn't tucked into her knickers and unlocked the door.

Polly could hear voices in the hall and tiptoed to the top of the stairs. Fingers crossed, David was just giving the earrings to Mark and she could stay safely out of the way until she heard the front door slam.

But no. Mark had let David in and was asking for his coat with a poise Bridget would have been proud of. If she wasn't quick, Mark would start offering hospitality, which might well take the form of a bowl of cornflakes. Polly resolved never to lend Mark money again and ran downstairs. She caught up with the party in the kitchen passage.

'Hello,' she said a little breathlessly, avoiding the use of his name. 'It's terribly kind of you to bring my earrings.' She smiled blankly, willing him to hand them over.

He didn't. She reversed a few paces, trying to draw them back into the hall, any thought of remaining aloof forgotten. But like a group of practised sheep faced with a sheepdog puppy, they stared at her and refused to move.

'Would you like a cup of coffee?' asked Mark. For a fourteen-year-old with a shaven head, he was remarkably polite. And he'd just blown his chance of a birthday present.

'Well –?' David's enquiring eyebrow forced Polly to endorse the invitation.

She produced a moderately welcoming smile. 'Yes, do have some. Mark' – she might as well make use of the little toe-rag – 'why don't you take David into the sitting room while I make it?'

'Actually,' said Mark, 'I've got to do my homework.' He nodded to David, beamed at Polly and disappeared.

Polly waved David into the kitchen and anchored him to the table with an invitation to sit down. This social interlude wasn't on her agenda. A brief, chilly 'thank you' on the door step as he handed over the earrings was more what she'd planned. But now he was here, she didn't want him wandering about.

She contemplated opening the wine she had brought for Bridget. Some alcohol might help, and coffee always had an unfortunate effect on her bladder. But the man was a wine merchant, and Tesco's cheapest would probably do unpleasant things to his sensibilities.

So she searched Bridget's cupboards for coffee beans and, not being a coffee fan herself, it was a while before she tracked them down in the fridge.

'What brings you to this part of the world?' she asked as she ladled beans into the electric grinder. Then wished she hadn't. Now she would have to wait for his answer before she could switch the button. He was mercifully brief.

'I was delivering some wine to some friends.' He crossed one long, corduroy-covered leg over the other and settled back to watch Polly flit about.

She pulverized the beans, then searched for a coffee-making appliance which took less than fifteen minutes to function. She knew there was one, but where? Bridget's kitchen was almost as familiar to her as her own, but her guest's Rock-of-Gibraltar calm was making her forget where everything was kept. And Alan, gadget-mad, had apparently bought an example of every new coffee-maker which appeared on the market. Every one of Bridget's fitted cupboards seemed stuffed with them, and they all seemed ridiculously complicated. At home, if she made coffee at all, Polly used an enamel jug and a spoon which worked perfectly well. At last she found the cafetière, which was the next best thing.

She took quick, covert glances at him as she poured on

the boiling water. He was wearing a lovat-green cash-mere (Polly was sure it was cashmere) sweater she would happily die for. She was quite sure Melissa had given her the run-down on his financial status, but although she couldn't for the life of her remember what she'd said, he had the sort of confidence which goes with generations of wealth. Not for him the flamboyant exhibitionism of the yuppie. What had he thought of Thalia's fabulous dining room or her stuffed moose heads?

None of his clothes were new – he might well have inherited his shirt (slightly worn at the cuffs, she noticed) from his father. But his father had probably bought his shirts in dozens from Jermyn Street and they would last several lifetimes.

His shoes, which were very large and tripped her up as she crossed the room to the fridge, had the high gloss created by years of regular polishing. No quick dab of face cream or furniture polish for the Locking-Hill footwear. Polly had the feeling that you could call on him at any time, day or night, and he would be the perfectly dressed English gentleman. A mother-in-law's dream.

Polly unearthed a packet of brown sugar and shov-elled some into the bowl she had given Bridget for her birthday. She set Bridget's Christmas present cups and saucers, which matched the bowl, on to a beechwood tray. She decanted a selection of home-made biscuits on to a plate (again, one of her own make) and found teaspoons. What was it about David which made her cluck about like a wet hen? she wondered irritably. Even Bridget was quite happy to plonk the tin down on the table and let people rummage about in it. But here she was, laying out flapjack and shortbread in orderly rows.

She'd be hunting for doilies and cake forks next. She heated the milk.

Making proper coffee from scratch takes a long time, even without interference from the last word in continental devices, and Polly dragged it out as long as humanly possible. But she did eventually have to declare it ready and face her visitor.

'Shall we go through to the sitting room or stay here?' The children might be in the sitting room, and as it was Mark who had got her into this spot he could damn well help her out of it.

'I think you should sit down, Polly. I'm sure you've had a busy day.'

Something about his deep, precise voice told her the wet hen was too reminiscent of the scatty escapee of dinner parties for him to forget the details.

She shot him a quick, thanks-for-nothing smile and put the tray on the kitchen table. Then she sat down, poured the coffee and offered him the biscuits.

He took a piece of shortbread and, annoyingly, managed to eat it without getting crumbs over his sweater. His nanny must have loved him – never a hair out of place and absolutely guaranteed not to speak with his mouth full.

'What lovely cups and saucers,' said David.

All her uncharitable thoughts dissolved. He couldn't really be a close friend of the Bradleys. He'd probably done the promise auction because it was for a good cause. She gave him her first genuine smile. 'Oh, do you like them? They're mine. I mean, I made them. I gave them to Bridget and Alan for Christmas.'

He examined his cup more closely. Polly was pleased with them herself. Breakfast size, they were cream-

100

coloured with hand-painted animals copied from a Shaker alphabet she'd borrowed from Cherry. 'They're delightful. So nice to drink out of.'

Polly basked in his praise for a sunny moment. She worked hard to ensure that all her pottery was pleasant to use as well as beautiful. It was good to have it appreciated.

'Are you a professional potter?'

He'd asked the right question, he hadn't used the dreaded word 'hobby'. Really, he was quite nice. 'Well, I take my pottery very seriously, but I don't actually earn my living from it, so I don't suppose I could call myself professional. But I wouldn't call myself an amateur either.'

'Do you sell much?'

Polly sighed. She could sell ice to Eskimos as long as she personally had nothing to gain by it. 'Not really. Though I occasionally go to a craft fair if I can get enough stock.'

'It's a pity. You're obviously very talented.'

Polly blushed. 'Thank you.'

'I'm sorry, I can't remember. Do you have a job, or do you concentrate on your pottery?'

'I have a job.'

'Oh?'

She thought frantically how she could divert him from asking for details. Not that she was ashamed of what she did, it just took so long to explain. Her mother always muttered vaguely about health-food shops when asked about Polly's career, but as everyone ended up thinking she owned a string of them Polly didn't think this ruse was quite her.

'Would you like some more coffee?' she asked. 'Have a

101

flapjack.' Bridget's flapjack was usefully sticky, and might keep his jaws out of action long enough for her to think of another topic of conversation.

'No flapjack, thank you. But I'd love another cup of coffee.'

He probably hasn't had dinner, thought Polly, pouring it, and doesn't want to spoil his appetite. But he took the hint and changed the subject.

'That's a very interesting Welsh dresser,' he said, and proceeded to discuss dressers as if he really cared about them. Polly gamely kept up her end of the conversation, tossing in extraneous bits of information with a liberal hand.

She was about to tell him that she'd made a very nice dresser herself, out of a washstand, a few orange boxes and a jigsaw, when Bridget's cat strolled into the kitchen and jumped on David's lap.

'What a nice cat,' he said, stroking the magnificent black creature. 'So much more friendly than Melissa's elegant queen.'

Polly's nervousness peaked, and suddenly she didn't care what David thought about her. She started to laugh. 'The trouble is, you're too well bred for her. What Melissa's cat likes is a bit of rough trade.'

David lowered the cat gently to the floor, and then stood up. She couldn't tell if he was offended or amused.

'Poor Melissa,' Polly went on. 'Was she dreadfully upset about those tom cats getting at her queen?'

David's expression was slightly less revealing than the average rock face. 'She said: 'Why can't that silly girl ever behave like a normal person?'

'Oh.'

He suddenly smiled, a little ruefully. 'You may be silly, but you're also very kind.'

'What?'

'The earrings were only an excuse. I wanted to thank you for looking after Patrick at the promise auction the other night.'

'But how did you know . . . ?'

'That it was you who rescued him?' His mouth lifted at the corner. 'I saw you near to him when he made his bid. And when he finally told me what had happened, I recognized his description of you.'

Polly wondered what form Patrick's description had taken, and just how unflattering it had been. 'I see.'

'It was very kind of you to feed him, and look after him.' He hesitated a moment. He felt obliged to give her the details, but obviously hated the thought of anyone knowing his private business. 'He'd run away from school.'

'I know.'

'He told you, did he? And did he also tell you he refused to go back, even though he hasn't been expelled at all, merely suspended?'

'Well, no. I got the impression he was fairly unhappy . . .'

He retreated behind a wintery hauteur. This was obviously no excuse. He probably believed that everyone was unhappy at school, but that was no reason to duck out of your responsibilities.

'He had no right to unburden himself to you. He'd do very well if he only kept out of bad company and did some work.'

'Don't be too hard on him. I thought he was a very nice boy.'

'Really?' David's expression snapped frostily. 'Well, you're the first ever to think so. And as I said earlier, you are a very kind person.' In spite of a half-smile forced into the granite of his displeasure, this sounded like a criticism.

'I did what anyone would have done.'

'No.' He shook his head, the smile growing to tease out the corners of his mouth, its very reluctance making it surprisingly attractive. 'Anyone else would have made an almighty fuss.'

'Honestly . . .' Her heart went out to him, a lonely, old-fashioned father dealing with a rebellious, much-loved son.

But he gave her no opportunity to express her sympathy. 'I'd better be going. Thank you so much for the coffee.'

At the front door, when Polly had retrieved his waxed jacket and he had shrugged himself into it, he put his hand in the pocket and produced a tissue-paper package.

'Your earrings,' he said.

'Thank you so much,' said Polly, taking them. 'They're only glass, you know. You really needn't have bothered. There are plenty more jumble sales where they came from.' She gave him a wide, reassuring smile and shut the door behind him.

Chapter Eight

She said nothing about her decision to climb down off the shelf to Beth and Bridget when she saw them the following Monday. Bridget had given her the third degree, and, abetted by her children, had found out more about David than Polly knew herself. She wasn't going to risk another grilling by declaring such a violent change of heart.

That evening she was going to a private view in Gloucester Docks. The fact that it was a long-standing arrangement she had almost forgotten about was neither here nor there. Not that it was not the sort of place you met people, but she was 'getting out more'. She planned to get back in pretty quickly afterwards, but it was a start.

So she didn't want Bridget searching her catalogue of eligible bachelors any more than she wanted Beth thinking of men who could give her a wicked time in bed. She could arrange her own social life, thank you.

All three women battled against the problems involved in kick-starting the week into action, but this Monday was brightened by Beth reporting that the tasty geezer of the other day was back.

'You should go for someone like that, Poll. He's got a lovely bum. And a really sexy leather jacket. Hair's a bit long, though.'

'Why don't you go after him yourself,' said Polly, 'if he's so wonderful?'

'Rob would kill me. And he's a bit old anyway.'

'You mean he actually shaves?' Polly sliced a cabbage into four. 'Wowee.'

'No, I mean old. Not as old as you, of course.' Beth lobbed a handful of used tea bags into the bin. 'He was walking without a frame.'

Bridget, who hadn't seen him the other day, took the opportunity to bring down some eggs from the storeroom upstairs. A few minutes later she re-entered the kitchen.

'He's about twenty-five, I reckon, Polly. His hair *is* a bit long and he's very attractive. But' – she lowered her tower of eggs carefully on to the work bench – 'don't either of you dare to have anything to do with him. He's dangerous.'

'And too young,' said Polly, banging the handle on the electric grater, grateful she hadn't let slip her recent change of heart as Monday ground relentlessly on.

Beth had been sent to the top of town for five pounds of carrots when the bell went later. Polly, who was by that time elbow deep in curried rice, was glad of an excuse to stop chopping peppers.

'Just coming,' she called, wiping her hands on the clean towel. Then she bounded out with a merry 'Can I help you?' on her lips.

Too late, she recognized her customer. Beth's 'tasty geezer' got the blast of charm Polly reserved for the over-sixties and under-sixteens. Back-pedalling hurriedly, she fiddled with the cake tongs, trying to modify her expression into something more restrained.

'Can I have my second cup of coffee, please?' he asked politely. 'And a slice of carrot cake.'

She allowed herself a moment's eye contact, long enough to note that his were the colour of cornflowers and went with an equally dazzling smile. For the first time ever, Polly's taste in men coincided with Beth's.

'With milk?'

'Actually it was a cappuccino.'

You can go off people. She thought of announcing that the free refill only applied to straight coffee, but instead she wrestled with the cappuccino handle, put the cup in place and switched on the water. He was astoundingly attractive, and Beth would help her with the peppers if she got behind.

She was showering the finished product with chocolate powder when Beth came back with the carrots. She gave the man a smouldering look, and winked at Polly.

Polly clenched her teeth, and carried the drink unsteadily to the counter. It was almost impossible not to overfill a cappuccino.

'And the carrot cake? It's so good here.' He watched her struggle to get it on the plate without messing up the icing. 'Did you make it?'

'No, it's bought in. Will that be all?' She told him how much he owed for the cake, and he offered her a twenty-pound note. Inevitably, she had to raid the shop till for pound coins, but she tried to be gracious about it. It wasn't his fault she was feeling harassed.

'Can I have an ashtray?'

'Of course.'

'I might see you again. I work for Cotswold Radio and I'm covering the demonstration on the roofs.'

'How interesting,' she said politely. What she meant

107

was, 'Please go and sit down so I can get back to my salads.' He may have been every woman's dream lover, but it was still Monday.

'So how do you feel about it?'

Right now, even the wanton destruction of her home town took second place to her more immediate anxieties. But she had to make it clear to this reporter that the local people were totally against there being a concrete and glass shopping mall in their town.

'Oh, I'm right behind the demonstrators. It would be a crime against our heritage to pull those buildings down. Whatever it takes to save them must be done.'

'You obviously feel very strongly about the issue. Why aren't you up on the roofs with the others?' He sounded critical.

Her guilt about not being with them made her snap. 'Partly because I have a living to earn, and partly because I can't stand heights.'

He laughed, as if she'd said something witty instead of the simple truth. Polly smiled back, through gritted teeth. Beth came out, ostensibly to check the tables. They both watched him take his coffee and cake and sit down. He wasn't particularly tall, but he had a swagger which oozed confidence. Polly wanted to kick him.

'See what I mean, Poll?' said Beth when they were back in the kitchen. 'Isn't he lush?'

'More your type than mine. He's too blatantly sexual for me.' She was annoyed with him for pricking her conscience.

'Rubbish!' He's just the type you need to show you what sex is really like.'

'I'm sure his technique would be perfect. I happen to consider that mere acrobatics is less important than being of like mind and having mutual respect.' A sprig of broccoli aimed at Beth emphasized this adult attitude.

Beth stuck her tongue out at Polly and scooped up some of the toasted cashews intended for the rice salad. Polly batted her out of the way and ate a couple herself. Beth had a lot of commonsense, if a rather earthy way of expressing it. It might be a good idea to try sex with a man who could find your erogenous zones without a map. But as the clock marched relentlessly towards twelve o'clock, leaving her struggling behind, she turned her mind to the important things in life.

At eight o'clock that evening Polly walked across the docks car park towards the *Wild Cat*, her high heels protesting a little on the concrete. She shivered inside her velvet jacket and tried to hurry, wishing she had put her British Warm on over the top.

In spite of rushing from the moment she left the café until now, she was, as usual, late. Her mother called her unpunctuality a psychological inability to arrive anywhere on time. Polly called it being busy. And this evening her mother was at least partly responsible for Polly's delayed departure. Simon would think she wasn't coming.

Polly and Simon had met while they were both at art school, and the relationship had ended at about the same time Polly had realized she wanted to work in three dimensions, and that form was more important to her than visual art. Simon had never quite forgiven her for either defection but they had remained friends. Since then, Beth had assured her that men only stayed friends after the romance was over if they thought they were still in with a chance. But whatever the reason, Simon had wanted her to be there for his big occasion.

There was a sturdy, land-lubbers' gangplank at the bow of the ship, but as Polly had approached from the stern she hitched up her dress and stepped aboard, ducking neatly under the rail.

She made her way along the companionway, admiring the teak-laid decks and tidy coils of rope. She reached a pair of double doors which opened to wide steps leading down to the main saloon. It was a beautifully fitted-out vessel. Simon had done well to get a sponsor who was so well connected.

Although she wasn't very late, the ship was already crowded. No doubt most people were there to see the inside of the star of the fish-finger commercials rather than the paintings.

Simon, sole exhibitor, was greeting people at the bottom of the steps. His artistically haggard expression lightened when he saw Polly. 'I'm so glad you're here, Poll. You look great. I knew you'd add a touch of class to the gathering.'

'You're quite classy yourself,' she observed, noting with relief that he had either borrowed or hired a dinner jacket and had got his ponytail under control. She put her arms round him and gave him a firm hug, feeling the tension in him. 'This is going to be a roaring success, I know.'

Simon looked disbelieving. Enormously talented and at times impossibly arrogant, he always lost faith in his work when it was framed and varnished and could no longer be fiddled with. 'The pictures are wonderful,' she added.

'You haven't had time to see them,' he grumbled. 'Come and find a glass of wine.'

'I've seen them all, lots of times.' She allowed herself to be tugged along. 'But this is the ideal setting for seascapes and boats. And the frames are superb.'

That should about cover it, she thought, and took the glass of wine he pressed on her. 'Oh look,' she said quickly, before he could press anything else, 'isn't that the mayor arriving?'

Simon shot a glance over his shoulder. 'Oh, yeah, I suppose I must go and say hello. But before I do, you know the guild's show and craft fair that's coming up?'

'I think so. What about it?'

'They've decided to have a small spot for non-guild craftsmen. I'm going to see if I can get you in.'

'Oh Simon . . .'

Simon patted her shoulder as one who had made it as an artist to one who hadn't – yet. 'You're very good. I'm well in with the committee. They should take my word for it that you won't let the side down.'

'Thank you, Simon,' she said, daunted by his confidence, and watched him steer his way through the crowd towards the mayoral party.

But Simon wasn't known for his reliability, and there was no point in getting het up about an event which may very well not happen. She might as well relax and look at the pictures. It was difficult to see them in such a crush, but she'd told Simon the truth when she said the ship was the perfect setting. And it seemed as though the exhibition was attracting all the right attention.

Including, she noticed, Beth's 'tasty geezer'. He was obviously working, holding a microphone under somebody's nose. She recognized the nose as belonging to a local sailor, famous for crossing the Atlantic at great speed and greater discomfort. It would be a coup for Simon if he bought one of his paintings.

She was amused, but not particularly surprised to notice that Cotswold Radio's roving reporter was one of the only men in the room wearing neither a dinner jacket nor a suit. He was still wearing what he had been that morning, though to his credit the T-shirt was clean. Beth was right about his jacket. It was rather sexy.

He had put down his microphone and was scanning the crowds for a fresh victim when he spotted Polly. Polly smiled slightly and watched him frown, think, and fail to come up with the required answer. Their customers often recognized the girls who worked at the Whole Nut, but few of them could ever work out how they came to know them.

'I've got it!'

Polly turned to see that he had made the connection and had crossed the room to tell her.

'The Whole Nut café!'

She gave him a smile as different as possible from the one he had inadvertently received that morning.

'I didn't recognize you at first. You look so different.'

'Good.'

It would be a poor show if she didn't. At work she wore a T-shirt, a wide denim skirt and white trainers, not to mention the apron. At work any make-up applied at seven in the morning had been steamed off by nine at the latest, leaving only a dingy shadow of itself under her lashes. Any glamour seen at the Whole Nut café was there courtesy of Beth.

Getting ready that evening had been a battle from start to finish. There had been a scant inch of odorous pink cream left in the tube with which to exfoliate both legs and her armpits. After squeezing, waiting, scraping and reapplying for what seemed like hours her legs felt stubbly about the ankle and cold. Her armpits were as nature intended, in the happy seclusion of her long-sleeved dress.

Her mother had rung while Polly was putting on her make-up, and carrying on this process with the receiver tucked under her chin was not easy. Polly had just explained how she must ring off now, a process which involved a lot of half-truths (Sylvia had never liked Simon), when Sylvia casually enquired when her daughter was planning to return Melissa and Sheldon's invitation to dinner. As Polly had no such plan and said so, the telephone call was further protracted.

When she had finally broken free her ear was throbbing, and she noticed that not only were her only pair of black tights laddered but Selina had gone to sleep on her black velvet dress.

These events, coupled with the very idea of inviting Melissa to dinner, left Polly so depressed there was nothing for it but to eat an entire packet of instant custard. And if it wasn't for her new resolution, she would have given up and had an early night instead.

But because she did want to make some sort of tottering step towards expanding her social life, and didn't fancy the recommended method of signing up for car maintenance classes, which inevitably turned out to be full of nuns, she had struggled on. It was nice to know her efforts had paid off.

She waited patiently while he decided between 'What's a nice girl like you doing in a place like that?', meaning the café, or, 'Do you come here often?', meaning the art exhibition.

He chose neither. He put his warm, dry hand into hers. 'Tristan Black, Cotswold Radio.'

'Polly Cameron.' She returned his ring-biting squeeze, but didn't add a soubriquet. He could make that up for himself.

'Can I get you another glass of wine?'

'No, thank you. I'm driving.'

'A soft drink, then?'

She hesitated. His blue eyes and black curls were not accustomed to being refused, and she was thirsty. 'Orange juice and fizzy water then, thank you.'

Tristan Black disappeared into the crowd, and Polly didn't really expect to see him again. Dynamic young radio reporters would quickly find more promising chat-up material than women who, while not actually old enough to be their mothers, could give them ten years, at least.

She examined the nearest picture, as usual mentally converting it into pottery and considering the effect. A tall ship might look rather well on the bottom of a flat, oblong-shaped dish, she decided. But they'd be a bit fiddly on a small surface. Oh, for a bigger kiln!

Inspired by a section of the ship's side, knotted and scored by years of hard work and now varnished into pure gold, she was trying to remember how to achieve that colour glaze when he returned.

'Here you are.'

She turned round. 'Oh! That was quick. I thought you'd be hours.'

He smiled, his talent for getting a drink under any

114

circumstance duly acknowledged. 'So what are you doing here?' he asked.

Polly put on a bland expression. 'Looking at pictures. How about you?'

'Oh, I'm working.'

She raised a sceptical eyebrow. 'Really?'

He had very white teeth, but Polly caught a glimpse of gold towards the corner of his smile. She found it curiously attractive.

'Well, I was. Now I'm enjoying myself.'

Polly was well aware she was being flattered and was annoyed to find herself warming to it. But she determined to keep her weakness to herself. 'You like pictures, then?'

He shrugged. 'I can take them or leave them. I say, you don't happen to live in Laureton, by any chance?'

Warily, she agreed she did.

'You couldn't give me a lift back, could you? My car's in dock.'

So that was why he was being so charming. She prevaricated. 'How did you get into Gloucester?'

'Took a cab.'

'Couldn't you take a cab home?'

He looked pained. Obviously Tristan Black wasn't used to having his requests for lifts refused any more than his offers of drinks. 'I'd rather not.'

Polly nodded. 'And I'd rather not give a lift to a man I don't know. I'm sure you understand.' She paused. 'And I'm sure you could claim for the cab on expenses.'

'Yeah, but I'd much rather go with you.'

She smiled dazzlingly. 'Of course you would. That way you can claim for the taxi anyway, and keep the money. There's sure to be someone else here going your

115

way.' The blue gaze stayed fixed, willing her to give in. 'I'm sorry, but I'm a single woman ...'

'I'm not a bit sorry you're a single woman ...'

'... and it's extremely silly to give lifts to strangers.'

He grinned. It was predictably disarming. 'Go on – live dangerously.'

Polly's idea of living dangerously was reading library books in the bath. 'No, thank you.'

But he wouldn't give up. 'Listen, suppose I can find someone here who can vouch for me, convince you I'm not a rapist or anything like that?'

'Why don't you concentrate on finding someone who can give you a lift home? Anyway, I've only just got here, I won't be leaving for ages.'

It wasn't what she told herself as she set out that evening. She'd promised herself she'd look in because Simon had asked her so particularly, and disappear as soon as she reasonably could. But she needn't tell him that.

'I meant later. I've got a few interviews to get.'

'Even so, the answer's still no.'

'You're a hard woman.'

'Yes.' She moved determinedly away. He was a brat – handsome, but definitely a brat.

As soon as he was out of sight, she found Simon and made her apologies. As Simon was wholly entranced by the daughter of his sponsor, he didn't protest. Polly congratulated herself on making an early, unaccompanied getaway.

Which was copping out of her self-inflicted responsibility. She should really have been more responsive to Tristan. He was young, attractive and apparently single. Instead, her old habit of fleeing at the first sign of interest had been too strong for her. She must do better next time.

Cross with herself already, it was particularly galling to run out of petrol going up Horsepools Hill. Filling up was one of the things she had had on her list of things to do, but knowing the car went for miles on 'E' and having been in a hurry, she hadn't.

Now she would have to walk a mile in the dark along a dangerous stretch of road on wobbly shoes to get to a phone box. She was searching in the back of her car on the off chance she'd left her wellingtons there, when a car pulled up ahead. The red light of a local taxi firm shone with grisly inevitability.

She tensed and watched a man get out and start walking back towards her. She groped for her can of WD40 out of habit, and because she was a sensible woman. But it was no surprise when Tristan Black tapped on her window, grinning with nauseating smugness.

She wound down the window.

'Got a bit of trouble?' he enquired.

This was her cue to smile and flutter and persuade the kind man to look after her.

'I've run out of petrol.' Her tone of voice was as frosty as the night air.

He leaned on the car door with his elbows, his body protruding dangerously out into the road. 'Can I give you a lift? In my taxi?'

She sighed heavily. She had managed to get the car well out of the way. It would be safe until she could get it sorted out in the morning. She might as well take her chance with him.

'That would be very kind,' she said, trying to ungrit her teeth.

'My pleasure.'

She clambered out of the car, aware that in doing so she revealed rather a lot of leg and the ladder in her tights, gathered up her bag and relocked the car.

'I said that you should get a cab. If I'd given you a lift you'd have been late home.'

She could hear him chuckle softly in the darkness. 'And I might have accused you of running out of petrol on purpose.'

'I don't think so,' she said with a haughtiness kept for special occasions.

He chuckled again, and took her arm. Unsteady on her heels, she let herself lean on it as they walked down the road. He was barely taller than she was, but his presence was unsettling. It was like having a panther for protection – you couldn't be sure when he'd give up protecting you and decide to eat you instead.

He opened the taxi door for her and she climbed in, hoping that he would sit in the front with the driver. He didn't. He got in beside her, bringing with him the smell of cold leather and French cigarettes.

The driver murmured something about a stroke of luck as he started the engine, and she murmured agreement. Just how lucky, she couldn't decide.

It wasn't a long journey back to Laureton, but she was aware of every inch. She held herself stiffly away from him, as if contact with him would singe her. Panthers might be deliciously furry, but it didn't do to stroke them – or let them stroke you.

'Where do you live?' inquired Tristan as they reached the outskirts of the town.

Polly thought quickly. 'Drop me at the bottom of the High Street, there's no need to go out of your way.'

To her relief, he didn't argue. But when the taxi drew up as requested at the bottom of the hill, which was pedestrianized, he got out too and paid the driver.

'Why did you do that?' asked Polly. 'Where do you live?'

'I wanted some fish and chips. How about you?'

Polly had eaten nothing but custard since she got in from work, and the thought of greasy chips with too much salt and vinegar was very appealing. And sharing a packet of chips with a man wasn't much of a threat to your virtue. And she must break herself of the habit of refusing every invitation automatically.

'Thank you. That would be lovely.'

If she sounded like her mother accepting the offer of a glass of sherry, Tristan didn't notice, and she found herself going with him into the steamy warmth of the chippy and waiting while he charmed the girl behind the counter with his ready smile.

They ate walking up the High Street, looking into the shoe shop windows towards the condemned buildings. As Tristan had said, they were now occupied. Relays of people camped out on their roofs, never leaving them unattended. It was too early to say whether this strategy would work, but it was certainly a statement which would create a lot of publicity.

Polly avoided looking to see who was maintaining a vigil on the top. She felt so guilty for letting her fear of heights prevent her from joining them. And even her efforts from the ground had been less than she felt they ought to have been.

Besides, she felt dreadful eating hot chips while the

protesters were probably frozen, in spite of their camping stoves and Thermos flasks.

If Tristan had been anyone else but a radio reporter, she might well have asked him to shin up the ladders and take them some. But some of the protesters couldn't be relied on to say the right thing and could be quite hostile to people they didn't know. Tristan could easily give his audience the impression that the protesters were left-wing hippies and put off some of their more conventional supporters. Polly didn't want to blow the whole campaign by inflicting him on them without warning.

They went up the High Street, past the seats and the sculpture in front of what was known locally as 'The Berlin Wall' and on towards where Polly lived.

Eventually they reached her gate. She stopped.

Tristan rolled his chip paper into a ball. 'You're not going to ask me in for coffee?'

'No.' She'd taken the first couple of steps, and that was enough for one night.

'Why not, as a matter of interest?'

'I don't drink coffee at this time of night.' She didn't.

'You could offer me tea, or even cocoa.'

'I could, but I'm not going to.'

'Why?'

'For all the reasons I didn't give you a lift.'

'But you had a lift with me, and you're quite safe.'

But was she? 'Sorry. I'm still not inviting you in.'

He shrugged. 'Next time, perhaps.'

'There isn't going to be a next time. I'll never run out of petrol again.'

'You will, you know.'

'Really? What makes you so sure?' He was probably right, but how did he know that?

'I'm psychic. Good night.'

He tossed his paper into the gutter, stuffed his hands into his pockets and walked off down the High Street, whistling.

Disgusted but fascinated, she picked up the paper and walked slowly down her garden path.

Chapter Nine

'You crop up in the most unexpected places.'

Polly nearly bumped her head on the roof of her car as she retreated backwards out of it. It was three weeks since they had shared a bag of chips, but she had no trouble recognizing the voice.

Tristan stood behind her. As a gesture to the freezing fog, he had added a scarf to the inevitable white T-shirt and leather jacket. He had his hands in his pockets, his feet slightly apart and his hips thrust forward. It was a characteristic gesture that was both threatening and rather attractive.

'I could say the same to you.' Polly straightened up. She had been stacking boxes of pots on the back seat. Her car was parked on the hill outside her shared studio, which looked particularly shed-like in the orange light of the street lamp.

'No, you couldn't. My work takes me all over the place.'

'Everywhere except to a radio station, it seems.'

He gave her his crooked grin, the glint of gold visible even in the semi-dark. He'd either perfected the grin to fit in with the false tooth, or had the tooth put there to add lustre to his smile. Polly hated herself for smiling back.

'Not at all. Didn't you hear my piece on the roof-top demonstration at lunchtime?'

'I only listen to Radio Four.' It wasn't true, but he needed suppressing.

He remained unsuppressed. 'What have you got in there?' He indicated the boxes.

'It's my work.'

'I thought you worked at the Whole Nut.'

Polly pulled herself up to her full, below average, height. 'That's my job. This' – she made a sweeping gesture towards the back of her car – 'is my work.'

Predictably, Tristan laughed. Polly laughed back at him. Her pretensions to being a great artist always amused her.

'What sort of work do you do?'

'I'm a potter.'

'Potter? Or potterer?'

'The former.' She was sensitive about the fact that she managed to do so little potting. His implication that she only played at it prodded her frustration.

'And you do it in there?' He gave the Shed a derisive jerk of the head.

'Yes,' she snapped, crisp as a gingernut.

Her asperity gave him further cause for amusement. 'Don't get so touchy, come for a meal.'

'No, thank you.' The words were an automatic reaction to his mockery. It was a pity. She was hungry and didn't feel like cooking.

'Why not?'

Something about him made her think. She had been refusing such invitations for so long it was a knee-jerk reaction. Perhaps she should accept, and punish his arrogance. He couldn't really want to take a clay-covered older woman, wearing dungarees, a great-coat and a woolly hat out for a meal. She'd call his bluff. 'Oh, all right then,' she said, trying to sound nonchalant. 'I'll meet you somewhere. I've got to get this lot home first.'

'Give me a lift?'

She released a long, shuddering sigh, and with it a great deal of in-built resistance to male advances. 'Climb in.'

If rape was really on his mind, he'd get bored long before he'd fought through the first layer of clothing.

He squashed himself into the car through the two inches of the door that opened, parked as she was, flush against the wall. He put his arm over the back of her seat in a way she couldn't really object to but didn't quite like either.

Though not a big man, he brought with him a highly charged aura which was more than the smell of leather and cigarettes. Tristan Black was confusing. Young, brash and anything but earnest, he would certainly be interested in a casual affair. He would equally certainly have the technique necessary to get her over her sexual hang-ups. And Polly was aware how strongly she was attracted to him. He was ideal.

But what was it about her that made him pay her so much attention? Was he really trying to pick her up? If so, why? There were plenty of sweet young things for him to seduce, so why bother with a less sweet older thing?

'When are you getting your car back?' Polly negotiated a pair of the mini-roundabouts which were a feature of Laureton.

'Tomorrow. Where shall we eat?'

'I've got to go home first. I'll need about an hour.'

'I'll wait while you get yourself ready.'

'I don't need an hour to run a comb through my hair,' she said icily. 'I've got things to see to.' She resented the implication that she needed so long to doll herself up to go out with him, especially as to really do the job would take much longer.

'What things?' He didn't believe her.

'My cat and my Rayburn, to name but two. And then there's my pots to sort out.' In fact, she intended to leave her pots in their boxes until the morning, otherwise she wouldn't have time for the all-essential bath. 'I'll meet you somewhere.'

'Why can't I wait at your house?'

Why couldn't he? Because it was a mess, and she never let strangers across the threshold? Not in his case. He could put up with the clutter, the dubious odours, the dust. But she couldn't have a bath in comfort with a strange man pacing about in her sitting room. Besides, she wanted to listen to *The Archers*.

'You'll be warmer at the pub. There's one up the road. I'll be with you as soon as I can. If you can't wait, don't worry.'

The handbrake went on with a decisive squeak. She climbed out, ushered Tristan up the hill towards the pub and watched to make sure he went there. Then she went into the house.

She raced through her chores, had her bath and washed her recently cut hair. With the aid of the right kind of spray-on gel, as recommended by Bridget's Mark, it curled and fluffed about her head in a gratifyingly trouble-free way. But she deliberately only put on just enough make-up to satisfy herself that she wouldn't frighten any passing children or horses. If he wanted to

125

take an older woman out for a meal, he could find out exactly what an older woman looked like before she got out her magnifying mirror and plastering trowel.

Polly walked up the hill to her local, uncertain if she would be relieved to discover that Tristan had eaten a plate of pie and mash and departed, or disappointed. She had a nasty suspicion she was in danger of what used to be referred to as 'losing one's head over a man'.

Her highly developed sense of self-preservation told her she should be grateful if Tristan had sauntered out into the night looking, if not for pastures new, at least for pastures younger. But the rest of her knew that if he had she'd be thoroughly ticked off.

It was not a smart pub, but it was one she could go into on her own without feeling uncomfortable. If he wasn't there, she could have had a drink and a chat anyway. If he was, it was fate leading her astray.

She pushed open the outer door and immediately saw Tristan, thoroughly at home among the regulars. He was leaning against the bar, all his casual confidence on display. A desert boot was propped on the rail and leather-clad elbows rumpled the towelling drip-mat.

In the way of all good journalists, Tristan was chatting to the landlord, constantly, almost unconsciously, sifting through mindless chat for the hint of a story. He had a ruthlessness about him which was quite capable of thrusting a microphone under the nose of a weeping widow and asking for her reaction to her husband's brutal murder. He would go far – quite how far in her particular direction he wanted to travel she had yet to find out.

She gave a general smile to the people who had turned on hearing the door open. Little prickles of something murmured in the pit of her stomach. Hunger pangs, she told herself firmly, and joined him.

'Polly!' He said it as if he was really pleased to see her. 'What would you like to drink?'

'Hello, Tristan,' she said casually, mastering the prickles. 'You still here? Gin and tonic please, Reg.'

'Of course I'm still here. Why wouldn't I be?' He appeared genuinely indignant.

She shrugged, impressed with her casual manner, and clambered on to the bar stool next to his. 'I thought you might have got hungry and eaten already.'

'I had a packet of crisps.' It was almost as if he was sulking. Then his self-righting ego operated and he shot her a grin that was practisedly wicked. 'Now I want something more substantial.'

If I were Beth I'd know exactly what to read into that remark, she realized, sipping her drink. But because I haven't played these games for so long I've forgotten the conventions. I can no longer speak the language. She busked it. 'Really?'

He produced a packet of Gauloises, offered her the packet and lit one. 'I'd like to go to the Old Grey Ewe.' He took a deep, tar-filled pull on his cigarette. 'I've heard the food there is good.'

'Do you really need food, with all that nicotine to keep you going?'

'Would you prefer me not to smoke?' He moved the cigarette so it was no longer under her nose.

She shrugged and refrained from replying that she didn't care if he burst into flames. 'It's none of my business. Where is the Old Grey Ewe?'

'At Ewestone, nearly at Cirencester. We'll call a cab.'

Polly inspected her slice of lemon. This talk of cabs and

Cirencester was unnerving. When she'd agreed to have a meal with him, she'd assumed he meant somewhere local, within running-away distance from home.

And was the taxi so he could get her drunk, or a responsible attitude to drinking and driving? Hard to say, but if she'd known he planned to go out of Laureton she wouldn't have had the gin.

'Another?' Tristan indicated her glass, and nodded to Reg without waiting for her answer. Reg burrowed in the bucket for more ice and Tristan burrowed in his wallet. He found a card with the name of a taxi firm on it at about the same time as Reg put a new drink in front of Polly.

Polly tipped the remains of her tonic into the gin, aware that she was entering strange, potentially dangerous territory. Tristan had crossed to the phone and was ordering a cab. Before it arrived she would have to decide if she was brave enough to get on the roller-coaster or not.

Two gin and tonics on an empty stomach had lowered her resistance and she decided to go for it. Playing with fire can be a lot of fun, and wasn't necessarily dangerous. And anyway, by now, she was too hungry to turn down the offer of a meal, especially one guaranteed to be fattening.

'Good night, Polly,' said Reg, as the taxi driver appeared in the pub.

''Night, Reg,' said Polly, trying not to feel the disapproval which accompanied this casual remark. 'I'll be in tomorrow.' To prove that I'm safe and sound, she added silently.

'Reg seems very fond of you,' said Tristan, climbing into the taxi next to her.

'He's very good to me,' she agreed.

'He fancies you.'

Polly sat back and digested this. Firstly, it had never occurred to her that Reg's kindness was anything but fatherly. And secondly, Tristan had not sounded pleased. It couldn't be jealousy precisely, more a male dislike of any other male paying the accompanying female attention. Interesting that he should feel about her like that.

The Old Grey Ewe was buried so deep in the country it was a miracle anyone discovered it at all. But as there were several cars parked outside it, and the taxi driver had known where to come, it was obviously popular with the cognoscenti.

The odour of stale chip fat, cigarette smoke and spilt beer hit them as they went through the door. Tristan steered Polly to a table, brought more drinks and a menu.

' "Piping Hot Pizza 'N' Chip's," ' Polly read from it aloud. 'Who is Chip, and which part of his anatomy is he prepared to sacrifice?'

'What would you like to eat?' Tristan, obviously not so particular about the standards of grammar in pubs today, overlooked this sally.

Polly concentrated harder. 'I'll have the "Crunchy Coated Jacket Spud with Bangers 'n' Beans", or what we call at the Whole Nut a potato. And a salad.'

'I'll have curry and chips,' said Tristan. 'Another drink?'

Polly hadn't finished hers yet, but as a well-trained feminist she got to her feet, purse in hand. 'It's my round. What are you having?'

'I'll have a Scotch and ginger ale.'

Polly was surprised to discover just how many of

Sylvia Cameron's prejudices she had inherited. Her mother would die before she referred to whisky as 'Scotch'.

'Shall I order the food at the same time?'

Tristan smiled. 'Yes, but don't pay for it. This is on me.'

Gold star for Tristan. Then she remembered the expense account and cancelled the gold star.

'So.' She set the drinks down on the table. 'How are you going to describe me on your expenses sheet?'

He drew his glass towards him and placed it carefully on a chance to win a holiday in Florida disguised as a beer mat. 'You know, something tells me you don't exactly approve of me.' He regarded her with eyes as innocent as forget-me-nots and as sexy as hell.

Polly looked into them, swallowed silently and acknowledged that one part of her approved of him very much. But she wasn't going to tell him that. He was quite perceptive enough without help from her.

'It's not that I don't approve of you, Tristan. I don't understand you.'

'What's to understand?' He made an open-handed gesture indicating he was an honest, salt-of-the-earth working man with not a shred of deviousness in his character.

Polly was not convinced. 'Why have you gone to so much trouble to pick me up?'

'What do you mean?'

'You know perfectly well what I mean. You don't need me to explain.'

'And I'm sure you don't need *me* to explain. You're an attractive, intelligent woman I want to spend time with.'

Mmm, thought Polly. It was good, but not *that* good. 'Yes, but why?'

'Why not? I enjoy your company, I –' His pause was deliberate, but she couldn't help prompting him.

'You what?'

'You'll probably slap my face.'

It was obvious that far too few of his previous female companions had slapped his face, and he was pretty confident that she wouldn't either. 'Go on, then. Tell me.'

'I don't half fancy you, Polly.'

Polly didn't raise her hand, she raised her glass and drained it slowly, using the time to pull herself together. 'How very flattering,' she said at last, managing not to sound flattered at all.

'No, really.' Tristan was put out that his compliment hadn't bowled her over with gratitude. 'You have a luscious body.'

Even if the word 'luscious' did remind her of overripe pears, she *was* secretly thrilled that her thirty-five-year-old body had the power to excite a twenty-five-year-old man. Then she wondered how much of her body he had actually laid eyes on. As far as she knew when Tristan had been about it had always been fairly well camouflaged.

'Have I? Which bit, exactly?'

'Your legs.' He chuckled with studied sexiness which, annoyingly, was still sexy. 'I love watching you get in and out of cars, Polly.'

'Oh.' Her legs, eh? Flabby thighs must have their fans after all.

'So what are we going to do about it?' husked Tristan, in the manner of the Hollywood Greats. 'Your body, I mean.'

131

Polly made an airy gesture. 'Slap a preservation order on it? Declare it a site of special scientific interest?'

Secretly she resolved to overcome her resistance to organized exercise and get into shape. If people actually looked at her legs, she'd better make sure she kept them up to scratch. Even if it did mean going through the boring agony of an aerobics class.

None of this showed on her face, and Tristan was not expecting such an off-hand reaction to his handsome compliment. But any protest was interrupted by the arrival of the food. Regarding it, Polly abandoned any half-formed plans to diet as well as to exercise.

Two massive oval plates loaded with food groaned under the weight of plastic boxes of condiment and raw onions. The chef didn't have much faith in his use of seasoning, thought Polly disdainfully. But she noted with approval the proliferation of scarlet serviettes around each knife and fork. She may be sniffy about the incorrect use of the apostrophe, but she wasn't above filling her handbag with pub napkins.

'You're not taking me seriously, Polly,' said Tristan after the complicated rearrangements necessitated by the hugeness of the plates and the smallness of the table.

She shrugged, high on the discovery that she could still, after all, play the game. 'What's to take seriously?'

'I am! I want a relationship with you, Polly.'

'Define "relationship".'

He shifted a bottle of vinegar and a salt cellar to make room for his elbows on the table. He obviously wanted to look meaningfully into her eyes, and found his style cramped by crockery. The look, when he finally managed it, was not meaningful, but it was effective.

132

'It's two people who enjoy each other's company, in every way. Let's not play semantics.'

He plunged his fork into a pile of chips without looking away.

He must eat in pubs a lot, thought Polly, and turned her attention to her crunchy coated jacket.

'Another drink?'

They had finished eating, and Polly, once a waitress, always a waitress, had put the plates and cutlery into a neat pile.

'I don't think . . .'

'Or shall I call a taxi to take us home?'

Did he mean their respective homes, just his or just hers? But before Polly could phrase her question, Tristan had gone off in the direction of the pay phone.

Polly fiddled with the stack of empty condiment cartons, contemplating Tristan's expectations and her own and how they differed.

For however devastated Polly was by his incredible sex appeal, flattered by his attentions, desperate to make love with a man who knew what was what, she was not going to bed with him tonight. In spite of the gin.

Tristan was a man any woman would fantasize about, but Polly had very firm ideas about fantasy. Rule one was that it belonged between book covers not bed covers – not on the first date, anyway.

By the time he had returned she had decided against asking him outright about his plans for the end of the evening. There are more subtle ways of getting home with one's honour intact.

In the event, he didn't threaten her honour. Polly was quite disappointed. He didn't even put his arm round her in the taxi. When they got to her house, he walked with her to her gate, wrote her telephone number carefully on a cigarette packet, and watched her write his on an envelope. He made it very clear that they were going to see each other again. And then he gave her a swift, hard kiss on the cheek, leaving her wanting more.

Because, for such an everyday event, that kiss was surprisingly exciting. Lots of men kissed Polly's cheek, lots of men wore pleasant aftershave, but this casual peck promised things Polly rarely experienced. Tristan would know how to kiss like an expert. Polly would stake her life on it.

This restraint was a very shrewd move on his part. The missing kiss tantalized Polly long after his taxi had ticked away.

That night Polly decided to ring Bridget the next day and tell her everything. It was not in her nature to be secretive, it wasn't fair to keep such delicious gossip to herself and she might well need some motherly advice.

Far more to the point, if she didn't tell anyone, she was bound to get found out. Tristan was sure to come into the café and demand cut-price carrot cake, just to embarrass her.

'I might come to aerobics with you on Thursday, Bridget,' said Polly on the telephone.

'Oh? And you rang to tell me?' They usually managed to communicate more than adequately at work.

'Well, you know. We're always so busy, I thought I'd probably forget the details. Now I can write them down.'

'Well, okay. It's on Thursday. At eight. At Portland House. Got that?'

'Yes. Actually, Bridget, there was something else I wanted to tell you . . .'

'What?'

'I went out with Tristan Black. You remember? The one who works for Cotswold Radio?'

There was a silence while Bridget fought the desire to utter dire warnings. She lost. 'Poll, are you absolutely sure you know what you're doing? I mean, he's so . . .'

It was not easy to pacify her friend when Polly knew perfectly well that all Bridget's fears were justified. Polly *didn't* know what she was doing, she *was* hopelessly naïve and vulnerable. She *could* easily get in way over her head. But she wanted to take the risk.

'I'll be all right, Bridget, honestly,' she finished.

Bridget sighed deeply. 'There are heaps of nice men you could go out with. I could arrange –'

'I'm going out with Tristan, Bridget. Maybe not for long. But I really can cope.'

'If you say so. But I'll get my extra-bulky shoulder pads out anyway.'

Polly laughed and said goodbye. Bridget was convinced it was going to end in tears. Her mother would cry at the mere sight of Tristan. But she felt happy that she'd made a positive decision. Let the devil take the hindmost . . .

Chapter Ten

At the door of the youth club where 'Dermot's Aerobics' jogged its way to fitness three times a week, Polly got cold feet. She admitted it to Bridget.

'Hold on to that feeling. In a moment there won't be an inch of you that's cold. Come on.'

Bridget, who had been nagging Polly to come to aerobics for ages, was surprisingly unenthusiastic about her coming now. It was Polly's motives that bothered her. Fitness for its own sake had a certain nobility. Improving your muscle tone so you could have a fling with a toyboy hadn't.

Half a dozen women stood in twos and threes about the room. Dermot himself was playing scraps of tape on a ghetto blaster and stretching his long legs. He was wearing black lycra cycling shorts, a T-shirt and very white sports socks. His already considerable height was added to by trainers the size of small cars. Even Polly recognized the brand name on the instep.

In spite of this, he was not the over-confident muscle man Polly expected. In fact, when Bridget introduced her he seemed almost shy. 'Hello,' he said to Polly. 'If this is your first time, just do what you can. It's important to stop if you feel it's too much. Keep marching on the spot until you've got your breath back. We aim to do only moderate aerobic exercise.'

Polly welcomed this practised speech with a smile, leaving Bridget to exchange a few words with Dermot. She could stay at the back being 'only' and 'moderate' and let the eager beavers concentrate on 'aerobic exercise'.

But not if Bridget had anything to do with it. She took hold of Polly's shoulders and moved her firmly to the front of the room. 'If you can't see what Dermot's doing, you'll never follow. There's no point in coming if you're not prepared to work.'

Bridget was obviously determined that Polly should suffer for her folly. And if keep-fit classes left her unable to walk, perhaps she'd think twice before entering a relationship with a man so thoroughly user-unfriendly.

Polly knew Bridget very well. She sympathized with her good intentions, but herself had no intention of swerving from her downward path. Meekly, she allowed herself to be positioned where she could be kept an eye on.

People began to drift in. Mostly female, they all had that look which declared them as having meaningful careers. Nothing so mundane as waitressing or office work for them. They were teachers, social workers and psychotherapists to a woman.

The three or four token men who came in the wake of some of the women appeared less dynamic, but no less unnerving. They were so bouncy. They danced about on their toes as if they would spring into the air like spaniels the moment someone held up a biscuit.

Polly shifted uncomfortably in her T-shirt and black tracksuit bottoms. She had bought the track-suit bottoms, with a matching top, in a hurry from a market stall. They were remarkably cheap. But the top had hidden the trousers, and it was only when she got them home that she discovered the words 'I'M THE BOSS' emblazoned in green lettering down the legs. She had them on inside out.

The psychotherapists wore black leggings with outsize T-shirts bearing Green slogans; proper trainers and jolly socks adorned their hairless, still-tanned, well-toned legs. Their long, abundant hair was confined with cheerful, Liberty-print scrunchies, and, apart from one pair of stars-and-stripes shorts, they none of them wore high-cut, highly coloured lycra leotards. This was not a class to show off how much you spent on leisure wear, this was where you sweated away for an hour and then carried on with your high-powered, meaningful life. They all seemed to have perfect figures.

'Nobody but me looks like they need to be here,' whispered Polly, tying up the laces of the trainers she had borrowed from Bridget's Mark.

Bridget, who had the same greyhound look as the others, whispered back, 'They look like that because they exercise. Now come and get a step.' She took her fitness seriously.

A step proved to be a square of cork raised a few inches from the ground, horribly reminiscent of a set of bathroom scales. Bridget explained that using this step burned up more calories and gave you more low-impact exercise than merely bouncing about on the floor.

'It looks like a form of torture devised by anorexics for normal women,' muttered Polly as the music began.

To his credit, Dermot didn't display his fitness. He did everything in a laid-back manner; and it was all easily achievable, even by the totally non-fit. The greyhounds worked far harder, pumping their knees and elbows up and down with boundless enthusiasm, sweat streaming down their unmadeup faces. Polly, whose make-up was reduced to a smear of black and whose feet were doing everything except what everyone else's were, hated them all, including Bridget. Particularly as she guessed they were all several years older than her.

'Now we've warmed up, we'll go on to the step.' Dermot made it sound like a treat. 'Keep marching while I change the tape.'

To Polly's surprise, everyone kept marching, although the teacher's back was turned and he wouldn't see them have a quick skive. This was a class for the Serious Minded. No dilettante fitness fanatics these. These people Cared About Their Bodies in the same way they Cared About The Environment. Polly wiped her face on the sleeve of her T-shirt and joined in.

The male presence in the class was a mixed blessing. They made everyone work harder (you couldn't be seen to be less able to keep going than a Mere Man), and they were hopelessly unco-ordinated, which made Polly feel better. But on the other hand, they took up a lot of space and sweated on to the floor. They also smelt. It was not, decided Polly, stepping up and down with a different foot to everyone else, necessarily an unpleasant smell. It was just very masculine and very strong.

After what seemed like hours, the steps were gathered into a corner and the five minutes of high-energy exercise began. It was a killer. Polly, who had discovered a clock in the corner, kept giving it sidelong glances and getting out of step.

'I'm not sure my bra is up to this,' she panted, clutching on to its straps to lighten its load. It was her Christmas bra, and Polly was still washing it by hand in her bath. She didn't want to over-extend it so early on in its career.

'Never mind your bra,' snapped Bridget, now quite red in the face. 'You haven't got stress incontinence to contend with.'

'What the hell's that?'

'It's what happens if you have babies and don't do your pelvic-floor exercises.'

Polly gulped, and tried frantically to get back into rhythm. Had she got a pelvic floor? If she had, she certainly didn't exercise it.

At last the class was 'warmed down' and invited to collect mats which appeared to be made out of the same polystyrene supermarkets sold meat on. By now the whole class was steak-red and Polly was forcibly reminded of a butcher's window as, for a blissful moment, they lay down.

This time Polly wasn't fooled. She knew that nothing in the class was restful, and it was certain that this brief reprieve only heralded more intense torture.

She was right. Biting back her cries of pain as she tried to locate muscles on her inner thigh, Polly wondered why, for the second time, she'd let herself be fooled into thinking fitness was a good idea.

A couple of years earlier, Polly and Bridget had gone to a yoga class. They were going to centre their minds and stretch their muscles and become younger and fitter. The class had been taken by a couple, a man of uncertain age and unbelievable elasticity and a girl, easily as supple and beautiful as the dawn.

Bridget had turned out to be fairly supple herself and improved weekly. Polly, when she should have been ensuring that her hand and arm were in perfect alignment and that her weight was on the outside of her foot, used to speculate on the beautiful couple's sex life. They must be one of the few couples on earth for whom the Kama Sutra was more than just a curiosity.

After six weeks Bridget had mastered the lotus position and Polly had decided the gain wasn't worth the pain. She didn't enjoy standing for hours in positions of great discomfort. Particularly not upside down. Shoulder stands were her least favourite.

This was the posture to be practised every day: it put back what the wicked world took out; it was of special benefit to women.

But not, Polly decided, to women with breasts. For no sooner had she hoisted her legs and lower back into the air when her bosom and all its accompanying flesh fell out of her leotard and hit her in the face. To remain there, suffocating, for ten minutes before you could come down into a plough, which merely broke your neck, was quite reminiscent of being sat on by a sumo wrestler, and only fractionally less unpleasant.

The wonderful girl told them that if they had their periods they were absolved from shoulder stands, but a monthly dispensation was not enough for Polly. She gave it up.

But this time it had been her idea to come, not Bridget's. This time she had an incentive for this suffering.

Tristan had only glimpsed her legs, and then they'd been wearing two pairs of tights. Under the black tights with the ladder, Polly had been wearing a tan-coloured pair. This was partly for warmth, and partly for the flattering effect. What her legs looked like in the cold (very) light of day was less pleasing. And if Dermot couldn't tone them up for her, no one could. Polly turned on to her front, stuck her bottom in the air and tried to do a press-up. This time she would stick with it. It was part of her plan. Get the body in trim while it was still rescuable, then the prospect of taking your clothes off in front of a man may not be so blush-making.

Polly was limping sweatily to the car behind Bridget when she was stopped by a cheerful shout.

'Hi, Poll,' said Mac. 'Haven't seen you for a while. Have you designed those posters yet?'

Guiltily, Polly pushed her wet hair out of her eyes. 'Sorry, no. I've been frightfully busy . . .'

'Never mind the excuses. The push is on. We've found how much those bastards are offering to pay for the land. It's a ridiculous price. If what they want to put up is so in fucking keeping, like they make out, why are they offering so much? They'd never get their money back. It's bloody suss. You must get to the meeting tomorrow night. Bring your drawings then.'

'I will. I'm dreadfully sorry I haven't been lately.'

Mac grinned. 'Cut the crap, girl. Just get yourself into gear.'

Only a madman would go to a supermarket at six o'clock on a Friday night, but if she was to turn up at the meeting, as she had promised Mac she would, she would have to face it. And as Polly slid her car in between a Japanese version of a Range Rover and a BMW, she knew she would not be alone in her insanity. Many, many others like her would be dashing in on their way home from work.

Except this time she would not be dashing. How

Dermot had the nerve to imply that his class would keep you fit, she hadn't a clue. Keep you crippled seemed more like it.

Usually she confined her trips to Tesco's to less popular times, but this was an emergency – Selina had gone off her cheaper brand of cat food and would starve to death unless offered something more expensive.

It was odd, thought Polly, disconnecting a trolley (you couldn't lean on a basket) from its fellows: if she personally had nothing in the house but dried peas, she wouldn't shop on a Friday night. But for her cat she risked bruised ankles, a migraine headache and the serious lowering of spirits which goes with crowds and the spendomania which overcomes people who are tired, hungry and in no fit state to shop. And all for a cat. Perhaps her maternal instincts were stronger than she'd realized. An unsettling thought.

Not even Polly, whose financial circumstances were a natural protection from impulse buying, could escape from Tesco's with only cat food. Thus she already had a few items reduced for quick sale in her trolley before she approached the pet-food aisle.

It was here that she spotted Melissa.

The aisle was packed, her line of retreat was cut off. She was far too stiff to run away, so frantically she considered fighting her way over the walls of tins into detergents and cleaning materials, or finding her woolly hat, which she'd stuffed into the bib of her overalls, and pulling it over her face. A spark of sanity made her opt for inspecting the label on the most gourmet feline titbits and praying Melissa wouldn't recognize her. She kept her head well down and prayed.

'Polly!'

143

Polly's heart sank into her wellington boots, which didn't even have the social nous to be green.

'Melissa! How nice!' she said weakly. Looking up she saw David Locking-Hill heave into view behind Melissa. 'David! Look who it is.'

Polly was already far too hot and trusted her blushes would go unnoticed. 'Hello,' she said in a small voice.

'We were just saying – weren't we, David? – how we hadn't seen you for ages. We didn't really get to talk last time, did we? And I'm dying to see your dear little house.' Melissa waited expectantly.

Polly had an out-of-body experience and heard her mother's daughter speak. 'You must come to dinner. I'm sorry I haven't asked you before –' Her sentence trailed away with a series of 'busies', 'rushed off my feets', 'don't often entertain' and ended with a cough.

'That would be lovely, wouldn't it, David?' Melissa's gaze marched briskly up and down Polly's working clothes. 'When?'

Polly reasserted herself quickly and determined not to let Melissa put her on the spot again. 'I'll ring you and arrange something. How's Sheldon?' she added firmly.

If she'd hoped (and she had) that she'd caught Melissa and David indulging in a safe but highly unusual form of illicit sex which involved supermarkets and crowds of people, she was in for a disappointment.

'Oh, he's tracking down the mascarpone so Maria can make *tiramisu.*'

Maria? Surely Melissa's maid was called Consuela? Perhaps she had a colony of them.

'Golly.' What the hell was *tiramisu,* and had she really invited Melissa to dinner? 'So did you just happen to meet each other here?' Polly gestured to David and

Melissa, still hoping to make at least one of them uncomfortable.

'No, we bumped into him delivering wine to an old pal of Sheldon's and invited him back for kitchen sups. He's out so often we were glad to catch him in. Then I remembered we hadn't any coffee beans. David very sweetly suggested popping in for some, but then I remembered the *tiramisu* recipe and thought I might as well get the ingredients.'

'How clever of you to remember what they were.' Polly curled her toes inside her wellingtons.

'Oh, I've always had a jolly good memory. Sheldon calls me his walking Filofax.' Melissa laughed brightly.

'How romantic,' said Polly dryly, thinking that Melissa's memory was a damn sight too jolly good. And even if you were owed dinner invitations, it wasn't quite the thing to remind people, especially not at Tesco's.

'He'd have to call you his walking sieve. You were always forgetting things at school. Darling, what have you got on?'

'Working clothes.'

'Working? Oh, you mean your *pottery*.' Melissa took in another eyeful of Polly's dungarees and was about to say how nice it was for her to have a hobby when Sheldon appeared, sparing Polly from having to ram Melissa with her shopping trolley.

'Why, it's Polly!' Sheldon sounded pleased with himself for having recognized her. 'How are you?'

'She's promised to have us all over for dinner. Won't that be fun?'

'Absolutely.' Sheldon searched Polly's dungarees for the ample breasts he knew to be in there. 'Terrific.'

'And David,' Melissa went on.

Polly looked at David. His expression was so bland it was almost telling. He wouldn't come to her dinner party, that was for sure.

'Well, it's been such fun running into you.' Polly pushed her trolley determinedly forward as if she intended to make her words literal, and Melissa stepped out of the way. 'I need to get some of this cat food.'

'Cat food.' Melissa's friendly expression hardened. 'That reminds me, it really was incredibly irresponsible . . .'

'I must get on,' said Polly. 'I'll be in touch, Melissa.' With your shins, she thought resentfully, and started to load her trolley with Selina's culinary cravings.

She was wondering if she could face another aisle to get some *fromage frais* when Sheldon tapped her on the shoulder. 'The cat was all right, you know. She had an injection the next day.'

Polly warmed to him. 'How kind of you to tell me.'

He hastened towards the others and then Polly looked up and saw Mac. He had obviously witnessed the whole encounter and found it highly amusing.

Polly pulled out her woolly hat and threw it at him.

When Polly finally extricated herself from the jaws of commerce and the supermarket car park, she set off for Bridget's house. With luck Alan would be there, and he would give her a gin and tonic to give her strength for the meeting. Alan had a way with a G and T that was quite his own. It didn't matter how hard Bridget or Polly tried, they could never get that magical balance of gin, lemon and ice which exalted the tonic to the heights of ambrosia. She needed a treat after what she'd been

146

through, and she could ask Bridget and Alan for dinner at the same time.

Usually Polly was happy for procrastination to steal as much time as he liked, but as she stood in the queue at the checkout she had decided to arrange Melissa's dinner party for the following Saturday.

Such rapid action had several advantages: *a*) it was highly unlikely that Melissa and Sheldon would be able to come, in which case she could invite another couple and have a jolly time with Bridget and Alan; and *b*) in the unlikely event that Melissa and Sheldon were free, the house would still be fairly tidy should her mother descend for her biannual visit which was due soon.

But she did need to make sure Bridget and Alan could come before she got in too deep.

'. . . So you see, I would be really grateful if you could come,' she finished, sinking into their down-filled sofa.

'We're not doing anything next weekend, are we?' Alan handed Polly her drink. 'Polly's dinner parties are always fun.'

Bridget took her drink, but didn't speak.

'Oh, come on, Bridge! I need you. For moral support!'

'Your morals certainly need a bit of propping up,' Bridget conceded. 'They're wobbling way off-centre.'

'Poppet?' Alan looked confused.

'Bridget's referring to my toyboy,' said Polly. 'She's worried I'm going to make a fool of myself over a man ten years my junior.'

'And are you?'

'Of course not. I hardly know him. And I'm not going to invite him to this dinner party, Bridget. I'm inviting

David Locking-Hill. As instructed. You can't pass up an opportunity to get a look at him, surely?'

Polly didn't mention her doubts about whether David would come, relying on Bridget's curiosity to see the man her children described as being the last bastion of the stiff upper lip to make her get her off her high and disapproving horse.

It didn't let her down. Bridget sighed deeply. 'Of course we'll come, and I'm not being funny about your toyboy, I just worry about you.'

Polly sighed also, exasperated. 'I don't know, you try and pair me off with every anorak-wearing introvert you encounter, but when I find a man for myself you worry.'

'Because you're so naïve,' said Bridget. 'I'm frightened you'll be taken advantage of.'

'I'm thirty-five and an independent woman,' said Polly, on a sticky wicket.

'Thirty-five, independent and naïve,' agreed Alan.

Polly drained her glass. There seemed no defence she could offer. 'I must fly. I've got a meeting to get to. So you'll come tomorrow week, at about eight?'

'Hadn't you better check Melissa can come first?' said Bridget. 'You don't want the fag of a dinner party without the advantage of being able to cross someone off your list of people you owe hospitality to.'

Polly considered denying having a list, then she abandoned her dignity. 'No, come anyway. I need to tidy the house for my ma.'

It was a pity she couldn't ask Tristan as David's stand-in, she thought. It would be so wonderfully insulting to flaunt a toyboy under Melissa's disapproving nose. She might get crossed off her list for ever. Bridget's disapproval was more serious.

When Polly unearthed Melissa's number the following morning, she had her message ready. Other people's answering machines saved her a fortune in phone bills, and Melissa's saved her having to talk to her torturer direct. And if Melissa and Sheldon couldn't make next Saturday, Polly could reasonably leave it for weeks, even months, before inviting them again.

Melissa rang back that afternoon when Polly was in the bath, and hung on persistently until Polly got to the phone.

'Polly, I got your message. Saturday would be lovely. Now, have you invited David, or do you want me to? I'm seeing him tomorrow.'

It was a tempting offer. Polly hated ringing people she didn't know, and the very thought of phoning the Locking-Hill establishment made her shiver.

'That would be very kind.'

She replaced the receiver feeling momentarily ashamed, but then decided if Melissa was going to inflict this dinner party on her the least she could do was invite the guests. Besides, she was busy. She had promised to design some leaflets for Mac to rally support for the occupation of the buildings, and had not been able to do them in time for the meeting the evening before.

She drew a rough sketch of the buildings and then started on the lettering.

WILL YOU SEE YOUR TOWN DEMOLISHED?

She hoped not.

Chapter Eleven

'I've brought the ice cream.'

Mark stood on Polly's doorstep wearing Pavarotti-sized jeans and several T-shirts. It was early on Saturday morning, and very cold. Polly was in her dressing gown but with a woollen scarf round her neck and fur-lined boots on her feet. She pulled Mark in quickly, so as not to let her heat escape.

'Thanks. Which kind did you bring?'

Polly had taken advantage of the post-Christmas cream glut which afflicts all supermarkets. She had bought several pints of it at half price, turned it into ice cream and stored it in Bridget's freezer. At times like these her inability to pass up a bargain paid off.

'Chocolate and caramel.' Mark followed Polly into the kitchen. 'Mum said one lot wouldn't be enough.' He put his newspaper-wrapped packages on the table. 'And I've come to help.'

'I can't afford help.' Polly knew Mark too well to credit him with any motive other than the purely mercenary.

'S'all right, won't cost you a thing.'

Polly slid the kettle on to the hotplate. Her grumpiness, like her dressing gown, enveloped her from neck to ankle.

She had been up for over an hour and was bitter about

missing her lie-in. Usually she loved entertaining. Usually she invited people she really liked. This time she resented the time it took to get ready and, after going to the protest meeting, guilty for consorting with people who, if not quite the enemy, could be accused of fraternization.

Yesterday had been her day for the Shed. She could have spent the morning wedging and preparing her clay, and thrown a respectable amount in the afternoon. But no, she had felt obliged to spend the whole day in the kitchen, cooking and cleaning for people who had been to school with and who entertained socially despoilers of the environment.

It was her mother's fault, she decided. You can shrug off only so much of your upbringing. The aproned housewife with a suburban desire to conform to other people's standards will eventually shame the rebellious slut into dusting the tops of doors and cleaning inside the sink overflows.

'It'll cost somebody something,' she said.

'Mum. I owe her loads.'

'It's kind of Bridget, but I can manage. I cleaned yesterday.'

'Mum said you'd say no.' Mark started juggling with an egg, an apple and a salt cellar. 'But she said I must make you accept. Or I'd have to slave for her for weeks.' He took a bite out of the apple as it passed in front of him. 'I'd much rather work for you. You don't go on about homework all the time.' He grinned.

Polly found herself grinning back. Bridget and Alan's household had a complicated credit system, devised by Mark, whereby favours could be demanded in return for 'favour pounds'. These had to be paid back, in labour.

Mark had once spent a long time explaining to Polly how it worked. Now she decided to accept what he said lest he explain again.

'Okay, then. I won't look a gift horse in the mouth. And, yes, you may have an apple.'

'Got these rich people coming round, then?' He took another bite.

It was one way of defining them. 'Yes.'

'What are you giving them to eat?' Mark, taking after his mother, was interested in food.

'Vegetarian food.'

He made a face. 'Are they vegetarian?'

'No, so what?'

Mark took another egg to replace the apple core. 'So, what ya having?'

'Cheese soufflé for one thing, so don't you dare drop my eggs.'

'Drop them?' Mark, affronted, took another two. 'Look, I can do five.'

Polly closed her eyes for a second, then confiscated the eggs.

'What else are you eating?'

'An aubergine thing. Risotto, salad.'

'Pud?'

'Homemade ice cream and oranges in caramel.'

'Ooh. Posh, eh?'

'I hope so. It took me hours to peel the oranges, not to mention slicing them and turning them back into oranges with cocktail sticks.'

'Sounds all right.'

'I've-given up caring. Now, are you here to help or to juggle the ingredients?'

*

At lunchtime, Mark went out for fish and chips but Polly was too strung up to eat. While Mark ate, telling her hair-raising stories about the goings-on in a modern comprehensive school, Polly concentrated on setting the table.

She dug out her favourite tablecloth, two remnants of curtain material sewn together, which gave the table a rich, medieval feel. Then she started hunting for matching silver. There was nothing so certain to harass a hostess than trying to find a clean pudding fork at the last minute. And none of Polly's forks was clean. When at last she found it, she dumped all the cutlery into a bowl with soda crystals and tin-foil to remove the tarnish. Mark could polish it for her after lunch, while she revved the Rayburn to its hottest. Usually she loved cooking with solid fuel. Today she would have killed for a cooker you could just turn on.

Once the table was set with silver, glass and table napkins (bought at a car boot sale, excellent value), Polly turned her attention to the sitting part of the evening.

But no matter how she arranged and rearranged the two sofas and two chairs, she herself would have to perch on the arm of one of them. But as long as Melissa got to sit by the fire, and no one got pierced by a sofa spring, Polly didn't care. She draped and safety-pinned the collection of bedspreads which served as sofa covers and turned her cushions cleanest side out.

At six, Mark went home and Polly retired to the bath with a glass of wine. At ten past six she dripped downstairs in a towel and had another. At seven she awoke with a start, suddenly aware that while she had agonized over every other detail of the dinner party, she hadn't decided what to wear.

'I've got my priorities all wrong! Most women would think about their clothes before anything else.' She padded into her bedroom and opened her wardrobe door.

Absolutely nothing seemed suitable. It was all either too hippy, too avant-garde or in need of cleaning. Her black dress would have done, if she hadn't worn it at Melissa's and at the promise auction.

In desperation she started pulling things out, holding them against herself and flinging them on the bed. Memories of Melissa at school constantly straightening Polly's collar, tugging her skirt about and ordering her to tie back her hair were horribly fresh. And she couldn't guarantee Melissa wouldn't still do it.

Eventually she found a garment which consisted of a blouse and a pair of knickers joined together. She had bought it because it was only three pounds and the blouse part looked nice. It was hell to get on, made going to the loo a major undertaking and the neckline was rather more revealing than it might be, but by some miracle of modern science it didn't need ironing. She hunted for something to go with it.

From under several other layers of clothes, she retrieved a mid-calf-length bottle-green velvet skirt which she had bought at a jumble sale. Even at the time it had seemed unlikely she would ever wear it, but she couldn't let so much good velvet go to the rubbish tip.

She clambered into both and then returned to the bathroom where she layered on jewellery and make-up with her usual lavish hand. The effect was very sixties deb, but provided she stood up straight there was something tidy about her ensemble which should keep Melissa's twitching fingers at bay.

It was while applying her second coat of mascara that

she realized she was swaying a little. She wasn't usually so susceptible. It was probably a combination of too hot a bath, too little lunch and nerves. But whatever the reason, there was nothing she could do about it.

'You'll just have to concentrate very hard, and hope it wears off,' she said out loud. Then she poured a dollop of Chanel No 19, which had been a present from her mother, down her cleavage and returned to her bedroom to look for clean tights and her tidy shoes.

Polly was brushing her teeth when, dead on eight, the door bell rang. She had been counting on injury time – those golden moments between the hour of the invitation and when the guests actually arrive – when mountains can be moved. She wiped her mouth on a towel and went down to answer it.

It was Bridget and Alan.

'Thank God it's you.' Polly licked toothpaste from the corner of her mouth. 'I was just thinking how rude it was of Melissa to arrive so punctually.'

'You asked us to come right on eight, so we'd be first,' Bridget pointed out. 'And you're not wearing any lipstick.'

'Hell, I must have left it all over the towel.' Polly patted her hair and pulled at her skirt. 'Do I look okay otherwise?'

'I doubt if anyone else can look so good on so little money,' said Bridget serenely, taking off her coat and revealing an elegant little number in biscuit-coloured silk jersey. 'And if they did, I'd hate them. Shall I take this upstairs?'

'Please.'

Alan kissed her. 'You're not looking your usual

155

cheerful self.' He handed her two bottles. 'Perhaps these will cheer you up. It's Fitou.'

'If they fit you, I'm sure they'll fit me,' said Polly grimly. 'Come into the kitchen and we'll stick these on the Rayburn to warm up.'

Alan, knowing full well that Polly was quite capable of putting wine in a microwave, thanked heaven she hadn't got one. 'Did you say one of your guests is a wine merchant?'

She scraped at the foil on the bottle with a corkscrew. 'Uhuh.'

'Then please don't talk about warming the wine up.'

Polly made a face. 'Not if it upsets you, Alan. But "*chambrer*ing" it sounds so affected, don't you think? Especially when it's "kitchened".' Alan's pained expression made her take pity on him. 'Don't worry, I'm on my best behaviour tonight. I'm not going to drink a thing except fizzy water.'

'That's going a bit far, isn't it? You can usually put away a fair bit before you dance on the tables and tell blue jokes.'

'I never dance on the table, Alan, but I had a couple of glasses while I was in the bath and can't take any chances. Mark was brilliant, by the way.'

'Good,' said Bridget, coming into the room. 'I'm glad he's useful for something other than light entertainment and colourful backchat. I hung your clothes in the wardrobe, Poll. I hope you don't mind, but Melissa's got to put her coat somewhere.'

The contrast between Melissa's elegant boudoir and her less than elegant bedroom made Polly shudder. 'Absolutely, and besides,' she added more cheerfully, 'Selina's got to have something to sleep on.'

'That cat,' said Alan, who was a dog man, 'is as much a liability as Bridget's.'

'I know.' Polly put homemade croûtons into home-made dishes. 'But she's the mark of a spinster. You can't be single and female and not keep a cat.'

'A cat, yes,' Alan went on. 'But does it have to be incontinent?'

'Oh, God! She hasn't made a mess, has she?'

Alan made a face. 'I'm sure it's only a matter of time, but no, not yet.'

'Then don't make me nervous.'

Polly refused to allow anyone to be squeamish about the less appealing aspects of Selina's declining years. But if there was anything unsavoury about it was sod's law it was Melissa's Bally shoe it would end up on.

'Take no notice of him, Polly.' Bridget scowled at her husband. 'And put some lipstick on. You were right about the towel. I turned it over.'

As the minutes past eight ticked away, Polly got more and more nervous.

'The house looks very cosy, really homelike,' said Alan.

Polly inhaled sharply. 'It is not homelike! It is pristine, asceptic, positively minimalist! Mark and I have spent most of the day eradicating all trace of human habitation.'

'Sorry,' said Alan meekly. 'I just meant it looked nice – and tidy. People always feel at ease in your house, Polly.'

'It does look beautiful,' agreed Bridget. 'Not actually minimalist, but very uncluttered – for you.'

Polly fiddled with the tiny vase of snowdrops which nestled among the candlesticks, jugs and odd bits of family silver on the mantelpiece. 'I'm sorry to snap. But

157

it's always the same. I kill myself cleaning, I sweep every hint of my personality into black plastic sacks and people say it looks homelike. I want it to look like a museum!'

'You don't really.' Bridget helped herself to a handful of croûtons. 'You like your house the way it is, otherwise you'd live differently. Face up to the fact and relax.'

Polly couldn't. Usually, when her guests actually arrived, her tension snapped and she thoroughly enjoyed herself. But she knew this time her tension wouldn't have a chance of snapping until the Melissa entourage had gone.

'You will keep Melissa out of the kitchen, won't you?' said Polly for the umpteenth time.

'I've said I'll do my best,' said Bridget. 'But I can't promise. Your kitchen has a siren quality about it. It lures people in.'

Polly sighed. 'And that's normal people. I don't suppose I'll keep Melissa out of the roof space.'

At that moment they heard the sound of voices cursing the honeysuckle.

'Ah!' Alan raised a dramatic hand. 'They've reached the Catcher in the Eye. Battle is about to commence.'

'Oh, shut up, Alan,' said Polly and Bridget in unison. Then there was a knock on the door.

Polly opened it. Her welcoming smile was a death-mask impression of her usual cheery grin.

'Hello, Melissa, David, How lovely to see you. So you came in one car. Did you find it all right? Do come in, Sheldon.'

Sheldon, at the front of the group, seemed reluctant to cross the threshold and thus blocked the way for the other two. None of them was small and when they were all crammed in together it made Polly's doorway tinier than ever. Eventually they got themselves inside.

'Let me take your coats, everyone.'

She smiled vaguely as the men draped massive overcoats over her waiting arms. To her relief they also produced bottles of wine, which they gave to Alan who had appeared to receive them. Bringing wine to dinner parties was certainly not done in the best circles, but Polly's circle couldn't afford to be particular.

Her knees buckling slightly under the weight of winter menswear, she held out her hand for Melissa's coat.

Melissa shivered in her Persian lamb as if she would prefer to keep it on.

'Actually Polly, if you don't mind, I'll come up and powder my nose,' she said. 'It'll save you carrying it.'

'Of course,' said Polly. 'Alan, Bridget, do introduce yourselves. And Alan, be a dear and organize drinks and put another log on the fire.' The fire was already roaring up the chimney, but Polly hated to think of people being cold in her house. Her mother always felt cold, no matter how much she revved the Rayburn and stoked the fire. And that was in August.

Polly led the way up her twisty staircase, hardly able to see over her armful of coats. She had known Melissa would want to come upstairs and hoped she wouldn't keep her talking too long.

'Darling!' Melissa sounded genuinely horrified. 'My walk-in wardrobe's bigger than your bedroom! You haven't even got a dressing table!'

'It's in the bathroom.'

Melissa didn't hear. 'And where do you keep your clothes?'

Polly indicated her small but adequate cupboard, and prayed Melissa wouldn't open the door.

'It's like when we were at school!' Melissa went on, horrified.

Yes, thought Polly, but at school, we had to keep our wardrobes tidy. Here I can pack in as much as I like. She watched Melissa take out a lipstick from her clutch purse.

'Actually, Melissa, the bathroom is better for putting on make-up.'

'Oh, don't worry about me, Polly dear. I'll be fine. I'm sure you've got things to do.'

Polly left Melissa grimacing in front of a very spotty mirror with no light. If she had let her, Polly would have shown her to the bathroom, which was large, well lit and warm.

But at least her shock at the appalling conditions in which Polly kept her clothes distracted her from other aspects of Polly's bedroom which might give rise to comment. Like the fact that the bed was supported by bricks, and there may well have been an apple core or two among the pagoda of bedtime reading which teetered on her bedside table.

The men leapt to their feet as Polly appeared.

'Please don't get up. Have you all got drinks?'

As one, they indicated their full wine glasses.

'What about you, Polly?' said David. 'Where's your drink?'

The wine Polly had drunk that evening was still rushing round her head. Until she had a chance to eat, she'd better not have any more. 'I'm fine, thank you. Ah, here's Melissa.'

Melissa picked her way down the stairs and came into the sitting room.

'Melissa! Come and join us round the fire.' She ushered Melissa firmly to where Bridget and Alan, obedient to their briefing, had saved a place for her. 'Now let me get you a drink.'

'Darling,' said Melissa, when she had sunk into the sofa and accepted a glass of wine, 'this cottage is delightful! But so tiny! How on earth do you manage?'

'Well, there's only me in it, most of the time.' Polly perched on the arm of the sofa.

'Even so . . .'

'Have a croûton,' broke in Polly quickly, lest Melissa had discovered that Polly shared her bedroom with a small colony of woodlice and was about to announce the fact. 'How's your glass, Sheldon?'

'Have you come from far?' Bridget asked Melissa.

'Stony Vale.' Melissa named the deeply rural area known to some as Millionaire's Hollow. 'Not bad, really.'

'And is it difficult to get baby-sitters so far into the country?'

'No,' said Melissa. 'We have a nanny.'

Bridget, who had once said she'd no more get a nanny for her children than a mistress for her husband, said, 'Jolly convenient.'

It was going even more badly than she'd feared. Polly yearned to retreat into the kitchen to clear up a bit and get her soufflés into the oven, but etiquette required she exchanged at least three gobbets of conversation first.

'Were my directions all right?'

'Frankly, they were hopeless,' said Melissa. 'If it hadn't been for David's expert navigation, we would never have got here. You never were much good at "joggo", were you?'

'Which way did you come?' asked Alan, who hadn't heard this abbreviation of 'geography' before but had written the directions for Polly.

'You'll have to ask David. I got totally confused after the first wrong turn.'

Polly decided not to wait to see if Alan confessed authorship, or how David rescued them from darkest Gloucestershire, and fled.

David came in to the kitchen just as Polly was holding her bowl of egg whites upside down to see if they were stiff enough. Fortunately, they were.

'Oh, hello.' She replaced the bowl and spooned a dollop of cheese and egg mixture into it. 'Can I get you anything?'

'I came to see if you needed any help.'

'Oh, no! I've got it all under control, thanks.' Aware that she had sounded over-horrified she gave him a shaky smile as she made figure of eights in her egg white. This usually simple task suddenly became fraught with difficulty.

But instead of taking the hint and leaving her to it, David crossed the room in two strides and, like everyone else who ever entered her kitchen, leant against the Rayburn.

The room had rarely, if ever, been so tidy. Yet suddenly every flaw leapt to her attention. Thanks to Mark, her drying underwear was no longer hanging loopily from the *batterie de cuisine*, but she wished she hadn't declared so sniffily that a dresser was for use not for ornament and had removed the less decorative items.

The dresser was directly opposite him, and it was

unlikely that the nit comb, bunches of keys, onions, lemons, etc. would escape his attention.

'This is a lovely room.'

Polly dropped the spoon in her surprise. 'Oh, do you like it?'

'Why, don't you?'

'Well, of course. But I'd hardly expect you to.' She had him down as a steel and white Formica man.

'Why not?'

Polly shrugged. 'It's so – unstructured.' It wasn't quite what she meant, but it was the best she could do in the circumstances.

'What are you making?'

'Cheese soufflés.'

'Aren't they terribly difficult?'

Not usually, no, but with you watching me like a hawk, yes, terribly. 'Not at all,' she said, mendacious but polite. 'It's a popular myth.' She scraped the last of the mixture out of the saucepan, wondering how she could make him go away without seeming rude. 'You seem to make a habit of sitting about in kitchens watching me do things,' she said.

'Do you mind?'

'Oh, no,' she lied. 'It's just that it's not what I'm best at.'

He raised a speaking, but totally silent, eyebrow.

'Cooking, I mean.' She burbled on: 'I'm a far better potter.' Did many people boast out of sheer embarrassment? 'Not to say that I'm much good at that.' Oh, shut up, Polly.

'Did you make these?' He indicated the ramekin dishes she had struggled so hard to make alike.

163

'Yes. And the plates. In fact, I made almost everything except the glasses.'

'Talking of which, can I fill yours?'

Heaven forbid. 'Oh no, only Perrier for me, thank you. But let me do yours.'

She reached for one of the bottles on the back of the Rayburn and remembered he was a wine merchant.

'You probably disapprove terribly of me heating up the wine – putting wine there to *chambrer*, but . . .' She shut her mouth and poured the wine before she could talk herself into more trouble.

Before I met David, she decided, doling out portions of soufflé mixture with gritted teeth, I never really knew what 'taciturn' meant. Now I have it personified, in my kitchen, while I am trying to give a dinner party.

At last she got the dollops of mixture roughly equal, without slopping too much over the edges.

'Excuse me, please. I need the oven.'

He moved about two inches, and she stepped around his feet to open the oven door. With luck, if she tripped over him often enough, he would take the hint and leave her alone. He didn't.

But surely, if she left the room herself he would feel obliged to follow.

'Come on. Now those are in, let's go and join the party.'

Chapter Twelve

'Party' was something of a misnomer. Bridget was accepting Melissa's well-meaning advice on how to deal with difficult teenagers with every appearance of gratitude, although she must have known by then that Melissa's own children were four and six. And Alan was talking to Sheldon as if they really did have something in common. But the atmosphere didn't exactly crackle.

Which left Polly, desperate to get back to her cooking, to make small talk with David.

'Are you going on holiday this year?' Polly had read somewhere that that was the classic opening conversational gambit for hairdressers.

It worked only up to a point. 'I'll probably go to France a couple of times, but not on holiday.'

'On business then?'

David nodded.

This really required some intelligent questions about the wine trade. Polly, woefully light on these, and in agonies about her rice which she was sure was burning, took a wild stab. 'To visit vineyards?'

David shook his head. 'Probably not. I like to visit my *négociant* at least once a year, and see if he's got anything new to show me. But I don't often get time to visit individual vineyards.'

'Oh? I thought wine merchants spent weeks lurching drunkenly from one vineyard to another.'

'Not solvent ones.'

She sensed a certain antipathy towards drunken wine merchants and suspected it would extend to drunken potters.

She ate a garlic-flavoured croûton to clear her slightly muzzy head. 'So no holidays at all?'

'Maybe. I do have a small property in France, and there are sometimes things I need to see to.'

She could bear it no longer. 'I've got things to see to, too. In the kitchen. Please excuse me.'

The rice, in the warming oven, had developed an extra crispy crust, not present in cookery-book risotto, which was quickly stirred in with a fork. But the soufflés were perfect. Little brown hillocks of foam billowed satisfactorily above the rims of her ramekin dishes. She slid each dish on to a plate and loaded plates on to a tray. She was poking her aubergine dish with her finger to see if it was hot enough when David appeared. She wiped her finger surreptitiously on her skirt and handed him the tray.

'Tell them it's ready, would you?' She put the aubergines into the top oven, praying that by the time she came to take them out they would be hot but not burnt, and picked up the two remaining soufflés.

Polly hadn't gone so far as to write place cards, but she had followed her mother's advice and worked out where everyone was to sit.

Her seating plan put her next to Sheldon, who was bound to peer down her cleavage at every opportunity, but at least she was spared David, who wouldn't peer but might not talk either.

'Goody, cheese soufflé, my favourite,' said Alan from

the head of the table, when everyone had shuffled about and stepped on each other's feet getting to their places. 'How's your glass, Melissa?'

'I always thought soufflé sank if you didn't eat it immediately,' said Melissa, obviously put out that in spite of the shuffling it hadn't.

'Not little ones,' said Bridget, who'd taught Polly how to do them. 'They're usually very well behaved.'

'Polly?' Alan poised the bottle over her glass.

She shook her head. 'I'll fetch the water.'

'This is *delicious*,' said David, sounding faintly surprised.

Polly smiled somewhat sourly. No thanks to him if her soufflés were like biscuits.

'Very nice,' said Melissa. In spite of Alan's constant attention to her glass, she showed no signs of relaxing. She shot a quick glance at David, strong but silent at her side. 'I never cook for company. I think being a hostess is a job in itself.'

'But Polly seems to manage to do both,' said Bridget, who for some reason was not being her usual accommodating self and was obviously annoyed on Polly's behalf.

Alan took a quick, surprised glance at his wife. 'Without even a husband to help,' he said, covering up.

'I don't need a husband,' said Polly. 'I can borrow Bridget's.'

Melissa gave her a sharp look as if to warn Polly against borrowing Sheldon. If Melissa only knew, Polly wouldn't have him gift-wrapped.

'It's a pity you don't cook for company, Melissa,' said David. 'You do it so well.'

Melissa coloured slightly, and it dawned on Polly that Melissa really wanted David for herself. This was probably why she was constantly introducing him to women he was unlikely to respond to, like Polly. Thus he would realize how well Melissa was suited to him, and regret that she was unobtainable.

'You do, Melly, really,' said Sheldon, and received a sharp look of his own for his pains. Obviously she was 'Melly' only in private.

Polly glanced sympathetically at Sheldon and realized she shouldn't have. He smiled back and squeezed her knee.

'Do you cook?' Polly asked Alan, knowing perfectly well that he did.

He responded valiantly. 'Yes, but only bread-and-butter cooking. Bridget's the professional.'

'Oh?' Melissa turned to Bridget. 'Do you cook for dinner parties, buffets, things like that?'

'I cook at the Whole Nut café, with Polly,' said Bridget firmly, lest Melissa mentioned directors' lunches.

'I see.' Melissa had come to terms with Polly's menial occupation, but was surprised that someone as apparently competent as Bridget shared it.

Anxious about the next course, Polly started to gather plates. 'If you'd hang on to your forks, please.'

'How continental,' said Melissa. 'Such fun.'

'Yes, isn't it?' said Polly, knowing that Melissa wouldn't give a sandwich to the gardener without two sets of cutlery. 'If you'd be a dear and take the tray, Sheldon.'

Sheldon leaped to his feet and managed to get his hand on her waist as he manoeuvred past her in the kitchen. As she put down her plates, he encircled her from behind and breathed down the front of her blouse. She shook him off. 'Please, Sheldon, I must get something out of the oven. Do go and sit down, I can manage now.'

She peered in the oven, sure she could feel Sheldon's eyes on her bottom. As she feared, the oven had been too hot. The top was burnt, and cheese sauce had bubbled like a hot spring all over the bottom of the oven. She'd be lucky to get it out without third-degree burns.

She grabbed a towel and managed to get the dish on to the kitchen table without dropping it. Then she looked up and saw Sheldon staring lustfully at her breasts.

Teeth clenched, she fought the temptation to cover him in scalding sauce. 'Please stop staring at me like that.'

'Sorry, Polly, but you have got magnificent . . .'

'I also have a large quantity of very hot dinner in my hands. Unless you want it in your lap, go back to the table.'

Chastened, like an unruly but well-meaning puppy, he slunk out of the room.

Polly took off the burnt sauce with a spoon and scattered the dish with chopped parsley. She put more parsley on the risotto and turned her attention to the salad.

She'd chosen to do a watercress, celery and orange salad because it always sold so well in the café. She had the ingredients prepared, and only had to assemble them and add dressing. She was mixing it all with her hands when she realized that she was giving her guests oranges for pudding. It was the sort of mistake Melissa would never make, but she wasn't going to pick out the bits of orange at this stage. It would have to do.

Typically, when she could have done with a bit of help to carry in the dishes, her guests remained seated firmly at the table. Perhaps they'd overheard what she'd said to

Sheldon and didn't dare go into her kitchen. At last she was organized and went back to face them.

She hadn't been out of the room long, but it was too long for the fragile condition of her dinner party.

'I think it's selfish of people to stop progress just for the sake of it,' Melissa was saying. 'I mean, think how many jobs will be involved in having those shops replaced with new ones.'

Bridget was pleating her napkin as if her life depended on it. 'So you feel they should be bulldozed?'

'Absolutely. They're a complete and utter eyesore. They're what's keeping Laureton the tatty little town it is. I never go near the place if I can help it.'

Bridget's tact, already strained to breaking point, snapped. 'But you couldn't help accepting Polly's invitation to dinner in Laureton?'

When she realized what she'd said, Melissa was horrified. 'Of course – I didn't mean –'

'Don't be silly, Mel.' Polly shifted the candles to make room for her dish, wishing Bridget would simply ignore Melissa's unfortunate remarks. 'We all know what you meant. But I must disagree. Restoring those shops would create just as many jobs as tearing them down and rebuilding.'

'But you don't agree with those ghastly protesters, surely? They *look* so frightful. David, you agree with me, don't you?'

Polly couldn't bear to hear David condemn the buildings and couldn't trust him not to. She copped out. 'Sorry, Melissa, I must get the salad and the rice.'

The subject had changed when Polly finally forced herself to come back, but the conversation was just as sticky. Bridget, no longer snappy, was getting heated.

'You really think it's sensible to decide children's careers for them while they're still at *primary school*?'

Melissa looked confused. 'Oh, no, *prep* school.'

Any minute Melissa would tell Bridget that both her children were going to boarding school when they were seven, and soft-hearted Bridget would say something Polly would regret.

'Hand me those plates, Sheldon,' said Polly briskly. 'I'll serve up. Melissa, help yourself to salad. David, have the rice before it disappears to the other end of the table. Alan!' She shot him a desperate look. 'Give everyone another glass of wine.'

At last everyone was served. Sheldon forked through his aubergine as if looking for something. He caught Melissa's eye and eventually said, 'What kind of meat is this, Polly? Not goat, is it?'

Polly sighed. 'It isn't meat, it's vegetable.'

'Oh.' Sheldon slumped, disappointed, in his chair.

'Are you and Bridget vegetarian?' Melissa asked Alan.

'Oh, no,' said Alan blithely. 'Are we, chicken?'

The 'chicken' in question gave him a look, which, while it would not have actually killed, would have left a very nasty bruise.

'So,' went on Melissa, 'why are we eating "veggie" tonight?' The inverted commas were audible.

'I'm on a diet,' said Polly, relying on Melissa knowing as much about calories as she did about style. The truth – that Polly couldn't afford to entertain if she gave people meat – would embarrass everyone.

'So everyone else has to be too?' Sheldon sounded more hurt than annoyed.

Polly removed a tiny stone which had somehow found its way into the rice. 'It's good for you, Sheldon.'

'How are your boys, David?' asked Melissa, having inspected a forkful of watercress salad for an unnervingly long time. 'I think you handle them marvellously. Young people nowadays are so *ungrateful*.'

'Haven't they always been ungrateful?' suggested Polly mildly, relieved that Melissa hadn't found a snail in her watercress.

'Not at all. I was always aware how hard Mummy worked to make my season a success.'

'You mean your *social* season?' Alan was impressed. 'Queen Charlotte's Ball? I don't think I've ever met anyone who "came out", before.'

'What about that pair of antique dealers?' said Polly. 'I thought they were quite good friends of yours. They must have been to any amount of queens' balls.'

Sheldon giggled. Melissa ignored this deviation from polite conversation and reverted to her topic. 'And they dress so appallingly. That's one of the reasons I think it's important to pack them off to a good school as soon as possible. I know David agrees with me.' Melissa leaned forward confidentially. 'I remember Angela telling me, years and years ago, that David put his boys' names down for his old school the minute they were born.'

Poor Melissa. It seemed she couldn't open her mouth without making someone acutely uncomfortable. Surely if she knew that David's old school, whichever it was, hadn't done the trick for one of his boys she wouldn't have mentioned it.

'I think the whole public-school system is antiquated and downright cruel,' said Bridget. 'I think you send your children to the local comprehensive and have done with it.'

Polly bit back a sigh of frustration. Bridget was

172

obviously so hellbent on debunking Melissa that she had started to deviate from the truth. Certainly she sent her children to the local school, but one of the reasons she and Alan had moved into the area was the excellence of the schools. She was also a governor, and spent a lot of time keeping the school up to scratch. Her 'having done with it' took a great deal of effort and dedication.

'And as for school uniform,' Bridget went on, developing her theme, 'they don't have them on the continent, you know.'

Melissa didn't know, or care. 'Of course,' she said kindly, 'if you can't afford to –'

'It's not a matter of affording,' said Bridget icily.

'Yes it is,' said Alan. 'We couldn't possibly afford to educate our children privately.' He tried to change the subject over Bridget's protest that no money on earth would induce her –

'David agrees with me,' said Melissa. 'The right school is all-important.'

'Actually,' said David, sounding tired, 'Patrick's just dropped out of school.'

There was a stunned silence. Melissa broke it.

'Oh, David, I'm so sorry.' She put her hand on his and squeezed it.

'His son hasn't died, Melissa,' snapped Bridget. 'He's only left school! Good for him!'

However much she agreed with her opinions, Polly wanted to hit her friend who, without being bland, was usually guaranteed not to ruffle any feathers. And here she was, ruffling for all she was worth.

'It's *so* ungrateful.' Melissa shook her head sadly.

'Not really,' said Polly. 'If David's son had his name put down for a school at birth, you can't call him ungrateful if he didn't like it. He didn't have any choice in the matter.'

'Polly dear . . .'

'I think young people nowadays are much more aware than we were about the environment, social issues . . .' Polly ignored Melissa and said her piece for the younger generation. 'And Mark,' she finished, 'Alan and Bridget's son, worked for me today and I didn't pay him a penny.' It was the literal truth, after all.

'I don't suppose that was any great hardship,' said David. 'How old is Mark? Fourteen? Fifteen? A very susceptible age.'

'Susceptible to what?' snapped Mark's mother. 'Chicken pox?'

'To the charms of a very attractive older woman. I think perhaps Polly has a gift with the younger generation.' The thought appeared to give David little satisfaction.

'It isn't quite . . . Mark doesn't –' Polly shut her mouth, hoping someone would finish her sentence for her. She was flattered by David's description of her, but disgusted by his implication and furious that her attempts to stick up for Patrick, albeit obliquely, should have earned such an ambiguous reply. Yet she didn't feel capable of explaining why Mark was willing to work for her without admitting that he was as mercenary as the next young person.

The entire company waited for her to continue.

'I – I meet a lot of young people, and I think they're great,' she finished lamely.

'I dare say you do.' David eyed her coldly, as if liking young people was a socially unacceptable habit.

'There's plenty to be said for the older chap, Polly,'

said Sheldon, batting for David. 'Experience counts for a lot in one particular department. Send a boy to do a man's job and you'll end up with a very disappointed lady.'

Polly surveyed him through narrowed lids. 'You mean, "There may be snow on the roof but there's a fire in the cellar"?'

Sheldon thought about it. 'Exactly. Trouble is,' he chortled happily, 'my roof needs re-thatching!'

Polly and Bridget exchanged glances. 'Never mind, Sheldon,' said Bridget, who, to Polly's relief, had climbed down from her high horse about education. 'Baldness is supposed to be a sign of virility.'

Polly caught sight of David's very thick head of hair, and wished she could get so drunk that she wouldn't be able to remember this terrible evening. The appalling hangover might be worth it. Unfortunately, her upbringing was too strong for her.

Desperate, she changed the subject. 'Do you like gardening, Melissa?'

Before Melissa could reply, there was a knock on the door. Polly fought her way past everyone to get to it, and flung it wide.

Tristan Black stood on the doorstep. His black leather jacket had taken on the hue of shining armour. His devilish smile had an angelic quality. 'Can I come in?'

By that time Polly would have welcomed a tribe of Jehovah's Witnesses riding pillion behind the US Cavalry. Tristan could have been a long-lost friend, missing presumed dead, by the way she flung her arms round his neck.

'Do. I'm just about to serve pudding. Everyone – this is Tristan Black. He works for Cotswold Radio.' Polly saw

Tristan take in the situation at a practised glance. 'Introduce yourselves, everyone. I'll get Tristan a glass.'

She left the room as Tristan was shaking each person by the hand. When she returned she found him seated at the table. He had heaped Melissa's side plate with salad, what was left of the rice and a piece of bread.

'Hope you don't mind, Polly. I haven't eaten.' His grin was still dazzling, even with his mouth full.

'So, what do you do?' Tristan looked into Melissa's eyes while he took her knife to spread butter on his bread. 'Something fascinating, I bet.'

Melissa laughed coltishly. 'I don't work outside the home. I suppose some would say I was just a housewife.'

Tristan shook his head. 'Not "just" a housewife, Melissa. Running a home and family is a very creative thing to do, as I'm sure Sheldon would agree.'

Sheldon nodded. He had to live with Melissa.

'And Bridget.' He turned his brilliant blue eyes in her direction. 'I know you. You produce that wonderful food in the Whole Nut café. It's the best in Laureton. This salad is to die for.' He winked at Polly, picked up a bottle of wine and tipped it into the glass she gave him.

She smiled weakly back and sat down. He had a cat-like ability to make himself at home, and she envied it. She noted how he used people's names, frequently and immediately. Any minute he would have Alan and Sheldon eating out of his hand, just as Melissa and Bridget were.

She was not so sure about David. Squeezed between him and Melissa she could observe him closely. Outwardly his expression was calm, yet she could almost see his antipathy to Tristan coming from him in waves, like dry ice.

'How do you come to know Polly?' David asked.

'We met at the Whole Nut, and later on the *Wild Cat*. Have you seen that ship? Not content with being a floating gallery, it's now fitting out to take passengers around the world. Do you sail?' As if aware that he had yet to win David round, Tristan kept his attention on him.

'I have done. I have very little time for it now.'

'Pity. Modern life is so stressful. There's nothing like the wind in your hair and the spray on your cheek to make you feel at one with the world.'

'You put it so well,' said David.

Tristan gave up and turned his attention to Alan. Polly decided it was time to see to the pudding.

She had forgotten to take the ice cream out of the freezing compartment to ripen. It was rock-hard. Knowing she would be better off being patient, she thrust the dish of ice cream into the oven. A few seconds later she rescued it, only fractionally too late. But the oranges, piled into a pyramid on a stemmed dish which had somehow got cracked in the firing, looked splendid. And who cared if the ice cream was a bit soft? She had an ally, dragging her dinner party back from the brink of failure. Only David disapproved, but he was dreadfully stuffy anyway. He was bound to despise media types like Tristan.

Tristan was in mid-anecdote, his balanced tones taking his audience by the hand and leading them where he wanted.

Of course, he was a professional. He was trained to know how to read an audience, how to make his story spicy but not offensive, gossipy but not slanderous.

He broke off when Polly arrived. 'Not only is she

beautiful, but she can cook!' He dipped a finger into the melting ice cream and licked it. 'Food for the gods!' He scooped up some more with Melissa's spoon and carried it to her lips. 'Taste this! Couldn't you eat the whole bowlful?'

Melissa protested girlishly as Tristan fed her another spoonful. 'It is very nice, Polly.'

Melissa was so entranced by Tristan that she overlooked the appearance of oranges twice during one meal. Bridget's lips were twitching and Alan seemed quietly amused. Polly looked at David, to see his reaction to the extra guest, and caught his eye. He gave her a small, cold smile, which spoke volumes of disapproval and distaste. For a moment Polly regretted Tristan's sudden appearance.

Eventually the witching hour sounded. Built-in babysitter or not, Melissa and Sheldon leaped to their feet the moment Polly's grandfather clock struck twelve. Bridget and Alan leaped likewise, and by twelve-fifteen, after a flurry of thanks and hugs, her invited guests had gone. Only David hadn't kissed her, but had confined his farewell to a handshake, his thanks to an icy platitude. It left Polly feeling suddenly empty.

Chapter Thirteen

Tristan had his feet up on the sofa and appeared settled for the night.

'That was the most dreadful dinner party I have ever had anything to do with.' Polly sank into the opposite sofa, picked up someone's wine glass and drained it.

Tristan picked up another glass and found a half-full bottle. 'Who were those people?'

Polly closed her eyes. 'People I owe hospitality to, and Bridget and Alan. Did you get enough to eat?' She didn't move. 'There's more in the kitchen.'

'I wouldn't mind.' As she didn't stir he went on, 'But I can get it. You must be tired.'

She was almost asleep.

She heard Tristan come back and build up the fire. By the time she opened her eyes, he had a loaded plate and had turned out the lights. Candles flickered at variance to the flames from the fire, but otherwise the room was in darkness.

Polly felt better for her rest and curled up to watch him eat. He was an appreciative diner. His compliments were acted out rather than spoken. He wiped his plate with a piece of French bread, and then got up. 'You really are a wonderful cook, Polly.'

'Sometimes.'

He took his plate out to the kitchen and came back

with a bottle of wine. He refilled her glass and sat down beside her. They watched the flames for a while and then he put his arm round her. She felt awkward in his embrace and tried to relax into it.

'That was an amazing rescue job, Tristan,' she murmured. 'I don't know how to thank you.'

'Don't you? I'm sure you can think of something if you put your mind to it.' His hand slipped under her chin and Polly realized he was going to kiss her. It was fairly inevitable, and in the time it took for his lips to reach hers she had decided it was fairly nice, too.

His lips were firm, practised, he knew what he was doing. Polly dragged up her response from the mists of time and kissed him back. They sank deeper into the sofa. Her blouse gaped and his hand wandered delicately inside the lapels. The smell of leather and aftershave filled her nostrils. It was pleasant to be cuddled after such a stressful evening, but somehow she couldn't respond.

I'm too tired and strung up, she decided, pushing his fingers away and struggling upright.

'Tristan, I like you very much, but I'm not ready yet.'

Tristan continued to try and lift her breasts out of the cups of her bra. 'Of course you're not ready, I've only just started.'

It took Polly a moment to understand. 'I mean, I'm not ready to go to bed with you. I don't know you well enough.'

Tristan straightened up. He swept back his hair with an impatient gesture. 'We're both too old for necking on the sofa.'

Polly rearranged her blouse, feeling a great deal too old for anything else. 'I know, it's just . . . I find it difficult

to – go any further – until I know someone really well.'
Which was true. The fact that she hadn't known anyone
really well for a very long time was irrelevant.

'The best way to get to know someone is by making
love to them, don't you think?'

'Probably, but it's still too soon to jump into bed.'

He raised his hands in an open, supplicating gesture.
'Who said anything about jumping?' His voice was
gravelly, and his eyes crinkled.

Polly sighed. 'Why did you come here?'

'Do you want the truth, or the fancy answer?'

'The truth, please.'

'All right, I'll tell you. I was walking back from the
pub. I saw the cars outside your house and shadowy
figures behind the curtains, and my curiosity got the
better of me.'

'I see. Well, it couldn't have been more opportune. I
was desperate.'

'Yet you don't want to reward me?'

'Not like that, no. I'm too damn tired. And as I said,
it's too early in the relationship.'

'I see.'

His forbearance made her feel guilty. 'I'm sorry if I've
misled you, Tristan. I never meant to.'

'No.' He sighed deeply. 'But I do very much want to
go to bed with you.'

Polly got up. 'At least you're honest about it.'

He joined her standing in front of the fire, and put his
hands on her shoulders. 'But now I've come clean about
my evil intentions, can't I persuade you to change your
mind?'

For a moment she wavered. He was very persuasive,
very sexy. 'No.'

181

He sighed again. 'A cup of coffee then?'

He's taking it very well, she decided, in the safety of the kitchen. He must be a lot nicer than his handsome-devil looks make him appear. She got out her secret packet of Abernethy biscuits as a sop to her conscience.

'Well, Polly,' he said eventually, 'if you won't go to bed with me, come to a party next Saturday.'

'A party?' After seeing him crunch his way through half a packet of her favourite comfort food, her conscience wasn't nearly so troubled. She opened her mouth to refuse but shut it again as she remembered she was supposed to be getting out more. And she owed him something. 'All right.'

He grinned. 'Good, I'll ring you with the details and pick you up.'

'So you do have a car, then?'

'Of course.' He got up, stretched broadly and yawned. 'I'd better go, seeing as you're not offering a bed for the night.'

She walked with him to the door and let him kiss her again. Perhaps I'm just out of practice, she thought.

'See you at nine on Saturday, Polly.' His gently husky tones caressed her cheek.

'Bye, Tristan, and thanks for tonight.'

He gave her a look which could have earned him money in the movies. 'I'll take a rain check on your gratitude, sweetheart.'

Polly shut the door behind him with a bang.

'Am I destined to spend every Saturday evening looking through my wardrobe for clothes I haven't got?' Polly demanded of her cat.

Selina continued to wash herself noisily, and didn't reply.

'At least for my dinner party,' went on Polly, 'I knew what I would have worn if I'd had it. But God knows what I'm expected to roll up in for Tristan's party.'

She rummaged about in the bottom of the cupboard, where clothes which had slipped from their hangers had to wait to be rescued until Polly wanted to wear them again. 'Hey! My jeans! I wonder if I can get into them! Let's see if all that aerobics and suffering has made me any slimmer.'

Polly stripped off her clothes and put her legs into the jeans. Then she lay on the floor, and inch by inch forced up the zip. She did up the button and got to her feet. She walked stiffly to the mirror in the bathroom.

'Mmm. Not too bad. But what about from the back? Can my bottom stand such exposure?' She screwed her neck round as far as she could and surveyed the least favourite part of her anatomy.

Either the tight, black lycra-enhanced denim was acting like a corset or those buttock exercises had instantly paid off. Because her rear view was a lot less offensive to her critical gaze than usual. Breathing was a bit of a problem, of course. But jeans always shrank a bit when they were washed. They'd loosen up as the evening went on.

Back in the bedroom, her elation at fitting so snugly into her jeans was dampened by the problem of what to wear with them. Eventually she settled for a full-sleeved silk blouse and a velvet waistcoat. It was not high fashion, but hopefully it was non-fashion and wouldn't peg her too accurately as a post-hippy-feminist craftsperson. She didn't want to feel like Tristan's older sister.

Having made the decision, she returned to the bath-room to put on her make-up, and make a selection from the strings of beads hanging by the mirror. It took a lot of thought. Finally she opted for undoing the blouse, for sex-appeal, and three long necklaces for glamour. Large silver earrings, boots pulled over her jeans and a large-buckled belt was a touch Calamity Jane on a night out, but the alternative was starting from scratch and she was already running late.

To her surprise, Tristan was punctual. David Locking-Hill would arrive the very moment he said he would, but she didn't expect it from Tristan.

'Hi!' She pulled the door open. 'Come in.'

'It's a foul night,' said Tristan, looking her over with an assessing eye.

'And do I pass?' Polly thought she might as well hear the opinion he was forming with such thoroughness.

'The first test, with flying colours.'

His eyes narrowed into a smile with enough of the predator in it to make her nervous. Fortunately it was quite a long time before she'd be obliged to take the second test.

'I haven't overdone it, with the jewellery?'

'Nope.'

'Or the make-up?' She'd started on a new tube of mascara and it had gone on rather thickly.

'You've got wonderful eyes, Polly.'

Polly blushed. He had a way with words.

'I'll get my coat.'

As a gesture to her new image, she shunned her trusty British Warm for a jacket passed on to her by Mark. She hadn't worn it before, not feeling the blouson style was flattering to her hips and it was not very warm. But it went with her new look, she would be in a car and parties were always hot.

His car turned out to be an elderly American Studebaker. She clambered in, and hoped they weren't going far. Her jeans were dreadfully tight.

'So who's giving this party?'

'An old mate of mine in the music business. He's forming a new band. I told him I'd check it out, and if it's any good put it in my "What's New in Town" show.'

'I thought we were going to a party, not a concert.'

He gave her a fond look. 'We are – but his band are playing at the party, you know? For the music?'

Polly decided to keep her conversation to the entirely general from now on. She was so un-cool. She thought the music for parties came from records, or at least CDs.

She kept up her silence until she realized they were nearing the common.

'Where are we going, Tristan?'

'The New Inn. It's great for gigs.'

She phrased her next question carefully. 'Are you working tonight?'

He flashed her the grin. 'I'm always working, sweetheart. But with you at my side, business is always a pleasure.'

Hmm, thought Polly, pleasure for whom? The New Inn was a pub in the middle of twenty acres of common with a bad reputation. Polly had only been there once, and that had been at lunchtime. She had told Beth about it at the café and Beth had been shocked. 'Even I wouldn't go there, Polly,' she'd told her. What Beth would say when told that Polly had been there on a Saturday night would be picturesque and to the point.

Still, she was a big girl now and was with street-wise

Tristan, at home in every situation. Nothing very dreadful could happen – could it?

Although it was still early, the party was up and running, judging by the music pulsating from the buildings and the number of cars in the car park. She mentioned it to Tristan.

'Oh, yeah, it's a twenty-four-hour do. We'll be in on the last eight hours or so.'

'Oh.' It had been a very long time since she'd been to an all-night party. She wasn't sure she had the stamina.

'Come on, Polly,' said Tristan, hauling her out of the car into a puddle. 'Let's go and have a good time.'

He hung on to her arm as they made their way to the back entrance of the pub. They were passing the kitchen when a girl shot out and grabbed hold of Tristan. She was tiny, blonde, and dressed in black leggings, a purple lycra bra top and a filmy overshirt. Her eyes were circled with black eyeliner and she had a stud in her nose. Given a good wash, thought Polly, who was possibly twenty years older, and less unflattering clothes, she'd be divinely pretty.

'Hey, Tris! Cheers! Glad I caught you. You know that rave I told you about –?' The girl glanced doubtfully at Polly. 'You mind if we speak alone?'

Tristan looked at Polly and shrugged. 'Will you be all right, sweetheart?' Polly's misgivings must have shown, because he hailed a passing hell's angel. 'Hey, Spike! Buy my old lady a drink, will you?' He thrust a fiver into the man's hand and disappeared into a storeroom with the diminutive waif.

Polly followed her escort into the main bar with extreme reluctance. Here the band had their amplifiers turned up so loud it reverberated in her breastbone.

'Whatdya want?' he shouted over the music.

'Lager,' she shouted back.

He gave her order. 'And a Pernod and black.' He handed over the note and put the change in his pocket. 'Seeya!' he said, and disappeared into the crowd.

Polly was reluctant to admit that coming had been a mistake. She took off her jacket and tried to relax her features into a pleasant expression. She tried not to feel cut off from the crowd, but her clothes, her class and her personality seemed enormous barriers. The wall of noise made communication beyond the simplest body language impossible. Rashly she attempted to inhale naturally, as if the fumes did not rasp her lungs. As she did so she realized that tobacco was only partly responsible for them. She even twitched her feet in time to the music. But eventually she gave in and admitted she wanted to go home.

It's probably because I'm over thirty, thought Polly, the music ripping through her body like a circular saw. I haven't got enough wax in my ears, or something. And my clothes are wrong. I should have stayed in my clay-covered dungarees. Then I would have been totally inconspicuous.

She took a sip of warm lager and made a second admission. She was more than a little panicked at being stranded without her own transport, miles from anywhere in a pub notorious for the number of times it had been raided by the police. If only Tristan hadn't deserted her.

She couldn't really blame him. He *was* a journalist and she was a grown woman, supposedly independent. She should be able to cope with being on her own in a strange place without an escort, even if she was the only person there who wasn't drunk or stoned. But all her feminist strength seemed to have drained away, leaving her with a pathetically feminine desire to be protected. She looked at her watch. Tristan had been gone for half an hour. Surely he couldn't be much longer!

She attempted a smile at the man opposite her. He acknowledged her overture with a confused frown and turned away, probably thinking her part of his hallucination.

He was, like most of the people there, what Bridget's Mark and anyone else under seventeen, would call a crusty. Now she had the opportunity to examine one at close quarters, she could see why. This one had hair which seemed to be formed from teased rope and sofa stuffing. His clothes hung in shreds, exposing large expanses of grey flesh and greyer underwear. He had had his nose pierced, probably in unhygienic circumstances, and his teeth hadn't had contact with either a toothbrush or dental floss for a very long time. An odour of unwashedness emanated from him through the almost suffocating smoke. He probably grew hallucinogenic mushrooms as a cash crop.

The thickness of the smoke started to bother her. Would anyone notice if there was a fire? How long would it take to evacuate the room? She glanced at her watch again. It felt like hours since she had last looked, when in fact it was only minutes.

Polly's fears became more and more irrational. Eventually she convinced herself that the building actually was on fire and she was about to be trampled to death by a hundred hobnail boots.

She decided to find refuge in the car park. If Tristan ever emerged from the cupboard and remembered he'd brought her, he could find her. But as he'd been gone for nearly an hour, he may well have forgotten all about her. In which case Polly might start thinking about how to get home. It was probably still pouring with rain, but she had her jacket and it would be safe there, and comparatively quiet.

Fighting her way past a man in a large cowboy hat, a whitefaced, black-eyed damsel in leather fringes and a brace of unconscious teenagers who stood no chance of survival if there actually was a fire, she finally made it into the fresh air.

She breathed in several lungfuls, musing on the effects of passive dope smoking, and put on her jacket. Then she noticed a car with its bonnet up.

She had been in a similar situation too recently herself to ignore it. She moved out of the shelter of the porch and slithered across the mud-slicked car park.

'Can I help you?'

She found the rain beating down on her quite refreshing, but the poor student bending over the car engine with a torch probably didn't.

He looked up and brushed back a lock of gold hair which had escaped from its ponytail. 'I may have fixed it.'

They recognized each other at the same moment – which said a lot for Patrick Locking-Hill. He was wearing more or less the same clothes as he had the first time she had seen him, his kneecaps protruding from his jeans like bones through a shroud, but Polly's 'Calamity Jane' outfit was far removed from a little black dress and pearls.

'Oh, hello,' he said, obviously embarrassed. His jacket was soaked. Phrases like 'outgrown his strength' floated into Polly's mind as he slammed the bonnet shut and got into the car, anxious to get away from one who'd met him for the second time in unfortunate circumstances. The engine produced a plaintive whine and stopped.

'What about a push?' she suggested after watching him repeat the procedure a few times. 'I'm sure you could get some people from inside to help.'

A certain bitterness about his mouth made it seem doubtful. Perhaps the ex-public schoolboy had not fitted in well with the crowd inside.

'Nah.' A tiny spark of hope emerged from his desolate expression. 'But perhaps if you sat in the driving seat I could bump start her down that slope.'

Polly looked in the direction he was pointing and could just see through the rain that the gradient of the land did alter slightly at one point.

'We could try, I suppose.'

She was not convinced, but she felt sorry for Patrick, whose cultured voice clashed so violently with his tangled hair and multi-pierced ears.

She climbed into his dilapidated Fiat Panda and pulled the seat forward so she could reach the pedals. Patrick took his place at the rear of the car.

'You know what to do?' he shouted. 'Keep your foot on the clutch and when –'

'I know what to do!' she shouted back.

Polly had long since accepted the male inability to credit the female with any mechanical knowledge whatsoever, even if the female in question had had her licence at least fifteen years longer than he had. But it still annoyed her. She waited patiently for the car to move.

They bumped and ground their way along, until Polly wondered if Patrick intended to push her and the car all the way back to Laureton. Then at last the car picked up speed, Polly did her bit and the engine started.

When Polly had driven it round the car park and back to where he waited, he came to the driver's door to thank her.

As he spoke, a waft of best bitter fumes hit her. Polly, about to get out, stayed put. He wouldn't like it, but she couldn't let David's son drive in that condition.

She braced herself. 'If you've been drinking, I really don't think you should drive.' She silenced his protest with a hand. 'I'm not being priggish, I'm sure you're quite capable of driving' – she crossed the fingers of her hidden hand – 'But this place isn't exactly known as a temperance hotel. You're almost bound to get stopped. Out here in the middle of nowhere everyone comes by car. If they're down on their quotas,' she added, hoping a bit of anti-pig feeling on her part might endear her to him, 'they come here and breathalyse everyone.'

He sighed deeply and kicked at the ground with his Doc Marten. 'How else can I get home? The old man'll throw a fit if I don't show up.'

'You could ring him and explain. After all, it's the responsible thing to do, if you've been drinking. You could stay with a friend.'

'What friend? I haven't got any he approves of.'

'Take a taxi?'

'And pay with what? They don't do it for charity, you know.'

If she'd had enough money, she'd have given him the fare. But £2.50 wouldn't do it. 'Would your father collect you?'

The boy shook his head. 'No way.'

'Are you sure? Most fathers would rather collect their sons than have them drive home drunk.'

'Knowing that I've had a drink at all will be enough for him to kill me. He went ape-shit about the last time.'

Polly, wishing she'd stayed in the comparative safety of the drunken, drug-crazed fire-trap from which she had escaped, felt that David was probably justified.

'Yes, but I'm sure he'd rather you rang and . . .'

'I'm not ringing. I'll hitch if I have to.'

And who do you imagine would be foolish enough to pick you up, dressed like that and drunk into the bargain? she wondered, but had the tact to keep her doubts to herself.

'Listen, I haven't been drinking much. I'll drive you home.'

'You're just as likely to be breathalysed as I am,' he said sulkily.

'True, but I'm less likely to be found positive than you are. Get in and wait for me. I've got to leave someone a message.'

She took the car keys with her and plodded her way across the car park and got as far as the pub kitchen. There she wrote a note for Tristan on a serviette and persuaded one of the staff to give it to him. Then she picked her way back to Patrick's car, and her own escape.

Patrick was able to give Polly very clear directions, and she was awarding herself Brownie points for her kind action when the car slowed to a halt.

'Oh *shit!*' Patrick banged the dashboard with his fist before glancing apologetically at Polly.

'It's all right. I use that word myself sometimes,' she said. 'What do you think the problem is?'

He gave her a look which erased her feelings of goodwill and told her he thought her an idiot. It was faintly familiar. 'We've run out of petrol.'

'Oh. Well, now we'll have to ring your father.'

'No way! We can walk from here. Or at least I can. There's no need for you to come too.'

It was Polly's turn to be scathing. 'Thank you very much. There's nothing I like better than spending the night alone in a broken-down vehicle. I do it every holiday.'

'Sorry. I didn't think.'

'No, well, you've got a lot on your mind. But at least your father won't shout at you if I'm there.'

Polly caught a gleam of white as Patrick grinned. 'No, he'll probably shout at you.'

A quiver ran through her as she bitterly regretted not wearing her coat, turned up the collar of her jacket and climbed out of the car. 'Nonsense! He'll be overcome with gratitude.'

'Yeah. That's what'll make him so pig sick.'

It took them half an hour. After the first five minutes, Polly realized her boots would never be the same again. After ten, she wondered if she would. Her jacket was already soaked and now even her bra felt damp. And her jeans had tightened into straitjackets, making them almost impossible to move in. Patrick walked fast, his long legs and his well-shod feet striding confidently over the muddy verge. Polly struggled along behind, risking a twisted ankle at every step, aware that only the punishing pace protected her from hypothermia. Every now and then he would wait for Polly to catch up, but the moment she did he moved on so they never walked together. He was sulking, she realized, in anticipation of a row.

The compassion she had felt for Patrick when she first saw his plight, and that had developed as he explained his situation, had vanished long before they got to the top of the drive which led to the Locking-Hill residence. By the time they reached the front door of a small but very beautiful stately home all her pity was for herself.

Her hair was plastered to her head, her teeth were chattering so loudly she could hardly hear herself think and the combination of mascara and rain which filled her eyes so painfully was making it difficult to see. It would take a mountain of heartfelt gratitude to restore her spirits.

Patrick pulled a brass knob and a bell jangled inside. At the sound of bolts being pulled back and keys being turned, he shot her a quick glance of complicity. The door opened.

'What the hell –' Anger, relief and then confusion flashed across David's face in quick succession. The anger remained, controlled but evident. 'Polly! What are you doing here?'

She blinked water and mascara out of her eyes. 'I brought Patrick home.'

As she spoke, Patrick, with the stealth of a practised villain, stepped past her and took the elegant staircase in four bounds, like an oversized dog. David gave him an exasperated glance and turned his attention back to Polly.

'And why was that necessary?'

Polly, who was still standing on the door mat, dripping freely, took exception to his tone. 'It's not for me to tell you, suffice it to say that it was.' She glared at him, forestalling his argument. 'We ran out of petrol.'

'I see.' At last David took in her bedraggled appearance. 'You'd better come in.'

Chapter Fourteen

His marbled hall made Melissa's seem positively poky. It could have swallowed up the entire floor area of Polly's house and had room for seconds. A vast fireplace, which reached almost to the roof like a small slice of the Elgin Marbles, was covered with disapproving cherubim. The furniture all seemed to be antique and there was undoubtedly a Mrs Danvers character somewhere about who dedicated her life to rubbing elbow grease and Antiquax into the heirlooms until the house was bequeathed to the National Trust.

'I'd better take my boots off,' she said after a quick glance round. 'Or your housekeeper will go mad.'

David was obviously not as considerate of this person's sensibilities as Polly, and watched with irritation as she struggled to pull off her mud-impacted boots. Eventually he lost patience altogether, picked her up and staggered with her to an armchair.

Polly wanted to growl and hiss, like a cat removed from a favourite spot, but as the spot he had dumped her on was preferable to hopping from foot to foot on the door mat she didn't.

He removed her boots in two efficient tugs, wiped his muddied hands on a pristine white handkerchief and regarded what his son had dragged in with evident distaste.

'Let me take your coat,' he said coldly, and took it, pulling it from her arms with more irritation than courtesy. 'Come by the fire and dry yourself.'

Polly padded in the direction he indicated, wondering how much longer she would be able to contain her own anger. His attitude and her situation were equally intolerable. She'd put herself out to save his son from committing a criminal offence. And instead of helping Patrick out with mitigating circumstances while he explained himself to his irate father, she was left to face the irate father on her own.

Her feet left wet footprints on the marble floor, and she hoped his sitting-room carpet was suitably pale so she could leave footprints on that too. There was certainly a fair amount of mud in the hall. If there was any justice in the world, tomorrow Mrs Danvers would give him the kind of forelocktugging earful which would make any Englishman squirm.

The Englishman in question opened the door for Polly and ushered her into his drawing room.

Only the area by the fire was illuminated, the rest of the room was in shadow. Firelight danced on a highly polished parquet floor softened by worn Persian rugs. What little furniture there was had evidently been there for generations. A vast oak chest spanned the space between two sets of French windows, which were draped in rich brocade faded to the most delicate eau-de-Nil. A console table against the opposite wall supported a table lamp. There were pictures on all the walls: a series of botanical prints of apples, ancient maps and family portraits coexisted happily with some very modern impressionistic paintings.

It had none of the opulence of Melissa's designer

drawing room. It was even faintly shabby. But it was the kind of shabbiness even Melissa would recognize as class. The quantity of engraved invitations on the mantelpiece was daunting.

The fire at least was welcoming. A button-backed chesterfield was placed a respectful distance from it, so Polly plumped for the wing-backed armchair which was far closer, ignoring the reading lamp, the open book and other signs which told her it had just been vacated by the master of the house.

'Can I get you anything?' David's anger was cocooned in politeness, but only just. 'Tea, coffee? Something stronger?' he added as she didn't respond.

The angles of his face looked very severe as he towered over her. He was wearing a Guernsey sweater and corduroy trousers which somehow enhanced the breadth of his shoulders and the athletic length of his legs. His feet were slightly apart and he had his hands on his hips. It was a dominant posture. If she'd been any younger, any drier, or in any way to blame for the situation, she'd have been frightened of him. She looked him straight in the eye.

'Something stronger. Much stronger.'

For someone so adept at hiding his feelings, his features had suddenly become remarkably expressive. Disapproval was etched instantly into every line. He barely managed to keep it out of his voice.

'What? Whisky? Gin? I haven't got any vodka.'

'Whisky. Please,' she added, thinking at least one of them should hang on to their manners.

He crossed to a rosewood side table on which reposed a silver tray, which no doubt some Locking-Hill had won for rowing, a couple of decanters and some glasses.

'I'm afraid I haven't got any ginger ale, so which would you like, water or soda?'

'Neither, thank you.'

'Well, what would you like in it?'

'Nothing. I like it on its own.'

He poured a drink for himself at the same time and returned to the fireside. 'I didn't think you drank.'

Polly glowered acidly. 'I don't "drink", as you so delicately put it. I'm just very wet and very cold, and happen to want one.' She glanced down at what he'd given her, and saw not the faint wetting of the glass she was expecting but a good two fingers of whisky. She took a sip. Unless her taste buds deluded her, it was an unblended malt, as smoky and peatflavoured as a turf fire.

She forgave him slightly for his comment and crossed meanness off his list of faults. Then she thanked him, somewhat belatedly.

He took a sip of his own drink and folded himself in the chair opposite, his legs stretching towards the fire. 'Now tell me how you came to rescue my son from a tricky situation for the second time.'

Polly took another sip of her whisky and settled back. The fire had at last penetrated the worst of the damp, and the alcohol was beginning to release its potency. Another fifteen minutes and she'd feel fine.

'Shouldn't you be asking Patrick that?'

'Patrick and I have a communication problem. Finding anything out from him takes a long time.'

'Perhaps it would be time well spent.'

His eyebrow flickered, 'Perhaps, but it's not time I have at the moment.'

Still she hesitated.

'I'll tell him I forced the information out of you,' he suggested dryly. 'He won't have any problem believing me, I assure you.'

'Do you bully your son, David?'

His eyes narrowed. 'Did you kidnap my son, Polly?'

It was an appalling suggestion. 'Of course not! What do you take me for, a cradle-snatcher?'

'If the cap fits.'

'It does not fit!' Then Tristan's image nudged her conscience, and she blushed. Damn him and damn her revealing complexion.

'No? I thought you had a preference for the young.'

'Socially, yes, sexually, certainly not!'

David had obviously drawn the right conclusions from Tristan's late arrival at her house, but equally experienced some difficulty in drawing a distinction between a sophisticated man of twenty-five and a newly hatched schoolboy.

Feeling she'd gone a bit far, she tried to backtrack. 'David, Patrick is perfectly sweet, but I can't imagine he's much more than eighteen years old.'

'He's seventeen, actually.'

It got worse and worse. 'And you're accusing me of picking up a mere' – she fought for the right word and lost – '*child*?'

'He wouldn't like to be described as that. And I'm not accusing you of anything, I'm trying to find out the truth. Something in which you are offering no assistance whatever.'

Two can play at being pedantic. 'I beg your pardon,' she said icily. 'I don't wish to be obstructive.'

'I'm glad to hear it. So do tell me how you came to

meet him.' He settled into his chair as one prepared to hear a fairy story.

She opened her mouth to speak, but took another sip of whisky instead. Did David know that Patrick went to unsavoury pubs and got drunk in them? Judging by what Patrick said, and his performance so far, he wasn't exactly up for a Liberal Parent of the Year award. Patrick could find himself cut off without a shilling, or whatever it was that parents did these days.

'You might just as well tell me the truth, Polly. It can't be any worse than what I'm imagining.'

Polly gave up the fight with her conscience. 'It isn't anything very dreadful. I was at the New Inn, on the common. I came outside for some fresh air and saw Patrick trying to start his car. Of course I didn't know it was Patrick at first, I just thought he needed a hand. He wanted me help him bump start the car, and I did.'

'So why did you come home with him? Did you need a lift yourself?'

Trust David to put his finger on a very tender spot. 'Not exactly.' She would have found some way of getting home without Tristan. 'But I – I thought Patrick may have been drinking.' She paused. 'He's very like you to look at, you know.'

'Yes.' The knowledge didn't seem to afford him much gratification.

'Anyway, I couldn't let the child of anyone I knew drive when they were – had been drinking. That place is notorious. The police are always raiding it.'

'I know.'

'So I offered to drive him home.'

'And were you stone cold sober yourself?'

'Christ Almighty! What is this? I rescue your son from

201

a very tricky situation, and for my pains have to go through an interrogation worthy of Inspector Morse! And, no, I don't suppose you would consider anyone who'd had half a pint of lager sober, but a breathalyser would. And nor was I stinking of spilt beer.'

'What about your own car?'

'I didn't have my car with me.'

'So you ran away with my son, not having transport of your own?'

'No! I left a message!'

'So your motives were purely altruistic?'

She dragged her tattered dignity about her. 'Mark Twain said there's no such thing as an unselfish act. But given that a middle-aged woman is much less likely to get stopped by the police than a seventeen-year-old boy, I did what I'd have done for the child of any of my friends.' Which of course counts you out from now on, she added to herself.

For the first time, possibly in his life, David was amused. 'I could call you a lot of things, Polly, but not middle-aged.'

'Good.' She huddled back into her chair, nursing her glass, and glared at him. 'We ran out of petrol and had to walk for the last mile or ten.'

'I see.'

'I hope so. I don't take kindly to being accused of cradle-snatching, not to mention kidnapping and driving while under the influence of alcohol.'

'Well, I apologize for that. But what I want to know now is what the hell were *you* doing at that dump?'

'I was at a party.'

'The same party as *Patrick*?'

She shrugged. 'I suppose so.'

'Wasn't the company a little young for you?'

'No.' She had felt out of place for a thousand reasons, but she had not been the oldest person there.

'Who did you go with? That poser from local radio?'

Polly clenched her teeth. 'What, may I ask, has that to do with you?'

Their eyes locked in anger for long seconds.

'The New Inn is no place for the likes of you, Polly.'

He was undoubtedly right, but she wasn't going to concede a single point. 'Even if you knew me well enough to judge, which I doubt, it's my business, not yours. And don't you dare pigeonhole me. I'm an individual, not a type.'

David got up from his chair and kicked the logs in the fire. Polly's experienced eye told her they didn't need kicking. 'Then I apologize again,' he said. 'And I'm sorry I wasn't more gracious about your kindness to Patrick. As a parent, you can't help worrying.'

Sympathy and whisky combined to swamp her irritation. 'I'm sure.'

'And now I suppose you'll give me a few handy hints on how to get on with the younger generation.'

'Me? Why the hell should I? What do I know about it?'

'You were singing the praises of "Youth Today" the other night.'

Polly chuckled. 'I love them until they're about fifteen, then they start to go off. Over sixteen they inhabit a different planet, and I don't speak the language.'

He sighed ruefully. 'Total lack of experience doesn't usually prevent people from giving advice.'

'How many other children have you got?'

'One. Another son. He's at university at the moment.'

'You must be very proud.'

203

'Yes. He worked hard. He should do well.' He sighed again. 'What Patrick's going to do with his life, God alone knows.'

'I dare say Patrick has some ideas.'

'If he has, I'd be delighted to hear them. But as you said, he speaks a different language.'

He looked so drawn and anxious Polly longed to help him. 'Not as different as all that,' she suggested gently.

'About as different as it always is between father and son, I'm afraid. Now –' He snapped back into his role of host. 'What are we going to do about you?'

Polly's hackles rose again. 'There's no need for *you* to do anything. I'm quite capable of looking after myself.'

'Are you? I'm glad to hear it. So how do you plan to get home?'

'Well, I –' She stopped and ran through her options. She could call a taxi. She could ask him to drive her home. She could stay the night. She could walk to the nearest hotel and wash up to pay for her bed.

The taxi seemed the best idea, only she didn't have enough money, either on her or in her pot at home. If only David was the sort of person you could borrow money from. The very idea made her cringe. If she wasn't such a soft-hearted fool, she wouldn't be in this abominable situation. She took a deep breath.

'Would you mind very much driving me home, David?' He didn't reply, so she went on: 'I realize it may seem a bit of an imposition, but I wouldn't be here if it wasn't for Patrick.'

'My dear Polly, I'm only too aware of the favour you've done me and Patrick in seeing he got back safely, but I'm afraid I couldn't possibly drive you home.'

'You couldn't? Why not?'

He indicated his glass. 'I'd already had a drink before you came, and knowing how strongly you feel about drinking and driving, I couldn't take the risk.'

If it had been anyone else in the world, Polly would have deeply suspected this virtuous statement. And as the hotel plan wasn't really viable, she would have to ask David for the taxi fare home. A lot of scruples she hadn't previously noticed made this incredibly difficult.

'Lend us a fiver, David.'

David raised a eyebrow, and shrugged. 'I can't help you, I'm afraid. I'm right out of cash.'

Having steeled herself to ask him, she wasn't going to accept a refusal. 'You can't be.' The house oozed wealth from every beeswaxed pore. There must be a wad of tenners somewhere about. 'What about the kitchen? Don't you keep money for the milkman somewhere about?'

'I pay monthly, by cheque.'

'The paper boy. Don't you have to pay him?'

'No, I pay the newsagent. And for someone so pernickety about whose business is whose, you're asking a lot of very personal questions.'

Polly blushed, but refused to give up. 'I just can't believe you couldn't rustle up enough money for a taxi if you really tried.'

'Do you want to search me for loose change?'

She was about to get him to turn out his pockets to see if they had enough between them, but his supercilious eyebrow forced her to drop the subject. She slumped back in her chair, simmering with irritation.

David appeared almost sympathetic. 'I think you'll have to resign yourself to staying the night. The guest bedroom is considered tolerably comfortable.'

205

'I'm sure.' She shifted awkwardly in her rapidly shrinking jeans. They'd have to be surgically removed if she didn't do something soon.

He must have noticed her wriggling. 'Why don't you come and look at it? You could have a bath and get out of your wet clothes.'

'I haven't any dry ones.'

'I'm sure I can find something to lend you.'

Polly regretted that age and dignity made it impossible to reply with suitable sarcasm. The chances of him having anything which would fit were minimal. And he didn't seem the sort of man who would keep his late wife's wardrobe intact after all these years.

She allowed herself to be guided up the stairs, along the passage to the end of a corridor. The thought of getting out of her jeans was beginning to obscure her objections to staying the night.

'Here we are.'

He flung open the door to reveal a large double-bedded room. Seeing the bed she was reminded what her fate may well have been if she'd stayed with Tristan. At least there wouldn't be any danger of anything like that with David. He'd probably never propositioned a woman in his life. He and Angela probably hadn't been to bed together until safely tucked up in the honeymoon suite at Claridge's.

She looked around her. The walls were pearl-grey, offsetting the white paintwork. The carpet and curtains were a delicate dove-pink which brought out the richness of the mahogany chest of drawers and desk. It was all extremely refined and understated.

'There's an electric blanket on the bed, which I'll put on.' He bent and switched something which also turned on the bedside lights. 'But we'll need to find sheets and things.'

She followed him back into the passage to a huge airing cupboard. Its light went on immediately he opened the door, and the shelves were neatly labelled, single sheets, double sheets, pillow cases and so on.

He hauled out a duvet the size of a small marquee. 'I'm pretty sure this is the duvet for that bed.' He handed it to Polly. 'What else do we need?'

The duvet was as light as it was large and was undoubtedly filled with pure goose down. The mere feel of it made Polly long to curl up and go to sleep. 'Why don't I find the bedlinen?' she suggested. 'You must be tired and I can manage.'

He regarded her thoughtfully. 'Actually, I'm starving hungry. When did you last eat?'

Polly thought for a moment. She'd eaten a Mars Bar when she got in from the Shed, but she'd missed lunch. It was a long time since her toast and Marmite. Her stomach rumbled as if suddenly realizing it was hungry. 'Well, now you come to mention it . . .'

'What about some scrambled eggs?'

'Sounds wonderful.'

'Why don't you get sorted out here, have a bath and then come down to the kitchen? I'll get you a dressing gown.'

He disappeared down the passage while Polly scanned the airing cupboard shelves. Was it David or the late lamented Angela who'd insisted on a place for everything and everything in its place?

She pulled out a perfectly laundered linen sheet. It weighed a ton. None of your polyester-cotton for the Locking-Hills, it seemed. A pretty, floral cover from the shelf marked, 'Duvet covers, double,' went with a couple of frilled pillow cases in the same fabric.

'Here you are. This will keep the draughts out, anyway.' He handed her a dressing gown straight out of a West End production of a Noël Coward play. It was maroon silk with navy-blue facings and cord. It would have been almost anklelength on David.

'Thanks.'

'Bring your clothes with you, and I'll put them somewhere to dry. Come down to the kitchen when you're ready.' He grinned. She hadn't known he could grin. 'I won't actually put the eggs on until you arrive.'

Polly smiled shyly back. 'Good.'

'Don't forget you'll need towels. They're here.'

He clapped a hand on a stack of shelves named after bathrooms. Polly soon found hers ('best spare'). They were white with pearl-grey lace edges and pale pink embroidery. Patrick's (labelled 'boys') were bright green. David's were a discreet, masculine navy-blue with no frilly bits.

As she might have expected from the towels, the bathroom was decorated to match the bedroom. A little safe for Polly's taste, but exactly what you'd expect from someone who labelled their airing cupboard shelves and colour-coded their towels.

Even the soap and bath foam toned in tastefully. The bath foam came in a pale grey bottle with a white dove as its top. She unscrewed it and took a tentative sniff. It was surprisingly nice. David's 'Mrs Danvers' must have continued to buy the bathroom goodies that Angela had, to keep her colour scheme intact.

Forbidding herself to have any more *Rebecca* fantasies, but continuing to speculate about the housekeeper's jealousy of any woman who threatened to replace David's first wife, Polly turned on the tap. Then she tipped a lavish amount of foam into the hot water that was gushing into the bath and started peeling off her damp clothes.

It was bliss to be free of her constricting jeans, her clammy blouse and her tights, which had developed a hole since she'd put them on and were cutting painfully into her big toe. She bundled her jeans and blouse into a corner, but flung her bra, pants and holey tights into the mountain of foam. At least she'd have clean underwear tomorrow, if she did have to fight her way back into her jeans which were now encrusted with mud as well as too small.

Then she climbed in on top of the clothes and bubbles, and wallowed in the scented water. Her eyes closed, and her thoughts drifted off on a whisky cloud.

Would Tristan mind her walking out on him like that? Or would he console himself with his tiny, dirty informant? Perhaps he already had, in the cupboard, and had emerged with his white T-shirt covered in grubby marks. And if he had, would he try and find Polly, apologize profusely and do his damnedest to seduce her too?

She found it hard to resent Tristan. He had behaved like a cad, but then he *was* a cad. She'd known that the moment she saw him. And nor did the thought of him making love to that little girl upset her. She'd been very attracted to him, no doubt about that. But now the thought of making love to him, or letting him make love to her, no longer seemed a probability, or even a possibility, she felt nothing but relief.

She dipped her head under the water and washed her

ears. David could be guaranteed to behave like a perfect gentleman at all times – when he wasn't behaving like Mr Barrett of Wimpole Street. And even then, she decided, surfacing and shaking water out of her ears, there was something rather noble about him. Poor Melissa. What a shame for her she was shackled to Sheldon.

Polly reached for the shampoo and started to wash her hair.

Chapter Fifteen

The kitchen was, as she had predicted, as different from hers as possible, given the two rooms performed more or less the same function.

His was huge, of the operating-theatre school of interior design, aggressively hygienic and totally intimidating. The floor was pure white quarry tiles, a surface so hard that anything you dropped would break into a million pieces. And only a Mrs Danvers would tolerate standing on such an unyielding surface all day, or be prepared to keep it clean.

Nothing was on display: not so much as a jar of spaghetti, copper pan or pot of parsley growing on the window sill.

Polly spotted at least two built-in ovens, though more may have lurked behind those snow-white doors. She'd have bet money on everything gliding out at you on runners whenever you opened a drawer or cupboard.

Two combination hobs winked at her under downlighters so bright they'd probably give you quite a good tan. A trio of stainless-steel sinks gleamed likewise, daring you to rinse a coffee mug and spoil their pristine surface. There was enough naked work surface to land a small plane on, and you could easily cook a banquet without being pushed for space.

But would you want to? Either David was very brave

when he elected to cook anything as messy as scrambled eggs, or he had Mrs Danvers under his thumb.

David had his sleeves pushed up and was beating eggs in a bowl. The light shone directly on to his head, making his hair shine and the angles of his face very steep. For a moment Polly watched him before she glided silently towards him on her bare feet, clutching the skirts of the dressing gown so she wouldn't trip.

He couldn't have heard her come in because his expression when he first saw her was one of extreme shock.

'Ah, Polly! Here you are. I was about to put the eggs on. Two or three?'

'Two, please. I put my clothes in the airing cupboard, if that's all right.' She hadn't known whether to file them under 'S' for soaked or 'M' for muddy. 'Can I do anything to help?'

'Would you like to cut some bread?'

'Not really. I can't do it straight.' She'd better admit it. Her wedge-shaped slices would drive him mad and she'd get crumbs on the floor.

'Oh. Then perhaps you wouldn't mind finishing this and I'll do it.' A built-in breadboard slid out of somewhere with a built-in breadknife to match. 'I've cleaned the worst of the mud off your boots, put newspaper in them and put them in the bottom oven of the Aga to dry. With a good dose of polish tomorrow, they may well survive.'

Trust David to know how to handle muddy boots. He'd probably learned it in the Army Cadet Corps at school. She took over the whisk.

'It's awfully kind of you to go to so much trouble.' She smiled gratefully, but privately she found such excessive politeness as intimidating as his kitchen. On balance she preferred him rude and overbearing.

'Have you put in salt and pepper, or would you like me to do it?' she asked, matching his civility point for point.

'No. They're in that cupboard, next to the hotplate. Here, let me pass them.' He crossed the room and opened a tall, narrow cupboard which contained the clutter most people kept on show, like a spice rack. He extracted salt and pepper mills, which were probably Italian, and matched the quarry tiles.

'Oh,' he said abruptly, as she ground pepper into the eggs. 'You haven't got any underwear on.'

Polly promptly dropped the pepper mill and clutched at the lapels of her dressing gown which had gaped open. How much of herself had she exposed, and for how long?

'No – I'm afraid . . .'

He brushed aside her apology. 'I shouldn't have mentioned it. Do you like butter on your toast?'

Polly relaxed her grip on her chest area. 'Yes, please.'

For a moment there she'd thought David was going to make a suggestive remark. But then the idea seemed ridiculous. She couldn't suppress a giggle.

He shot her an inquiring look. 'I was just remembering –' Her brain strained to think of a funny incident she could reasonably relate. 'The last time I bought butter, I left it on the Rayburn to soften and Selina sat on it.'

It hadn't been funny at the time, and the joke hadn't improved with keeping, but David smiled politely. 'Shall we take our eggs into the drawing room, by the fire?'

'What a good idea. It's so cosy there.'

Then, relieved that she wasn't going to have to eat her

213

supper terrified lest her porcelain plate slip on to the merciless quarry tiles, Polly gave him a beaming smile.

He returned one considerably more restrained and tipped the eggs into a pan which sizzled on a hotplate.

'The secret of scrambled eggs is not to stir them more than absolutely necessary,' he said.

'Did your old nanny teach you that?' Polly imagined nursery suppers made over an open fire, high above the rest of the house.

He shot her a look which queried her sanity. 'No, my first girlfriend, actually.'

Polly realized she had made a lot of huge assumptions on very scant evidence. 'Oh. And how old were you then?'

'Seventeen.'

'Patrick's age.'

'Yes. And she was thirty-five.'

It took Polly a long time to think of a reply. 'I wonder if Patrick's girlfriend teaches him to cook.' What she really wanted to know was what else David's girlfriend taught him.

When the eggs were piled in buttery heaps on the toast, David put them on to a tray already loaded with plates, napkins and knives and forks. 'Would you mind very much opening the door?'

Polly, determined to be polite and not annoy David by sitting in his chair, sat on the sofa, adjusted her dressing gown and accepted the plate of scrambled eggs he handed her. Rather to her surprise, he sat next to her.

He cleared the magazines off a double footstool and put the tray on it.

'Do start.'

Polly's plate slid about her lap as she dug her fork into a bit of toast. 'I didn't realize how hungry I was,' she said when she finally got it to her mouth. 'Delicious scrambled eggs.'

'I'm flattered. Coming from such an accomplished cook, that's high praise.'

Hoping he wasn't being sarcastic, Polly smiled weakly and then tried a soupçon of sarcasm herself. 'But you did have an excellent teacher.'

'I did. By the way, did I thank you properly for such a pleasant evening last Saturday?'

This was taking good manners way too far. He was definitely being sarcastic, in spite of the blandness of his tone.

'Really, David, anyone who describes that dinner party as "pleasant" has either a severely limited vocabulary or needs their head examining. And, yes, you did thank me.' In retrospect, his chilly words of gratitude seemed rather hurtful.

'It was a very entertaining evening.'

'You didn't appear terribly "entertained" at the time.'

'No? Well, Englishmen find it difficult to show their feelings.'

Polly swallowed grimly, horribly aware that somewhere along the line she had got David badly wrong.

'And the food was excellent,' he added kindly.

'In spite of being vegetarian? And burnt?' Her knee seemed to have escaped from her dressing gown, and she twitched the silk back into place.

'Certainly.'

'I don't think Sheldon thought so.'

'Ah, Sheldon.'

Polly waited to see if David was going to indulge in

some harmless gossip about Melissa's husband, but he didn't. She was disappointed. She liked gossip.

They continued to eat. His white teeth crunched through the toast like an army marching through undefended countryside. Polly cut little forkfuls, and clutched on to her dressing gown while she chewed. It seemed to have taken on a life of its own, closely connected to that of the eel. A gentleman to the last, David appeared not to notice her struggles.

'I should have made tea. Would you like some?' he said.

'No, don't bother. I can't drink –' She nearly found herself telling him that if she drank tea after nine o'clock she'd have to go to the loo in the night.

'What about some more whisky? I think I'll have some.'

'Oh, well, yes please.' She suspected that if she refused he would change his mind, and she needed him out of the way for a moment so she could sort out her dressing gown once and for all.

She got up when he did, put down her plate then wrapped the dressing gown tightly round her so only her collar-bone appeared above the navy silk. She tied a double knot in the belt and sat down again.

This done, she was able to accept her glass and resume her supper with some degree of confidence.

'Now,' he said, when he was seated once more. 'Tell me about this party.'

'Do you really want to hear about it, or do you want an opportunity to disapprove of me?'

'My dear Polly, you must think me very ungallant.' His smile was more than a little mocking. 'Why on earth would I want to disapprove of you?'

'I don't know. I just thought it was your latest hobby.'

'I can't imagine why you thought that, Polly. Please tell me about the sort of places my son disappears to on a Saturday night.'

Polly gave him a narrow-eyed glare, covered her knees and started to describe a scene similar to Dante's Inferno with music. She was letting her powers of description run riot on the man who'd bought her a drink with Tristan's money when she realized that, although David was looking at her intently, he wasn't listening to a word she was saying. She struggled on for a word or two and then dried up.

'Excuse me.' David removed her plate from her lap and put it on to the footstool. 'I'm afraid I'm going to have to kiss you.'

The next moment Polly found herself thrust back into the sofa cushions, one of his arms round her waist, the other supporting her back. Losing her balance she clutched at him, but instead of pushing him away found her arms wrapping tightly round the roughness of his sweater.

For a moment, she struggled. But only until his mouth touched hers and her eyes snapped shut and refused to open. His jaw was hard against her cheek, his hand, buried in her still-damp curls, was strong, holding her still. Then any desire to fight him melted.

At first he kissed the corner of her mouth with tender, exploratory kisses. His cheek was rough against the softness of hers, and his sweater prickled where it grazed her skin. But her senses seemed to slip away from her as she breathed in the dizzying combination of his after-shave and his own male scent; an explosive cocktail of pheromones and citrus.

His breath whispered across her skin as his mouth settled decisively on hers, opening it like a flower. He tasted of whisky and his kiss had all the fire and force of the spirit. But like the whisky his passion was controlled, tamed by ancient skills and half-forgotten alchemy. Her last conscious thought was that she must be very drunk. Then she gave herself up to pure sensation.

After her initial shock of finding herself in his arms, she kissed him back with a hunger she had never even dreamed of. His mouth delighted her, she revelled in his skill as all his concentration centred on her mouth. His tongue probed hers with delicate mastery, teasing the softness of her lips, her teeth, her tongue, until her bones turned to water and the last of her inhibitions drained away.

He nudged past the lapels of the dressing gown and found her breasts. His hands encircled their opulent fullness and caressed her sensitized nipples, sending shock-waves of longing tingling through her.

When at last he drew back they were both panting, and Polly realized when it came to kissing Tristan was the merest amateur.

'Polly . . .' David's voice was husky and his breathing shallow. 'Oh, for God's sake –'

He pulled her into his arms again and didn't try to speak for some time.

Polly had found her way under his Viyella shirt and had pulled it out of his trousers. David had already shed his jumper, but there were still these maddening little buttons between her and the wonderfully sculptured body she wanted to see as well as touch. Her fingers didn't seem to work as well as usual.

David took pity on her plight, and with a fine disregard for the consquences tore off his shirt and sent buttons pinging in all directions.

This was an improvement. She could now admire the dusky triangle of hair enhancing the curves of his pectorals. And she could see the definition of the muscles explaining the strength of his arms, and the width of his shoulders.

She explored his torso with her potter's hands, feeling the silk of his skin over the marble-hard musculature which proved that for a wine merchant he spent a lot of time keeping fit. Perhaps he worked out with weights.

But there was this belt round his waist, and the buckle kept sticking into her. Her fingers fumbled ineffectually, plucking at the silver pin.

When he swept her hands away she thought he was going to help her again and take it off himself, but he didn't.

'It's my turn.' He tackled the knot at her waist, first with his fingers then with his teeth, until at last he released it and pulled open her robe.

'Christ, you're beautiful.' His gazed roved reverently up and down her body, lingering over her full breasts, her rounded belly and the curve of her thighs beneath the darkness of her pubic hair. 'I've spent a lot of time lately thinking about your body. I didn't know the half of it.'

Embarrassed and flattered, she *felt* beautiful under his admiring gaze. 'Have you really been thinking about my body? I thought it was only Sheldon who did that.'

'I imagine almost every man you meet thinks about it.'

'I've always thought it was a shade too Rubensesque for modern tastes.'

219

'Don't fish for compliments. Rubens was an artist, and curves like yours will always be in fashion.'

He drew her legs across him so she was almost sitting on his lap. His lips hovered over her breasts before he took her nipples into his mouth one at a time. She arched her back so he had better access and sighed softly as he turned the whole of her front into an erogenous zone.

His fingers, which had been shadowing the actions of his mouth on her other nipple, began to wander below her navel.

Polly wriggled upwards, to encourage him in his downward path.

'I don't think this is a very good idea,' he breathed.

Something in Polly died a little.

'I think we'd be much better off upstairs.'

Polly gave a breathless laugh as he scooped her into his arms and got unsteadily to his feet. Then he strode out of the room and carried her upstairs.

When he finally dumped her on to the spare room bed, his chest was heaving and his breath was coming in short gasps.

'If you want to change your mind about this, now would be a good time to tell me.'

Polly slid under the duvet to find the sheet beneath her hot from the electric blanket.

'I haven't changed my mind.'

She almost lost her nerve as she watched David strip off his trousers and pants in one swift glissando. She only dared to take quick, covert glances at his member which rose so splendidly above the tautness of his stomach and the length of his thighs. It was like watching a Greek statue come to life – magical, but awesome, more than a little frightening.

But when he joined her in the warm bed, and she felt the silken caress of skin against skin, all her doubts and fears were swept away by simple passion. He pulled away the dressing gown so she was totally naked, and the duvet followed so he could admire her body with all the concentration of a connoisseur gazing longingly at a work of art.

His lovemaking was shocking. It was so intense, so lacking in the restraint which characterized him. His enjoyment of her body made her enjoy it too. Parts of her she had disliked, he worshipped. Parts she had ignored, he discovered, tended and brought to the peak of excitement. Under his caresses, his whispered exclamations at her beauty, she flowered, opening herself to him emotionally and physically.

And she was greedy for him. Once she'd got over the shock of the size of his penis, she wondered at it, stroked it and adored it. It was as if it was created just to satisfy the need which grew, like a tidal wave, slowly at first, but which culminated into a wordless, mindless, flood of emotion, and which left her panting out of control.

As she felt herself reaching an orgasm for the first time in her life, she clutched at him, digging her nails into his shoulders, scared of losing her mind, frightened of the way ahead.

He sensed her fear and soothed her, holding her tight, so the moment of fulfilment, essentially solitary, was triumphant. And afterwards he let her come down to earth safe in the strength of his arms.

Only after she had stopped shuddering did he finish his own journey, and, still inside her, slumped on her body, his sweat slicking against her own.

It was then she started to cry. At first the tears slid

from beneath her lids discreetly, but as emotion overcame her she started to sob in earnest. Her shoulders heaved, she hiccuped, she sniffed. Her whole safe world had collapsed about her, leaving her weeping in the wreckage. She was devastated.

'What's the matter?' Totally confused, he blotted her tears with the duvet, pulling it round her shaking shoulders.

She couldn't answer, but continued to gulp.

'Are you all right?' he asked a bit later.

She gave him a withering look. 'Of course I'm not all right!'

Now that she was able to speak, David felt it safe to leave her, and went to fetch a length of loo-paper from the bathroom. 'Here.' He handed it to her. 'Have a good blow.'

She blew, so that although she still felt the world shifting on its axis was no very good thing, she could at least breathe.

'What am I doing here, David?' she wailed.

'Crying your heart out. Or is that too obvious an answer?'

'You never make jokes. Don't break the habit of a lifetime now.' She trumpeted again into the soggy wad of tissue.

'Are you angry with me, Polly?'

She rounded on him. 'Of course I'm angry with you! What did you bloody well think I'd feel? Grateful?'

'Well – I never feel it's quite the done thing to ask, but I had got the impression you enjoyed yourself. Obviously I was wrong.'

'You weren't *wrong*,' she went on furiously. 'It was –

you were – marvellous. It's the situation I'm so upset about.'

'What situation are you referring to?'

'What situation do you sodding well think?' He was being so frightfully calm about it, she wanted to shock him into some sort of reaction. 'We are in bed together, isn't that situation enough for you?'

'It's more than enough.' He was still maddeningly unruffled. 'But why are you so upset? Are you worried you might get pregnant?'

The thought hadn't occurred to her. Now that it was thrust into her consciousness, she rejected it. 'Pregnant! Of course I'm not going to get pregnant! It's a ridiculous idea.'

'Why, are you on the pill?'

She was affronted. 'No. Why would I be?'

'Difficult periods, perhaps?'

Although he was the father of two sons, Polly found it difficult to imagine that David had ever heard of periods. She glared at him.

'I do realize I should have taken responsibility for the contraception,' he said. 'But I'm afraid I got totally carried away. And if I hadn't' – he almost smiled – 'I'd have felt a bit awkward knocking on Patrick's door to see if he could lend me a packet of three.'

'Patrick!' She was so horror-struck, she overlooked this lapse into jokedom. 'What is he going to say when he sees me at breakfast?'

'He's never up in time for breakfast.'

'But how would *you* feel if the situations were reversed, and he brought home a floozy for the night?'

'I hate to point this out, but he *did* bring home a floozy for the night. And I didn't object at all.'

'David,' snapped Polly. 'If you turn out to be developing a sense of humour, I shall cut my throat.'

'Are you worried about being unfaithful to that Cotswold Radio character?' In three words, he reduced Tristan to the status of a celebrity hand puppet.

'No.'

'So didn't you sleep with him after we left on Saturday night?'

'Kindly keep your nose out of my affairs, David.'

'Forgive me, this affair looks like belonging to me too.'

She looked at him in horror for a moment, then she started crying all over again, turning for comfort into the softness of the pillow.

After a moment, David got up. Polly waited to hear him leave the room, but instead she heard the water running in the bathroom. He came back a moment later.

'Polly, why don't you have a nice, soothing bath, and I'll make you some hot milk? You're obviously suffering from shock.'

A bath might well be a good idea. It couldn't wash away the past couple of hours, but it would soothe her aching body.

'Thank you,' she said into the pillow. 'That would be lovely.' She didn't move until she'd heard him go out.

Chapter Sixteen

The hot water embraced her. It was barely two hours since she'd had a bath, but she felt like she had climbed back into the safety of the womb after a violent shock in the outside world.

Somewhat to her surprise, her body still looked the same. The curves and hollows which had so delighted David still looked like the billowing thighs and the dimpled knees she had forced into her black jeans with such determination. Her breasts, floating about in the bubbles, which had contributed so freely to her downfall, were the same which threatened to black her eyes if she bounced too enthusiastically at aerobics.

Yet in herself, she felt she'd suffered a terminal blow to her equilibrium – a blow she wasn't sure she would recover from. But as she had no tears left, and while her mind was unclouded by the sobs and heavings of the previous fifteen minutes, she tried to analyse why she was so upset.

She hadn't been raped. She hadn't even been seduced; there'd been no courtship, no pleading, no gradual erosion of her resistance. If at any time she'd asked David to stop, he would have stopped. There'd been no moral – or should that be immoral? – pressure. So it wasn't that.

And she'd seriously considered sleeping with Tristan,

so it wasn't the thought of ending her years of celibacy which had turned her emotions upside down.

What she had to ask herself was, if she had gone to bed with Tristan, and it had been as mind-blowing, would she have been so thrown?

Polly rubbed her face on a towel, considering hard. Frankly, no. She'd *expected* Tristan to be good in bed. Beth had insisted that younger men were better – and even Bridget acknowledged that Tristan was sexy. If he had pressed the right buttons and got the right mechanical response, she would have coped.

But deep down, Polly had felt that sex with Tristan would probably have been just as much of a non-event as it had been in the tent in France all those years ago. So sleeping with Tristan would have only reinforced her prejudices and left her emotionally untouched.

So it was David who was at the cause of the upset. The thought of David, who had been so tender and caring, who had run her this bath, who had taken her to heaven and back, brought her anger back in a rush.

For thirty-five years, more or less, she'd been happily celibate, convinced that however much sex did for other people she could do without it.

And po-faced, stuck-up, stuffy old David Locking-Hill had had the brass neck to prove her wrong. He had seduced her on the sofa, swept her up to bed and dismantled her most firmly held convictions. How dare he?

And how, she demanded of her red-faced reflection, which stared back at her from the mirror tiles round the side of the bath, how had she let herself get into this ridiculous situation? She was such a bloody fool, she should be locked up for her own protection.

The word 'protection' caused another upheaval in her precarious emotional state. She *could* get pregnant – if not as easily as a seventeen-year-old girl, as easily as any careless thirty-five-year-old. Frantically she tried to remember where she was in her menstrual cycle. But without Bridget to refer to, she had no idea. She was probably slap bang in the middle.

One thing she did know, abortion was for other people. So was adoption. And could she possibly bring up a child on her own? And would her mother be half so thrilled to have a grandchild if it was born out of wedlock? On reflection, Polly decided she would. She'd make a big deal about it, but in the end she'd come up trumps, buy a pram and be as proud as possible.

Somehow this thought offered a smidgen of comfort to Polly.

'And I might not actually be pregnant,' she said aloud in the steam. 'And I can always ask Beth about the morning-after pill on Monday.'

Just how she'd slip this into the general conversation, along with asking Bridget when she was due for her period, she'd work out when she'd had some sleep.

She went back into the bedroom, swathed from head to foot in towelling in case David was waiting for a second round. He wasn't there, but she noticed that the sheet had been changed.

Exactly why had he done that? To spare the blushes of Mrs Danvers? Or had his wife been fastidious, and refused to sleep in the same sheets they'd made love in?

Taking no chances, she crawled into bed, still wearing the towels. There were enough sheets in that airing cupboard to keep a whole orgy from having to sleep on the damp patch.

David found her there a little later. He had obviously showered as his hair was damp and unusually ruffled. He was wearing a dark-blue towelling robe which stayed done up. She regarded it resentfully. If he'd lent her that, instead of that slithery thing, she'd be fast asleep right now, her world still intact. David was carrying a mug and a T-shirt.

He handed her the mug and put the T-shirt on the bed. 'I brought this for you to sleep in, in case you feel the cold.'

As if anyone who lived in her house could feel the cold in his centrally heated palace.

'And I found you a new toothbrush.'

'Thank you.' She couldn't meet his gaze.

'Is there anything else you're likely to need?'

She would desperately need some sort of moisturizer to put on her face, but it was unlikely he was able to provide it.

'No, thank you.'

He stretched out on top of the duvet next to her. 'Are you up to a bit of straight talking?'

'No.'

He ignored her. 'You reacted so strongly when I said the word "affair", I wondered if you'd been badly hurt by one.'

'No.'

'Is there anyone serious in your life at the moment?'

'No.' She sipped her milk.

'Then I was wondering if you'd like to come to France with me.'

'I beg your pardon?'

'I asked you if you'd like to come to France. On

business. I'd do the business, of course. You'd come along for the trip.'

'But – *why*? You've never as much as asked me out to *dinner* before.'

'I've got to go, and thought you might like to come too – no strings attached.'

Some distant memory of conventional good manners stirred. 'Um – David – it sounds wonderful – but I really can't get away from work now. And there's my cat and things . . .'

'Don't panic.' He picked up her hand and held it in his warm, dry one. 'You're perfectly entitled to refuse the invitation. I just didn't want not to see you for a whole month.'

'A month!' Polly freed her hand. She wouldn't see him for a whole month! For a moment she was devastated. Then she pulled herself together. 'I could never have gone away for so long. I thought you meant a long weekend.'

'But you still refused?'

'Yes. Not really – I mean –'

'It's all right, I understand. I don't have casual affairs either.'

'David, I don't have affairs at all.'

'Don't you, Polly? Then how do you feel about marriage?'

She couldn't have been more surprised if he'd asked her how she felt about suicide pacts, or more horrified. But it was important to consider her response. If she answered unguardedly, she may find herself saying something she'd regret.

'In general, or for me personally?'

'Both.'

'Other people can do what they like. I'm not getting married, not now, not ever, no how.'

He tucked a wisp of hair tenderly behind her ear. 'Fair enough. I take it you don't want me to spend the rest of the night with you?'

'No, thank you.'

'Then I'll say good night. Sleep well, little one. Don't forget to finish your milk.' He bent and kissed her cheek, then turned out the bedside light.

Polly lay in the dark, trying to sum up her thoughts. He was amazing. One minute he was the sort of sexual athlete she'd previously only read about in American doorstoppers, the next he was tucking her up and all but reading her a story.

How on earth did she get involved with such an anthropological freak? Bloody Melissa, that's how.

'That woman has a lot to answer for,' she said out loud. And then she fell asleep.

Polly heard someone, probably David, go past her door. She glanced at her watch and saw it was half past eight. Not late for a Sunday, but as she knew she had no chance of sleeping any more, and David might need to go somewhere, Polly thought she'd better get up. She felt numb, almost apathetic, as if she'd used up her entire stock of emotions and would have to wait for them to renew themselves before she could feel anything again. It was a restful state of mind.

She found her clothes were dry, but so stiff with mud she couldn't bear to put them on. But at least this time she had her underwear and David's T-shirt to wear under the dressing gown. She brushed her teeth and her hair, but had to rely for make-up on what she'd put on the evening before.

Her most pressing problem was her face, which after so much washing felt Sahara dry. She'd have to search the kitchen for whatever Mrs Danvers put on her hands after sanitizing the work surfaces and use that.

But Polly was heartily grateful that this apocryphal person was unlikely to roll up on a Sunday to cook David's bacon and eggs. And if he was like any other normal seventeen-year-old, Patrick wouldn't be up for hours. So it was only David she would have to face. And if he could produce a pair of jeans she could roll up a few times, she would ask him to drive her home.

The very thought of Sunday in her untidy little cottage, with her cat, the omnibus edition of the Archers and her old, happy-go-lucky celibate self disturbed her short-lived peacefulness and threatened to make her cry all over again. Would anything ever be quite the same? Now she had had a truly erotic sexual experience, could she go back to her spinster's life quite so happily?

David was cooking bacon when she came into the kitchen. He was wearing a pair of worn green cords, an open-necked shirt and bare feet. He looked up from the frying pan. 'Good morning, Polly. Did you sleep well?'

He seemed in an unnecessarily sunny mood, considering he couldn't have had more than five hours' sleep. He hummed softly as he went to the fridge for eggs. Polly could barely summon a smile.

'Are you being polite, or do you really want to know?' Her voice was husky. She never spoke before her first cup of tea if she could help it. And if David was going to spend the next hour oppressing her with civilities, she would ring up a taxi, direct it to Bridget's house, and ask her to pay. Right now.

'I really want to know.'

'Very well, actually,' she conceded grudgingly. 'Surprising though it may seem.'

'All that crying wore you out, I expect.'

Not only the crying. 'I dare say.'

'Are you hungry? – I really want to know.'

'I never eat breakfast.'

David shut the fridge door and crossed the room to her. He took her hands and drew her across to the kitchen table. He pulled out a chair and made her sit down.

'Polly, we could pretend that what happened last night didn't happen, but I think that's a little childish, don't you?'

Polly looked up at him with anguished eyes. 'Sometimes being childish is the only way I can cope with things. I'm sorry, but I'd prefer it if we did pretend it hadn't happened.'

He put his hands on her shoulders and started to massage them. 'But *why*? You admitted you enjoyed yourself. I think we could be great together.'

'In bed, do you mean?'

'Of course.'

How much 'greater' did he want it to be? 'Well, I did explain. I don't have affairs.'

'And if I suggested more than an affair?'

'What more is there? You're not suggesting we move in together, are you?' In spite of her distress, she couldn't help laughing.

He released her shoulders and went back to his bacon, which was spitting over the polished steel. 'No, not exactly. Perhaps you're right. Perhaps it would be better to pretend nothing ever happened. How many rashers of bacon do you want?'

He had an unnerving way of changing the subject practically mid-sentence, which lowered her resistance. If he was set on cooking her breakfast, it would be easier to give in and eat it.

She turned out to be surprisingly hungry, and ate the bacon, mushrooms, tomato and fried egg he put in front of her. She drank two cups of tea he made specially for her. She even managed a piece of toast.

'Anything else I can get you?' he asked, wiping the last of his toast round his eggy plate in a surprisingly human way.

'Some clothes would be nice. And if Mrs Dan- your housekeeper has any handcream or anything I could put on my face . . .'

'I can manage the clothes, but you'll have to ask Monica about the handcream yourself.'

It didn't seem quite right that David should refer to such an august figure as Mrs Danvers by her Christian name. And the thought that she might appear at any minute and discover the young master had a woman in the kitchen was truly horrifying. 'She doesn't come in on Sundays, does she?'

'Oh, yes. In fact, I think I can hear her now.' He got up from the table and went across to the window.

Panic-stricken, Polly joined him. Down the drive came a motorbike. On the back of it was a black-clad figure who would have looked at home at the party last night.

'That's your housekeeper?'

'That's Monica, yes.'

The motorbike stopped, the figure swung its leg over

the saddle, pulled out the stand with its booted foot and started to unbuckle its helmet.

'Why does she come in on a Sunday?'

'Double the money. She's saving up for a Harley. You know – the motorbike?' He put his hand under Polly's chin and gently closed her mouth. 'My old nanny used to say that was the way to catch flies.'

'I don't believe you ever had an old nanny.'

He assumed a hurt expression. 'But of course I did. She looked after my boys when they were babies, too.'

Polly heard the back door start to open, and in spite of Monica being as far from the Mrs Danvers of her imagination as it was possible to be, she still didn't want to be caught in David's dressing gown. 'Do you think you could find me something to put on?'

'In a minute. You must meet Monica first.'

'*No!*' she squeaked.

But it was too late. Monica, still in motor-biking leathers, strolled in. She had exchanged her boots for black socks and looked about nineteen. 'Hi, Dave. Hello!' she said to Polly.

'She calls you Dave!' Polly squeaked under her breath.

'Polly,' David drew her forward firmly. 'This is Monica. Monica, Polly. She rescued Patrick from the New Inn and brought him home.'

'Pleased to meet you. I heard there was going to be a rave up the New Inn last night. I wanted to go myself, but me mum couldn't look after me little girl, so I couldn't. Pity. I heard there was a terrific rumble – the police came and everything.'

'Monica, Polly's clothes got covered in mud. I don't suppose there's anything you could do about it?'

'What sort of clothes?'

234

'Oh, it's all right!' Polly insisted. 'I'll manage. The shirt'll be dry anyway, and I'm sure David will lend me some jeans.'

'I could give the shirt a quick wash and tumble dry it,' said Monica who, in spite of having the spiky, bleached hair of a punk seemed to have a very unspiky temperament. 'Where is it?'

'In the airing cupboard,' said Polly, deciding it wasn't for Monica's benefit that David had changed the sheet.

'Tell you what, David. I'll wash it out, and you take Polly round the garden while it dries. Then I'll get on. Don't suppose Patrick's up yet?'

Polly protested that she was quite capable of washing out her own shirt, but was ignored by Monica and David who were discussing what Monica should do for the rest of the day.

She was slipping out of the room, trying not to be noticed, when David stopped her.

'Get your clothes and give them to Monica, then I'll find you something to put on.'

If you're used to having servants to look after you, giving one a bundle of mud and asking for it to be washed would come easily. Polly felt very awkward about it. She fetched her clothes, and tracked Monica down in the drawing room. She was polishing the legs of a table, and was wearing a Walkman. The buzz which came from it seemed to indicate that Monica was into rap.

Polly cleared her throat. Monica switched off the Walkman at her belt.

'Here are my clothes. They're frightfully muddy, I'm afraid. But don't feel you have to wash them, I can easily do it myself.'

Monica took the clothes. 'Have you got a washing machine?'

'Well, no, but . . .'

'Then I'll put them on a quick wash.' She examined the shirt. 'That'll come out all right, but the jeans will need another go.'

'They're so dirty, I hate to ask . . .'

'If you'd washed rugby shirts what've been in a bag six weeks, you wouldn't call these muddy. Dave said something about you wanting some handcream?'

'It's for my face, actually. It gets terribly dry if I don't put moisturizer or something on it.'

'So does mine. I've got some Nivea. Any good?'

'Brilliant.'

'Come on, we'll get these put in the machine.'

She followed Monica's boyish figure along a series of corridors to what would now be called a utility room. It might have been an old dairy.

'Have you worked for David long?' she asked, as Monica twisted dials and poured in liquid detergent.

' 'Bout three years. Since I fell for my little girl.'

'Did you work for his wife?'

'Oh, no. She wouldn't have had anything to do with a punk like me.' She grinned. 'Dave's all right. He lets me sort out what needs doing, and I do it in me own time.'

'He told me you're saving up for a Harley.'

'Yeah, that's why I come in most Sundays. He doesn't mind, and me mum can look after the baby.'

'What's she called?' Polly would have bet money on Kylie.

And lost. 'Anne. She's a nice little thing. I'll show you some pictures if you come again.'

'Monica, I know it's really none of my business, but does David often –'

'Have women to stay? No, he don't. Pity. He could be quite tasty if he dressed right.'

Polly thought he was quite tasty dressed wrong, or even not dressed at all. 'So you wouldn't mind if he married again, or had someone to live with him?'

'Not if they didn't get in my way. Here's the Nivea. Will your shirt shrink if it goes in the tumble dryer?'

'I don't think so. It's very kind of you ...'

''Snot kind at all. I get paid for it!' Monica gave Polly another wide grin, picked up a duster and left.

It's just as well I'm not vain, thought Polly, when half an hour later she set off with David to visit the garden. She was wearing one of David's cashmere sweaters, a pair of his jeans pulled in with a belt and rolled up at the ankles, an old waxed jacket and a pair of wellingtons which Patrick had at school and which were still too big for her. Her own boots were still stuffed with paper in the Aga.

Next to her, David, who was going out for a formal lunch where he had to make a speech, had changed into a dark suit and white shirt. Which, a small part of her admitted, he looked wonderful in.

But when she saw the garden she forgot her scarecrow appearance. David led her out through the back door into a walled garden which would have once supplied fruit and vegetables to the house. There were still espalier fruit trees on the south-facing walls and there was an ancient glass greenhouse which on closer inspection was found to contain a vine.

'It's fantastic. Don't you love it? Who keeps all this up?'

David manoeuvred her out of the glasshouse, which was trailing cobwebs on his suit. 'Well, not Patrick and his brother, that's for sure. Angela liked garden design, but we always had gardeners to do the actual work. Now a firm comes in a few times a year to keep it tidy.'

It seemed a terrible waste that no one was interested in such a historic and beautiful garden. Keeping a garden tidy was not enough. But she didn't say so. In her experience men only gardened on television. Even then, she suspected there was a team of women who actually did the work after the programme was over.

He seemed surprised at her enthusiasm. 'Come and see the rest of it.'

He opened a gate in the wall and stood behind her as she gasped at the beauty of the view.

Lawns swept in voluptuous curves down to a ha-ha. Beyond it lay the most perfect wooded valley. Behind this rose a hillside clothed with trees and dotted with cottages of golden stone. These were connected to civilization by a network of roads so steep and so narrow Polly could hardly make them out. With leaves on the trees, they would only be visible when the sun shone on the windows of the houses.

He led her on a tour which included everything her gardening heart could dream of. Pleached hedges, south-facing walls, an arbour. There was even a herb garden planted in crescents and half moons round a fish pond.

She found primroses tucked under a rosemary bush six feet across. A pink viburnum smelled so sweetly that David broke off a sprig for Polly to tuck in the zip of her jacket. A drift of snowdrops, like a lake, led to a stand of beech trees. A patch of vivid irises etched in yellow and white made Polly exclaim in delight and fling herself to her knees, not noticing she was getting mud on David's trousers.

'And they smell, too! What variety are they?'

'I'm afraid I can't help you.'

Polly gazed up at him, enraptured. 'Any garden can look beautiful in spring or summer, but one like this, which enchants even at the end of winter, is worth all the rest put together.' She got up and brushed at the mud, ensuring it got rubbed well in. 'You're very lucky to live in such a beautiful place, David.'

'Am I? I've lived here more or less all my life. I suppose I just take it for granted.'

'You can't take such beauty-for-granted! It's wicked!' Then she remembered that his wife had died, and that under his stiff upper lip, and his fantastic sexual energy, he might be deeply sad. 'It can't be the same for you now Angela's dead,' she finished gently.

'No,' he confirmed. 'It's not the same. Perhaps I needed someone's fresh impressions to see it properly.' He took hold of her arm again. 'Come on, Polly, show me the rest of it.' She puzzled over this statement for a moment before saying, 'I'd like to inspect the outbuildings.' David guided her round the side of the house. 'These are the stables.'

A long, barn-shaped building, with loose boxes sufficient for at least half a dozen horses, were obviously no longer in use. Next to it there was huge tack room. There was an old tortoise stove which must once have made it extremely cosy.

'Did you and Angela ride? With such wonderful facilities, it would have been a shame not to.'

'I did, but Angela didn't and the boys have never

shown any interest. If I'd had daughters it would probably have been different.'

Polly laughed. 'It would have been if Bridget's little girl is anything to go by. She lives and breathes horses and ponies. I sometimes take her to the stables to ride. She certainly wouldn't let you get away with having all this empty.' Realizing she may have been tactless, and that doubtless David would have loved to have been twisted round a daughter's finger, she changed the subject. 'These would make fabulous workshops. You could let them out to local craftsmen. You'd make a fortune! But of course it would be an awful nuisance, having the place full of people.'

'Yes, but perhaps one, chosen person wouldn't be too intrusive.'

'No. Someone who makes jewellery, perhaps. Something nice and quiet.' Or a lucky, tidy potter who had no personal connection with the landlord.

'If it's not too difficult a question, what would you consider to be a reasonable rent?' David asked.

'For the whole stables, or just the tack room?'

'Would the tack room be big enough on its own?'

'Oh, yes, it's ideal. You could put in a new stove, if that one doesn't work. It's light. There's plenty of space for shelving.'

'So how much do you reckon?' She told him. 'And is that what you pay?'

She shook her head. 'Good Lord no, but my studio, the Shed we call it, is nothing like as large or luxurious. No, I could never afford premises like these, unfortunately.'

Then, suddenly worried that he might think she was angling for special treatment, she went on, 'If the Laureton Trust manages to buy the shops they're

240

threatening to pull down, I might get workshop space in there.'

'Will they buy them?'

'If they can raise the money.' She changed the subject. 'How is Patrick going to get his car back?'

'We'll take a can of petrol in my car and you can drive it home, if you don't mind. Or we could wake him up and make him come too. It's his own silly fault he ran out.'

'Oh, no.' Polly didn't want to spoil the congenial atmosphere between them by adding a recalcitrant adolescent. 'I'd be more than happy to drive his car back. Then I really must get home.'

David smiled. 'I'll fetch a can.'

Chapter Seventeen

❦

David switched off his car's engine, which purred into silence.

If he thinks I'm going to ask him in for coffee he's got another think coming, thought Polly. After experiencing the aseptic qualities of his house, no way was she going to let him in hers. She hadn't tidied so much as a mug since the dinner party, and Selina would almost certainly have ignored the catflap and disgraced herself, just to show her resentment at being left alone all night.

She ran hastily through a list of reasons why she couldn't invite him in and failed to come up with anything acceptable. And for some unknown reason, she suddenly wanted to put her arms around him, lay her cheek against his crisp white shirt front and feel the firm, warm flesh beneath.

'David . . .' she began, moistening her lips and scanning the car door for the handle. Like everything else about him, his car was unnaturally kempt, lacking the plethora of sweet papers, till receipts and car park tickets which littered her own.

And what did you say to the man who gave you your first orgasm? 'Thank you very much, I had a lovely time'? Polly fiddled with her seat belt, still trying to locate the handle. Whoever designed the car did not intend to allow its passengers a quick exit.

'Polly, I know we agreed that we'd pretend last night didn't happen, but I want you to promise me one thing . . .'

Oh God, he's going to make a speech about letting him know if I'm 'in trouble'. If ever you need money, just come to me . . . She'd *die* rather.

'What?'

'That if I ring up and invite you out to dinner when I come back from France, you won't burst into tears.'

She regarded him through narrowed, suspicious eyes. 'Why would you do that?'

'As a return match for the other evening, of course.'

'I think the scrambled eggs covered it. And the breakfast.' Not to mention what went on in between.

'Sorry, that doesn't count. It has to be a proper meal in a restaurant. So do you promise?'

Polly sighed. 'I promise not to cry, but I don't promise I'll accept your invitation.'

'Very well, I'll content myself with that.'

Then he swung his long body out of the car and came round to her side. Her door opened and she found herself drawn to her feet without making any effort to move. He propelled her up her garden path and came to a smooth halt at the front door, in spite of the roses and honeysuckle.

'Thank you for rescuing Patrick for me. For the second time.' Then he lowered his head and kissed her. It seemed to go on for a long time. Afterwards, as she watched him stride back down the path, she wondered if kisses like that could possibly be damaging to the ozone layer.

Polly let herself into the house and was instantly leapt on by Selina. After stroking her for a bit, Polly hitched

243

her up on to her shoulder and picked up a postcard which had been pushed through the door.

It was from Simon. It was telling her that she had been accepted as the non-guild member, and that the craft fair was in three weeks. For a moment sheer panic made her forget her other preoccupations, like her hungry cat or whether she was pregnant.

It was a terrific compliment to be chosen, but for a moment Polly felt as if she'd been given the lead in *Madama Butterfly* at Covent Garden – flattered but filled with doubt. Could she actually sing?

She went into the kitchen and filled the electric kettle before opening a tin of cat food. She'd have to have a cup of tea before she could face the cosmic shocks that life had thrown at her since yesterday.

She did craft fairs reasonably regularly. But this one was different. The whole thing was extremely prestigious. Only her very best work would do.

She put the tea bag in a mug and opened the fridge for the milk. Seeing the bottle, Selina miaowed loudly, demanding that the milk be given to her. Without thinking, Polly poured it into her dish and realized a moment later that there was no more.

'My brain's gone. It's had too many shocks in too short a space of time. My first orgasm and my first major pottery breakthrough in twenty-four hours.'

She stood in her kitchen, staring at a pile of washing-up that had been there for three days. Usually it just looked like a few dishes in a bowl of cold, greasy water. Now it looked like a symbol of her life so far. She had to get out of the house before she sank into a serious depression.

Her co-user wasn't always enthusiastic about using the

Shed on a Sunday and a hasty, pleading phone call convinced her that it was a cold, nasty place and she would be better off at home. The Shed would be free for Polly in an hour.

In that hour she forced herself to light the Rayburn and deal with Selina's protest statements. The washing-up could wait until there was some hot water.

Then she piled several more jumpers over David's cashmere and fled to her work for comfort.

The recently vacated Shed was warm. Polly should have been grateful, but somehow she was used to coming into it cold and warming it as she warmed herself and prepared her clay.

She pulled off her overcoat, her ancient Aran sweater with the unravelled cuffs, and the jumper her mother had knitted her which was too short and too wide, but left David's cashmere. It was light and unbulky, and as she somehow felt that her tumult of feeling was all his fault it would be poetic justice if she got clay on it.

She made tea, using a teaspoon of dried milk. She tidied her shelves. But still the energy of the place was wrong – or was it just different?

There was a large cardboard box of christening mugs and milk jugs and a couple of teapots. She picked up a coffee pot. It was part of a breakfast set, and each huge cup had a picture of a different farmyard animal on it, each one a comparatively rare breed. The pot bore a Gloucester Old Spot pig.

Polly held it in her hand, admiring it. It was a beautiful piece which should sell well. But looking more closely, she saw a tiny flaw in the glaze. No one would notice and if they did, well, slight irregularities were a feature of hand-made pots. But Polly watched, helpless, as her hand lifted the pot and flung it at the wall.

The noise as it smashed against the rough brick and the clattering as the shards landed on the floor had the effect of cold water on Polly's muddled spirits.

As she picked up the broken pieces she realized why she'd deliberately destroyed such a pleasing thing: her life had changed, her work needed to change too.

The artist in her wanted to smash all her pots, so she would be forced to create something entirely different for the craft fair. But she had struggled against penury for too long. Whatever new, as yet unconceived, creation she produced might be hopeless and might not sell. And while she mentally forbade herself to show any of her old stuff at the craft fair, she might need this to fall back on.

But she heaved the box into the lean-to which usually housed black plastic sacks filled with rubbish. She filled another box with every half-made pot she could find, so she wasn't remotely tempted to do a few mugs 'in case'.

When she went back into the warmth of the studio, it had become her space again. She collected three pre-wedged, weighed balls of clay and started kneading them together. The resulting lump might very well be too heavy for her to throw.

She had no idea what she was going to make, but the rhythmic pressure as the weight of her shoulders came down on her right wrist, the slow turning with her left hand, the press-release, press-release, was as soothing an activity as she could think of. She counted the turns. Only when she had reached a hundred and fifty did she consider the clay ready.

She detached her brain from the activity of her hands

and watched as they centred the clay firmly on the wheel and caused the ball to rise into a cone. She saw her left hand press outwards and upwards on the inside wall of the pot supported by the corresponding crooked forefinger on the right. What she was producing was three times the size of the two-pint jugs or teapots which were the largest things she usually made.

With a horrible fascination, she watched a large-bellied, narrow-necked vessel, which would be bound to 'squat' if she made the tiniest mistake, appear on her wheel.

Then she no longer left it to her potter's instinct. She applied her brain, stopped the wheel, and decided to build the rest of the pot by hand.

Two hours later she realized she had spent all afternoon producing a pot, albeit a pot like no other she had ever made and even to her own eyes utterly beautiful, which would take up the entire kiln.

She found a pencil-end and the back of a till receipt and worked out how many such pots she could make, glazed and decorated, by the craft fair. Even working long, late hours, stealing kiln time from her friend, she would be hard put to come up with more than six.

She was mad even to think of it. But she didn't think of it, she just decided that was what she was going to do – produce six beautiful, large vessels which would not be aimed at the casual buyer, would not have appealing animals on them, would not be remotely saleable except to those who wanted them as works of art. She was glad not to think about it, because it was such a ridiculous idea that she'd talk herself out of it in seconds.

As she drove home at midnight, stiff with cold and aching in every muscle, she wondered which was more ridiculous – the fact that she had gone to bed with David Locking-Hill and may very well be pregnant, or that she had turned her back on a very nice line of merchandise to produce 'art' – something she had always sworn not to do.

She took time off work the following day to go to the doctor. And the doctor, although she had never seen Polly before, listened to her embarrassed, halting, highly edited account of why she needed the morning-after pill.

Without further probing, the doctor explained how it worked, agreed that this was the best thing to do and wrote out a prescription.

After work Polly took the pill home, re-read the accompanying literature and then flushed the whole lot down the loo. Feeling a lot better, she made out a chart of roughly how many days there were before her next period as far as she could calculate and put the question of her possible pregnancy out of her head.

If she was pregnant, it was fate. She would accept it. And no doubt she would love the baby the moment it was born, and would one day be grateful to David Locking-Hill for turning her life upside down. Then she rang her friend to check that she'd already left the Shed and would have no objection to Polly using it. As she got in the car, Polly reminded herself that she never had any energy, either physical or creative, after a day at the café. She was mad to even attempt to do any work.

By the time she parked the car, she had convinced herself that what she was going to do was to drag back the boxes of finished pots she had so carelessly tossed into the lean-to. She had come to her senses, she would make proper, saleable items. After all, it was her coffee-sets and christening mugs for which Simon had got her a place at the craft fair. They probably had lots of 'artist' potters. They probably wanted someone producing things which you could use – for more than bunches of dried sticks. She should squash her huge pot and make something sensible with the clay.

But when Polly put the lights on and saw her pot drying nicely, she realized she couldn't. Something, probably David Locking-Hill, had forced her to free herself from her cosy, restrictive ways into a new, frightening, unpredictable way of working. And she couldn't go back.

With a sigh of resignation she started preparing the clay for the next day. She would quite likely work herself into a state of exhaustion and end up with nothing but enough glazed and decorated shards to drain several dozen flower pots. So much could go wrong, at any stage. Pottery always had an element of risk, but to increase the risk rather than minimize it was pure insanity.

Usually, before a fair, the days whizzed by her like scenery from a high-speed train. The struggle to produce enough work, the long hours she had to spend potting and the pleasure of being creatively occupied gave her a buzz like no other.

But this time, she just felt driven. She cut her days at the café down to two a week, haggled, nagged and bribed more studio time from her friend, and spent almost every waking hour at the Shed.

But however hard she worked, there was always fallow time – when she was waiting to open the kiln, stirring glazes, wedging clay – for her mind to wander back to the night of madness which had triggered off more, different madness.

She felt strangely lonely. She had no time or energy to socialize, but she wanted someone other than Selina to confide in, to share the success of her first firing, to tell that she had managed to make some huge plates, slip-trailed in the manner of Thomas Toft, with thick, basket-weave patterns. And she wanted someone to hug – not the sisterly, affectionate hugs she shared with her women friends, but a bone-crushing bear-hug, which would finish with a passionate kiss and would lead eventually to bed.

But in spite of this unfamiliar, aching emptiness, when Tristan turned up at the café a few days before the fair, looking incredibly charming and sheepish, Polly had completely forgotten the circumstances in which they'd parted. She was hard put to think of his name. He, on the other hand, had no trouble remembering hers. But then, as she'd remarked before, he was trained for it.

'Polly, you must hate me.' He leaned on the counter, the personification of a reformed, deeply apologetic rake. 'I would have got in touch before but I've been in Ireland, working on a programme.'

Polly felt so immune to his abundant charm, she smiled at him benignly. 'Of course I don't, Tristan, why should I?' Then it came back to her. 'I was a little hurt,' she fibbed. 'But I'm not one to hold a grudge. And I did abandon you.'

Relief flooded Tristan's handsome features. 'I feel such a heel. I never meant to be so long with that girl. But you did get home all right? I meant to ring . . .'

'Oh, I was fine.' Sort of.

'I really would like to make it up to you.'

Polly couldn't help feeling he'd put in an extra word by mistake. He actually meant, 'make up to you'. 'Do you?' she said.

'Really. I want to take you out. This Saturday. Somewhere nice. There's a place on the river.' He mentioned a restaurant much starred and frequently mentioned in the guidebooks. 'Are you busy this Saturday?'

She should have said 'yes', but some devil urged her to tease him a little.

'What's the assignment, Tristan?'

He was offended. 'No assignment, Polly.'

'Then how do you propose to get a table? That place is always booked solid.'

He grinned, his gold tooth winking jauntily. 'I had a cancellation. Do come. I owe you a decent meal after that fiasco.'

'I'll think about it, Tristan.' Saturday was the day of the craft fair. She would certainly need a square meal afterwards, but was an evening of Tristan's ebullient company too high a price for white truffles and quails' eggs? She didn't want to commit herself. 'I may be busy. Can I ring you?'

'Sure.' He jotted a number on the back of a printed card. 'This is where I'm staying in Laureton – in case you've lost my number.'

'Fine.' Polly tucked the card in her pocket. 'I'll be in touch, then.'

'Make sure you are.'

His smile smouldered so hotly, Polly feared for her plastic apron. He was the very picture of a man who had had his cake and now wanted his rum baba. Did she really have the energy for him?

The telephone was ringing as Polly got through her door that evening. If it was Tristan harassing her, she'd give him a flea in his ear. Selina always had plenty to spare. She was too tired to make definite decisions.

She let the phone ring while she took off her coat and pulled a pile of papers off the chair. It was probably her mother. Polly hadn't spoken to her for ages and felt guilty, but dreadfully tired at the prospect of describing her activities in a way that would satisfy her mother's anxious, inquisitive heart.

It was Melissa. 'Polly, can you come to dinner on Saturday?'

No way. Certainly not. Frightfully short notice. 'I'm dreadfully sorry, Melissa, I can't.' She'd rather risk a sordid struggle in Tristan's car than face another of Melissa's tastefully selected gathering of friends, especially after a day on her feet. And that was saying something.

'You're not going out, are you?' Melissa didn't sound her usual efficient self, in fact she sounded agonized.

'I've got a craft fair on, and I may well have to go out. If I don't, I shall need an early night.'

But Melissa was clearly too desperate to take the hint. 'It's just that I've invited David Locking-Hill's son, Patrick, to stay, and I can't think who to invite with him.'

'But isn't Patrick quite young?' Polly couldn't remember how much she was supposed to know.

'A teenager. I wouldn't have asked him, but I promised David I'd keep an eye on him while he is in France. You know, to help him stay out of trouble, after he was expelled from school. So I invited him to stay the weekend. I didn't think he'd come.'

'But he's going to?'

'Only for dinner and the night on Saturday, thank God. And between you and me, Polly, it's probably only because he's eaten all the freezer meals the housekeeper made, spent the money David left on drink and is after a free feed.'

Highly likely. Polly was surprised how much Melissa had picked up about 'Youf Today' since they'd last talked. 'Oh, surely not.'

'You'd never think he was David's son. He's a real layabout. He never opens his mouth except to eat, and grunts whenever you ask him a question.'

Polly could imagine it. 'He sounds awful. I can't think why you invited him.'

Melissa sighed deeply. 'I feel I owe it to David. It's hard for him bringing up those boys on his own. And Angela was my best friend. But quite frankly' – Melissa snapped out of her reverie of dutiful self-sacrifice – 'I'm beginning to regret it. So I thought I'd ask you to help me entertain him.'

'It's a very flattering invitation . . .'

'Oh, don't tease, Polly. I can't think who else to ask, and I need *someone* to support me.'

'What about Sheldon? I mean, you don't have to organize a whole dinner party for him, do you? Cook a huge shepherd's pie and let him eat it in the kitchen.'

'No! That would be even worse! I feel so awkward if people don't speak, and I never know what to say to young people. You're so good with them.'

'I'm not really. And I'm sure you're worrying about nothing. You could send out for pizza or something, and a gory video, then you wouldn't have to make conversation.'

'I couldn't possibly! What would David say?' His good opinion was clearly extremely important to her.

'Does it matter? He obviously thinks Patrick is old enough to be left on his own. It's very nice of you to ask him at all. David's hardly going to complain if you don't lay on a huge great reception for him.'

Melissa sighed again. 'Oh, please come, Polly,' she pleaded. 'You could bring that charming Tristan we met at your house.'

A smile began to creep its way across Polly's mouth. Exposing Tristan to Melissa's deficient entertaining skills was about on a par with him exposing Polly to the New Inn et al. It would be an elegant revenge, one which would ensure that Tristan got out of her life for ever, with no hard feelings on either side. 'Could I? Well –'

'I'd be eternally in your debt, really.'

It was hard to resist a plea for help – especially from Melissa, who'd probably never issued one before.

'Okay, Melissa, I'll come.'

'I don't suppose you'd stay the night? Then you can be there at breakfast . . .'

'No, Melissa.'

'But you will ask Tristan?'

'I'll ask him, but I can't promise he'll accept.'

'Oh, good. With both of you there, I'm sure the evening will go swimmingly.'

As Polly expected, Tristan jumped at the chance of seeing Melissa and Sheldon's cosy corner of Millionaire's Hollow. He may well have been equally eager to avoid paying for a meal at a notoriously expensive restaurant. But Polly doubted this; it was unlikely he was going to pay anyway.

Now all Polly had to do was to decide whether to be

open about staying at David's house that night. She could bundle David's clothes into a bag and say, 'Here you are, Patrick, give these back to your father for me.'

Or she could ring Patrick and warn him to say nothing about it.

Eventually, although lying made her nervous, she decided on the latter course.

Because if Melissa found out that Polly had twice rescued Patrick from a difficult situation, she would be achingly jealous and Patrick's life would be made miserable by her attempts to outdo Polly. What Melissa didn't know wouldn't hurt her. Besides, Polly was in no hurry to return David's clothes. His jumper was wonderfully warm.

She had just come to this conclusion and was leafing through the telephone book when the phone rang again. This time it was her mother.

'Darling?'

'Hello, Mummy, are you all right?'

'Bit down, actually. Audrey's gone on a cruise and I'm feeling rather at a loose end.'

Audrey was Sylvia Cameron's bosom pal. 'Will she be gone for long?'

'Another couple of weeks. In fact, I was wondering if I could come and stay.'

'With me? When had you in mind?'

'Tomorrow.'

'Tomorrow!' This was all a girl needed to send her to the loony-bin. 'Oh, darling, I'm frightfully busy. There's a craft fair on this weekend, I'm working every hour God sends and I'm going out to dinner on Saturday evening.' She hesitated. 'Though I suppose I could always cancel that.'

'Where were you going?'

'Melissa's.'

'Oh, you can't possibly put Melissa off, she's been so good to you.'

'Has she?' Good at getting her into a whole heap of trouble.

'Of course. Your social life's come on no end since you two met up again.'

Sometimes Polly wondered if her mother knew her at all, but then realized it was probably Melissa she didn't know. When Sylvia had last seen her, Melissa had read pony books, had glossy plaits and excellent manners. Nothing else about her had penetrated.

'That's nice of her to ask you,' her mother went on. 'I thought when you had them the evening hadn't gone very well.'

'No, it didn't, but she's got – a young friend to stay, and she thought I could help entertain him. She said I could bring Tristan.'

'Tristan?'

'You know, I told you. I've been out with him a couple of times.'

'He's not that nice one with the double-barrelled name?'

'No. He's the one in local radio.' And how do you know David's nice? You haven't met him.

'Well, I could always stay at home while you two go out. What a pity you haven't got a television set. Still, I could always do the mending.'

Polly closed her eyes. 'That sounds terribly dreary. Why don't you come *next* week? I won't be so busy and we could have a nice time together.'

'The thing is, the men are coming in to fix the central

heating next week and I have to be around to supervise. It's really this week or nothing.'

At almost any other time Polly would have remained firm with her mother, explained this week was totally out of the question and suffered a month or so of her mother's hurt feelings. But she couldn't help remembering that she might need her mother on her side in the near future.

The answer was simple. She'd get Melissa to let her bring her mother. While she didn't usually relish sharing her social life with her nearest relation, her mother could hardly spoil a dinner party already destined to be as roaringly successful as the last couple she'd been at.

'I tell you what, Mum . . .'

'I wish you wouldn't call me that, darling. It's so common.'

'. . . I'll give Melissa a ring and ask if you can come too. I'm sure she'd be delighted to see you.'

'Oh, sweetheart, that would be delightful. But please don't put Melissa out. I can easily stay at home.'

'No, no, Mummy, I wouldn't hear of it. Let me telephone Melissa and I'll ring you back.'

'Darling, I'm so looking forward to seeing you.'

Melissa was delighted at the prospect of seeing Polly's dear mother again. When Polly finally escaped, she found out David's number, and tried to phone Patrick, but he wasn't in. She left a message on the answer-phone asking him to ring her and retired to the bath.

Chapter Eighteen

'So where's your work?'

It was seven o'clock in the morning. Simon had arrived to take Polly and her pots to the craft fair in his van.

'At the Shed. I didn't want to bring it home.'

It was early enough for Simon not to be annoyed by this bit of information since there was plenty of time. But he was surprised.

'Why not?'

'My mother's staying. Please don't wake her up.'

Simon grinned. 'She never did like me. But what's wrong with your stuff? Have you painted scenes from the *Kama Sutra* on a tea-set? I'm not sure the guild would like that.'

Polly shuddered. She still hadn't managed to rid herself of the notion that indirectly sex had had something to do with her change in potting style. It was one of the reasons she hadn't brought her pots home. She hadn't the energy to go through a lot of made-up explanations to her mother. 'No. Come and see. The Shed's on our way, anyway.'

Polly picked up the plastic box of sandwiches that her mother had insisted on making for her, and the flask of tea. Polly wouldn't drink the tea, but it had pleased her mother to do something practical for her daughter who, she said, was looking quite grey with tiredness.

When Simon saw her six pots and six huge plates, he didn't speak for a long time. Polly concentrated very hard on peeling flaking paint from the walls with her thumbnail. There was more of herself in those six pots and plates than in every mug or jug she'd ever made before. She respected Simon's judgement. He was an artist, not a potter, but he knew what was good and what was merely self-indulgent.

Half thrown, half hand-built, the pots were over two foot high. They had been dipped in a yellow-gold glaze as warm and transparent as amber. The glaze was not entirely even, and in some parts seemed to Polly to have the depth and intensity of an Italian sun. It was the first time she had made anything which didn't have an obvious use. She could have made them into bread crocks, but giving them handles or lids would have added to the time they took to dry out. But they were strong enough to put things in and were firm on their bases – practicality hadn't given way to art completely.

In contrast to the extreme simplicity of the pots, which relied on their shape and rich glaze for their beauty, the plates were highly decorated with trailed slipware. A stylized horse with an arched neck and flowing mane pranced in the middle of each one. The edges were criescrossed with thick white slip. It was a haphazard, primitive design which depended on quick, bold strokes. None of the careful painting which went into her tea-sets would do here.

'Mmm,' said Simon eventually. 'How much are you charging?'

She produced a handwritten sheet. The prices on it

terrified her, but each of the pots had had to be fired separately. If she didn't sell them, she wouldn't be able to pay for the electricity. And yet no one would pay that for a pot. No one *could* pay enough for the pain that had gone into their creation, the long, long hours she had worked, checking, waiting, praying. By rights they should be tortured, agonized shapes –

Yet as she looked at them through the critical eyes of Simon, she saw simple, happy pots which would grace any room in any house.

Simon took out a pen and added noughts and ones to Polly's figures. 'Good girl,' he said. 'I knew you wouldn't let me down. Now, let's get them loaded up.'

Having done so, they set off in Simon's van away from the hills to where the Severn flattened out the landscape.

After the strain of production, Simon's uneffusive but genuine approval was enough to make Polly decide that, come what may, she would enjoy the craft fair.

The financial consequences if she didn't sell anything were unthinkable, but she had crossed a personal Rubicon and she had no anxiety left over for anything else.

When they arrived at the stately home which was the setting for the craft fair, Polly discovered that the fair was divided. Most of it was the general run-of-the-mill craft of which she was usually part. But the owner of the house, whose daughter was a glass engraver, wanted a section of the fair devoted to 'art'. And thanks to Simon, Polly now found herself in this section.

'So why have the guild decided to let in the likes of me?' asked Polly, patiently holding up a picture which Simon was trying to hang.

Simon made a tiny mark with a pencil and took the

mirror plate out of his mouth. 'A couple of our main potters have got major exhibitions on elsewhere. And there's all this space to fill.' He gestured to half a tent, which, at half past eight in the morning, only had three lots of exhibits: Polly's pots, Simon's seascapes and a great deal of engraved glass.

'It was kind of you to ask me, Simon.'

Simon looked at her speculatively for a moment, and Polly was suddenly terrified that he was going to try and restart their long-defunct relationship.

If he had been going to, something about Polly changed his mind. He was very intuitive. 'Just giving a fellow artist a helping hand.' He kept his gaze intently on her. 'You know, there's something different about you, Polly. What is it? I wonder.'

Go on wondering, thought Polly, behind a particularly bland smile. 'It's probably because of my change in style. I'd got awfully inhibited by those little saleables I always did.'

That should have been enough explanation for an artist, but it wasn't. 'Yeah, but what made you change it, just like that? You'd been making mugs for ages. Are you seeing someone?'

Literally she wasn't and shook her head. But she wondered for the millionth time how much her volte-face could be put down to her encounter with David. Simon, a man, and therefore convinced that no woman could be fulfilled without a man in her bed and her life, would no doubt say David was totally responsible. Personally, she was happy to credit him with that first coffee pot, flung against the wall in sheer frustration. After that her inspiration was entirely her own.

261

'It's probably my age, Simon. Oh look, there's Rhoda with her silver. I'll go and give her a hand.'

The setting-up of a show was Polly's favourite part. She loved watching the marquees and tents change from mere stretches of canvas, coir matting and trodden grass into little rooms, each one representing the work and character of its occupier. They ended up as varied and individual as people's houses, in spite of the fact that the basic dimensions were the same.

'Hello, Rhoda,' said Polly.

Rhoda, who was elderly, looked like a television grandma and bred Yorkshire terriers, regarded Polly rather severely. 'Hello, dear. Are you in with us today?'

Polly nodded apologetically. 'It's something to do with the space. They wanted another potter in here.'

Rhoda looked across at Polly's pots which were displayed on a simple structure of planks and bricks. 'Is that your work?'

'Well, yes. A bit of a departure from the usual, I know.'

'Mmm. You'd be better to stick to what you know. It's foolish to start changing your style.'

Polly shrugged and smiled. 'Did you bring any of your dogs today, Rhoda?' Polly's confidence was usually fairly precarious, but as Simon had approved of her new style, and she had always considered Rhoda's silver dogs and cruet sets the epitome of dullness, she was unmoved by Rhoda's lack of enthusiasm.

'No, Petronella's in season and Peregrine's unwell. I've left them with Daddy.' She was referring to her husband.

'Oh, I'm sorry,' said Polly, grateful that she wouldn't have to spend all day watching people gooing over dogs that might snap at any moment. 'Would you like any help?'

Rhoda, who hid amazing, wiry strength behind a veneer of fragility, gave Polly a valiant smile. 'Thank you, dear. That would be kind.'

Rhoda's silver looked at its best on yards and yards of blue velvet which Polly wanted to wear. But instead of draping it around herself, she obligingly draped and pinned it over the series of boxes on which Rhoda displayed her work. As well as Yorkshire terriers, in all sorts of endearing postures, Rhoda made a lot of small silver birds – robins, wrens and tits – which peered irritatingly at you from burnished eyes and cost an enormous amount of money. Polly imagined they mostly became expensive, unwanted wedding presents, and were kept permanently in their boxes, not nice enough to pass on, too valuable to give to a tombola.

Once Rhoda was happily established, her ancient vacuum flask and *The Yorkshire Terrier Year Book* at the ready, Polly excused herself and went to see how the rest of the setting-up was going.

She walked out into the March morning. A silvery sun, filtered by layers of cloud, shone with restrained determination, melting the mist which had billowed from hedges earlier.

The house was a handsome, locally designed building which included an orangery. It was saved from its rather austere proportions by the beauty of the soft, pinky-grey bricks of which it was built. The gardens were huge but well under control, like a well-trained guard dog. Neither house nor garden showed any tendency towards bad taste, like Cannongate Manor. But both houses lacked something that David's house had in abundance. Whether it was the southerly aspect, the golden stone or its owner Polly didn't take time to consider. For a craft fair, this house was perfect.

Narrow sections of tent ranged in three sides of a rectangle in a paddock at the side of the house. The space in the middle was taken up by a few hardy, well-insulated outside exhibitors. Fences made of elastic, wicker sculpture and 'poolside art' enlivened the usual range of garden gates and wrought-iron work while their creators breathed warm breath into the cold air and hugged their hands round steaming mugs.

A few very expensive antique dealers had space in the house itself, but everyone else, condemned to trade al fresco, felt their work was flattered by the grandeur of the setting.

Polly walked round the marquee to the less high-falutin end of the event. Here were the food stands selling everything from homemade fudge and sparkling apple juice to flavoured coffee beans and cured chitter-lings. These were laid out daintily on a tray by a pretty girl in a striped apron and boater. They were plaited together into ropes, and were, according to the girl, eaten just as they were, pink and revolting.

'You don't actually eat those things, do you?' asked Polly, with horrible fascination.

The girl smiled and shook her head. 'But then I don't eat the sausages either. I'm a vegetarian.'

Polly worked her way through the food stalls, meeting old craft-fair hands and tasting cubes of hand-made cheese. This was the time when people exchanged news and gossip, boasted of successes and toned down their failures.

She emerged, smelling strongly of a sample of the ambiguously named 'Countryside Scent' with which she had misguidedly sprayed herself, at the stall of an old friend.

This stall was sheer Enid Blyton fantasy. Its owner had created a 'forest floor' with greengrocer's grass and modelling clay. Miniature 'woodland creatures', mostly Squirrel Nutkin lookalikes, rabbits and owls, peeped from behind mossy logs and clay toadstools. A tiny battery-driven stream gurgled merrily over tufa rocks. Lanterns made from Christmas tree lights hung from the branches of a gnarled old oak tree, which was once the inside of a roll of carpet.

Everything displayed was created from 'nature's bounty', which actually meant wool pulled off barbed-wire fences, feathers from dead birds and a lot of mossy old sticks and pine cones.

'Polly, me old fruit. I thought you'd given this effing craft fair a miss!'

The creator of these lucrative flights of fancy used language which was as earthy as her raw materials, but a lot less whimsical.

She was very tanned and wrinkled, and wore an aggressively hand-knitted sweater the colour of slurry and a pink cotton headscarf. These, with her bright eyes and curly grey hair, made her look very like the sweetly pretty animals she sold in such numbers.

'I'm up the other end,' said Polly guiltily. 'Goodness knows why they put me there.'

'Oh.'

Polly sensed a slight withdrawal of the woman's warmth. 'So, how are you? Husband still giving you a hard time?'

This was the right question. Any coldness vanished as the woman started on her favourite subject.

'Who does he think I am? "The Elves and the effing Shoemaker"?' the woman demanded, not expecting an answer. 'I'm not working my arse off night and day just to make enough for stuffing and paint! Not to mention the effing hundred quid for the stall. So when he told me there was a three-day event coming up, I told him what he could effing do with it. How are you doing, Polly dear?'

'Well –' Polly always thought of her as 'Effie' and found it difficult to remember her real name, which was Cynthia. Fortunately Cynthia interrupted before Polly could make a fatal slip.

'How did you get your stuff here?' Cynthia was extremely nosy, but also extremely kind. You couldn't take offence at her inquisitiveness any more than you could at her language.

'Simon Kepple gave me a lift in his van. But if I'd had to hire one, I don't know if I could afford to come.'

'But your stuff always sells.'

It was true. Lots of people came to craft fairs for a day out, if the weather was neither too hot nor too cold. And most of them wanted to buy something. They often didn't mind much what it was, as long as it wasn't too expensive and not difficult to carry home. If they weren't the type to buy two baby rabbits huddling together under an oak leaf, they had previously often managed to find just the thing for their goddaughter or friend or mother-in-law on Polly's stall.

But she was unlikely to attract that sort of market now her creations cost three figures. Polly stared glumly at a mole coming out of a woollen hole, regretting the boxes of doublehandled christening mugs, animal napkin rings and brightly painted milk jugs which could now be turning themselves into the electricity and materials she had squandered in the cause of 'personal expression'.

'I don't know if it will this time. I've rather changed my style.'

'Have you, dear? Why did you do that? If you've got a good selling line, you're best to stick to it. You don't think I like making cutsie-wutsie animals out of cowpats, do you? But they pay the effing bills.'

'I know –'

'Oh, look,' said Effie. 'Here come the effing public, bless 'em. And there's an effing punter wanting another stuffed owl for their effing niece, if ever I saw one. See you, love.'

'See you, Cynthia.'

Polly stayed long enough to watch her foul-mouthed friend be perfectly charming to the woman in question and eventually wrap the largest of her stuffed owls and slip the money into the leather bag she wore round her neck.

I bet she's making an effing fortune, thought Polly before regretfully returning to her own works of art and the more genteel conversation of Rhoda.

Her initial euphoria caused by Simon's approval had worn off. Effie was right. She'd had a good line, she should have stuck to it.

She rubbed her arms for comfort as she walked through the stalls. Somewhat defiantly she'd put on David's cashmere jumper again, having discovered for herself why such things were so expensive and so desired. It was because they were so warm. Which, she insisted, was why she was wearing it. Not because it was his, and the smell of his aftershave clung to it.

No one had yet got past the stalls of wooden 'treen'

flower pots and love-spoons, papier-mâché plates and pokerwork firescreens to the 'arty' end. Polly wondered if they ever would.

But when she saw her pots, golden in a shaft of artificial sunlight courtesy of one of Simon's spotlights, her spirits lifted a little. They may have been a ghastly mistake, but they were beautiful.

Craft fairs always made her want to eat. It was all right when she was busy, but in the inevitable lulls (and this one threatened to be all lulls) she yearned for sugary things. She should have been grateful that today the homemade sweet stall was too far to walk for the privilege of having your fillings pulled out. But she felt deprived of her sugar fix.

She got out her neatly made sandwiches and offered one to Simon, who was deep in *The Deptford Trilogy*, and started on the rest. Rhoda was too self controlled to eat her lunch before one o'clock, and the glass engraver had still not shown up.

Polly was beginning to wonder if she could creep under Rhoda's blue velvet and catch up on some of the sleep she had missed over the past weeks when a man appeared.

He wore a dark-blue overcoat and shiny London shoes. Although he looked out of place among the Barbours and tweed jackets which were beginning to throng the fair, he examined her pots with professional thoroughness.

'Hello,' she said, blowing crumbs of ham sandwich at him. 'Can I help you?'

He ignored her enquiry and Polly finished her sandwich in peace, idly wondering whether David would eventually go bald, like this man had, and if he did would it make him any less attractive?

She was halfway through her third sandwich when the man came up to her. He had looked at each pot and plate with enormous concentration and now he applied that concentration to her. Then he produced a card.

She put the card in her pocket, and met his gaze.

'Is this all?' he asked.

Polly forced back her apologetic explanation. 'Yes.'

'And how long did it take you to produce it?'

This was usually a difficult one. Not this time. 'Three weeks.'

'So you're slow?' He sounded disappointed, and started to move away.

'No!' She called him back with urgency in her voice. 'I'm quick, really. I'm just part time. I have a job, and a shared workshop.'

'Pity. I'm on the lookout for high-class pottery for one of the big London stores. But we'd need to have things on a regular basis.'

If only he wouldn't be so discreet, and tell her which London store.

'Presumably you'd want the same stuff all the time?'

'Oh, no. Of course, there are bound to be orders, but the whole point of this section of the shop is that everything is original and individual. You could make what you liked, as long as you kept your spot full.'

It sounded too good to be true.

He went on: 'I was wondering if you ever did anything big, or do you like to keep things manageable?'

Big? What did he mean by big? These were the biggest things she'd made since she'd left college! She could see that Simon had put down his book and was mentally urging her to great things.

'Oh no, I *yearn* to build something a decent size. But I'm restricted by only having a small kiln. I can't afford to fire it with only one or two big pieces in it.'

'It's a shame. You'd do well. Couldn't you get a loan to set yourself up properly?'

Polly shook her head. 'Not really. I haven't the collateral.'

'What would you make if you were free to do anything?'

She made a wide, expansive gesture. 'Oh – pots big enough to hide Ali Baba's forty thieves – garden urns – bowls two foot across. I want to try raku – you know? When you bring the pots out while they're still white hot, and bury them in sawdust or water. You get fantastic glazes.' She ended on a deep sigh. 'It's hard to do in the back garden of a small cottage.'

The man was too businesslike to be sympathetic, but his expression definitely softened.

'It would be a shame if you never managed to reach your full potential. But if your situation should alter, let me know. You've got my card.'

'Thanks.'

Polly watched him work his way down the aisle. He would probably find another potter whose work was original and geared to what people wanted to buy, and who had a kiln the size of a house. Not for a long time had she so minded being poor.

Unable to face either Simon or Rhoda, who were looking at her with blatant curiosity, Polly said, 'I must get a drink. Anyone else want one?'

She galloped to where a couple of gallant souls sold

drinks and snacks in aid of an environmental charity as fast as she could, given that there were a few hundred people in her way, all of whom had to be got past politely in case they were potential customers.

On her way back, partially revived by a couple of gulps of hot chocolate, she related her sad tale to Effie.

'It's good news really, it shows my work is good enough to sell in the London shops. But how can I possibly afford to make any more big stuff without something to pay the bills with?'

Effie offered her a rusty tin containing miniature paving slabs studded with porridge oats.

'It's always the effing same. You need a bob to make a bob, but how do you get hold of the first effing bob? Couldn't your mum lend you any?'

'She needs all her capital to live on, and she's very good to me really. I couldn't ask her.'

'Something'll sort itself out, you'll see.' Effie patted her hand. 'What you need is a nice man who's willing to keep you.'

No, I effing don't! thought Polly, secretly furious, wondering if a day spent in Effie's company would permanently disbar her from polite society. 'Like yours does, Cynthia?'

Effie laughed, revealing much-filled nicotine-stained teeth. 'No, ya silly girl, I said *nice* man. And a rich one.'

Effie was right, of course. Marriage to a rich, indulgent man would be the answer. But although a man who was certainly the former sprang easily to mind, she doubted if he was in any other way suitable. She tried hard to put thoughts of him out of her mind.

But stubbornly they lingered, and almost as tenacious

271

as the memory of his sensitive fingers and strong, muscular body, were his stables.

In her head she had already converted them. She had installed a wood-burning stove, put up a whole wall of wide, deep shelves and fitted a sink with hot water as well as cold. What a pity David didn't know about it.

In theory, she wouldn't have to marry him to get her hands on a workshop next to a peach-covered wall. He might easily decide to convert the stables himself, and then she could rent one.

Here painful reality crept in, like a leaking hot-water bottle in a warm bed. Even if she could somehow afford the rent on a place like that, it would be too far for her to travel. At least with the Shed she could call in on her way home from work, if she needed to. And she could barely afford to rent that – half of that.

The man's card, still tucked in her pocket, became like a cruel joke. Without capital, she could do nothing. And unless her circumstances changed she would never get any capital.

Her lifetime's ambition was thwarted for the want of a few thousand pounds. Her resolution to enjoy the fair come what may dissolved into tiredness.

She watched enviously as Simon sold a picture to a man who had been in the Navy. He and his wife were retiring to the seaside and wanted the right sort of picture, ready to hang. It was a pity they didn't want the right sort of pot ready to put things in.

She spent the rest of the day hatching up unlikely schemes for obtaining vast sums of money. The trouble was she was temperamentally unsuited to safe-breaking, and her maths wasn't up to embezzlement. The only practical thing she could do was to make a piggy bank and cut back her meagre expenditure still further. Simon was doing no better so they decided to pack up early.

'Just hand me up that last one, Simon,' Polly called over her shoulder.

'How much is it?'

Polly turned round in irritation. Its price was of purely academic interest now. She'd have to give her pots and plates away as presents.

But instead of seeing Simon standing there with a pot in his hand, it was the man from London, his shoes as shiny as his pate.

'Er – hang on, I'll look.' Polly plunged her hand into her pocket, brought out the scrap of paper and made a hasty deduction before telling him.

The man smiled. 'You'd get more for them if you sold through a London shop. But as I'm buying this for my own collection, I'll accept the discount.'

He hefted the pot into his arms and pulled out his wallet. Polly watched, fascinated, as he handed her enough notes – thanks to Simon's inflated notion of her worth – to cover the electricity and have some over.

She was so dazed she hardly said goodbye to him. She could do it. She had sold a pot to a real, discerning person. She was a potter.

Chapter Nineteen

Polly was in ecstasy all the way home, until they passed the condemned buildings. Then she had a severe attack of conscience. Perhaps she should give the money to the fighting fund. Although it was unlikely actually to tip the balance, every contribution brought the protesters nearer to success.

She discussed her dilemma briefly with Simon. He told her she was an idiot and changed the subject.

Her mother was waiting for her when Simon dropped her home. Out of respect for Sylvia Cameron, he declined to come in. Polly, who was still smarting from his reaction to her selfless notion, was grateful.

She was also grateful she wasn't obliged to explain to her mother how it was that although she had come home with a large amount of money, she had actually sold only one item. For some reason she didn't want to explain that she had given up making christening mugs.

There was a pot of tea on the newly cleared table, and a plate of egg and cress sandwiches. Polly kissed her mother fondly.

'Oh, Mum! My favourite! How lovely! I'm starving, and God knows what time we'll eat tonight. You are a dear.'

Sylvia Cameron smiled and patted her hair. 'I thought

you'd be tired,' she said, gratified. 'And I remembered you like egg and cress.'

'Lovely!' She put another dainty triangle into her mouth. 'And I can never wait for the mixture to go cold before I eat them.'

'Don't talk with your mouth full, Polly dear. Have a cup of tea.'

When Polly had eaten all the sandwiches, and thoroughly enjoyed being treated as if she'd just got in from school, she toiled up the stairs to the bath. In spite of the glow of success which surrounded her, she seemed even tireder than usual after a fair. When she got into the bathroom, she discovered why.

But although she should have been overcome with relief to see the red stain on her knickers, her bubble of happiness deflated, almost as if she were disappointed.

She banished the thought that she wanted David's baby any more than she wanted any other baby, and went to fetch her towel. Half an hour in the bath would work like a couple of hours' sleep.

But as she sank into the water, she realized she was quite looking forward to going to Melissa's that night, and wondered why. The combination of Tristan, her mother and Melissa would usually have sent her into the deepest depression. It wasn't the thought that she had sold a pot, because she certainly wasn't going to tell anyone. So what was it?

A flash of honesty, which, like lightning, she usually managed to avoid, told her she wanted to see Patrick again. Another told her why: she was missing David like mad, and seeing his son was somehow better than nothing.

*

When Polly opened the door to Tristan, her energy was much restored.

'Hello, Tristan.' She let him brush her cheek with his designer stubble. 'Come and meet my mother ... Mother, this is Tristan Black, he works for our local radio station. Tristan, this is my mother, Sylvia Cameron. She's staying with me for a few days.'

Polly hadn't told Tristan in person that her mother would be making three in the car, but she had left a message for him at the number he'd given her. But if he hadn't got it, you would never have guessed it from his attitude to Sylvia.

'Polly's mother?' He took her hand, and for a moment Polly thought he was going to kiss it. 'I would have said Polly's sister was nearer the mark. It's a pleasure to meet you.'

Sylvia Cameron, who was a terrible snob and prided herself on being able to spot a phoney at fifty paces, found herself fluttering daintily as Tristan smiled deep into her eyes. 'And you – er – Tristan.'

'Are you lov -' A glance at Polly decided him against referring to Polly and her mother as 'lovely ladies'. 'Are you both ready?'

'I'll fetch my coat.' Sylvia went upstairs to Polly's bedroom, hers for the duration.

'I'll put mine on,' said Polly, who had been sleeping on the sofa for the past three nights. 'Did you get my message, Tristan?'

'About your mother coming with us? Yes. She seems a sweet old bat.'

While somehow it was all right for Polly to refer to her mother as an old bat, she didn't like Tristan doing it.

'We're going in her car.'

After the last time, Polly refused to go anywhere with Tristan without her own means of getting home, so Sylvia had volunteered to drive. It was probably because Polly's car was so messy and, Sylvia felt, unreliable, but it did at least mean Polly could get roaring drunk if she felt like it. Or, more likely, fall asleep on the way home.

'I'll take you in mine. There's plenty of room.'

'I dare say, but with my mother coming I'd rather we had our own transport.'

Tristan was hurt. 'Polly! Last time was a one-off, I promise. I'd never do that to you again.'

'No, Tristan, you won't. In fact, I don't think we'll be seeing each other after tonight. We don't have very much in common.'

'But Polly – we have the most incredible sexual energy going on between us! You can't just ignore it!'

'I can. In fact, I hate to say this, but I haven't even noticed it. You're extremely attractive and I was flattered by your attention, but really, we're finished.'

Tristan rocked on his heels considering his best course, and decided to play it cool. If he didn't, he would blow his opportunity to see Melissa's dream home. 'Fair enough. It's nice of you to take me to Melissa's. I've never been in one of those houses.'

Polly managed to restrain herself from patting him on the head and telling him he was being a brave, good boy. 'I thought you'd enjoy it.'

Sylvia came down the stairs looking very smart in a red wool coat with a fur collar. She could never understand Polly's scruples about wearing fur. 'But it's dead, darling,' she would say. 'And it died years and years ago . . .'

And at least Melissa wouldn't give Polly black looks as

277

if her mother's lack of environmental awareness was somehow her fault.

'Mrs Cameron -' Tristan came forward. 'You look delightful. So do you, Polly,' he added more coldly.

'Let's get into the car then, shall we? I'll sit in front and give directions, Mother.'

Melissa greeted them with open arms and took Polly and Sylvia upstairs herself, leaving Consuela to deal with Tristan.

'Dear Mrs Cameron, it is so good of you to come.' She turned to Polly. 'He didn't arrive until after six, although I invited him for teatime. But quite frankly, it's a mercy! He hasn't said *a word* since he got here. Sheldon says it would be perfectly all right to offer him a glass of beer, but I don't think so. I mean, he's not actually eighteen yet, is he?'

'Isn't he?' Polly hadn't managed to speak to Patrick about not recognizing her, so she would have to rely on Patrick's reluctance to communicate to protect her privacy.

'And he's just standing around wearing those dreadful black clothes. I mean, he went to a decent school, why is he so *gauche*?'

'Perhaps he's shy,' said Polly.

'Well, *I* don't seem to be getting on very well with him. Anyway, I thought after supper we could play some games. Like we did in the old days at dinner parties. Do you remember, Polly?'

Polly had only been to one of Melissa's dinner parties, 'in the old days'. When the meal was finally over, everyone had gone into the drawing room and done Scottish dancing. Polly, who had refused to go to the classes which were held during the school holidays, was the only one who went wrong. Everyone thought it wildly funny, except Melissa who clapped her hands and got cross. 'But not Scottish dancing?'

'No, no. Not with your mother here.' She smiled at Sylvia as if she was a hundred and twenty years old instead of barely sixty.

Sylvia smiled back. At last she was getting the measure of Melissa.

When they reached the drawing room Patrick and Tristan were holding glasses of beer. Patrick looked at Polly as if he had never seen her before in his life, and merely nodded when Melissa made the introductions. Polly couldn't decide if this was stupendous acting, or he really had forgotten her. He had been extremely drunk the first time they had met. But he hadn't been so far gone at the New Inn as to forget his rescuer, surely?

Grateful for his reticence, but hurt – after all, she had pulled Patrick out of two very nasty messes – she greeted Sheldon with a kiss. 'Have you recovered from those aubergines?'

Sheldon flushed. 'Of course. What can I get you and your mother to drink?'

'You'll have to ask my mother. I could murder a gin and tonic.'

She had murdered two of them, and her mother had drunk two glasses of sherry, before Consuela announced dinner. Melissa had chickened out of entertaining such a motley collection of guests in the kitchen, so they all trooped into the dining room and found their place cards.

Polly was put next to Patrick. 'I hope you don't mind,' Melissa had whispered. 'But you're so good with . . .'

'Young people. I know.'

Consuela came in with a tureen of soup which looked reassuringly like Heinz tomato. She placed it carefully in front of Melissa and left. Melissa proceeded to dole it out with the efficiency which had gained her a head-girlship at school while Sheldon circled the table with a bottle. He filled Polly's glass to the brim. Sheldon was beginning to grow on Polly. His insatiable lust apart, he was a nice chap.

'Dig in!' Melissa trilled. 'I hope this is all right,' she said across Tristan to Polly's mother. 'But I gather it's what young people like best.'

'Is your father away for long?' Polly asked Patrick.

'A month.'

'So when's he due home?'

'Next week.'

'And have you missed him? Or is it nice to be able to play your records – er, music – at full blast?'

'It's all right.'

His reluctance to talk gave her a nasty attack of déjà vu. It seemed only yesterday that she had sat in this very spot trying to make conversation with Patrick's father. 'Then you're not lonely?'

'Not really.'

Polly gave up. Melissa was right. Patrick was extremely hard work, but the soup was very comforting.

'Monica looks after me.'

Polly nearly dropped her spoon. Patrick had made an unprompted remark.

'And Monica is . . .?' she asked, willing him not to betray her.

He gave her a very reminiscent look. 'She's the housekeeper. I thought you knew that.'

Melissa looked questioningly at Patrick. 'How would Polly know that, dear?'

Polly took a large gulp of wine.

Patrick shrugged nonchalantly. 'I thought Dad might have mentioned it.'

Polly exhaled slowly. 'This is delicious soup, Melissa. My favourite.'

'Good!' Melissa continued brightly. 'Shepherd's pie to follow! You do like shepherd's pie, don't you?' she asked Patrick, faintly pleading.

'S'all right.'

'And ice cream and hot chocolate sauce for pudding.'

Melissa had apparently got her ideas of what 'young people' liked from the kiddies' section of a service station menu. Polly, grateful that at least they'd been spared fish-fingers, wondered if there would be chips and baked beans with the shepherd's pie.

'Super,' said Polly. 'Everyone likes that, don't they, Tristan?'

'They sure do, Melissa.' Tristan flashed his gold tooth in an endearing way. 'You really know how to create an atmosphere.' Then he engaged Melissa in conversation as only he knew how.

Patrick looked Polly in the eye for the first time ever.

'I'm really, really glad,' he said in a voice so low she could barely hear it, 'that that woman can't ever be my stepmother.'

'But she means so *well*!' Polly whispered back.

'Exactly.' Patrick tipped back his antique dining chair, causing it to creak alarmingly, and drained his glass.

'Right!' Melissa got to her feet. 'Back to the drawing room. We're going to play some games!'

Polly took her mother upstairs to powder her nose.

'Are you all right, Mum?' she asked when they were out of earshot, forgetting it was common. 'If you don't want to play party games, we could always make an excuse and leave. I'm dreadfully tired.'

Her mother wouldn't hear of it. 'Oh, no! I'm having a lovely time. Melissa's such a nice person, and she's gone to such a lot of trouble for that oafish boy.'

Polly was on the side of the oafish boy. 'A touch patronizing, perhaps? I mean, Patrick's seventeen and she's treating him as if he were seven.'

'But she means well. Do you think this lipstick suits me?'

She means well, thought Polly, admiring the lipstick. Put that on Melissa's headstone, it's what everybody says about her. But what would they put on mine?

Back in the drawing room, Polly accepted another glass of red wine. Her period had begun to make its presence felt and she could do with the extra iron.

'So what are we going to play? Polly?'

Melissa looked hopefully at Polly, whose heart sank. As 'O/C. Young People' it seemed she was expected to organize the games.

She had often helped Bridget with her children's parties, but Bridget always provided a list of games, a cassette player and a bag of sweets if anyone got restive. Melissa hadn't been so considerate.

She thought frantically.

'What about "Give us a Clue"?' suggested Sylvia, to Polly's grateful surprise.

'Oh, yes,' agreed Melissa. 'How do you play it?'

By the time everyone understood the rules, Patrick had disappeared behind a book, apparently for the duration.

'Come on!' Polly hissed at him. 'Melissa will be terribly upset if you don't join in.'

'What does she think I am?' he asked her. 'A kid?'

'Yes! But it's not her fault, she just doesn't know any better. So be a dear and put up with it. Tristan's playing.'

'Tristan's a prat,' said Patrick. But he untangled his lower limbs and swung to his feet.

'You pick your team, Patrick.' Melissa was determined to give the guest of honour the best of everything.

'Okay. I'll have Polly and Tristan.'

'Oh, but you can't have Tristan. That means Polly'll have two men!'

'So?'

'Oh, very well, then. Sylvia, you come and sit by me. We'll let them go first.'

Tristan, predictably, was brilliant at it. Patrick's performance was hindered by using images unrecognizable to the over-twenties, and Polly got by. It was Sylvia who excelled in the other team, because she stuck doggedly to her point and went on acting out a word in different ways until her team had caught on.

'Time for oranges and a team talk!' called Sheldon, when everyone had had a turn. 'Sylvia, you're the star, what would you like to drink?'

Polly was glad to see her mother stick to Perrier. She herself had already had too much to drink for safe driving, and didn't want to stop now. Melissa's dinner parties, she decided, were heaps better if taken well oiled.

A few more rounds of 'Give us a Clue', and the party started to flag. Melissa looked at Polly, who mentally ran through Bridget's list. Dead lions, musical chairs and pass the parcel weren't quite right. And she wasn't sure if her mother really wanted to squash herself in cupboards to play sardines. Which left charades.

'I'm not playing charades unless I can dress up,' said Sheldon, who had also had quite a bit to drink.

'Don't be difficult, Sheldon,' Melissa snapped, not liking the idea of her party thundering up the stairs to ransack her walk-in wardrobe.

'I'm not,' he went on. 'You've got loads of clothes you never wear.'

'It is more fun to dress up,' said Tristan, giving Melissa a blast of blue-eyed charm. 'Haven't you got any jumble?'

'Jumble! That's a brilliant idea,' she said. 'I sorted out some for the hospice, and my mother gave me a huge trunkful when she moved into a Rest Home. A lot of it came from Granny. I haven't even looked at it yet. It's in the spare dressing room. You'll have to come up.'

They went and instantly started to rummage through, pulling out ostrich feathers, bits of fur and lace, wonderful circular petticoats and beautifully tailored coats and skirts.

Polly wanted to take it all home immediately, and wondered whether, if she made a donation, Melissa would cut out the middle man and let her have it direct, rather than require her to go to the actual jumble sale. But she didn't embarrass Melissa by asking.

There was a lot of dubious underwear in Melissa's bags, doubtless Sheldon's optimistic Christmas presents, and some interesting early specimens of Crimplene. Melissa found the Laura Ashley she wore to Glyndebourne the first time she went with Sheldon, and became almost tearful.

Then Tristan said he wanted face paint and forced

Melissa to give him some old lipsticks and a blue eyeshadow which she was still wearing, but which Polly told her, *sotto voce*, did nothing for the colour of her eyes. Sheldon insisted on keeping up the alcohol levels in people's glasses and everyone got terribly rowdy, even Melissa.

And no one would even think about choosing a word until they had tried on everything and decided what they looked best in. But eventually they were herded downstairs by Polly's mother and divided back into their groups to pick their words.

Patrick, as team leader, wanted 'gestalt', but was talked out of it on the grounds that 'alt' wasn't really a word, and the thought of acting the whole thing would have daunted Meryl Streep. Tristan wasn't allowed 'media', either.

Polly couldn't think of anything except 'cupboard' and their team had to ask if they could consult a dictionary. Melissa allowed them one volume of *The Concise Oxford Dictionary* on the strict understanding they put it back in the right place. They ended up with 'mountaineer'. Patrick fancied himself as Van Gogh.

Patrick's team was in full flow when Consuela opened the door and ushered in David.

His entrance couldn't have been more effective if he'd turned up at a vicarage tea party wearing scarlet tights and a black cloak dressed as the demon king. In fact, he was far more startling as the only one who wasn't dressed up.

His gaze panned his audience, who stared at him in silence. It paused at Polly, who was wearing the Laura Ashley which was surprisingly low-cut. It went on to Tristan, in a Crimplene two-piece and garden-party hat, who had one arm round Polly's waist and the other on her thigh.

Patrick, who had his head swathed in lavatory paper and was draped round Polly in a way which suddenly felt improper, wriggled free. His father's gaze took in the rest of the party, and swung back to his son.

'Hi, Dad,' said Patrick.

The silence broken, everyone unfroze and Melissa bustled forward, apparently having forgotten that she was wearing a rather unlikely camisole with suspenders which flapped over her dress.

'David! What a marvellous surprise. Do come and join the party. I invited Patrick to stay for the weekend as I thought he might be lonely.'

'How kind, Melissa,' said David. 'I'm sure he was delighted to come.'

Melissa gathered those she could trust around her. 'David, come and meet Polly's mother. Sylvia, this is David Locking-Hill. David, Sylvia Cameron.'

Sylvia, whose dressing up had extended only to a lorgnette and a cigarette-holder, rid herself of her props and prepared to be enchanted.

'How do you do, Mrs Cameron?' David reached down from his great height and took her hand. 'I'm so pleased to have the opportunity to meet you.'

Sylvia gave a small sigh, discernible only to Polly, who, from the other side of the room, knew that her mother thought David wonderful.

'I think you know everyone else, don't you?'

'I do, indeed.' His eyes fixed on Polly. 'I confess I'm surprised to see them all here. I was only expecting Patrick.'

Patrick grinned. 'You're back early, Dad.'

'I got everything done and thought I may as well come home.' David accepted a glass from Sheldon, who was coping better than most with David's sudden appearance. 'I saw Patrick's note to Monica when I got home, and thought I might as well come too.'

'We're delighted you did, David. Would you like anything to eat? Come into the kitchen, let me find you something.'

'I ate on the plane and had a snack when I got home.'

'Are you sure?' Melissa had worked very hard to get all those ill-matched guests under her roof. But now David was here, she seemed ashamed of them and wanted to distance herself and David from the group.

'Quite sure.'

He kept his gaze on Polly, who suddenly felt very hot and released herself from Tristan's embrace which had been surprisingly tenacious.

She caught her mother's eye. 'I think perhaps we should go. It's getting late.'

David intercepted her frantic glance. 'Oh, don't let me break up the party. You're having such a good time.' He turned abruptly away from Polly. 'How long are you in the area, Mrs Cameron?'

Chapter Twenty

❦

Polly slipped quietly upstairs to change into her own clothes. Her back was aching and she was desperately tired. And it wasn't only her back which ached. Seeing David again, so cold, so different from the last time, gave her a pang which would make the severest period pain seem like nothing. She hunted about in Melissa's bathroom cabinet until she found an aspirin. Now her head was beginning to throb too.

She went back down to fetch her mother, but the party sounded so noisy, and it was so quiet in the hall, that she stayed there. She was enjoying the peace when David came out of the drawing room.

Polly stiffened like a cat confronted by a strange but possibly very fast dog. Her instinct was to flee but her good sense told her she'd never make a clean getaway.

'Hello, Polly. How are you?'

His tone was still glacial, and she could see from his eyes that he was as coldly furious as it was possible to be. But why?

She used the same chilly tones as he did, and kept her manner just as detached. His icy rage was infectious. 'Fine. Did you have a good trip?'

'Very successful, thank you.'

'Good.'

'Your mother has just told me you've been at a craft fair. How did it go?'

'Very well, thank you. There was a man there from London who said he would buy everything I could make, provided I can make enough.'

'And can you?'

'Possibly.'

'Oh. Are you pregnant?'

Polly thought she'd misheard. 'I beg your pardon?'

'I asked you if you were pregnant.'

'No, thank you.' Thank you? Golly, her mother had a lot to answer for.

'Are you sure?'

'Quite.'

'I came back early to find out.'

'You could have telephoned, if you were so anxious to know.'

'Of course I was anxious! But I didn't think it right to just ring up and ask.'

'Very delicate of you. Now you can breathe a huge sigh of relief and forget all about me.' The thought of him doing it stabbed her and she clenched her teeth to keep back the tears.

'Can I? I don't think it's as simple as that.'

Her nails bit into the palms of her hands. 'Yes, it is. I'm not pregnant, there's no abortion to pay for or to persuade me to have, and no threat of child maintenance.'

'If you had been pregnant, would you have had it terminated?'

Polly hesitated. Not because she had any doubts about the matter, but she didn't want David to misconstrue her reply.

'Well?'

'No.'

'Why not?'

She shrugged. The tears were very near the surface now. If her voice broke, she was lost. She took a deep breath. 'I just couldn't. Don't take it personally. I'd feel like that if I were pregnant by anyone.'

'I see.'

Bitterly painful though this conversation was, Polly felt compelled to keep it going.

'What would you have done if I had been pregnant?'

'Married you.'

She flushed. 'I wouldn't have.'

'You would, you know.'

She lifted her chin, a hair's breadth away from collapse. 'What makes you say that?'

'Because even you can't go on being a bloody fool for ever.'

Anger flooded in to the rescue, and suddenly she was furious. 'Who the bloody hell are you to call me a fool?'

He shrugged. 'Another bloody fool.'

'You said it! And you *must* be a fool if you're even *suggesting* marriage to someone you can hardly even be civil to.'

'If you want civilities from me, keep that poncing little upstart's hand from up your skirt and your arms from around my son!'

'I don't want anything from you, you arrogant, stiff-necked *prig*! I'll put my arms round who I like because it's nothing to do with you! God! If I didn't know better I'd say you were jealous. Of your son?'

She watched the rage shudder through him. If she'd been a man he would certainly have hit her. There were the sounds of people coming out of the drawing room, but he ignored them and advanced towards her as she backed away.

'What you know about me could be written on the point of a pin. But I don't intend you should live in ignorance for ever!'

He reached for her, but before Polly could find out if he meant to kiss her or shake her, the door opened and Melissa, Sylvia and Patrick came out of the drawing room. David let his arm drop, and Polly found she was shaking so hard her teeth were chattering. She turned away so no one would see what had happened.

Patrick came over and spoke to his father while the others went upstairs to find their coats. Tristan and Sheldon could be heard laughing in the drawing room.

'Dad, I'm supposed to be staying the night with Melissa, but can I come home with you?'

Polly, trying to get her shivering body under control, listened for his answer. She expected David to swear at Patrick and tell him that if he'd made an arrangement he must stick to it. But he didn't. 'Fine,' he said shortly. 'I'll square it with Melissa.'

Polly turned round in time to be seared with a blinding look of what was probably hate from David before he went to speak to his hostess.

Patrick and Polly confronted each other in the hall.

Not only did Patrick seem aware that David and Polly had quarrelled, he seemed to think it was mildly amusing.

She transferred all her pent-up rage to Patrick. 'Your father is the most bullying, domineering, insufferable . . .'

'Yeah, he's good when he's angry, isn't he?'

'Good?' demanded Polly. 'He's –' Her fevered brain

searched for an epithet bad enough to describe him, and failed.

Patrick grinned. 'I know. It's best to give in. Then you've got that strength with you rather than against you.'

Polly made a gargantuan effort to calm down. 'You've changed your tune, haven't you? I thought you and David were at each other's throats most of the time.'

'Yeah. But then we're father and son. We have to fight out the old Oedipus thing. You know? He's the chap who murdered his father and married his mother. There's no need for you to put yourself through that confrontation.'

Polly took a series of calming breaths. 'Patrick,' she asked when she felt more in control, 'what are you planning to read at university?'

'Psychology.'

'A very sound choice. Now if you don't want to be an orphan, be a dear and go and find my mother. If I run into your father, I won't be held responsible.'

'No need to worry about that, Polly. He's a black belt in karate. You'd never get near him. On the other hand, he might well lose his temp —'

'Go, Patrick, or I'll stab you with my hatpin!' she hissed, and heard him laugh as he ran up the stairs.

While he was gone, she removed Tristan from Sheldon's whisky and sat with him in the car until her mother arrived.

'Well, that was very pleasant,' said Sylvia as she buckled her seat belt and turned on the ignition. 'I do think David Locking-Hill's a charming man. Don't you, Polly?'

Polly, who was in the back, curled herself into a very

small ball. 'No!' she squeaked as if she was being strangled. 'I don't!'

'I'm sure he thought you were charming, Sylvia,' said Tristan. 'This is a nice little car.'

'Thank you, Tristan,' Polly breathed, and closed her eyes.

She had intended to doze in the back of the car, but felt so churned up she couldn't.

Why had he been so cold, so *angry* with her tonight? Was he jealous? The thought warmed her for a few precious moments. Then reality reared its ugly head and she realized he was probably tired after travelling all day. To arrive at Melissa's expecting a quiet drink and his son and to find a group of people dressed in women's clothes and laughing hysterically had probably been extremely irritating. And he wouldn't have been able to take it out on anyone else.

This explanation was entirely logical, but didn't quite fit in with what Patrick had said.

'It's best to give in. Then you've got that strength with you rather than against you. There's no need for you to go through that confrontation.'

Wise words for a public school drop-out.

When they arrived home, she got rid of Tristan in record time. But her mother was harder to dispose of.

'Such a nice man, that David,' said Sylvia, filling her quilted hot-water bottle with agonizing slowness. 'Do you suppose he's related to the Yorkshire Locking-Hills?'

Polly wanted her bed more than anything in the world. A discussion on the more remote branches of David's family was not going to keep her from it. 'I really couldn't say, Mother. Now if you don't mind, I've had a hell of a day and I want to go to bed.'

Sylvia retreated to Polly's bedroom, muttering that she had not brought up her daughter to use language *like that*.

Polly collapsed on the sofa, laughing weakly.

On Monday morning, she brought her mother a cup of tea in bed and said a fond goodbye. They both knew exactly how long they could live together without quarrelling, and that time was up at midday. Polly was off to the café, and Sylvia was going to depart at her leisure.

The visit had gone unusually well. Possibly because Polly was so busy she had been home only late in the evening. By that time she was perfectly content to be cosseted, mothered and fussed over, and let the accompanying criticism float over her exhausted head.

Sylvia had enjoyed looking after her daughter when she was too tired to be independent and feminist and prickly. She had also greatly enjoyed Melissa's party. In Oxford most of her social life involved bridge and sherry, or white wine and intellectuals. Party games were a new departure for her that she rather liked.

She was also enchanted by David. He was a man you could lean on. He would be able to get a taxi in the rain, know what to tip the porter and whether the garage bill need really be so high. If there was anything in the power of positive thinking, David Locking-Hill would be her son-in-law before the year was up.

But although for once Sylvia had had the tact to keep these dreams to herself, Polly had had no difficulty in interpreting them. They were the dreams her mother had always indulged in.

It was bliss to come home on Monday evening to a

house empty but for Selina. It was wonderful to know that her mother would have changed the sheets on Polly's bed, and that she would be able to sleep on them. The sofa had become terribly uncomfortable. Her mother had washed up every last pot and pan, and left a bottle of sherry on the table. She had also 'tidied up' in a way which would take Polly weeks to sort out.

That was the trouble with being untidy. People always assumed that there was no method in the heaps of things which littered every surface. They thought that any sort of order was better than nothing. But it wasn't. It would take Polly a long time to extract the telephone bill she intended to pay (eventually) from the heaps of opportunities to win a fortune or to buy four best-sellers for fifty pence each.

But Polly had not yet got het up about this. She was still feeling gratified to be on her own again. Sufficient unto the end of the month was the evil of her mother's desire for order.

Polly put another log on the fire, poured herself another glass of sherry and settled back in the sofa. For once Selina wasn't clamouring for attention, being curled up on a cushion shedding flea eggs on to the velvet in her sleep. 'The sheer luxury of living alone,' Polly said out loud. She couldn't help remembering the saying: 'Guests are like fish, they go off after three days.'

She had a bath so hot she nearly blacked out when she got out. She put on her slipper socks, nightie and dressing gown and got the sofa cushions perfectly positioned for maximum comfort. She had even tracked down her book, which she had left open face down, where her mother had tidied it away in the bookcase and found her place. Then there was a knock at the door.

Polly almost didn't answer it. But as it came again she got up with a groan. It might easily be her neighbour wanting to borrow some milk, but she put the chain on the door before she opened it. It was David.

'Hello, Polly. Can I come in?'

She gulped. 'I'm not dressed –' She was also scarlet in the face from the bath, and had no make-up on.

'We need to talk.'

'To each other?'

'Of course.'

Reluctantly she unhooked the chain. At least the house was tidy. And although he had asked to come in quite politely, he sounded extremely determined to do so. The chain was only a gesture to security. If pushed, the hasp would pull away easily from the woodwork.

And although she was ready for bed, she was clothed to the neck. Her winceyette nightie had a piecrust collar and her dressing gown was wrapped well over and stayed done up. A less seductive figure had rarely been presented, but she clutched at her neck as she opened the door.

It was raining, and it clung to his hair and the shoulders of his overcoat. The smell of the night air came in with him and around his huge, glistening figure. Her sitting room seemed to shrink to the size of a doll's house.

Polly felt herself shrink likewise. She knew he was a lot taller than she was, but without her shoes it seemed like several feet.

It made her nervous. 'I must go and get some clothes on.'

His gaze flicked her up and down, taking in the

winceyette, the woolly socks. 'You seem perfectly decent to me.'

Decent, yes. But Polly would have felt happier with her knickers on. 'I won't be a minute.'

She fled upstairs to her bedroom and found a pair. But now what? Should she pull on some clothes, put on some make-up and hope he had forgotten how red-faced and shiny she had looked? Or would that be obvious, as though she cared? She compromised with a bit of powder, a quick flick of mascara and a thorough brush of her hair. But she decided against clothes. It would take for ever to decide what to put on, and he might think she didn't trust him. And rather disappointingly, in spite of the frisson his sudden appearance had caused her, she did.

She stood at the bottom of her stairs watching his tall figure rooted in the middle of her sitting room like Nelson's Column on a village green. When she'd had her dreadful dinner party she'd spent all day rearranging the furniture and taking out the bits she could do without so the room was as well-organized and spacious as possible. But now everything was as usual, highlighting exactly how small her cottage was.

'I came to apologize,' he said.

She had argued and re-argued their last conversation in her head, and each time her put-downs were more witty and more cutting. And here he was, presenting her with the perfect opportunity to recite them.

If she'd been anyone else, if she didn't know he wouldn't move from his prominent position until invited, and that most men never learnt to apologize, she might have done it. She might have stood on the bottom step of her staircase and harangued him in the elegant, sophisticated way she had rehearsed.

But as it was, she set aside her hurt and anger in her desire to get him to stop towering over her small world.

'Do sit down. Let me take your coat.'

She took it from him, heavy and damp and scented with aftershave. She put it over the back of a chair and pointed to the armchair by the fire.

Even without his coat he was big, and nearly as formidable seated, his legs bent double.

'Can I get you something? A glass of sherry? Tea, coffee, cocoa?'

'No, thank you.'

Deprived of her opportunity to escape to the kitchen, she forced herself to sit opposite him and lose the height advantage gained from being on her feet.

'As I said, I came to apologize.' He straightened his legs gingerly, like people do on trains, reluctant to kick the person opposite.

This was agony. She made a small, fluttering gesture with her hands, then forced herself to keep still. 'Really – there's no need.'

'Yes, there is. I was boorish, rude and overbearing. I'm sorry.' He apologized with the same calm integrity he did everything. And smiled, very, very slightly at the corner of his mouth.

Polly found a lump forming in her throat, and coughed. 'My mother didn't think you were boorish and rude.'

'I wasn't, to her.'

'No.'

'I came to explain, as much as anything.'

'You don't have to –'

'I was disappointed you weren't pregnant.'

His words went through her like a bolt of lightning. 'Why? Do you want more children so badly?'

He shook his head. 'Not really. I didn't think about the child. I just know I was disappointed when you told me there wasn't one.'

She had been disappointed too. 'I would have thought you would have been relieved.'

'So would I. It was a shock to discover I wasn't. It was one of the things that made me so angry.'

'What was the other?'

He heard her. He was looking at her with great intensity, but he didn't answer.

She sat in silence. He crossed one leg over the other, awkward in the tiny chair. 'You have a very generous, loving heart. I don't suppose you've ever felt possessive about another human being,' he said at last.

'But I haven't got anyone to feel possessive about.'

He heaved himself out of the chair and paced about the room as well as he could given the amount of furniture.

'Nor have I, damn it, but I *feel* possessive. I felt so damn jealous when I came in and saw you in that dress with that little twerp's hand up your skirt . . .'

'It wasn't really up my skirt . . .'

'. . . I could hardly stop myself pushing his gold tooth down his throat. I was even jealous of Patrick!'

She suddenly remembered his thirty-five-year-old girl-friend when he was seventeen, who taught him to make scrambled eggs. 'There's –'

'You keep telling me there's no *need* for this and no *need* for that. But I'm telling you there is.'

'But . . .'

He ground to a halt behind the table and placed his hands on it and confronted her. 'How would you have felt if, after what we'd shared, the situations had been reversed? If you came into a room and saw me with my arms around another woman?'

'I've got no right –'

'We're not talking about "rights", I'm asking you how you'd *feel*. Think about it.'

Polly didn't need to think very hard and tried to match his honesty. 'I'd be hurt.'

'Hurt? Is that all? You wouldn't feel angry? Cheated? As if someone were taking something that was yours?'

At this moment Selina, disturbed by the noise, opened her golden eyes and gave him a look so disapproving he was forced to laugh.

'That's rather a dramatic way of putting it,' he went on. 'I dare say you'd say that we are free agents and no one has the right to own anyone else. But it's how I feel.'

'David –' Polly felt short of breath. Her heart was hammering as if she'd suffered a bad shock.

'What I'm saying, in an extremely clumsy way, is that I care about you. And I want the right to punch the nose of any man who looks at you or touches you in the wrong way.' He half smiled. 'I'm not saying I'd do it, I just want to feel I'd be justified if I did. I want to be able to sweep you up and take you home –' He knocked into the table with his thigh. 'Preferably right now. This house is so damn *small*!'

She uttered a stifled protest.

Hearing it, he made a rueful, apologetic face. 'Sorry, I didn't mean to be rude. It's a charming house, just right for one.'

Seeing him like a tiger in a cage, hardly able to move,

only able to take a pace and a half before he had to turn to take a pace and a half back again she was forced to agree with him.

'I know what you mean. It's ideal for a single woman, but would be too small for a couple.'

He perched on the arm of the chair opposite her, his foot swinging. 'My house, on the other hand, is far too big for a single man and two sons who will leave home at any moment.'

Polly nodded. 'Perhaps you should sell it.'

'I can't sell it! It's the family home. I have to keep it for my sons. The answer would be to put someone else in it.'

'I don't think one person would make much difference in a house that size. It would take a small school, at least.'

'Polly, are you being deliberately obtuse? Did you hear what I said?'

She moistened her lips. 'I heard, but I'm not sure what I heard. And I didn't know how to react.'

He sighed. 'I'd make myself clearer but, knowing you, if I did you'd either run away or burst into tears. Do you always cry so much after making love?'

'No, I don't think so.'

'So why did you?'

She shook her head, afraid that she was going to cry again.

He noticed. 'You really are the most lachrymose creature.'

She cleared her throat. 'At least I won't die of a heart attack. People who express their feelings are much healthier than those who bottle them up.' Her glare suggested he was a chronic anal retentive.

He laughed tenderly in the same way he had teased her after they had made love. 'It's not that I object to you crying, it's just that it's hard to watch you without taking you in my arms. And right now that would cloud the issue.'

'What issue?'

'Promise not to cry?'

She growled.

'Well then, this is not a proposal, it is a statement of fact. I want to marry you.'

Chapter Twenty-one

The idea was so preposterous she didn't feel a bit like crying. It was like something out of a historical novel – or should that be hysterical? A marriage of convenience arranged between a spirited but impoverished heroine and a wicked, wildly attractive hero to give said hero an heir to his vast estates and massive fortune. She stifled a giggle.

'Why? You've got two perfectly good sons to keep the Locking-Hill family from dying out, you've got Monica so you don't need someone to darn your socks for you. You must lead a very ordered, comfortable existence. Why would anyone in your position want to get married?'

'I don't, not as such. I want to marry you.'

'If you want more children, you should go for someone much young –'

'As you said, I've got two sons, though "perfectly good" is somewhat debatable. Children really don't come into it.'

'I may be rather slow, but I still don't understand. You could have any woman you want at the drop of a hat. You don't have to marry anyone. What on earth is it about me that would make you want to give up your freedom?'

'Not your stiff upper lip, that's for sure.'

'So?'

'Anything I said now would come out like a declaration of love, which is even more likely to make you cry.'

She gritted her teeth. 'Let's leave my mawkish habits out of this. Tell me why you want to get married to me?'

'Because, to quote my son, I'm shit scared you'll go off with that –' He hesitated.

She helped him out. 'Prat? I'm also quoting your son.'

'For someone who left school before doing A levels, he does have a way with words.'

'His silences are pretty potent, too,' said Polly. 'He terrified Melissa.'

'She should play with children her own age. But we were talking about Tristan.'

'I'm not going to marry him, if that's what's worrying you.'

'Oh, no. He won't marry anyone without a rich and influential father, that's for sure.'

Polly wriggled indignantly. But with David stalking about, there was no room for her to release her frustrations in action. 'That's not fair. Tristan may not be . . .'

'Why were you with him at Melissa's?'

'She asked me to bring him.'

'Oh, really?'

His scepticism seared her. She could have set his mind at rest with the information that she'd told Tristan she didn't want to see him again. But why should she?

She shrugged. 'Ask her.'

The muscle at the corner of his mouth clenched. For a thousand reasons, he couldn't.

Polly went on quickly; there wasn't the space for him to get angry. 'What I don't understand is, if you're' – she hunted for the word – 'keen on me, why you didn't ask me out in the normal way?'

'Because, in case you've forgotten, we've already been to bed together, without there being any sort of court-ship, normal or otherwise. It does make it rather difficult to go back to dinner dates and trips to the opera.'

'Does it?' She rather fancied the opera.

'You may not like to admit it, but we shared some-thing very special that night. When I saw you with – Tristan on Saturday, I felt stabbed in the back.' He picked up the bottle of sherry on the table and examined the label absently, considering how to continue.

'I know this is my cue to remind you that you don't owe me anything, and for you to go on about being consenting adults and all that crap. And not being Patrick, I don't have the fancy arguments to confuse you into saying what I want you to say. Which is why –' He took a deep breath and let it out slowly. 'Which is why I have a suggestion to make.'

'Go on, then.'

'I suggest that we see each other, as often as we like, but say nothing more about marriage, for, say, a month. In the meantime you think about it. Think about having your own workshop on the premises. Think about being able to work at your pottery full time. Think about having the capital to set yourself up with a new kiln, or wheel or whatever it is you need. About not stubbing your toe every time you cross the room,' he added irritably. 'Then, when you've thought and the month is up, you can give me your answer.'

'I told you I'd made a breakthrough in my pottery. A really prestigious London shop has shown interest. The buyer actually bought a pot – for himself, personally. It may take time, but I don't need to marry you for your money.'

His smile suddenly made him look very like Patrick. 'Good. I made the proposition as attractive as possible, but I didn't think you were a fortune hunter. But you need some capital, to really get yourself going.' It was a statement of fact, and quite undeniable. 'Without me and my money, you'd make it eventually. With it, you'll make it much sooner.'

Because he was right, she went on arguing. 'I might be more inclined to marry you if you were poor. Perhaps you should give your money and possessions away.'

'That would be foolish.'

'Are you never foolish?'

'Not usually, no.'

'Then why have you come up with this ridiculous marriage idea?'

He chuckled. 'It could be your bad influence. Or it could be that I'm fed up with Melissa parading nubile young women in front of me.'

'She paraded me in front of you.'

'Yes, but you must have realized by now she didn't really expect us to get on.'

'I'm not sure that we do get on. We have opposing views on almost everything. And some of your friends . . .'

'Which friends?'

Polly shook her head. This wasn't the time to get into an argument about the appalling Bradleys and their attitude to old buildings. 'Never mind. But it isn't just that, it's your whole lifestyle. You have more engraved invitations on your mantelpiece than I have car park stickers in my car. I haven't been to a formal ball for years and years. I've rejected all that. I couldn't go back to it now. We come from different worlds.'

'Then wouldn't it be a good idea to see each other more, so we can find out what we agree and disagree about? The things we have in common, as well as the differences between us?'

'It would be much easier to fill in a questionnaire.' And a lot less heartbreaking.

His expression softened. 'But not as much fun.'

'Fun! Do you think it would be fun, fighting all the time, arguing over which newspaper to take, who to vote for? You wouldn't like it if I stuck anti-hunting posters all over the house when you had the MFH to dinner.'

He laughed. 'Don't you take anything seriously?'

'Not if I can help it,' she said crossly. 'It's a major difference between us. You are a very serious person. I'm essentially frivolous and superficial.' Her words were so much at odds with her expression that she was forced to smile.

'Don't you take your work seriously?'

'Of course, but that's my *work*.'

'And what about the environment, do you have superficial feelings about that?'

'No.'

'Your kindness? Your love of people? Children? Half-baked adolescents? That's just a frivolous little whim, is it?'

'No, but –'

'So you're serious about some things, and not others. So am I. I'm looking forward to finding out where we differ and where we agree.'

'You sound like a legal document! This is all very well

in theory, but I don't know . . . I mean, there are bound to be – well – drawbacks.'

'Such as?'

She took the bull by the horns. 'Sex, for one thing.'

'I've always been rather in favour of sex.'

'I'm sure. But where does it come in your plan?' What she wanted to say was, did he expect that after every date they went on together they would end up in bed?

He got up again, took his one and a half paces and turned back. 'I suppose you'd like me to say I won't lay a finger on you until the month is up, but I'm afraid I'm not as noble and high-minded as you might think.'

He managed to look both, and extremely sexy at the same time. 'And nor has having you once dampened the fires of my lust. Knowing that under that strangely unattractive garment you have the body of a fallen angel is a cross I'll have to go on bearing for a bit longer. No, I can't make any promises about sex, Polly. You'll have to take your chance. But I won't ever ask you to do anything you didn't want to do.'

'You didn't ask before.'

'And you didn't say no before.'

'I was drunk,' she countered.

'Rubbish! You may have had a fair amount of whisky, but you weren't drunk. Don't fall back on that old chestnut.'

No, what she had fallen back on was a huge, warm bed. It had been bliss.

'If I say no?'

'I'll say good night and goodbye.'

'For ever?'

He nodded.

He betrayed no emotion, as if not seeing her ever again

was a perfectly acceptable solution to the problem. On the other hand, the thought of not seeing him again was horrible.

'Oh, very well then,' she said grumpily.

'Very well what?'

'I'll agree to go out with you, for a month, and consider your suggestion. But I must tell you, David, I think it very unlikely I'll accept your –' What sort of offer was it? Bizarre? Lunatic? Incomprehensible? 'Kind offer. I am very happy being single.'

If she'd expected him to fall down on his knees in gratitude, she was in for a disappointment. He merely said, 'Good. I'll be in touch.'

He bent, kissed her cheek, picked up his coat and swept out of the door, leaving a huge empty space behind him.

For the second time in three days, Polly went to bed in a highly emotional state. But instead of wanting to cry, she just wanted an action replay of that entire encounter so she could make sure she hadn't dreamt it.

David had asked her to marry him – no, he'd told her he wanted to marry her. He seemed to think there was a difference. Perhaps there was. And he wanted them to go out together for a month to see how they got on.

Well, at least it gave her time to frame her answer. She hated hurting people's feelings.

Of course she should have let him walk out of her life for ever. That would have been the decent thing to do. But she couldn't bring herself to. The three weeks he was away were so empty, knowing she wouldn't run into him, wouldn't hear his voice on the end of the phone. The thought of not ever seeing him angry, hearing him laugh, and (now she did want to cry) never feeling his strong arms crushing the breath from her body again was torture.

She had taken the easy option. She would enjoy her month, and then she'd let him down as lightly as she could. He'd never said he'd loved her, although he did seem to come pretty near it a couple of times; she may have misunderstood. He would recover in no time. Melissa would find another, more suitable bride for him, and he would be as good as new.

And her? How would she react when their time was up? It was hard to say. She had always thought if she made it as a potter, her life would be totally fulfilled. Now this seemed a real possibility. One swallow might not make a summer, but one pot could be followed by a series. But would earning her living by her wheel be as satisfying as it seemed from this distance, or would there always be an empty space in her life?

And if a one-night stand counted as a past, she even had one of those. She could tell her – she hesitated – her what? She didn't have any young relatives likely to produce children she could treat as nieces and nephews. And she didn't have children of her own, and probably never would.

Bridget's children were special to her, of course. She could tell them when they were grown up of how she'd had a brief fling with a wonderfully rich man, but rather than sacrifice her freedom she had refused to marry him. Would her reasons stand up thirty years from now? Or would those young things regard her with pity and mutter how Polly had always been *very* eccentric, not to say completely mad?

She'd miss Patrick. She hadn't spoken to him much,

but she cared about him. She wanted to know why he'd told her he was planning to read psychology at university when he'd left school before A levels. She wanted to sort him out, to make sure he did his exams. His relations with David were obviously sticky. Patrick needed a kindly older woman as a catalyst.

Of course, his house and garden were a dream she longed to know better. She wanted to see the trees when they were fuzzed with the green of spring. She wanted to see the blossom on the apple trees drop and turn into tiny apples which would eventually swell. She wanted to fill those wonderfully sheltered flower beds with the sort of tender plants that wouldn't stand a chance in her own tiny frost pocket.

She cuddled her hot-water bottle. These things were not to be. There was no point making herself miserable about them. The trouble was, she might well be able to live in his environment for short periods, but there was no way he could survive in hers. It wasn't enough for her to smarten up her act and follow about in his aristocratic footsteps, it had to be a two-way process.

The following evening, she worked on her books with the smart London talent-spotter in mind. But it was no good. However creative her accounting, she still couldn't afford to give up one of her days at the café in order to have more time to pot. She'd have to ask for a loan. But now she had that precious card, which was virtually proof that her work would sell, if she put up a good enough case her chances of getting one were reasonable.

If she married David, she wouldn't have to go business plan in hand to anyone. It was a shame her principles wouldn't let her take advantage of him.

When the phone rang and she didn't hear David's deep voice on the other end she decided against paying her phone bill and let herself get cut off. Then she tuned in to who was calling her. It was Mac.

'Polly, how are you?'

For most people this was a fairly normal way of starting a telephone conversation, but not for Mac. Something was up.

'Mac, what is it? Is everything all right?'

'No. My spies tell me Bradley's planning to send in the bulldozers next week. We're ten grand short of the asking price, and his offer's going to be accepted.'

'Oh, Mac! I feel so useless! You've all been up there, and I'm too cowardly to help.'

'Your posters were very decorative, but now's your chance to be a real heroine.'

'What do you mean?'

'We're desperate for people for this Saturday night. The days are sorted, but most of the usual bunch can't make it. At the moment it's only me and Jill. Not enough. If the police took it into their heads to make arrests, they could manage two of us easily. With a few more they won't try. Too dangerous. A protester might drop on someone's head.'

A ghastly foreboding crept up from the pit of her stomach. 'But there are loads of you. You must be able to find enough.'

'They've got other lives, Pol. Cathy's too big to climb the ladders now. The baby's due next month. Jack broke his ankle coming down last week. Dave's wife says she'll leave him if he doesn't spend a night at home. It's Phil's weekend for his kids and as he only gets them once a month he can't risk messing it up. Pete –'

'Oh stop it, Mac, you'll be asking me to go up there next.'

'Yes,' said Mac. 'I will.'

Polly exhaled a slow, shuddering breath.

'Sorry, Polly, I know you don't like heights, and I wouldn't ask if things weren't desperate. I'll be with you to hold you on. And we want people who aren't afraid to get arrested.'

Polly hadn't previously considered whether or not she was afraid of being arrested. Mac obviously thought she could cope with being dragged off between two policemen with total equanimity. Perhaps she could. What he didn't realize was just how bad was her fear of heights.

There's a difference between a faint dislike of clambering up rickety ladders, or looking over the edge of cliffs, and a real phobia. Polly even felt uncomfortable in tall buildings with proper walls. Knowing there was so much space between her and the ground made her frightened. 'Mac, I don't know ...'

'Please, Poll We need you.'

Her lips were already stiff with fear, and her stomach churned. But she knew that Mac would do anything for her, and the cause was so vital. She didn't want to seem a wimp in front of someone so intrepid. 'Okay.'

'Great, I knew we could depend on you. It's Saturday night we want you. They reckon that if there's any damage or anything, they've got all Sunday to clear it up. Come about nine. I'll be there. You can shout up, and I'll give you a hand.'

'Yes, Mac.'

Polly was trembling. The very thought of climbing on to a roof and staying there for the night had made her feel sick.

313

Her voice was still shaking when David did phone. He noticed.

'Polly, are you all right? You're not crying?'

'No, I'm not crying. What can I do for you?'

'You don't sound very happy.'

'No.'

'Well this may cheer you up. I've got tickets for *Don Giovanni* for Saturday. We'll have supper afterwards and stay the night.'

Polly felt bitter. 'You've got a *pied-à-terre* in town, have you?'

'No, I've booked into a hotel. We don't have to sleep together, if you don't want to.'

Polly did want to. She wanted very much to be swept up to Covent Garden in David's luxurious and speedy car, be transported to ecstasies by Mozart, be fed a dainty but sustaining meal, possibly oysters, prior to being transported to ecstasies by David. It sounded as near heaven as a sexual fantasy could be.

And this was even without the evening being an alternative to camping out on a rooftop with the dual fear of falling to her death or being put in prison.

'Oh, David.' She nearly was crying now. 'I'm terribly sorry, but I can't.'

'Why not? What are you doing?'

'I don't think I can tell you.'

'Why not?'

'You won't understand.'

'Try me.'

'Well, the shops in town, you know? The ones your friends – the ones they want to pull down in favour of a shopping mall?'

'Yes.'

314

'They're sending in the bulldozers. And most of the protesters can't go on. If there's no one there for a night, they'll either pull the buildings down altogether or make them so unsafe that even we won't climb on them.'

'Who's this "we"?'

'Some of us who want to see the buildings preserved have formed into a group. It's those of us who can't stand to see this town being pulled apart any more than it already has.'

There was an eloquent silence. 'And that includes you?'

'I'm afraid so.' It didn't come out as the conventional expression of regret that she'd intended.

'What do you mean "afraid"?'

'I don't like heights, much.' She had a feeling if she told David the whole story he'd get upset, which would start a whole new row about who had rights over whom, for which she had no stomach just now.

Another long pause. 'I see. But you're prepared to go up there anyway?'

'Yes.'

'What if the police come?'

'They can't do anything. Trespass is a civil offence.' What he didn't know wouldn't worry him.

'I see.'

Polly was beginning to find out where Patrick had learnt the art of the terrifying silence. She couldn't bear it any longer.

'I would very much prefer to go to the opera with you, David, but this is something I have to do.'

'But why you, Polly? There must be enough people without you having to do it.'

'No. One of the girls is eight months' pregnant, she's

315

been there every night since it began. She can't do it any more. Other people haven't seen their children for ages.' She decided not to mention the broken ankle. 'I must do my bit. It's climb up or shut up, David. The crunch has come, and I have to be there.'

'I see.'

She sighed. 'You'll have to take someone else to the opera.'

She willed him to say that he wouldn't go if she couldn't, but somehow wasn't surprised when he didn't.

'Yes.'

'It shouldn't be difficult finding someone.' He had probably planned the evening very carefully, and spent a huge amount of money. No man would take kindly to an invitation like that being turned down in favour of a cause he didn't believe in.

'No.'

He was probably changing his mind about everything even as they spoke. He would never align himself with someone who was prepared to break the law and occupy condemned buildings. He was far too conventional. He was probably beginning to see how vast the differences were between them, and would realize that they were too great. 'I'll be in touch, then, Polly.'

'Goodbye, David.'

'Goodbye.'

Chapter Twenty-two

❧

The buildings were shrouded in tarpaulins and scaffolding. They were only three storeys high and as unlike tower blocks as possible. But to Polly, they made the Telecom Tower shrink into insignificance.

A series of ladders had been lashed between platforms, which were fenced off by sagging ropes. One of the members of the protest group was well versed in the health and safety regulations, and in theory the way up was secure. But nothing short of a solid staircase, double handrail and a fitted carpet would make it safe for Polly.

On top of the buildings, Polly could see lanterns and torches, the glow of cigarettes. She could hear the low laughter of the protesters preparing to go home for hot baths and fish and chips. They had been virtually living up there for months, and leapt about on the rooftops like a troop of orang-utans.

Polly thought enviously of their casual indifference to their height above the ground. This was her chance to prove she was a real conservationist, and more than just a cipher who used unbleached recycled loo-paper and did her sums on the backs of envelopes. She had to set her personal fears aside, and go up and join them.

Polly was well wrapped up. She was practised in the art of keeping warm. Apart from many layers of tights and socks and trousers, she was wearing three jumpers, including David's cashmere one, and a thermal vest. She also had on a woolly hat which Bridget had lent her. It was supremely unflattering, but warm and less itchy than her own. She had a sleeping bag and two hot-water bottles.

She also had a packet of soggy salad sandwiches, a flask of hot chocolate and a tin of chocolate flapjack contributed by Bridget, who was right behind the supporters and had given money to the appeal fund, but wasn't prepared to leave her comfortable double bed, even for a night.

For Polly, the discomfort involved was minor. It was the thought of climbing up those rickety ladders and on to the roof that made her shake with fear. She was hoping the fact she wouldn't be able to see down would help.

'Mac? Are you there?' she called, hoping he wasn't and she could use his absence as an excuse to go home.

'Polly? Is that you?' Mac was as invincibly cheerful as ever. 'Want a hand?'

'Yes, please.' And a foot and several miles of guts to replace hers which had melted.

She listened to the sounds of Mac's descent with a strange detachment. In the few minutes it took him to reach the ground, time seemed suspended; she got a lot of thinking done. And she discovered that if she wasn't in love with David, she was so near it as makes no difference.

There was a thump, and Mac jumped the last bit, his working boots landing firmly on the pavement beside her. He put his arm round her and kissed her.

'Give us yer stuff. I'll take it up, and then come back for you. You okay? You're shaking.'

'Cold.' Her teeth were chattering, but Polly, just out of a scalding hot bath, actually felt as warm as toast.

It seemed no time before Mac was with her again. 'You go up first, then I'll be here to catch you if you slip.'

'Don't use words like "slip", please. Where do I start?'

'There.' He pointed to the bottom rung.

There seemed no alternative. Polly heaved herself on to it.

'Keep looking up, Poll It's not far, only three storeys.'

'Okay, Mac, no need to remind me.'

She started to climb in earnest, keeping her mind and her gaze on her goal. The rungs were quite large, but the ladders vibrated hideously, and every now and then the sole of her boot would slip a little. Living in daily contact with Laureton's steep and many hills kept Polly fairly fit, but by the time she reached the platform at the top she was panting hard and sweating under her clothes.

'Hello, Polly. Mac said you were coming.'

She was totally disorientated, but momentarily less scared. She had made it.

'Who's that? I can't see.'

'It's me, Jill. Come and sit down. Your stuff's here.' Jill lifted the blanket she was sitting under and patted the space beneath. Polly almost fell on to it.

'Is it only us, or are some of the others staying? She didn't know many of the protesters apart from Mac well, but Jill was an old friend.

'Just us, I'm afraid. That's why he had to ask you. At least it isn't raining – yet.'

By the time she was sitting next to her friend, with the blanket over her knees and a sleeping bag over their shoulders, Polly felt a little better. She couldn't see the ground, and she could catch up on Jill's news.

'I haven't seen you for ages, Jill.'

'No, well I've been up here for the last two months.'

There was an awkward pause. If she told Jill about her fear, Jill would want to talk it through, to try to help. But having her phobia related to something that happened to her mother while she was in the womb wouldn't help. It could well make it worse.

'I feel terrible I haven't been before but – I've been so busy.' She wasn't lying, she *had* been busy.

Jill may have guessed the real reason for Polly's absence and changed the subject. 'How's the pottery going?'

'Not bad, I went to a craft fair last week. There was a man looking for stuff for a London store. He said mine was exactly what was he was looking for. But what with being part time and sharing facilities, it'll be a while before I'll be able to follow it up.'

'What you need is a sugar daddy.'

'A what?' Was Jill a mind-reader? Did she know about David?

'You know, a rich old man who could set you up with your own equipment, let you give up the Whole Nut and get down to your pottery.'

It was said in Laureton that everybody ended up working at the Whole Nut sooner or later, but most people managed to escape in the end. Jill had escaped a couple of years ago to have a baby.

'Yes, but I'd miss the company if I did that.'

'But not the hours on your feet, the heat of the place in summer. Those boxes of vegetables you have to heft up and down those dreadful narrow stairs. It's hard work, Polly.'

'I know. But it's a job, and I love the customers and the

320

people I work with. Bridget sent some flapjack, by the way.'

'Oh, good. Did you bring a flask?'

'Yup, and two hotwater bottles, sleeping-bag, blankets.'

'And are you wearing plenty?'

'If I wore any more I wouldn't be able to move.'

Jill laughed. 'If I fell off here, I'd bounce!'

'Don't even joke about it, Jill.'

'Sorry. Let's get sorted out and try and get some sleep before the pubs chuck out.'

'You manage to sleep here?'

'Yup, if it's quiet. Saturday nights aren't, though.'

'Why not?'

'The skins lob cans and things at us. Nothing really violent so far, but it is unpleasant. It would be good if we had a few more men.'

'Jill, that's rather a politically incorrect statement for a feminist, isn't it?'

'No one's ever denied that men have an important role in society.'

'Haven't they?'

'Nope. There's a time and a place even for brute strength and ignorance. Pity you haven't got a boyfriend you could bring along, Polly,' she added dryly.

Polly was equally arid. 'Yes, isn't it?'

Fortunately, Jill's follow-up question was interrupted by the day shift.

'We're off, then.'

Two women and half a dozen young men loomed from the other side of the roof ridge, so loaded with bags and blankets they looked like a small group of refugees. 'Will you blow-ins be all right without us?'

'Are you offering to stay?' asked Jill.

'Nah – we just want to go off knowing you won't miss us.'

'We won't miss you. Go home to bed. Don't think about us freezing to death here.'

When the last taunt and joke was exchanged, and the ladders had stopped vibrating with the sound of Doc Martens thudding their way to safety, Jill propped herself up with blankets and cushions and closed her eyes.

Jill was a single parent who had left her children staying with a friend. But the pay-off was that she had to have her friend's children as well as her own on the following day.

Mac came up and settled in his corner. He'd been there all day, as well as several of the past nights, and was able to sleep anywhere.

Polly felt very alone. Her fear had abated sufficiently for her to replace it with thoughts of David. Knowing she could have been with him made her miss him terribly. She even wondered if she should accept his offer and marry him, but a moment later put this aberration down to an unreasonable desire for security caused by her present situation.

The chances of anyone's marriage working out were so slight. It would be lunacy to marry when they were so unsuited.

She pushed aside the thought that they were not so unsuited in bed. That wouldn't go on for ever, and after the honeymoon period was over she would have to spend the rest of her life being snapped at from behind *The Times* as she presided over the coffee pot at breakfast. No, if she'd rejected the idea of marriage as being stultifying at twenty, she wasn't going to let herself in for it at thirty-five.

Suddenly the sound of raised voices reached her. There was singing, a snatch of a football chant and the sound of breaking glass. The pubs were out.

Mac heard them too. 'With only a few of us here, they may not bother harassing us,' he said reassuringly.

As Polly had forgotten what Jill had said about the drunks lobbing cans at them until he reminded her, she wasn't reassured.

'Unless the Race Horse has got a whole new clientele,' she pointed out, 'they'll assume there are the same number of people as usual.'

'Yeah, well. I'll go and have a look.'

'Do you have to?'

'I need to know who it is down there. They might be mates of mine.'

Mac had mates in many surprising places.

'Be careful!'

Prickles of fear stirred in Polly's stomach as she heard him go. She didn't want to wake Jill unless she had to.

Voices floated up the ladders. Mac was returning, and there was someone with him. Perhaps he'd made a convert of a skinhead. If anyone could, it was Mac.

'Polly, it's a friend of yours.' Mac materialized out of the darkness and stepped aside to let the friend reach the top. It was David.

'David? What on *earth* are you doing here?' she whispered, her surprise masking her delight at seeing him.

'The same as you, I imagine,' he whispered back. 'Although "on earth" is something of an overstatement.'

323

Polly could have hugged him. 'I didn't think you were remotely interested in saving these buildings.'

'I wasn't, until you told me you were coming. I thought I'd better do some research.'

Jill stirred in her sleep. Polly pointed to her. 'Sit down,' she whispered. 'You'll freeze to death. I bet you're not wearing enough clothes.'

'I've got my skiing gear on, several jumpers and my Barbour jacket.'

'You should have worn a hat. You lose over a third of your body heat through your head.'

'I never wear hats.' He crouched down next to Polly and stretched his legs out gingerly. Then he put his arm round her shoulders and kissed her cheek. She was about to kiss him back when Mac broke in.

'Don't get too cosy, you two. I think there's going to be trouble.'

David stood and went to join Mac, who was leaning over to listen. Then, there was a terrific bang and the scaffolding vibrated violently as something knocked against it.

'Christ, a litter bin! They'll bring the whole lot down,' muttered Mac.

A bottle flew up but fell short, breaking as it hit the scaffolding.

'Much more of this, and there'll be a breach of the peace.' Jill had woken up.

'What's that mean to us?' asked Polly.

'It means the police will come along and arrest them, but they may arrest us too for causing it.'

'But we're not causing anything!'

Jill shrugged. 'They may say the drunks wouldn't be

chucking litter bins around if we weren't here to chuck 'em at.'

They strained to hear.

'I'm going down,' said Mac. 'See if we can get them to piss off quietly.'

'I'll come with you,' said David.

'Who's that?' asked Jill as the men clambered down.

'A friend of mine, David.'

'I thought you didn't have boyfriends.'

'He's not a boyfriend, really. I don't know why he came.'

'It is a good cause, Polly, perhaps that's why.'

'He's never been near these buildings before. He'd hardly even heard of the protest. He doesn't live in Laureton, you see.'

Jill chuckled. 'Are you sure he's not a boyfriend?'

There came the sound of shouting, and more broken glass.

'I hope they won't get hurt,' said Polly, trying to imagine David in a street brawl and hoping that what Patrick had said about him being a black belt in karate was true.

'I hope they don't put a window in, and someone calls the police,' said Jill. 'I really don't fancy the hassle.'

Just then a burglar alarm went off. 'Oh, shit!' said Jill. 'Someone's bound to get the fuzz in now.'

It seemed only a matter of moments before a flashing blue light could be seen reflecting off the opposite buildings. Polly heaved a sigh of relief. She hated the thought of David being beaten up by a load of drunken skinheads.

Mac came thumping up the ladders, panting hard.

'Get down as quick as you can, girls. We're going to be arrested.'

Jill started gathering her things with practised speed as Mac slithered down again, life-threateningly fast.

'Come on, Polly!' urged Jill. 'Get a move on! If we're quick, we can slip out of sight before the pigs know we're here.'

Polly didn't get a move on. She couldn't. 'I hate to tell you this, you'll think I'm an awful fool, but I –'

At that moment a helmeted figure appeared. 'Good evening, ladies. You're under arrest.'

The policeman was well scrubbed, and agonizingly young. He obviously wasn't expecting to find two women who could easily have known his mother. In different circumstances Polly would have liked to take him home and give him Marmite sandwiches.

'What for?' demanded Jill. 'Trespass is a civil offence.'

The young policeman pulled himself together. 'I'm arresting you for causing a breach of the peace. You have the right to remain silent . . .'

'Oh shit!' said Jill.

'. . . but I must warn you that anything you do say . . .'

Polly thought she must have fallen asleep and awoken as an extra in a police series. She couldn't believe the words she'd heard so often on television were actually being said to her.

'. . . can be taken down in evidence, and used against you. So if you don't mind coming along with me.'

Jill, as vulnerable to a dewy-checked boy dressed as a policeman as the next mother, abandoned any notion she might have had about being obstructive. Besides, she'd get a better night's sleep in a prison cell than on a rooftop on a cold night. She finished gathering her things and rolled up her blankets.

Polly, her fear mounting, did likewise, dreading the inevitable next step.

'Come on, love,' Jill put an arm on her shoulder. 'We may as well get this over with.' She started down the ladders. 'You can bring my stuff,' she said to the policeman, and disappeared.

'Come along, madam,' he said. 'Like your friend said, let's get this over with.'

'I'm terribly sorry, I can't.'

He was put out. 'Are you resisting arrest?'

'No!' Arrest sounded a positively cosy alternative to climbing down those dreadful ladders. 'I'm terrified of heights. I can't get down,' she explained.

The policeman looked nonplussed. 'Wait here.'

Polly sighed deeply, but refrained from asking where she was likely to go to when she was too terrified to move. The policeman disappeared over the parapet.

Another, older policeman appeared. He had grey hair, a moustache and the air of someone who'd very much prefer to be in bed but had a few years to go before retirement. 'Come along, miss. Let's not waste any more time. Just come down.'

'I tried to say. I can't. I don't wish to be obstructive. The thought of spending a night in the cells is wonderful. I just can't get down the ladder.'

He wasn't having any of this, not from a middle-class leftie sitting in the path of progress. 'You got up.'

Polly tried to sympathize. The police didn't have an easy job. 'Only with great difficulty. And going down is far worse.'

'Why did you come then, if you knew you couldn't get down?'

Why, indeed? But she attempted to show some backbone. 'It's a good cause. You should be here protesting, not arresting innocent trespassers.'

'Couldn't you carry her down?' The younger one looked at Polly. 'She's not that big.'

Their assessing glance made her feel like a sack of potatoes, but she didn't point out that she was heavier than two sacks.

The older one shook his head. He'd met her sort before. 'She'll get us on a charge of undue force. And it could be dangerous. She might struggle.'

At least he hadn't refused to carry her in case doing so permanently injured his back.

The young one hadn't thought of this, but hadn't run out of ideas yet. 'The fire brigade are on standby, we could get one of their blokes to carry her down.'

But the older one didn't like the thought of another service interfering in police business. 'They can't get up the High Street, not with all those skips in the way.'

'They could walk.'

'I'm not having that twit Geoff Hacker telling the whole pub we couldn't deal with one lady protester without help. I'd never hear the end of it.'

Polly began to wonder if she would have to stay on top of a listed building for ever, a sort of monument to the triumph of folly over good sense.

The older policeman regarded Polly, debating if she was the hard-nosed litigious sort he had come across at peace camps. He evidently decided she wasn't because he tried to reason with her. 'Listen, love. I'll take your stuff, you come slowly down behind me. You'll be fine.'

Polly shook her head. 'I'm sorry.'

The policemen consulted again.

'Are you married to either of those two men down there?' said the young one.

'No,' said Polly sourly, wondering what on earth that had to do with the price of fish.

'I think what my colleague is trying to say,' said the older one, who'd met her type before, 'is would it help if we got one of the chaps who were up here with you?'

Polly shrugged. 'I don't know, it may.'

'But surely, they're in the van by now,' the young one objected. 'We can't drag one of them out to get her down.'

'It's either that or us doing it,' his superior snapped. 'Do you fancy carrying her down them ladders? Not to mention sure as eggs she'll charge us.'

'Well, she can't stay here.'

Polly tried to think of something constructive to say. 'A general anaesthetic might be the answer.'

They looked at her consideringly. 'Nah, that'd mean a doctor, and all sorts.'

Polly wanted to cry. She had been joking.

'I'll go back down,' said the young one, 'and radio for advice.'

In the end they got David. He was rigid with anger and irritation at the situation, and had a nasty bruise forming on his cheek-bone. 'What's this about you not coming down?'

'I told you, I'm scared of heights.'

At least he didn't need any more explanations. 'I'll have to carry you, then. Stand up, and shut your eyes.'

She got groggily to her feet, to be instantly tipped over his shoulder.

The young policeman made admiring noises, and she heard the older one mutter something about that being the way to deal with uppity females.

At any other time in her life, Polly would have given him hell for this desperately sexist remark, but tonight she decided he was a hen-pecked husband and overlooked it. She had other things on her mind.

Then began the excruciating, tortuous, agonizing descent.

At last the sounds around her told her they were near the ground.

'You can open your eyes now,' David said. 'We're down.'

He pulled her off his shoulder, and then caught her as she staggered briefly. He steadied her shoulders, and then released her before she could topple into his arms and sob with relief.

Deprived of comfort herself, she decided to offer him some. 'Are you all right, David?' She put a hand to his cheek.

He removed the hand. 'I'm fine, thank you. What about you?'

'I'm all right now. Thank you for rescuing me.'

'That's perfectly okay, Polly. Now would you mind getting into the van so we can get this farce over?'

The older policeman, who had now joined them on the ground, muttered 'Hear, hear' into his moustache.

David helped Polly into the van, as if not trusting her to get in without a fuss. Polly started to get angry.

Because she was indirectly responsible for David being in such a ridiculous situation, she felt guilty. And because she knew perfectly well this sort of scene was anathema to anyone as upright and English as he was, and it hadn't occurred to her to ask him to join her, her guilt turned rapidly to resentment.

If he'd kept his aristocratic nose out of her affairs, he could be at the opera now, or eating a dainty little supper after it.

Instead, he was banged up in a paddy wagon with people with whom he had nothing in common, and was about to go to jail. He should have gone to London with some elegant sophisticate and left his country's heritage in the hands of those who cared enough to protect it.

She glared at him, managing to overlook the fact that if he hadn't come she might well still be up there.

Chapter Twenty-three

Jill and Mac were already in the van. The gang of youths had been taken off already. The younger policeman tossed the collection of bags and blankets in behind them, slammed the door shut and locked it firmly. Then they were off.

'Let's hope those skins are out of the way before we get there,' said Mac. 'I've had enough excitement for one night.'

'Have you been arrested before?' asked Polly.

Mac laughed at her naïvety. 'Anyone who's been on the snip as many times as I have has been arrested. It's nothing to worry about.'

Polly didn't look to see how David reacted to this information, and wondered if she should explain that 'on the snip' meant the wire-cutting adventures which went on outside army camps with nuclear installations. But she decided it was hardly worth the effort. At this rate their relationship would be over before he'd even so much as taken her out to dinner.

Fortunately, it wasn't far to the police station or Polly would have been sick.

Polly had only been to Laureton police station once, when she had found a purse in the street. But the building was famous in the town for its utter soullessness and the fact that it had no artistic or architectural connection with the buildings around it. One day it would be preserved as a perfect specimen of sixties glass and concrete. Until then, it glowered over the town with a faceless lack of interest.

The van swooped round some bends into an underground area. The doors were unlocked and Mac was taken out. Before the doors clanged shut again, Polly saw the words 'Loading Bay' painted on an arch. She felt more like a sack of potatoes than ever.

David went next, then Jill. They left Polly until last, but eventually she joined the others in a sort of reception area.

The policeman behind the desk had obviously had a hard time with the skinheads. His expression relaxed somewhat seeing David, the picture of middle-class respectability. The others he dismissed as time-consuming, but harmless.

'Right. I'm the Custody Sergeant, and I've accepted that the charge under which you were brought here is valid. You will be cautioned, and your possessions taken away from you and placed under lock and key in a sealed bag. Could I trouble you to turn out your pockets, sir?' He looked at David.

Polly peered interestedly at the contents of David's pockets. They were sensible, inoffensive things, like car keys, some loose change and a clean handkerchief. Apart from her house keys, her own pockets were full of dirty tissues, till receipts, bits of string, half a very sticky packet of throat sweets, a few coppers and a cup handle.

Mac, who had already disposed of his stash of dope, glibly produced a handful of nails and not much else. Jill had a selection of plastic toys, a purse and her house keys.

The Custody Sergeant swept each person's things into individual plastic bags which were sealed with much ceremony.

Polly signed her inventory which had listed her sandwiches as 'comestibles' and asked if her woolly hat could be added to her things. It was making her ears hot.

The processing took for ever. It was so painstaking, so nit-picking and included embarrassing questions about height and weight. She glanced at David to see if he expressed shock at her replies, but then realized he had better reason than most to know exactly how heavy she was.

A diminutive WPC, who was too fine-boned and pretty to be in such a rough occupation, frisked Jill and Polly with dainty efficiency. The men were searched by a constable with a matter-of-factness born of long experience. And eventually all the forms were filled in and all the questions were answered.

They had declined the services of a solicitor. Mac and Jill told the others that summoning one wouldn't get them out any quicker, and would only prolong the time before they were put into cells and given an opportunity to sleep.

Polly didn't look at David as he and Mac were put into a cell. She would have to live with his silent reproaches for ever, and she didn't need a dagger-like glance to tell her how fed up with her he was.

Jill and Polly were put in together. Jill was a mine of information.

'They'd separate us if they could, but they've probably got prisoners from all over here, and only so many cells. Those skins would take up a fair few of them. We're only here on a breach of the peace, so there's nothing we can collude about.'

'How long will we be held, and what will happen?'

Jill shrugged. 'Dunno, but it's my guess they'll throw us out in the morning. Otherwise they have to keep us here until Monday, take us to the magistrates and slap an injuction on us. I wouldn't mind, I really wouldn't, but I'm so depressed at the thought of those buildings being pulled down.'

Polly sat huddled on the bench, her knees close to her chest. 'I know.'

'And we only needed another ten thou. That's nothing to a rich person. Pity we don't know any.'

'But it would be too late now, wouldn't it?'

'Maybe not. The council might decide that their plans are too unpopular, decide not to press charges and sell the land to the trust. If the trust could come up with enough money, the council would be only too pleased to back out with dignity.'

'Oh.'

'Well, I'm going to get my head down. I've got all those brats to look after in the morning. I wouldn't mind, but Sonia's kids always beat mine up.'

'She won't make you have them now, will she? If you've been in jail all night?'

'Oh yes she will. Nothing for nothing, that's her motto. So, if you don't mind, I'll get some kip.'

To her surprise, Polly also felt remarkably sleepy. It must have been something to do with the fact that there was absolutely nothing else she could do. And because she was very tired.

As Jill had predicted, they were released early the next

morning without charge. They were let out into the sunshine, clutching their plastic bags.

'Well, I'm off,' said Jill. 'I've got kids to look after.'

'Take the flapjack,' insisted Polly. 'With luck, it'll stick their little jaws together.'

Jill tucked the tin into her gaily coloured raffia bag. 'Thanks. Rot their little teeth as well.'

'Do you want a lift anywhere?' asked David.

Jill shook her head. 'Sonia lives just over there. Thanks, though.' She smiled at David in a way which told Polly how very attractive she found him. Polly was surprised to find she didn't like it.

'What about you, Mac?'

Mac shook his head. 'No thanks, mate. I'm local too. You get home and have some breakfast.'

He bounded off up the hill leaving David and Polly confronting each other.

Polly didn't know if she should make her escape while she could. David might easily be hopping mad with her and hiding it under a thick veneer of reserve.

'Let's go home,' he said eventually. He took hold of her bundle of blankets and sleeping bags, arranged them into a more convenient package for carrying and tucked them under his arm. 'Come on.'

He couldn't be as cross as all that. She went with him to where his car was parked, near the buildings. 'I can walk from here, David. It's only a step.'

He regarded her down the length of his scornful nose. 'Just get in the car, Polly.' Then he unlocked it, threw her belongings in the back and opened the door for her.

Dispirited, she got in. She didn't want to go home to an empty house. The whole escapade had been so traumatic, and so utterly futile.

'It's dreadful that after all that those buildings are still going to be torn down,' she said, as they drove away. 'It'll rip the heart out of the town completely. But thank you for trying to help. I'm sorry it went so wrong.'

He glanced at her. 'I think you were very brave to climb up there when you were so frightened. It showed real courage.'

His praise warmed her. 'Thank you.'

'A pity it was totally unnecessary.'

'What? It wasn't unnecessary! It may have been totally useless, but it wasn't unnecessary! I would never have forgiven myself –'

'Shut up a minute, and listen.'

Incensed, Polly shut up. But he didn't immediately speak. He sent his car leaping up the hills and round the corners until they were out of the town.

'I'm still listening. It hasn't done me a lot of good yet.'

He shot her his tantalizing half-smile. 'No, but it will.'

'Go on, then.'

'I'd prefer to wait until we've had a shower and some breakfast.'

Polly looked out of the window at the hedgerows speeding past. 'Very well.' She was hurt that he had referred to their quixotic exploit as 'unnecessary'. It was such a niggardly word.

David parked his car at the back of the house and breezed in through the back door. Polly decided to leave her things in the car and followed more slowly. Monica was in the kitchen and with her was an older woman who had to be her mother, they looked so alike.

David was obviously delighted to see her. 'Mrs Kidd! It isn't spring cleaning already, is it?' he asked.

'I came early,' said Mrs Kidd slowly, 'to make sure Monica's still doin'a good job.'

'Oh she does. An excellent job.' He turned to Monica. 'Who's looking after Anne?'

'Er dad. My dad's there too.'

'Just as well. Mrs Kidd, allow me to introduce Polly Cameron. Polly, this is Mrs Kidd, who used to look after us when my wife was alive. She's known the family a long time.'

Polly did her best to smile. Mrs Kidd's scrutiny made her feel the personification of an unsuitable fiancée. Which, considering she wasn't any sort of fiancée, was galling. 'How do you do, Mrs Kidd?'

'Mustn't grumble, Miss – Cameron.' Mrs Kidd would obviously die of shame if she found out that her daughter called her employer Dave and his friend Polly.

'Is Patrick home?' asked David.

'No,' Monica said. 'He left a message on the machine to say he was staying over at a friend's and would be back tonight.'

Mrs Kidd's stoic expression told her she knew all about children who stayed out all night, not to mention employers who came home in the morning with no explanation.

But David appeared unmoved by his son's social life, or Mrs Kidd's disapproval. 'Would you like some coffee?' he asked Polly.

Polly shook her head. 'I'm dying for a cup of tea.'

'Would you like me to make it, Mr Locking-Hill?' asked Mrs Kidd.

'No, thank you. I'll manage. I'm going to cook some breakfast, too. Don't let us hold you up.'

Mrs Kidd gave Polly another critical examination,

giving very low marks for her jeans, her layers of jumper and her unbrushed hair. Deprived of the opportunity to criticize her table manners, Mrs Kidd reluctantly moved away. 'I'll be waxin' the dining-room chairs, then, if you want me.'

When she had left the room the atmosphere lightened. 'We've spent the night in prison, Monica,' said David.

'You never! What for?'

'Causing a breach of the peace,' said Polly. 'They let us off.'

'Bugger me. Better not tell me mam,' said Monica, and disappeared after her mother with a vacuum cleaner so high-tech and complicated it probably ran off nuclear fuel.

Polly felt a lot better after a cup of tea and a couple of pieces of toast, but declined David's offer of eggs and bacon. It would make the stove so greasy.

'Now,' she confronted David. 'Are you going to tell me why camping out on the buildings is so unnecessary?'

David sighed the long, drawn-out sigh of someone who has spent the night in a small cell. 'I'd rather wait until we've been to bed.'

Polly was horrified. 'What! How can you even *think* about sex, on a Sunday, with Monica and her mother in the house?'

He laughed. 'Actually, my dear, I wasn't thinking about sex. I just thought we both needed some rest. But, of course, now you've put the idea into my head . . .'

'David, please! Mrs Kidd might – or Monica – come back at any moment.' The noise of the Hoover was getting near.

He smiled sleepily. 'You can use the spare room. We

can both have a bath and a few hours' kip, then I'll take you out to lunch.'

Polly subsided, and then chuckled. 'A bath would be nice. Although it's all I ever seem to do at your house.'

He gave her a look which was both quizzical and so piercingly suggestive she felt herself blush. 'Not quite all, Polly. Unless you've forgotten.'

'No, well –' Of course she hadn't forgotten. It was a memory which would warm her for ever.

David rose from his chair and came round the table to where she was standing and gazed at her with explicit intensity for long minutes. Then he pushed his hands up the back of her clothes and undid her bra. He moved round and took hold of her breasts, weighing them with his hands, caressing her nipples.

Polly felt herself begin to tremble. She couldn't believe she could feel so lustful in that gleaming, aseptic kitchen with Monica and her mother cleaning in the background.

Just when she thought she would explode with frustration, he released her breasts and unbuttoned her jeans. He undid the zip and put his hand on her stomach, warm and comforting. Then his palm moved slowly downwards until his fingers could gently probe between her labia and find the entrance to her vagina.

Although her brain cried out that this was not the place, or the time, she knew she was already wet. She wanted to feel him inside her so badly she thought she would die. She closed her eyes and leant her head against his shoulder while with sure and sensitive strokes he brought her to a rapid, shuddering climax.

She sighed deeply as he withdrew his hand, and stayed leaning against him, trying to reorientate herself.

He held her against him while she recovered, then gently pushed her upright.

'Go and get some rest, Polly. Monica and her mother will be gone by twelve.'

Somehow Polly got herself out of the kitchen and found her way to the spare room. For someone who always thought she was frigid, she was turning out to be surprisingly highly sexed.

Polly couldn't sleep. She was clean, she was warm and she was extremely tired, but she couldn't let herself relax and sleep. The trouble was she was still excited by what had gone on in the kitchen. Sex was a drug, and David had made her addicted. By rights she should feel resentful. In fact she just wanted to get through the next couple of hours until twelve, and have another fix.

She decided to put her clothes on and have a look round the garden.

She needed to borrow a coat. Her own was on the back seat of David's car. But no doubt Monica would be able to find her one to borrow. If only she didn't run into Mrs Kidd by mistake.

She was lucky. Monica was in the kitchen on her hands and knees cleaning out a cupboard which had obviously never been dirty. She was wearing vivid yellow rubber gloves which brightened up her black leather no end. She heard Polly come in and turned round.

Polly was about to ask where she might find someone's old anorak, when Monica took a deep breath and started to get a load off her chest.

'I wish my bloody mother would go 'ome.' She rubbed the shelf so hard Polly feared for the Formica surface. 'Thinks she owns this place, she does.' Monica started loading Tupperware into the cupboard as if her life depended on it. 'She's very good to me, I'm not denying that. But I'm good at my work –'

'You certainly are.'

'I don't need 'er checking I've been cleaning the tops of the doors.'

'Well, I expect . . .'

Monica kicked the cupboard door shut with her pointed ankle boot. 'I mean, who taught me to bloody clean, in the first place? And now here she is, telling Dave she 'as to make sure I'm doing it right.'

'Mothers do tend to . . .'

'When will she realize I'm grown up now, and this is my job, not 'ers. She's not like this at 'ome. It's just 'ere! Bein' bloody nosy if you ask me.'

'About your work?'

Monica relaxed and then smiled for the first time. 'No, about you.'

'Me! Why would your mother be nosy about me?'

'Because she's nosy about everyone,' Monica explained. 'And anyway, my mother loved that stuck-up Angela. Thought the sun shone out of her back –'

'Really?' Polly interrupted quickly. 'It must have been very sad for her when she died.'

Monica's expression softened. 'Yeah, she was ever so upset. But that don't mean Dave's got to stay alone for ever, does it?'

'No, of course not.'

Monica grinned again. 'I mean, if he wants a woman . . .'

Polly cleared her throat and changed the subject. 'Did you know Angela well?'

'Not really. I used to come here with me mum, it's how

342

I learned how to be a good cleaner. But I never got to know her. She always made me feel I were makin' a mess, even if I wasn't. Though she was kind enough, and used to give me money at Christmas.'

Polly nodded sympathetically. If her mother worshipped the memory of Angela, and if Monica felt resentful about it, there weren't many people around Monica could tell.

People often told Polly their problems. She was sympathetic, uncritical, unthreatening, and never gave advice. Or, if pressed for it, she expected it to be ignored. But it wasn't often she was so interested in the confession.

'She used to get really upset if anything got broken or dirty. I remember me mum telling me how cross she was when the boys took a rug out into the garden and got it muddy. Turned out it were Chinese silk or somesuch.'

'Well, that would be upsetting.'

Monica moved to the next cupboard and pulled some baking trays and cake tins on to the floor with a deafening clatter. 'I reckon she loved things more than people, she did.'

'I don't suppose she did re –'

'Me mum took me to the funeral, and I felt ever so guilty because I couldn't cry.' Monica's cloth despatched a hundred per cent of all known germs at a swipe.

'I always cry at funerals,' said Polly.

The inside of the door, which was already snow-white, became sterile. 'She was so dainty, so perfect. 'Ad to 'ave clean sheets every day.' Monica sat back on her heels and considered. 'I don't think it could've been because she and Dave –'

'Monica!' Mrs Kidd appeared in the doorway. 'You should be workin', not wasting time talkin'.'

Polly was relieved that Monica couldn't finish her speculations, but resented Mrs Kidd telling Monica off in front of her.

She tried to take the blame. 'I want to look round the garden, Mrs Kidd, but I need to borrow a coat. I was just asking Monica.'

Mrs Kidd's glazed, reminiscent expression told Polly clearly that Angela would not have been so unprepared as to be without a coat. Polly was gearing herself up for a curt refusal, when Mrs Kidd smiled – rather tightly, but still a smile.

'But it's raining, Miss Cameron. Perhaps you'd like me to show you round the house first.'

Polly was complimented. 'Well, if you think Mr Locking-Hill wouldn't mind . . .'

'He won't mind, miss. You come with me.'

Like any visitor to a stately home who finds themselves alone with a keen guide, Polly felt obliged to make intelligent comments about everything she was shown. Her knowledge of marble fireplaces was severely limited and she was relieved when Mrs Kidd suggested they move on from the hall to the dining room. Polly was much more familiar with tables and chairs.

Apart from a massive mahogany dining table and matching chairs which shone like newly fallen conkers, the dining room was full of family portraits.

Some of them were very old. Some tiny and darkened; the ancestor who ran away from home to become a pirate could hardly be seen. But the modern ones were more revealing.

The portrait of David's father showed that he had

David's enigmatic eyes, slightly crooked nose and determined chin. Polly couldn't help wondering what other attributes they shared. There was a deeply contented expression on the face of David's mother.

'Old Mrs Locking-Hill is still alive,' said Mrs Kidd. 'She's a grand old lady.'

'She looks – very handsome.'

'And this – Mrs Kidd was approaching her pièce de résistance. 'This is Mr Locking-Hill's wife. Had it done when they were first married, he did.'

It was a pastel. It showed a young woman staring out over a landscape. She had a chiffon scarf round her neck and her eyes were very bright blue. Patrick's eyes. Her hair was the colour of barley straw and flowed about her bare shoulders, but Polly felt it had only been permitted such freedom for the painting. The woman was handsome in a way that is essentially English. She had good cheek-bones, a strong nose which some might have said was too strong, and a well-shaped mouth, a trifle on the small side. If the artist was to be believed, she had wonderful skin. The whole made a very beautiful picture.

'She's lovely,' said Polly honestly.

Mrs Kidd nodded appreciatively. 'She was Deb of the Year, had her picture in *Country Life* when they got engaged. Look.'

Like a magician revealing a rabbit in his top hat, Mrs Kidd produced an ancient copy of *Country Life* and flicked to the page. Underneath the photograph of a very beautiful girl, apparently naked except for a string of pearls, was her name. The Lady Angela Harecourt.

Polly didn't know quite what to say. Mrs Kidd obviously longed for Polly to comment on the fact that

Angela had had a title, but even to please Mrs Kidd she couldn't. 'What a lovely photograph.'

It was a lovely photograph. It was the sort that employed silk gauzes, artistic lighting and obscure camera angles. It would have made the most ravaged, worn-out hag look innocent and dewy-fresh. With Angela's good looks as a starting point, the effect was stunning. There was probably a silver-framed copy of it on David's desk.

Had it been a terrible disappointment to Lord and Lady Harecourt that their exquisite daughter had married a mere mister? Moving on to an old master, which according to Mrs Kidd had been in the family for generations, Polly decided not. David's ancestors were just as noble, but probably not as sycophantic to the right monarch.

'She was a lovely wife to him,' said Mrs Kidd, a trace of sentiment edging its way into her stern tones. 'Didn't have a job outside the home.' Mrs Kidd stopped being sentimental, and turned fiercely on Polly. 'I don't hold with women having jobs, not if they've got husbands who can keep them. And nor does Mr Locking-Hill, neither!'

While Polly thought it unlikely that David had confided to Mrs Kidd his views on this subject, she thought Mrs Kidd was probably right.

'Oh,' said Polly, in a way which was meant to silence Mrs Kidd on the subject.

'Yes,' Mrs Kidd said firmly. 'It was the way he was brought up.'

Polly smiled blandly, and Mrs Kidd took the hint and shut up.

Polly had already seen the drawing room, but she

allowed Mrs Kidd to show it to her anyway. Polly exclaimed in genuine wonder at the patina on the console table, and the shine on the silver. She allowed her attention to be drawn to the large number of engraved invitations on the mantelpiece.

'He's ever so busy, Mr Locking-Hill. Always attending dinners and suchlike.'

'Ah.'

'Yes. You see, he has his place in society to keep up.'

Polly had a sudden image of David, like Atlas, struggling to hold his 'place in society' above his head. In order that Mrs Kidd shouldn't see her disrespectful smile, she turned to the window.

She could have gazed for ever at the view from the long windows, although now the weather had worsened and she could see the rain scudding across the valley in sweeping grey curtains. But Mrs Kidd recaptured her attention. She was not so pleased with David's taste in art.

'Mrs Locking-Hill liked pictures you could recognize,' she said in front of something very reminiscent of Jackson Pollock. 'She wouldn't have given this house room.'

'No, well, everyone has different –'

'Very particular, was Mrs Locking-Hill.'

'Ah.'

'She didn't hold with books being kept in here, neither.' Mrs Kidd halted disapprovingly in front of a bookcase.

Polly scanned the shelves. David was obviously fascinated by the First World War and naval history, but read few novels. He had bound editions of many of the classics, but nothing at all by women.

'Did Mrs Locking-Hill read?' asked Polly, hoping that this paragon had a secret passion for Mills and Boons which would explain why she didn't keep them in the drawing room.

Mrs Kidd shook her head. 'Mrs Locking-Hill was a very busy person. Did a lot for charity.'

Obviously reading was only for the idle. 'How – wonderful.'

Mrs Kidd accepted the compliment. 'All her clothes – you know, after she died – went to Cancer Research.'

'And did she – er – die of cancer?' Polly wouldn't have asked if Mrs Kidd hadn't so obviously longed to tell her.

'No, it were a car accident. Killed instantly. Terrible shame.'

Polly bowed her head.

'And them two little boys left motherless. They were at school when it happened.'

'How awful.'

'James, now he's a real credit to his parents. But that Patrick –'

'That Patrick' chose this moment to come into the drawing room.

Chapter Twenty-four

Polly's first thought was that now she and David wouldn't be able to spend the afternoon in bed, and her second was that she was pleased to see Patrick He'd obviously changed his mind about staying with his friend until evening.

But Patrick, seeing Mrs Kidd and possibly overhearing her disapproval, merely nodded and reversed out of the room as quickly as possible.

Mrs Kidd inhaled eloquently. 'I won't show you the library,' she said, 'because that's where Mr Locking-Hill does his *work*.'

The emphasis she gave the word made it clear she did not consider Polly a proper person to witness it. In her eyes, women and work, except in a charitable or domestic capacity, didn't mix.

'Now if you don't mind, Miss Cameron, I've work of my own to attend to.'

'Gosh, of course. Sorry to have kept you. It was so kind...'

It was only when Mrs Kidd had left the room that Polly realized she hadn't asked for the guided tour in the first place. No wonder Monica was saving up for a Harley. With a mother like that, you'd need something fast to escape on.

Mrs Kidd hadn't seen fit to show Polly the really

useful parts of the house, like where everyone kept their coats, wellingtons and walking sticks. She contemplated seeking out the collection of disused pantries and larders which this sort of house would be sure to have, to find some sort of mac. But it was raining hard now, and she was beginning to feel tired. She decided to hunt down a cup of tea instead.

Patrick was in the kitchen eating, apparently, an entire packet of cornflakes out of a mixing bowl. He nodded but didn't speak.

'Hello, Patrick. Is it all right if I make myself a cup of tea? I don't suppose there's such a thing as a tea bag, is there?'

He finished his mouthful. 'In that cupboard. They're Monica's.'

Polly found the right cupboard and, eventually, a mug. 'I hope Monica won't mind,' she said, waiting for the kettle to boil. 'Her mother has just given me the tour. It's a lovely house.'

'Mmm.'

'Mrs Kidd was obviously devoted to your mother.'

'Mmm.'

'I'm sorry, Patrick, I shouldn't have mentioned it. That was very insensitive of me.'

''Sall right. I can't remember her very well.'

Polly was too curious to stop being insensitive. 'What was she like?'

Patrick was quite matter-of-fact about it. 'I said, I don't remember her very well. She always smelled nice.'

'That's what little boys always say about their dead mothers, isn't it?' said Polly hesitantly.

Patrick grinned. 'I dare say. I think, though I may be wrong, that she was rather a boring person.'

Polly had come to the same conclusion herself, but she was shocked to hear Patrick say it. 'Patrick, I'm sure –'

'I don't know, of course. It's just when Dad talks about her I feel my eyes glaze over.'

'You shouldn't let –'

'Not that he talks about her often. You wouldn't put the kettle on again, would you?'

Polly had made her tea and Patrick's instant coffee, and they were sitting opposite each other drinking it when David came in.

Patrick's expression changed. His matey if rather monosyllabic manner was replaced by the wariness of the young buck when approached by the head of the herd.

David smiled at his son in a friendly enough way, but it was hard to believe he was the same man who had brought her to ecstasy in this very spot only a couple of hours earlier.

'Hello, Patrick. We didn't expect this pleasure.'

'It's all right, Dad, I'm not staying.' Patrick scraped his chair on the quarry tiles and stood up. 'See ya, Poll.'

David turned his disapproval on Polly. 'Since when has my son called you Poll?'

Polly shrugged and smiled. 'Can't remember.'

David came towards her and put his hands on her shoulders as she stood up. 'I'm not sure that I like it.'

'Tough tit –' The rest of the word was stifled by his mouth, which achieved almost the same effect as his hand had earlier.

When she could speak she asked him what had been worrying her for some time. 'Why didn't you kiss me before?'

'I hadn't brushed my teeth.'

351

Polly laughed, still tasting his toothpaste. 'How gentle-manly of you.'

'What do you expect? Now, are you hungry? I offered you lunch.'

'I could be.' Polly wanted to go out. Staying in the house with David and not being able to make love was a new kind of torture.

He looked her over thoroughly. He would recognize his jumper at any moment. 'It'll have to be a pub lunch, you're looking so' – he paused, as if finding the right word was difficult – 'disreputable,' he said finally, very slowly, every syllable a caress.

It was hardly a compliment, but Polly found herself responding as if he'd touched her. Even his voice was turning her on now. How had she turned so swiftly from an asexual spinster into a sex maniac? She bluffed her way through her embarrassment. 'I can't possibly be. I'm wearing your jumper.'

'Are you?'

'And I've been wearing it for the past twenty-four hours or so. Didn't you notice? You must have too many jumpers.'

'When I look at you, I think not so much of what you're wearing as what you look like underneath.'

'David – *please*! Patrick's here, and I don't know if Monica and Mrs Kidd have gone.'

He had been massaging her upper arms, an area she'd never thought of as an erogenous zone before. Reluc-tantly he let his hands fall. 'I suppose you're right. And we do need to talk.'

For some reason, this made Polly feel suddenly depressed. He sensed it.

'What's the matter? You were nagging me to tell you

why you needn't have risked your life on that roof. Don't you want to know now?'

'Of course I do. It's just ...'

'You'd prefer to spend the time in bed?'

Polly blushed. 'I don't know how you can say that.'

'All it takes is practice. But then, I've been talking since I was quite a small child.'

'That's not ...'

'Come on, before I drag you upstairs.'

He took her to a pub famous for its double pies. Half the dish was a pie with fly-away pastry on top, the other half was cauliflower cheese. Because it was still early they managed to get a table upstairs, where massive old beams actually held the place together rather than forming tasteful backgrounds for horse brasses.

'I didn't see you as a pub person,' said Polly as he set down two glasses and two packets of crisps, 'But then I didn't see you as –'

'What?' He settled himself opposite her.

'Never mind. So, spill the beans.' She sipped her drink.

David adjusted his glass on its beer mat. 'You might not like it.'

'Go on.'

'The reason you needn't have climbed on that roof is that the buildings aren't going to be pulled down.'

'What do you mean? How do you know?'

'The trust has got enough money to buy them from the council.'

'How do you know?'

'I rang them before I came. I came to tell you.'

'Then why didn't you? You could have rung before I went up there and saved me all that angst!'

'I didn't know soon enough. These things take – I mean I couldn't get hold of the right chap in time.'

Polly felt rather let down. 'I thought you came because it was a good cause.'

'It is a good cause, none better.'

'But you didn't really come to protest.'

'No. Because by the time I got there, there was no need to. But I did nearly throw my back out carrying you down those ladders.'

Polly's lips began to twitch. 'And you did get arrested.'

'And I did spend the entire night in a very uncomfortable police cell. What will Melissa say?'

Polly began to laugh. 'And all to tell us the good news. Mac must have been over the moon when you told him.'

'I haven't told him. I wanted to tell you first.'

Polly took another sip of her drink. 'I'm surprised Mac didn't know about it being on the cards. He's in touch with the trust all the time?'

David hesitated and then shrugged. 'They'd only just got the money.'

'But Jill told me they were ten thousand pounds short!'

'Really?'

'How could they have got that and not told Mac?'

'I really don't know the ins and outs of it. Do you think we could order? I'm starving hungry.'

'No, of course, do let's.'

David took hold of her wrist, which was lying on the table, and began to stroke the inside of it. 'What would you like?'

Polly cleared her throat. 'A two-in-one pie, please. Small.' She was lying. She wanted to jump into David's car and race back to bed. To hell with Mrs Kidd and

Monica and Patrick, and anyone else who might be around.

'Fine. I'll order them.' Something about his expression told her he felt very much the same.

'If Patrick's still at home when we get there,' said David, driving dangerously fast, 'I'll give him money to fill his car with petrol. That should get him out of the way.'

'But he'll know *why*,' protested Polly.

'I don't care. I want you, Polly. Very much indeed.'

Polly sighed deeply with anticipated pleasure.

What neither of them expected was that when they got to David's house the drive would be full of cars.

'Hell!'

'Have you arranged a party and forgotten about it?' suggested Polly, horrified. 'Or are they friends of Patrick's?'

David shook his head. 'I very much hope I'm mistaken, but I think these people are from the press. And there' – his voice became redolent with doom – 'is your friend, Tristan.'

'Mr Locking-Hill!'

Men and women in macs and dripping hats surged forward. They were obviously very pleased to see him. They appeared to have been waiting for some time.

Tristan reached the car first, and opened Polly's door. 'Come and tell me all about it, Polly old girl. I really didn't know you and Locking-Hill were such an item.'

Polly opened her mouth to deny everything, but before she could speak David appeared and put his arm around her shoulders.

'If we could all go into the house,' he said, quiet but impressive, 'I will issue a statement.'

355

Patrick, who must have been listening from behind the huge front door, opened it at just the right moment.

'Let's go into the –' David hesitated. 'Kitchen, then we can have coffee.'

His arm clamped Polly to his side so she had to walk in step with him. It reminded her of being in a three-legged race.

They crowded into the kitchen. Polly released herself from David's grip and counted the people.

There was a woman reporter she vaguely recognized from the local paper and a photographer. Another pair introduced themselves as being from the Gloucester paper, and a reporter on his own from Cheltenham. Tristan seemed to be alone, but there was someone else who was fiddling with a tape recorder so there may have been two local radio stations represented.

David came to her. 'Can you help Patrick give them coffee while I think of something to say?'

'Of course, but why are they here?'

David paused, as if working something out.

Tristan forestalled him. 'Don't you know, Polly?' he said. 'Your boyfriend's the hero of the hour. He put up the money to save the buildings.'

The effect of not enough sleep, a pint of lager at lunchtime and severe shock hit Polly's knees at the same time. David pulled out a chair and she collapsed on to it and then leaned her head and arms on the table and closed her eyes.

She heard concerned, female voices wondering about glasses, water, and then David's sterner tones.

'She'll be perfectly all right if you leave her alone. Perhaps you'd better come into the library and I'll make a statement.'

'We'll need a statement from Polly, too,' said Tristan. 'After all, she got you into this.'

'But not now. This way, please.'

Polly listened to a dozen pairs of feet leave the room, and lifted her head. Patrick was still there. He offered a steaming mug.

'It's tea. I've never seen you drink coffee.'

Polly sipped it. 'I don't often. This is wonderful.'

Patrick let her drink her tea for a few moments and then pulled out a chair and sat opposite her. 'So what have you and Dad been up to, then?'

Warmed and cheered by the tea, Polly smiled. 'Do you want the long version, or the abridged?'

'Abridged.'

Polly thought. 'Well, we started on the roofs of those condemned buildings in Laureton, you know?'

Patrick nodded.

'And we ended up in the cells. But they released us without charge, so that was all right.'

Patrick looked at her intently. 'Are you telling me that you got my respectable middle-aged, middle-class paternal relation arrested?'

Polly shook her head. 'He's not middle-aged, and it was the police who did the arresting.'

A grin started at the corner of Patrick's mouth and extended until he could have advertised toothpaste.

'Well, well, well! This'll keep the old man off my back for a while. I've never spent a night inside. Been brought in a couple of times, but I haven't actually been charged.'

'We weren't actually charged either, I don't think. I've lost track.'

'But did you have your belongings taken off you and put in a bag?'

'Yes.'

Patrick was quietly thrilled. 'But why? And how did you get Dad involved?'

Polly rubbed her face to try and clear her thoughts. 'At the time it seemed perfectly plain. Now I really don't know.'

'Go on,' said the embryo psychologist.

'I went up there because I wanted to stop them pulling down those buildings. I'm scared of heights, but I felt so strongly that when they were short of people I had to take my turn. David came up –'

Mentioning his name suddenly made her want to cry. She cleared her throat. 'Your father came to tell us that the buildings had been saved. But before he could, some hooligans started throwing beer cans and litter bins. A shop window got broken and we were carried off on the pretext of causing a breach of the peace.'

'Doesn't sound very fair.'

'No. But they did let us out without charge.'

'Even so, I think you should complain.'

'I'm not into complaining.' She finished her tea. 'Patrick, have you got any petrol in your car?'

'A bit, why?'

'I think it's time I went home.'

At home there were more reporters. They were clustered under her honeysuckle, sheltering from the rain. Tristan must have passed on her address. Polly wished she'd got Patrick to take her all the way home instead of to the top of the road.

'Polly Cameron?' A man waved a ring-bound note-book at her. 'You were on the roofs last night and got arrested? Can you tell us your reaction to the last-minute reprieve of the buildings?'

'Well, I'm delighted, of course.'

'And have you known Mr Locking-Hill long?' It was a woman, no doubt looking for a woman's angle.

'Not very, no. Do you mind if I go in?'

'Just a few more questions, Polly.' Another man spoke. He was very young, and Polly discovered that she disliked her Christian name being used by people she'd never seen before in her life.

'Well?' She sounded remarkably haughty.

Two of them spoke at once. 'Did you know he was going to put up the money?'

'Was it due to your influence that he decided to support the cause?'

'I've no idea. I really don't think I can help you.' She wanted to get to her front door, but with the reporters sheltering by the honeysuckle her only route was through the rambling rose. She hesitated.

The young one, who had spots on his neck, saw her dither and pounced. 'And is it true you were arrested for causing a breach of the peace last night?'

'Yes.'

'You and Mr Locking-Hill?' The woman was eager to link them together.

'And others.' Polly hoped that would be the end of that. 'Can I go in now?'

They shifted about six inches from in front of the door. Polly fumbled for her key and opened it. As she went through they clamoured their last requests.

'We would very much like to hear the whole story.'

'Is there a romance in the air?'

'Are you two engaged?'

Polly turned to her audience. 'No comment.' She marched firmly into the house and tripped over Selina. Then she burst into tears.

When Polly pulled herself together, and had fed and comforted Selina, she realized the house was freezing cold. The Rayburn was out and there was no hot water. The effort of lighting the Rayburn or the fire seemed immense. Her pioneering spirit which had kept her going over the years seemed to have dispersed, along with her courage and independence.

She picked up the telephone.

'Bridget? Can I come over?'

'Of course! Are you all right?'

'No. Yes, I am. But I may want to stay the night.'

'What's happened to you, Polly? You sound traumatized.' Bridget did occasionally lapse into jargon.

'That sums it up pretty well. I spent last night in prison.'

Bridget's shriek caused Polly to hold the phone away from her. She brought it back in time to hear Bridget say, 'Shall I come and fetch you?'

'That would be great.'

The reporters had long since gone, but Polly felt so paranoid she didn't trust them not to be sitting in their cars waiting for juicy quotes.

When she saw Bridget's scarlet Volvo park behind her own car, she ran to greet her. Too late she realized that Bridget would ask far more questions than a whole pack of papparazzi. And she would have to answer them.

To be fair, Bridget held off for quite a long time. She gave Polly chocolate cake and tea, and only started her tactful interrogation when the children had disappeared to watch television and Alan had been dispatched to do some much-needed DIY. She fixed Polly with a sympathetic but very no-nonsense eye.

'You've been holding out on me, Poll.'

Polly sighed deeply. 'I know. I've been holding out on myself.'

'What do you mean?'

'I've been so confused. I haven't known how I've felt about anything.'

Bridget cleared away the tea cups, and got out a bottle of wine. 'I think you'd better start from the beginning.'

'. . . Of course, I can't accept,' said Polly when she had told Bridget everything that had happened since David's strange proposition. 'We come from different worlds. I've never wanted to marry, but if I did I'd want it to have a fair chance of working. And now my pottery seems to have a chance of getting somewhere, I don't want to mess up my life with emotional complications.'

'Oh.' Bridget's romantic heart was disappointed.

'And although in some ways it would be a lot easier to have financial support, I can't risk it going wrong.'

'So, is it the money? The fact that he's so disgustingly rich?'

Polly almost smiled. 'Partly. I mean, what David did was absolutely wonderful, but I can't imagine ever having enough money to just write a cheque for ten thousand pounds.'

'It's not *that* much.'

'Yes, it is. But it's not only that. You've met David, you know what he's like. But his home is even worse.'

'What do you mean?'

'It's even more stuck up than he is. He's got so many

invitations on his mantlepiece he could be at a "function" for every meal, if he wanted. He'd want the sort of wife who would be a credit to him, not one with clay under her fingernails.'

'I would have thought he could have decided that for himself. You are quite well housetrained really.' Bridget chuckled. 'But you'll be telling me next that he's got a housekeeper, like in *Rebecca*.'

Polly shook her head. 'No, I'd be okay there. His housekeeper is a single parent, very young and into black leather. She's saving up for a Harley.'

'A what?'

'A motorbike.'

'Oh. That's all right then.' Bridget was encouraging.

Glumly Polly collected chocolate cake crumbs on her finger. 'No, it's not. You should meet Monica's mother. She *adored* the first Mrs L-H. I'd have said she'd read the book and modelled herself on Mrs Danvers, but I'm sure Mrs Kidd never reads anything except knitting patterns and recipes. She thinks it's a waste of time.'

'You seemed to have got to know her remarkably well. How many times have you met her?'

'Only – gosh, was it only this morning? She gave me a tour of the house. She was there spring cleaning.'

'So she's not there all the time?'

'No. It's Monica who's the housekeeper.'

'Well then, what are you worried about?'

'Bridget, if it were only Mrs Kidd between me and a life of bliss –'

'And time to do your pottery, and a garden, and . . .'

'I wouldn't hesitate. But she's a symptom, not the disease.'

Bridget pushed her chair back and got up. 'It seems to me the only disease is in your head.'

'All those reporters asking me if we were engaged brought it home to me. I just can't do it.'

Then the phone rang. David had finally tracked her down.

'There you are! I've been worried sick. Why did you run away?'

'I couldn't face those people.'

'I might have known it. And you ran to Bridget because there were just as many people at your house?'

'More or less.'

'We need to talk, Polly. To each other. And soon.' He'd become incredibly steely in the intervening hours.

'Look, David. I'm going to stay the night with Bridget.'

'Tomorrow, then. I'll pick you up after work and bring you here.'

'No. If you want to meet me tomorrow, it must be at my house.'

There was a short, eloquent silence. 'Very well. I'll be with you at about eight. We can go out to eat.'

The thought of wading through a meal knowing what she was about to tell him gave her instant indigestion. 'No, David. I won't want to go out. Perhaps I could rustle up –'

'No, don't feel obliged to feed me. I'll eat first. At eight, then.'

His change in attitude forced Polly to the conclusion that either he had sensed what she was about to say or that he was going to say something similar. Saturday night's fiasco must have brought it home to him how unsuited they were as a couple. He wouldn't be disappointed by her decision.

363

On the other hand, it wasn't going to be at all easy to ask David, the epitome of upright decency, if she could please be his mistress.

Chapter Twenty-five

Anticipating his need to pace about, she had pushed her furniture against the walls and removed every extraneous item. She'd won the point. She'd forced him to meet her on her territory so she would be gracious and make things easier for him.

He'd probably be delighted at her suggestion. They were deeply attracted to each other sexually. He could whisk her about in his car, take her to the opera and other wonderful places, and make love to her as frequently as their shared need required. And he wouldn't have to alter his comfortable, tidy lifestyle one iota.

Why was it, she asked Selina, who had viewed Polly's furniture-moving activities with the gravest suspicion, did she feel so nervous about telling him?

About two minutes after David had got in through the door, she decided her anxieties were a premonition. He had in his hand a sheaf of newspapers.

When Polly wrested them from him she discovered he was a hero.

'"LOCAL BUSINESSMAN SAVES HISTORIC BUILDINGS,"' Polly read aloud. 'Good Lord!' She went on: '"Wine merchant David Locking-Hill, fifty-nine" – You're not, are you?'

'No.'

'. . . "Stepped in at the last minute to save Laureton's historic buildings. The row of shops which had been under threat of demolition for the past five months have been saved by a massive donation to the Laureton Trust, which has been campaigning to buy the shops. Mr Licking-Hall" – oops – "actually climbed on to the roof himself to tell protesters of his rescue" . . .'

'I've read it already.'

'. . . "but still managed to get arrested. His heroism didn't end there" . . .'

'Please, Polly.'

'. . . "he also rescued his fiancée" – fiancée!' Polly repeated, horror-struck. 'How dare they? These people are shameless! Can we sue?'

'I'm afraid not. You see, they got it from me.'

'You – told them, these newspaper people, that we were engaged?'

David nodded.

It was the ultimate treachery. 'How dare you? You had no *right*!'

'Calm down, Polly, it's no big deal.'

'Yes, it is! I am not your fiancée. Not now, and not in the future! And you had no right to tell those gossip-mongers that I was.' He seemed unconvinced of his crime. 'I'm not going to marry you, David. I've decided.'

'I only said it to protect you.'

'Protect me from what?' she demanded.

His expression reminded her that she'd run away leaving him to deal with the press alone. 'To protect you from some of what I have been experiencing ever since this absurd escapade began.'

But she refused to accept the blame for any of it. 'Let me remind you that it was nothing whatever to do with me. I didn't ask you to get involved. You did that on your own. And if you've got so much money lying around in loose change that you can sling the odd ten thou to charity, well congratu-bloody-lations. But don't try and make me feel responsible.'

David regarded her for a long minute. 'Like it or not, you are responsible.'

'How come?'

He went to the table and arranged the papers on it into orderly piles. He didn't even know he was doing it.

'I went to see Bradley.'

'Yes? How was your old buddy?'

David looked coldly at her. 'He's a Philistine.'

Polly could think of another, shorter word beginning with 'P' to describe Mr Bradley and his vision for Laureton.

'And?'

'At first he refused to tell me his plans for the site. When he finally agreed to show me, I realized why you are all so passionate about stopping the development.'

Polly waited for as long as she could, but he seemed to have ground to a halt. 'So you put up the money to save the buildings because you genuinely thought it was a good cause?' she prompted hopefully.

He considered his reply for an agonizingly long time. 'Not quite.'

'So why, for goodness' sake?'

'You can be incredibly stupid.' He said it quite mildly, in a way which defused Polly's anger at his high-handed announcement to the press.

'Can I?'

'You really don't understand anything.'

'Hardly my fault, if you don't explain.'

367

'I would have thought you could have worked it out without explanations.'

'Worked what out?'

'Why I spent ten thousand pounds trying to make it unnecessary for you to climb those bloody ladders, why I hauled you down them, why I spent the whole of Sunday afternoon trying to protect you from publicity. It's because, my sweet idiot, I love you.'

Polly thought she was going to faint. She collapsed on to the sofa and considered putting her head between her knees. But she couldn't get around to so much constructive activity.

David appeared to be fairly shocked himself. 'I don't think I've ever said that before.'

'Not even to Angela?'

'Not like that, no.'

She licked her lips. They seemed surprisingly unresponsive to her commands to move. 'I don't know what to say.'

He leant against the arm of the chair. His large body slumped a little. He seemed suddenly very tired. 'That tells me all I need to know.'

'What do you mean?'

'I mean, if you don't know how to respond to a declaration of love, it's pretty clear you don't reciprocate. Is that why you decided not to marry me?' he continued in flat, matter-of-fact tones.

'No – no, not really. We're just so unsuited. Our lives are too different to bring together. You live in a stately home with people like Mrs Kidd fussing round you, and I live here. And people like Mac are my friends.'

'I feel I know Mac pretty well myself, after spending a night with him.'

'Yes, but you wouldn't have met him if it hadn't been for me.'

'No, but . . .'

'Our social circles are too different, David. If I married you it would be like planting a rhododendron in a limy soil.' She saw that this didn't mean much to him. 'For a while the marriage would look okay, but then it would start to go yellow at the edges and eventually die. Because the soil conditions were wrong. If I transplanted myself to your world, I'd lose my identity.'

'Really? And what about my identity?'

'You're a man, you're strong. You haven't had to struggle to make a life for yourself like I have. If I married you and it went wrong, I'd have to start again from scratch. You could just carry on. I can't take the risk – not when it looks as if I can make it as a potter.'

He regarded her as though from a long way away. His resigned acceptance of her refusal was dispersing, to be rapidly replaced by anger.

'That probably sums up the difference between us fairly well. You can't take the risk, you had to struggle to make your life, I didn't. Actually, I think the only difference between us is guts!'

She tried to speak, but his expression stopped her. 'I may be a rich man now, Polly. But if I am, it's because I worked, and still work, bloody hard. I nearly lost the house to death duties, but I saved it – by taking risks. I could have lost everything, but I thought the chance worth taking.' His eyes condemned her as spineless.

'But you would rather stay in your safe little cubby hole and maintain the status quo than be forced to prove yourself. While you're here, you'll always have some excuse not to take your pottery seriously. Oh, I realize

you're good and that you've got London shops interested, but how long will it take for you to save up for a
bigger kiln, or whatever it is you need to really get
going?'

She tried to protest, but her vocal cords wouldn't
cooperate.

'You seem to think that marrying me would somehow
compromise your integrity as a potter. I think it's just a
fucking excuse so you don't have to be a potter! Because
without the inconvenience of my money you won't ever
have to do it every day, and see how it fares against
other, professional potters. No, stay poor, stay amateur,
safely single.' He took a long breath. 'When it comes
down to it, Polly, you simply don't have the courage to
take a chance and risk changing your cosy little world.'

Mercilessly he tore up her life into pieces, he who had
made love to her so tenderly, with such sensitive
understanding. In the course of a few moments he had
turned from her lover to her most relentless critic,
decimating her with calculated cruelty. She buried her
face in her hands in an effort to gather her thoughts.

'And if you even think of crying –' His voice was no
longer cold, it was level, conversational and intensely
threatening. 'If you shed so much as one tear, I shall slap
you!'

She looked up and flinched from his expression. He
was hurting, and needed to strike at the source of his
pain. He wasn't the sort of man to hit women, but then
again he wouldn't make empty threats, either.

'I'm the one who should be crying!' He knocked into
the table again as he crossed the room. 'I offered you my
heart, and you tossed it up in the air a few times then
you let it fall into the gutter. Because you don't need it.

You've got your safe little life, and that's enough for you.'

'David, it's not –'

'Heaven forbid that anything should threaten your cosy cocoon of cats and clutter and prejudice. It's unreasonable of me to suggest that you might care to sacrifice some of your personal space, your independence, your pig-headed belief that you can manage on your own. I can't imagine how I came to be so insensitive. Well, if you can manage without love in your life, so can I. Thanks for nothing.'

Polly dragged her voice back into service. 'Couldn't we – I mean, wouldn't you – couldn't we go on being lovers?'

This time she thought he really was going to hit her. His fist clenched, he drew it back but when it shot forward it was into the palm of his other hand. If it had landed, it would have broken her jaw. He breathed hard for long, shuddering minutes. But when he spoke again, he was quite calm.

'I didn't realize there was anything more insulting than an offer to remain "good friends". But I was wrong. There's the suggestion that you keep me on as a pet, a gigolo. A gigolo who pays. That really takes insult to an art form.'

He gave a mocking bow. 'I'm afraid I must refuse your generous suggestion, but please don't hesitate to make it to someone less scrupulous. It does seem a shame to let that wonderful body and all that erotic talent go to waste.'

He picked up his coat from where he'd left it and shrugged into it. It made him the size of an angry bear.

'Just remember, when you finally choose your stud,

that whatever he does to you, or you do to him, it won't be anything near as good as what we had. Because it'll only be sex which, when it comes down to it, is pretty turgid, run-of-the-mill stuff. You turned down the real thing for your petty independence. I hope it makes you happy.'

The sound of the door slamming behind him stayed in her ears for long minutes. Then the phone rang. It was the local paper wanting to do a profile on her about her efforts to save the condemned shops.

'Oh, piss off!' she hissed, and slammed down the receiver.

Polly walked slowly up the hill from the café. Her shopping bags were unusually heavy. In one of them was a bottle of whisky, bought with some of her telephone bill money. With luck, British Telecom would cut her off and she would never have to answer the telephone again.

But if they intended to, they hadn't done it yet. The darned thing was ringing its head off as she struggled through the door. She knew it was her mother: some ancient, maternal witchcraft had told Sylvia Cameron that her daughter had rejected one of the most eligible men in Gloucestershire (bearing in mind Polly was on to the second flush), and she wanted to know why.

'Hello?'

'Darling! You sound *dreadful*! What's the matter?'

Was it possible that Sylvia actually didn't know? 'I'm a bit tired . . .'

Sylvia's sympathy was but fleeting. 'I'm not surprised. The things you've been getting up to!'

'What things?'

'It's in the paper!'

'What paper?'

Sylvia told her. It seemed that the story had been picked up by some of the tabloid dailies.

'Well really, Mummy, if you will read the gutter press . . .'

'I didn't buy it, darling. I just happened to see it in the hairdresser.'

Polly considered suggesting that her mother went to a better class of hairdresser, but didn't get the chance.

'You and David Locking-Hill. Are you really engaged?' Sylvia demanded sharply.

'No.'

'Oh, good. It would have been so cruel of you not to tell me.'

Polly began to laugh weakly. 'I'd never do anything like that to you, Mum. I know how important . . .'

'It's a poor show if a girl's own mother is the last to know.'

'Yes.'

'But why did the paper say you were engaged?'

'I don't know! You know what papers are, they always get it wrong.'

'What a shame. Still, I expect he will marry you if you apologize.'

'Apologize for what?'

'Doesn't matter, darling. It's the women's role. Men can't apologize, you see, so the woman has to. Then the man can say, "Oh no, it was all my fault." '

'Mummy, you're mad!'

'He's such a nice man. So right for you, darling.'

'Mother dear, apart from the fact that there is nothing

373

in this rumour, and I am not going to marry David, he and I are *not* well suited. That's why I ref –'

'So he did ask you?'

Polly wondered how old she would have to be before she could hide things from her mother. 'It's no good. We're totally unsuitable for each other, it would end in a hideous painful divorce.'

'Nonsense, darling. All you have to do is be a bit tactful. Keep your feminist ideas to yourself. A man won't stand for too much independence in a woman, you know.'

'Mother, I have to go. There's someone at the door.' She spoke with the heartless briskness of a much-tried daughter.

There wasn't anybody at the door, but Polly had barely made herself a cup of tea before the phone rang again.

Resolving to hide it under a pile of cushions the moment she escaped, she picked it up. 'Yes?'

'Polly? Is that you? It's Melissa.'

It was, she supposed, inevitable. 'Oh. Hello.'

'What is all this in the papers? I tried to get hold of David, but apparently he's gone away on business. Are you and he really engaged?'

'No.'

'Oh, good. Because it would never work in a million years, you know.'

'But you introduced us.'

'I'm not the village matchmaker. I didn't expect you to get married.'

'Well, we're not.'

'Good. You'd drive him mad. You're too scatty. Angela was so –'

Here we go, thought Polly.

'Well organized. Nothing was ever so much as an inch out of place in that house.'

'It still isn't.'

'What?' Polly could practically see Melissa's ears picking up alarm signals. 'You've been there? When?'

'Only a couple of times.' But oh, how action-packed were those times!

'But I don't understand. I thought you said you weren't engaged.'

'We're not. You can visit a man's house without the protection of a ring, you know. These days. Mrs Kidd's a dear old thing, isn't she?'

Quite why she threw that in, knowing it would drive Melissa wild, Polly had plenty of time to consider while her friend indulged in mild apoplexy.

'You've met Mrs Kidd? Angela thought the world of her.'

'The feeling was mutual.'

'How did you get to meet her?'

Melissa could have been talking about royalty rather than a retired housekeeper. 'She showed me over the house. She seemed to think it was her role rather than Monica's.'

'Monica! That little punk David took in out of the kindness of his heart?'

Polly bit back the information that the little punk called her master 'Dave'.

'She's extremely good at her job. Mrs Kidd's her mother.'

'When did this tour go on?'

'Yesterday morning. When David was in bed.'

'You mean all that about the buildings and the police

and prison were true?' Melissa sounded as if she were speaking from a long way off.

'Yes.'

'And did he really carry you down off the roof? Like they said in the paper?'

'I can't answer for the paper, but yes, he did carry me off the roof.'

There was a long pause. Polly couldn't actually hear Melissa taking long, soothing breaths and fighting back the tears, but she could visualize it.

Eventually she spoke. 'If you don't make him happy, I'll never speak to you again!' Melissa slammed the phone down.

In films, thought Polly, piling blankets on to the phone as if she were trying to suffocate it, people take the phone off the hook. Try that nowadays and it screeches at you.

She put a pan of milk on the stove and added a spoonful of honey and a good dollop of whisky. The result was soothing and soporific. But it was no substitute for a pair of strong arms.

'It's the World Service for you and me,' Polly told Selina. 'It's a good thing we like it so much.'

In some ways, things began to get better. The press interest died away, the customers got their opportunity to tease her about it and then didn't mention it again. Even Beth eventually stopped singing 'Up on the Roof' every time she saw Polly.

But artistically Polly seemed stifled. The clay, which used to be a yielding and compliant ally, became perverse and stubborn, refusing to translate her ideas into tangible objects.

David's taunts about being afraid of having to test her

work against other, 'professional' potters rankled. His pride was hurt, and he had been trying to hurt her back. But was he right? Had the vicious circle of poverty, which made it impossible to devote enough time to pottery to make a living at it, really been a rubber ring which protected her from the roughness of the waves of real life?

She now accepted, though wouldn't admit it to a living soul, that she was deeply in love with David. She loved his stuffiness, his pedantic way of speaking, his formality, his tinder-dry sense of humour which so often took her by surprise.

She was also so sexually attracted to him that it was almost an obsession. She still couldn't understand why her suggestion they remain lovers had made him so angry. It seemed such an ideal solution. And surely it was women who were so hung up on commitment? Why was David so all or nothing about their relationship?

And while she fervently hoped she would finally settle back down into the life she had argued in favour of so hotly, she hadn't managed it yet.

Chapter Twenty-six

꧁꧂

Nearly a fortnight after David had stormed out of her life for ever, Polly was trying to summon up interest in her macaroni cheese which she'd made three days ago and still hadn't finished, when there was a knock on the door.

Even after she'd opened it, it took her a while to recognize Patrick. He had on a suit which was too big for him across the shoulders, some sort of regimental tie and a pure white shirt. His long hair was tied into a neat ponytail.

Once she was sure it was really him, she opened her door widely.

'Patrick! How lovely to see you! Do come in. Are you hungry? Can I interest you in some macaroni cheese?'

Patrick came in, but slowly, and Polly realized he was not his usual laid-back self.

'What's with the suit, Patrick? Have you been for an interview or something?'

He shook his head.

'Cup of tea, coffee, glass of wine?'

He shook his head again.

'So what can I do for you?'

At last he spoke. 'I came to see why you're being so tight to Dad.'

'What do you mean?'

'He's gone, you know.'

'What do you mean, gone? Melissa said something about him being away on business, but –'

'He's not away on business. He's gone AWOL.'

'I don't understand.'

'It means, "absent without leave".'

'I know *that*. But how has David done it?'

'He's walked out on everything. Left his business. Taken a permanent vacation.'

Polly felt she'd been punched in the stomach. She was far too upset to cry.

Patrick went on, 'It's funny, really.'

'Funny?' Polly had never heard anything less funny in her entire life. For David to turn his back on everything and disappear seemed as unlikely as the world to start spinning in the opposite direction. Yet it seemed he had done just that.

'Ironical, then.'

'What is?' It was no good hurrying Patrick.

'That of all the women who've chased Dad since Mum died he should fall in love with you.'

'Why is that so strange?'

She spoke softly, terrified that the wrong reaction would make Patrick revert to nods and monosyllables. She passionately wanted to hear every word he had to say about his father, and his feelings for her.

Patrick stared desolately into the fire. 'Because you won't have him. You've played so hard to get you're hardly in the same game, and yet for some reason you're the only woman I could stick being married to Dad.'

'Why?'

'For once our tastes coincide.'

She was horrified. 'Patrick!'

For the first time that evening a smile lifted the corner

of Patrick's mouth, making him look more like David than ever. 'Don't burst a blood vessel. I only said I fancied you. I've no intention of murdering Dad so we can have a bit of leg-over.'

'Patrick!'

'And I know you won't try and be a mother to me.'

Polly shuddered. 'I'd rather mother Damien!'

'Exactly. And you won't get into a paddy if I don't conform to what the privileged classes consider normal behaviour.'

Thinking about this, Polly conceded, 'Well, no. I suppose I wouldn't.'

'So don't you care about Dad? Too stuffy for you, is he? I can see he's not the perfect choice if you're into open marriages and all that shit. He's got some very old-fashioned ideas about things like that.'

'Of course I'm not into open marriages! I love David very much, but I can't marry him.'

'Why the fuck not?'

'Because –' She was tired of answering this question, and made a sweeping gesture as a short cut. 'Look at my house. It's mine, and I love it. But it's not the same as your house. We come from very different places, Patrick. And those things are important. I wouldn't give our marriage a snowball's chance in hell.'

'Because Dad lives in a big house, and you don't?'

'There's also my pottery. David would want a wife to be ready with his pipe and slippers when he got home. I wouldn't be willing to drop everything in order to cook for him. Oh, I'm sure he could cope with my pottery if it kept its place and didn't impinge on his comfort, but women married to men like David are expected to make a career of being married.'

'You've no evidence for any of that.'

Polly tried to explain. 'Patrick, you're probably too young to realize just how things have been for women over the centuries . . .'

'Yeah, right.'

'But men like David – I mean, men from David's section of society – expect a lot from their wives. They don't expect them to scrub floors or even necessarily iron shirts, but they expect to come first. Supposing, for example, David managed to wangle a couple of weeks off and wanted us to go somewhere. How would he feel if I had something important coming up, and couldn't go with him?'

'Disappointed?'

'Disappointed and resentful. He'd resent my work, I'd be torn between the two and miss out on both.' She took a breath. It seemed important to make Patrick understand why she was apparently so willing to break his father's heart.

'And what about the social side of things? I mean, I like entertaining as much as anyone, but on my terms, not according to a whole lot of outdated social mores when the ladies withdraw and leave the gentlemen to their port.'

'I hear what you're saying, but you've got Dad all wrong. He does his social duty, sure. But he doesn't really enjoy it. He's not into that formal crap. He only goes with the flow. If having you for a wife drove away the boring old farts, he'd be delighted.'

Polly shrugged. 'You might be saying these things out of loyalty to your father, or you might believe them. But you might be wrong.'

'And you're not prepared to take the risk?'

Once she would have had no hesitation – marriage was not for her. Now she was less certain, the arguments were less clear-cut. 'If I did and went to live with you in that great big house, my friends would never come and see me. I'd lose my support system. Then, if it went wrong, I'd have to start all over again. I'm too old for that sort of thing.'

'You're younger than Dad. He's obviously prepared to take a few chances.'

'But it's not him who'd have to make the adjustments.'

Patrick laughed incredulously. 'Wouldn't he?'

'Not in the same way. He wouldn't come and live in my house.'

'No, I suppose not.'

'And he walked out on me, you know. I was quite prepared for us to go on seeing each other.'

Patrick grinned. 'Dad's a little old for girlfriends.'

Polly was offended. 'I didn't mean as a *girlfriend* exactly . . .'

'You meant mistress?'

Somehow, coming from Patrick, it sounded tawdry. 'That implies that I'd accept money from him, which I never would.'

Patrick sighed. 'So it comes down to money, does it?'

Polly didn't know what it came down to any more. 'Sort of. I don't know.'

'He's rich, you're not. End of potentially happy relationship.'

Polly shrugged again.

'Would you have let money come between you if he'd been broke?'

'Of course not . . .'

382

'So what's the difference? Either money's important or it isn't. I don't think it is.'

Polly smoothed the bedspread which covered the arm of the sofa. It was loopy from Selina scratching at it, and was developing a hole. 'Nor do I, I don't suppose.'

Patrick sensed a breakthrough. 'And this "friends" thing. Frankly Poll, I don't know why you're getting your knickers in a twist. If your friends like you, they won't stop liking you because you move house. If they change towards you, they're not real friends. Whatever problems we two have, Dave's okay when you get to know him. They'd probably get to like him too.'

'Would they?'

He nodded. 'You did.'

Polly inspected her fingernails for a long time. 'All right. Tell him if he rings, I'll speak to him.'

Patrick stared at her, confused. 'But I can't! I thought I told you. He's done a bunk.'

The blood drained from her face as Polly looked at him in stunned, horrified silence.

'I thought when you said he'd gone on vacation, you meant he'd gone to your house in France.'

Patrick shook his head. 'No. But I can't get in touch with him unless he gets in touch with me. So far he hasn't. You'll have to go to him yourself.'

Doubt fell over Polly like a shroud. 'I don't think I dare. Besides, he'd never take me back, even if I begged.'

Patrick didn't contradict her. 'You would have to beg. He's hellishly proud. But he loved you two weeks ago and he probably still loves you. Surely it's worth a try?'

'I can't! I'd feel such a fool!'

'You are a fool. Don't be an even bigger one.'

Polly briefly considered mentioning something to

Patrick about respecting his elders, but as they seemed to have reversed their roles she decided against it. 'You're a lot of help, you are.'

'I am, actually. Which little boy scout has been keeping the family firm going in Papa's absence?'

'What, you? Or your brother?'

'No, James has got exams coming up and is too busy revising to help Dad out. It's yours truly, aka the Cavalry, who's keeping the restaurants, bars and off-licences of the South West in fine wine at reasonable prices. Hence the suit.'

'You look good in it.'

'It's not my scene, but I couldn't let Dad down. I hate the bastard most of the time, but blood's thicker and all that. Fortunately there's a chap to do the bits I'm too young to do, seeing as I'm under eighteen.'

Polly laughed. She felt better than she had for ages. 'So where is this father you're so devoted to then?'

'He's borrowed a bothy in Scotland.'

'I beg your pardon?'

'Well, shepherd's shack, really. It's on the shores of a loch and is miles from anywhere. It's over a mile from the road.'

'Good God!'

'We used to go there on holiday. It's great for kids. Lots of burns to dam, stuff like that. We cooked over an open fire.'

'But there has to be a cooker!'

Patrick shrugged. 'I can't remember. It's years since we went. We used to pee outside though. And wash in the burn.'

Polly shifted uncomfortably. 'Well, give me the address and I'll write.'

Patrick shook his head.

'Don't tell me. It's ten miles to the post office, and he won't know to collect letters even if he does go there?'

'You're getting the picture.'

'Oh. Then it looks like I'll have to wait until he comes back, doesn't it?'

'If you don't go and see him he may not come back. And that'll leave me a poor, defenceless little orphan.'

'Orphan I'll accept, but not little or defenceless.'

'Still. You'll have to go, Poll. If you love him, that is.'

Polly stared at the worn patch on the hearth rug for a long time. 'Yes, I love him. I'll go.'

Patrick's face lit up like a sunflower. 'Bloody impossible place to find. Will your car make it?'

The thought of her car having to pound up the motorway for ten hours or so at forty miles an hour made her shudder. It would be like asking Selina to go ten rounds with a pit bull terrier. 'Probably not. It's old and it's due for its MOT, and I know it needs welding before it has a hope of passing. What can I do? Borrow your car?'

'Nah. Mine's in worse nick than yours. You'll have to hire one.'

'There's the poor little rich kid talking. What with?'

Patrick rummaged in his pocket and produced an alarmingly large roll of notes. 'Here, borrow this.'

Polly's mouth went dry. 'Where did you get it from?'

Reading her mind, Patrick grinned. 'Selling crack, what do you think? Twit! One of the customers paid me. Call it petty cash.'

'Patrick, I can't use David's money –'

'Yes, you can. You can spend the rest of your life paying him back, in kind.'

385

'Sometimes, Patrick, I think you're not a nice boy at all.'

'Oh, Mummy, don't say that!'

Polly growled. 'Patrick, if you ever call me "Mummy" I'll kill you!'

Patrick tutted sadly. 'I can see you're going to be a really wicked stepmother.' Then he laughed. 'Hey, that's a pun. Do you geddit? Wicked means good, but it also –'

'I do speak the language, you know. And you can eat the macaroni cheese, or you can wear it. Make your choice.'

It was surprisingly easy to hire a car. The man was helpful and efficient until, inspired by his accent, Polly mentioned her destination.

Instantly he reacted as if Polly was planning to cross Siberia with only a Pakamac and a bicycle pump.

'Ye'll need better tyres than these.' He kicked the ones already in situ with derision. 'These'll nae be any guid tee ye North of the Border. Not if the weather turns nasty. Jimmy!' he roared. 'Put some decent tyres on this for the young lady. She's going North.'

Jimmy, also a Scot, insisted on checking Polly's road atlas and the route plan which Alan had painstakingly worked out, offering desperately complicated alternatives wherever possible.

By the time Polly escaped, deeply touched but also a little irritated by their paternal concern, it was nearly eleven o'clock, at least an hour later than she had planned.

That morning she had taken Selina to Bridget's, where she would spend most of the time on Cherry's shoulders and come back several pounds heavier than she went.

Something about Bridget's household encouraged comfort eating.

Bridget had sent her best wishes, Alan had planned her route and listed every junction, roundabout and hole in the hedge he could remember. He also told her which were the best service stations along the M6. After then, Polly was on her own.

Patrick had been round to tell her how to find the place, as well as he could remember.

'Here's the Ordnance Survey.' His finger jabbed at a patch of map which at first sight seemed to represent the Himalayas. 'And here is the loch.' A sickle of blue broke the unrelenting brown. 'The road goes here, but then you have to turn off. One of these tracks, I think.'

'But where's the house?'

'It isn't a house, Poll. It's a stone shack.'

'Well, whatever.'

'I'm not quite sure. You'll have to park the car and walk. We could ring the friend Dad's borrowed it off and ask for better directions, but he might drive over to Dad and tell him you're on your way.'

'And that would be bad?'

'I really don't know, but he might bunk off again and then you'd have driven all that way for nothing.'

She shuddered. 'Then let's not risk it. I'll just go.'

Polly stopped every two hours, and every time she thanked God and Patrick that she had hired a car, and Alan for his directions.

This car had an effective heater, efficient windscreen wipers and was fast. The weather was fine, she enjoyed the scenery and she negotiated the usually nerve-racking transfer from one motorway to the other without hazard.

Once on the M6, she put her foot down. The thought that she was flying up the motorway to meet her lover inspired her, until she noticed how rapidly the needle on the petrol gauge moved to the left, and how inflated petrol prices were on the motorway.

Shortly after Stafford, she stopped at a service station to fill up and count her money. She would have to be very careful and drive a lot slower. From then on she kept to sixty miles an hour, but stuck to her resolution to stop every two hours even if she could only afford a cup of coffee.

It was five when she reached the border, and to celebrate she allowed herself a Danish pastry to go with her tea. She looked round the shop to give herself a chance to stretch her legs. It was full of Scottish dolls, tartan rugs and heathery little creatures claiming to be tame haggis. Polly had never been to Scotland before, but even this touristy glimpse of it made her excited. She bought a packet of something called 'tablet', which turned out to be a sort of extra-crisp fudge, to give herself energy.

It started to rain just as the motorway ran out shortly after Carlisle, seamlessly continuing as a dual carriageway. But when the rain turned to snow on Beattock Summit, her excitement about being in Scotland slipped into anxiety. She had been driving for eight hours. She no longer thought of her ultimate destination, or what might happen if she actually arrived. She concentrated on the next place name on the list and thought about the tea or hot chocolate she would have when she found a roadside café.

Now these were hard to find, and she soon stopped being picky about the potential state of the lavatories. And her initial self-consciousness about being the only unaccompanied female with a Home Counties accent in a steamy café full of chain-smoking lorry drivers rapidly faded. All she cared about was the money and the car holding out.

It was past nine when she turned off the mountain pass on to a sheep track. It was snowing in earnest now, and she was grateful for the fuss Jimmy and his boss had made about the tyres.

She stopped the car and checked with the map that she was in the right place. There was a turn-off approximately three miles along the road. She had been at least that, and found no turning.

She briefly considered going back, but the thought of doing a three-point turn on a narrow road with deep ditches on either side of it dissuaded her. She'd been looking so hard for the lane or track, she couldn't have missed it. She made a mental note of the milometer and set off again. The needle of the petrol gauge was hovering on E. That meant she probably had at least thirty more miles left in the tank. It would be all right. It had to be. If she took a wrong turning, she could be prevented by the conditions from getting back on to the main road again.

The road led higher and higher up the hill which was becoming a mountain. Another squint at the map told her she'd gone too far.

'Four hundred odd miles too bloody far,' she said aloud, to comfort herself. And then wished she hadn't. The words hung on the air, emphasizing how alone she was.

Taking infinite pains, she turned the car at a passing place and set off back down. Patrick had talked about a loch being near. He talked about mountains only in terms of scenery.

If the conditions had been better, she'd have free-wheeled to save fuel. As it was, she crept along until the road flattened out completely and she was nearly on the Glasgow road. When she stopped the car to retrieve the map from where she had bundled it on the passenger seat and confirm that she was lost, it wouldn't start again.

'Oh, David. How could you do this to me?' She banged her fist on the steering wheel. 'Bastard!'

Chapter Twenty-seven

❧

The sensible thing would be to wait in the car until morning, and then seek help. For a while, Polly did the sensible thing. But the combination of boredom and anxiety was too powerful for her. She studied the map again, found her torch, retrieved her British Warm overcoat from the back of the car and decided to walk.

It would be easier to find the track on foot, she argued.

Up till then, she thought she'd felt every flake of snow and every breath of wind which buffeted the car and made her swerve across the road. It was only when she left the heated, draught-free carapace did she realize how much it had protected her from the fierceness of the elements.

The blizzard nearly knocked her over as she got out. She staggered, and debated whether to get back in again. People did die of exposure, really quite often. No. If the snow got worse, she could get back in the car. She retrieved her wellingtons; she pulled out her bag and put on her woolly hat, but left the bag. Three paces on, she returned and dug out the couple of jumpers she had thrown in. There were a few frozen moments as she stood in the snow without her overcoat as she put them on. Then she set off into the night, hardly able to walk for the amount of clothes she was wearing, glad of every item.

But she wished, the moment she switched it on, that she'd put a long-life battery in her torch instead of a rechargeable one which faded almost immediately.

'I wouldn't go through all this if it wasn't for David,' she spluttered into the wind.

And then, as the cold really began to bite, penetrating her many layers of clothes like water through a sieve, she realized she wouldn't *have* to go through all this if it wasn't for David.

At last, after retracing her steps several times, she found something which might have been the track. It seemed to lead straight up the mountain into the leaden sky, but as far as she could tell it was the right one. And it was better than patrolling the main road, knowing she couldn't possibly find the house until she had turned off.

Arriving no longer seemed a possibility, more a constant, unlikely dream, like winning the football pools.

Wellington boots are not made for walking long distances in. They pulled the socks she was wearing over her tights down under her instep, and she kept having to take them off to pull the socks up.

Several times, as she hopped from foot to foot adjusting her footwear, she longed to be able to stop fighting the elements and just lie down and die peacefully of hypothermia. How long, she wondered, would it take them to find her frozen body?

But once a little way round the mountain, she saw a light. It was dim and far off, but it meant some sort of civilization. If it wasn't David, she would settle for whatever kilted Highlander happened to open the door. She was past the point of being fussy.

Her heart lightened enormously when she saw David's car parked at the side of the track. The fact that the track ran out at this point, and the light was still the merest pinprick in the snowy night, and was probably miles off, didn't faze her.

Several times she fell. Each time her resentment towards him grew as she cursed her foolishness for coming. At last the shack came into view. She staggered the last few hundred feet. She had made it.

She barely had the strength to bang on the door, and her fist made no sound over the howling wind. Then she found a stone and used it as a knocker. David would hear her if she had to break the door down.

There was no reply. Polly banged harder, but although there were lights on in the house, there was no sound of movement. It was starting to snow harder, and although Polly didn't imagine she was in imminent danger of being buried in a snowdrift, she didn't want to stay out in the open any longer. Tentatively she tried the door. It wasn't locked. She opened it and called out.

'Hello! David! Are you there?'

No reply. She opened the door wider and went in.

It was a long, low room, with rough, whitewashed walls and a wooden floor. There was a fireplace at one end of the room, and a kitchen area at the other. The fire was made up and going well. Drawn by its dancing flames, Polly went into the room and shut the door behind her. There was no sign of porridge bowls on the scrubbed table which took up most of the kitchen end of the room. Otherwise it was pure Goldilocks.

One of the wing-back chairs was pulled closer to the fire than the other. On the table beside it was a book. It had a book marker in it, and was about fighter pilots in the First World War. It had to be David's. Anyone else would have left the book face down.

She realized she was desperately thirsty, and made her way to the kitchen end. A saucepan, which had recently cooked scrambled eggs, was soaking in the sink – another sign of David. She found a gas fridge with half a pint of long-life milk in it. She washed the saucepan, poured out some of the milk and added some water. By the time it had boiled she would have found something to flavour it with – cocoa, honey, and if she knew David at all, some whisky.

There was no honey, but she found some very hard white sugar in a bowl, which had probably been there when Patrick last spent his summer hols at the house. This, with a generous dollop of the single malt which would always remind Polly of that life-shattering night, made quite a soothing drink.

There was a small, icy bathroom tacked on behind the kitchen. In it there were other reassuring traces of David's presence – a navy-blue and gold-striped sponge bag, toothpaste, his aftershave. Polly took a quick sniff, and then wished she hadn't. It filled her with an aching longing and loneliness. Where was David?

She was glad to get back to the comparative warmth of the main room. David must be some sort of masochist to come here in this weather.

Polly paced about examining her surroundings. Mrs Kidd would die at the thick layer of dust on the window sills, and the general air of neglect. But although it was sparsely furnished, it could have been delightful.

There were the two wing-backed armchairs on either side of the fire, something halfway between a dresser and a sideboard along the back wall and a chest of drawers which Polly hoped was called a 'kist'.

A pair of antlers hanging on the wall by the door had

been turned into coat hooks by David's bathrobe. These and a small watercolour of a stag looking imperiously down at a loch reminded Polly of Thalia Bradley's opulent Highland ballroom, although the standard of the art was really the only things the two rooms had in common. The picture was faded and spotted with fly dirt and had obviously got extremely wet some time in its career, and one of the antlers was broken. But picturing Thalia in this spartan setting made Polly smile in spite of herself.

There was a three-quarter-size bed in the corner of the room round which hung a loosely woven curtain. Next to it, on a painted orange box, was a stack of neatly ironed handkerchiefs and a pair of silver-backed brushes. Polly checked the monogram on the brushes, and could definitely detect four intials, three of which she knew to be David's.

Gradually Polly began to feel warmer. She took off her British Warm coat and sat by the fire. After a while she took a couple of logs from the neat pile and added them to the flames.

Why wasn't David there? Where could he be? It was after ten o'clock. If she hadn't got lost, she'd have been here hours ago. But where could he possibly have gone at this time of night? To a ceilidh? It didn't seem David's sort of thing, but recently she'd come to the conclusion that, like an iceberg, you only saw one-tenth of David at a time. One of those other tenths could easily be a whisky-drinking, song-singing storytelling Gael.

She put another log on the fire. The silence was total except for the crackling of the fire, and she was reluctant to lose this comforting sound. Conscious that she was wasting precious fuel, which probably had to be transported for miles, she huddled by it so as not to waste its warmth. Inevitably, aided by the whisky and the soporific effect of the flames, she began to feel drowsy.

She had nodded off at least three times, each time waking up colder and stiffer than before. 'This is ridiculous!' she said loudly. 'I'll go to bed.'

Somehow she was reluctant to climb into David's bed alone, but even after a stringent search she failed to find anything as comforting and namby-pamby as a hot-water bottle. At home she often kept bricks in the Rayburn oven which she would wrap in towels and put in her bed before she got into it. There may have been bricks outside the house, but they would take a long time to heat in the ashes of the fire.

In the end, having used David's toothbrush and made up the fire with the remaining logs, she got into bed still wearing her tights and all her jumpers.

In spite of this precaution, the sheet and duvet were icy, mitigated partly by the fact that they smelled faintly of David. But in some ways, knowing that he had been here, emphasized the fact that he wasn't here now-. and could be anywhere.

She left a table lamp burning, partly for David's return and partly for comfort. But it took her a long time to relax sufficiently to get to sleep.

'What the bloody hell are you doing there?'

David's furious voice broke into her troubled dreams. She choked back her scream of fright, but her heart began to pound. She knew it was David, she recognized his voice instantly. But her body didn't get the message and started to shake violently.

He stood over her. 'I've been going out of my mind looking for you! I thought you were dead!' His outline was huge, enlarged by several sheepfuls of Aran sweater under his waxed jacket. 'How long have you been here?'

Polly licked her trembling lips. Her brain told her he had been worried, and finding her in his bed had made him correspondingly angry. But he wouldn't hurt her. Still, when she found it, her voice shook. 'Since about – a bit before eleven, I think.'

'I've been looking since nine! I couldn't find your car! I couldn't think what had happened to you, apart from that you'd sprained your ankle and were lying freezing to death in some goddamn bog!'

'I hired a car.'

'You hired a car? And why the fuck didn't Patrick tell me that? I found a car on the main road bloody miles away, but I thought it was friends of the McFarlanes. It never occurred to me it had anything to do with you.'

'But you didn't know I was coming.'

'Yes, I did. I rang Patrick, and he told me. He didn't tell me about the sodding car, though. I'll swing for that boy!'

'But he's been wonderful! He's kept your business going and everything.'

David's eyes took on a gleam which would have put Rasputin to shame. 'Don't you start, woman! You've put me through hell and back. I've been tramping about shouting myself hoarse looking for you, and you have the bloody nerve to turn up in my bed. Well, I've suffered enough. Now it's your turn!'

He flung off his jacket, letting it land on the floor. His sweater followed, and then he started on his shirt.

Polly watched, hypnotized, half thrilled, half terrified

as he stripped. His belt clattered across the wooden boards. His trousers dropped from his waist as if they were weighted. A moment later he stood over her, naked, rampant with fury and passion. He looked more than capable of rape, with strangulation and disembowelment for an encore. Polly's mouth went dry.

'For Christ's sake,' he ground out between clenched teeth, 'move up, woman!'

Polly moved.

'And why the fuck are you wearing all these clothes?' he added as he clambered into the bed beside her, letting great wafts of cold air in at the same time.

Shaking from released tension, Polly started pulling off the cashmere jumper he'd lent her so long ago. 'Your language seems to have gone off a bit since I last saw you, David.'

He abandoned the use of language altogether and fell on her with a roar, crushing her into the bed with his weight. His mouth ground into hers, and his hands tore into her hair. She couldn't move, she could hardly breathe; if he'd suffocated her, she would have died happy.

Their coupling was brutish, short, and very sweet. But once their first, fierce hunger was satisfied, they made love more slowly. They lingered along the path to ecstasy, with leisurely, unhurried caresses, kisses and little bites, until their need got away from them again and they rushed headlong to their shared goal.

Afterwards, Polly dozed in his arms. She was dizzy with happiness and fatigue. Then her stomach rumbled.

David chuckled into her hair. 'My poor darling, you must be starving. When did you last eat?'

'At the border, I think,' said Polly dreamily, not moving.

She had her head on his shoulder and her thigh between his legs. She had never in her life been so comfortable. She was hungry, but she didn't want to break the spell.

But he slipped away from her. 'I must make up the fire. This place gets freezing if it goes out, and it also heats the hot water.'

She cleared her throat. 'There may not be any logs . . .'

He brushed her cheek with a rough, affectionate gesture. 'There's some coal by the back door.'

'Thank goodness for that. This makes my cottage seem positively sybaritic.'

'And you accused me of not being able to live outside my comfortable, ordered environment. I'll make you eat your words.'

'A sandwich would go down a lot better.'

He laughed. 'When I've done the fire, I'll bring you some cheese and biscuits to keep you going while I cook something.'

It was a primeval scene, a naked man tending a fire. Polly watched him snap sticks and place them carefully on the dying embers. Then, as they caught, she watched the flames flicker over his body, highlighting the muscles and sinews of his thighs, the sweeping lines of his curved back, his high-arched feet. She longed for a piece of charcoal and paper so she could capture the picture for ever. And, not for the first time, considered taking up sculpture.

He straightened up and unhooked his robe from the broken antler. As he pulled it on, he looked at her lying in bed, staring at him. He hadn't said anything about marrying her. He might be seeing the sense of her suggestion that they should remain simply lovers. When she had made it, it had seemed the answer to all their problems. Now the thought was desolating.

'You're very quiet. Are you all right?'

Polly dragged herself upright, pulling the duvet around her. 'I'm tired.'

'You'll feel better when you've had something to eat.'

He brought her a plate of oatcakes, a tumbler full of whisky and some rubbery cheese. He sat on the bed watching her eat. She brushed the crumbs off her hands and watched him. He was staring into the fire, deep in thought. She longed to know what he was thinking about, but didn't feel she had the right to ask. Eventually her patience paid off.

'I'm sorry I rushed you,' he began, 'about us getting married. Of course it was far too soon in our relationship, but I panicked.'

'Why?'

He shook his head. 'I don't know. I mean, when I first met you at Melissa's, and you were so different from any other women I knew at the time, I was very attracted to you. You represented the part of myself – the wild side which Patrick seems to have inherited so strongly – which I've suppressed for years.'

'You mean your taste in art, and penchant for loud ties?'

He chuckled. 'They're a bit which got away from me.'

'But why did you suppress it?'

He seemed to welcome her prompting, as if glad of the opportunity to get something off his chest. 'My father died when I was eighteen. The house was pretty well falling down, and I had to work like the devil to get it back into some sort of order. Then when I met Angela, and later when we had the boys, I still had to work terribly hard to keep my family. Relationships seemed to get pushed aside in the effort of making enough money to keep –' He hesitated. 'Everyone happy. I think I did keep Angela happy. She always told me I did. But the boys missed out on a lot of fathering. And I missed out, too.'

He took a sip of whisky from her glass and went on: 'But you were so idiotic, like a puppy, foolish and irresponsible, but incredibly appealing. Adorable, really.'

Polly willingly accepted 'foolish' and 'irresponsible' along with the jam of 'appealing' and 'adorable'.

'Seeing you deal with Patrick so well at that promise auction made me realize that you weren't all fluff and no substance. After that, although I didn't actually ask you out, I did manipulate Melissa into making sure we saw each other again. And all I got for my pains was seeing you with that radio reporter.' He scowled at her reminiscently. 'But I still thought going to bed with you for a while would be enough.'

'But it wasn't?' she prompted again.

'No. When you started sobbing in my arms I wanted to protect you, for ever. That's when the panic set in. I saw you as my last chance of discarding the middle-class work ethics that the years had piled on and discovering the happiness I felt I was capable of. But I realize I had no right to rush you.'

'Have you changed your mind – about marriage?'

He turned to her instantly. 'No, why? Have you?'

'Yes. I mean, if you still want to marry me, I will.'

Almost before she'd finished speaking he crushed her in an embrace so tight she could hardly breathe. She stayed, her nose pressed against his shoulder inhaling his fragrance, for what seemed a long time.

'Thank God for that,' he breathed into her hair. 'Thank God for that.'

Later, as they lay in bed together, she snuggled more comfortably into his side. 'Did you come here knowing I'd follow you?' she asked.

'No. I just wanted to run away. But you were mad to come. All that way, and into a blizzard. When I think what nearly happened ... You took an enormous risk.'

Polly sighed, 'I know, but it was a risk I had to take. Otherwise you would have said I was a coward.'

He had the grace to chuckle ruefully as he remembered doing exactly that. 'That's a different sort of risk. Driving here was life-threatening.'

'Not half as life-threatening as marrying you.'

His gaze became infinitely tender. 'You won't ever regret taking the risk, I promise you. But we don't have to get married if you don't want to.'

'No? You seemed pretty insistent about it before.'

'Half a loaf, and all that.'

'I think perhaps we do have to get married.'

'Why? Your mother?'

'Yes. I couldn't do her out of the white dress, the church, the tears. Patrick can be your best man.'

'And Melissa can be your matron of honour.'

She laughed. 'She'd stick pins in me while I got dressed. She wants you for herself, you know. She'll probably never speak to us again. She'll cut us off her dinner party list.'

David smiled. 'Dire though her dinner parties are, I would be sorry to lose touch with Melissa.'

'I suppose I would be too. She's such a dreadful snob, but I can't help liking her.'

'Mmm. And I owe her so much.'

'Do you? What?'

'You, ya daft ha'p'ath! She introduced us, remember?'

'So she did. I bet she rues the day.' She thought back to that dreadful dinner party. 'No, I won't insist she dresses up in purple taffeta. I won't have a matron of honour, only little bridesmaids. Bridget's daughter, people who'd actually enjoy it. I think, when I get used to the idea, I'll quite like it.'

'What? Having a white wedding?'

'No, having a double-barrelled name.'

He pushed her back into the bed and kissed her ferociously. 'I was going to suggest you kept your own name.'

'Professionally I will, of course.'

'Would you want to keep on the cottage? Your Shed?'

'You wouldn't mind?'

'I wouldn't mind anything. Making you happy is all I care about.'

Polly sighed ecstatically as yet another preconceived notion of what David expected of his wives bit the dust. 'I don't think I could hack having a second home. It's very un-Green, you know.'

'Naturally,' he agreed solemnly. 'I was prepared to overlook that, for your sake.'

'You cheque-book conservationist, you! You've never had a Green thought in your life. But there's another reason why I think I'd better give up my home and my beloved Shed ...'

'What's that?'

She looked into his eyes, her own eyes lambent with

the intenseness of her love for him. 'I need a studio on the spot if I'm going to take my pottery -' He smothered the rest of her sentence with a growl and a kiss. 'Bitch!'

'What a way to speak to the woman you love,' Polly reproached him.

He kissed her collar-bone and continued a trail of kisses up her neck to her ear. 'Do you really love me?'

A line of poetry, *How do I love thee? Let me count the ways,* floated into her head. She kept it to herself.

'Why do you think I came haring up here to look for you?' she demanded. 'Wanderlust?'

David thought for a moment. 'I think lust came into it somewhere.'

'Mmm. You may very well be right,' she said, and kissed him.

Going Dutch

Katie Fforde

Love isn't always plain sailing . . .

Jo Edwards never planned to live on a barge. She's not even sure she likes boats. But when her husband trades her in for a younger model, she finds her options alarmingly limited.

Dora Hamilton never planned to run out on her own wedding. But as The Big Day approaches, her cold feet show no signs of warming up – and accepting Jo's offer of refuge aboard *The Three Sisters* seems the only alternative.

As Jo and Dora embark on reorganising their muddled lives, they realise they both need a practical way to keep themselves afloat. But, despite their certainty that they've sworn off men for good, they haven't bargained for the persistent intervention of attractive but enigmatic Marcus, and laid-back, charming Tom, who both seem determined to help them whether they like it or not . . .

arrow books

Thyme Out

Katie Fforde

When Perdita Dylan delivers her baby vegetables to a local hotel and finds that her unpredictable ex-husband, Lucas, has taken over the kitchen, she is horrified – particularly when she discovers he's being groomed as the latest celebrity chef and needs her picturesque, if primitive cottage, and her, in supporting roles.

Her life is further complicated when Kitty, her 87-year-old friend, has a stroke. Perdita needs someone to lean on – and Lucas seems so keen to help that she starts to wonder if he's really such a villain. Can she cope with all this alone? Or should she face up to the fact that 'You can't cuddle lettuces'?

arrow books

ALSO AVAILABLE IN ARROW

Stately Pursuits

Katie Fforde

Hetty Longden's mother thinks that looking after Great Uncle Samuel's crumbling stately home will be just the thing for Hetty's broken heart. Hetty doesn't mind; at least she can be miserable in private. But 'private' is a relative term in a village which revolves around the big house. Particularly when you are expected to thwart Great Uncle Samuel's awful heir, and his nefarious plans for his inheritance.

Pitchforked into the community's fight to save the manor, Hetty has no time to wallow. And once she has shared her troubles with one neighbour (Caroline: a very understanding shoulder, despite her glamorous appearance and impossibly long legs), and cast an appreciative eye over another (Peter: equally long-legged, but offering rather more practical help), she wonders if her heart is irretrievably broken after all . . .

arrow books

Life Skills

Katie Fforde

A combination of overwork and jet-leg propels Julia Fairfax into becoming engaged to a golf-playing wine buff called Oscar. But when she realises that she has fonder feelings for his adorable Labrador than for Oscar himself, she is forced to confront the fact that there is something drastically wrong. Ditching her fiancé and jacking in her job, she decides to revolutionise her life.

Her new career as a cook on a pair of hotel boats is certainly a departure, and teaches her more about life than how to get a couple of narrow boats through a lock. But even afloat, Julia's past catches up with her. Not only must she contend with the persistent Oscar (not to mention his frightful mother and her own mother's determined matchmaking), but also the arrival of her childhood enemy, the enigmatic Fergus Grindley . . .

arrow books